The Gypsy Storyteller

Also by Thomas William Simpson

This Way Madness Lies

THOMAS WILLIAM SIMPSON

WARNER BOOKS

A Time Warner Company

Warner Books, Inc., 1271 Avenue of the Americas, New York, NY 10020

W A Time Warner Company

Printed in the United States of America
First printing: March 1993
10 9 8 7 6 5 4 3 2 1

Library of Congress Cataloging-in-Publication Data

Simpson, Thomas William
   The gypsy storyteller / Thomas William Simpson.
      p.   cm.
   ISBN 0-446-51613-9
   I. Title.
PS3569.I5176G97   1993
813'.54—dc20   92-54125
                                                       CIP

Book Designed by L. McRee

For Jamie,
and again for Lorelei, who kept the Gypsy home

I must down to the seas again, to the lonely sea and the sky,
And all I ask is a tall ship and a star to steer her by...

I must down to the seas again, for the call of the running tide
Is a wild call and a clear call that may not be denied.

I must down to the seas again, to the vagrant gypsy life,
To the gull's way and the whale's way where the wind's like a whetted knife;
And all I ask is a merry yarn from a laughing fellow-rover,
And quiet sleep and a sweet dream when the long trick's over.

from John Masefield's "Sea Fever"

For, what other dungeon is so dark as one's own heart!
What jailer so inexorable as one's own self!

from Nathaniel Hawthorne's The House of the Seven Gables

The Gypsy Storyteller

THE NIGHT BEFORE HE LEAVES TO KILL A MAN, *Daniel Hawthorn stands in front of his bedroom window watching fireflies. It seems a reckless, almost suicidal thing for the fireflies to do: ignite the darkness, even for an instant, with the night woods swarming with predators. Daniel imagines swift-footed rodents and beady-eyed owls laying for the lightning bugs, lurking in the shadows for the winged beetles to flash their signals, to strut their stuff.*

And strut their stuff they do. Over and over. They have no choice. To find a mate they must light up the night. Dangers be damned. Copulate and propagate is the genetic message built into their tiny bodies, copulate and propagate.

The sexual urge is a powerful lure.

The Aerolineas Argentinas 747 touches down at Ezeiza International Airport late in the afternoon. Several flights and more than one passport later, he clears Argentine customs and takes a cab into Buenos Aires. It is July, winter in Argentina, cool and dry.

The driver drops him at the Plaza de Mayo. He walks across the plaza, past the Casa Rosada. He feels calm even though the image of fireflies keeps flashing in the bright angled light of the setting sun.

He spends the evening alone in the drab, second-floor apartment in the heart of the old city, La Boca. The apartment is above a small neighborhood grocery store. He can hear through the floor the murmur of conversation, the opening and closing of the old cast iron cash register.

He does not sleep well. But he lies perfectly still, his eyes closed, his breathing relaxed and steady.

Soon after dawn he showers, shaves, and dresses. He cleans the apartment, throws away all evidence of his life there. Off and on for almost two years he has occupied the two small rooms.

Now all that remains is an old, half-filled leather rucksack. He throws the rucksack over his shoulder and walks out through the open door.

He leaves La Boca, passes through San Telmo, then back across the Plaza de Mayo. He walks slowly. Occasionally he glances at his watch. He leaves the plaza, heads up Avenida Florida. The shopkeepers are opening their doors, sweeping the sidewalk, preparing for another day of business, buying and selling.

He crosses the Plaza de San Martín without even glancing at the massive monument of Le Libertador high atop his bronze stallion. He turns up Avenida Santa Fe and across Avenida Nuevo de Julio in a throng of commuters hurrying to work.

At the corner of Santa Fe and Libertad he turns right, picks up his pace. It is ten minutes before ten o'clock.

He reaches the corner of Libertad and Montevideo at five minutes before the hour. At the newsstand he buys a copy of La Nación. He glances at the morning headlines while he peers over the newspaper at the apartment building across the street. In the doorway of the apartment building, the doorman stirs.

This is Le Recoleta, the city's most fashionable and affluent neighborhood. This is where the best restaurants and nightclubs can be found. This is where foreign capitals have their embassies. This is where the wealthy reside in luxury apartments overlooking the Río de la Plata. This is where the Nazi lives.

At precisely ten o'clock the doorman stands down off his stool and stretches his arms over his head. He takes a quick look up and down the street. All is well. All is quiet. He walks out onto the sidewalk, takes a few steps to his right, and turns into the entrance of the apartment building's parking garage.

Daniel watches the doorman disappear. He knows from the many mornings he has spent on this street corner that the doorman will be gone for exactly fifteen minutes: fifteen minutes to drink his coffee and relieve his bladder and argue politics with the garage attendant.

Daniel tucks his copy of La Nación under his arm and crosses the street. He reminds himself not to hurry, to relax. At the front door of the apartment building he draws a plastic card from his shirt pocket. He slips the card into a slot beside the door. A buzzer sounds. The door unlocks. He pushes the door open and goes quickly into the lobby.

There is a direct elevator to the top floor but it can be controlled only with a special key. So he rides the service elevator to the thirty-first floor, the floor just below the penthouse.

He steps out of the elevator into a long corridor. There are several doors. He wants the door at the far end. He pulls on a pair of thin leather *gloves, takes a small pointed tool from his pocket, and slips the end of the tool into the door's lock. A few twists and turns, and the lock pops open.*

He goes through the door and up the stairs two at a time. At the top, another locked door stands in his way. He performs his magic.

His heart pounds so hard he feels as though he might at any moment explode. But he has come too far to turn back. Like the firefly, he has no choice.

He enters another corridor. There is only one other door this time, all the way down at the end. He begins to run. He runs as fast as he can, his arms pumping. And just before he reaches the door, he turns his shoulder. The impact of his body against the door tears the hinges right off the wall. He crashes to the floor on top of the door. But he is inside. He has reached the penthouse.

And there, across the living room, on the plush carpet in front of an enormous picture window overlooking the city of Buenos Aires and the Río de la Plata, is the old Nazi. He has only seconds earlier been screwing his wife's Indian housekeeper. But now the illicit sex scene is suddenly over. Trouble has exploded into the penthouse.

Daniel springs to his feet, moves forward. "Herr Heinrich," he says in German, "at last we meet." Then, quickly, he crosses the living room to the two naked bodies still lying on the floor, their faces puzzled and horrified.

From his leather rucksack Daniel produces a length of rope and a handkerchief. He ties Herr Heinrich's arms behind his back, then stuffs the handkerchief into his mouth. Herr Heinrich struggles, but the old man with the loose skin hanging off his wizened body can do nothing but submit.

"Come with me," Daniel says to the Indian housekeeper, a thin and tiny brown woman trembling with fear. She no doubt thinks he is going to rape her. He pulls her to her feet, leads her down the hallway to one of the bedrooms. "You're not supposed to be here," he says to her in Spanish. "You're supposed to be with the family, in Bariloche, on vacation, taking the sun."

"I no go," she says, "I no go."

He ties her up, makes her comfortable on the bed. Then he pauses for a moment to think. "When they find you," he tells her finally, "you tell them the Gypsies did this. The Gypsies. Do you hear? Do you understand me?"

She jerks her head up and down several times.

"Good." He rips the phone from the wall, closes the door, and goes back down the hallway to the living room.

Herr Heinrich rests on the floor, shaking, his eyes as big as moons.

Daniel reaches into the old leather rucksack. He pulls out a pair of tall, very shiny black boots. "Remember when you used to wear boots like these, Herr Heinrich?"

The old Nazi pees right on his own carpet. He tries to crawl away in a corner.

Daniel pulls on the boots. They slip on easily, fit perfectly. He takes a few goose steps around the room. "Makes a man feel powerful to wear boots like these," he says. "Makes a man feel invincible." He stops, kicks Herr Heinrich hard in the chest with the toe of the right boot. "Makes a man feel like God."

IN THE GREAT ROLLING THUNDER OF TIME, take a moment. I'd like you to do me a favor. I'd like you to imagine you're me, just for a while.

It's September 1990. You're living in New York City, Seventeenth Street, between Sixth and Seventh, a fifth-floor walk-up, a real hole in the wall. You're almost thirty-five years old, almost halfway to seventy, more than a decade and a half out of high school. You're a white male, middle class, some say well educated, reasonably sophisticated, gainfully employed, a true-blue professional in the eyes of the outside world.

You've prospered financially, like just about everyone else west of the Danube, during the avaricious eighties, but emotionally you're still riding the Broadway local between Union Square and Trinity Place twice a day five days a week, sometimes six.

See, there's this woman. Good God, there's always a woman.

You've known this one and been in love with her for almost twenty years, more than half your life. For twenty years she's been making you crazy. Don't get me wrong, she loves you, too, just not quite the same way you love her.

Get the picture?

I know, it's an old story. But aren't they all?

Anyway, you've seen her just once in the past year. She's been in seclusion, hiding out where no one knows her so she can work on her paintings without being disturbed. At least that's the reason she gave before packing up and moving out of her loft in Soho. You, however, believe the paintings are only the tip of the iceberg. You feel sure you smell a rat. But then, you've always been slightly paranoid.

The two of you have communicated during this year, but not often and never with any real satisfaction. For you the entire enterprise has been a most trying and humiliating experience.

Still with me?

Okay, so the seasons pass, fall and winter. You see her for a few days in the early spring. You talk it over, again, at great length. You decide only to talk more later. You agree to spend a week together at the end of the summer, in September, after the crowds have gone back to the mainland, at an old seaside house on the island of Nantucket, a house your family has owned since 1933.

All through the summer you wait for this reunion. Finally the time comes to leave the city and head for the island. You arrive a day or two early, make sure the place is clean and fully stocked with wine and cheese and plenty of fresh shrimp. She loves Chardonnay and scampi and ice-cold shrimp cocktail with lots of horseradish sauce.

Early on the morning of her arrival you drive across the island to the village to meet the ferry. You arrive with plenty of time to spare. You take a walk up Main Street, over the rough cobblestones. You buy the *Globe*, read the headlines, try to relax.

You walk out to the end of the wharf where others have gathered to welcome friends and family. You see the ferry from Hyannis in the distance, just beyond the entrance to the harbor. Your heart pounds. Your thoughts race. Your expectations soar. You can't stop hoping that this week you spend together will, once and for all, stabilize and solidify your relationship.

You plan, for the fourth time—or is it the fifth time?—to ask her to marry you.

The ferry whistle blows as the ship enters the harbor off Brant Point. A little girl screams and plugs her ears. You try not to look nervous, just calm and cool in your faded Nantucket reds and white button-down oxford. You take a deep breath, run your fingers through your hair.

The ferry swings wide, then reverses its engines and backs slowly up to the wharf. You try to find her among the crowd shuffling for position as the deck hands secure the ship to the bulkhead. She's nowhere in sight, but you figure that's because she'll need assistance leaving the ship. She is blind, you see, stone blind, perceives not a shadow even in this blaze of bright morning light. Or so she would make you think.

The gangplank is moved into position. The passengers begin to disembark. Your heart pumps now at full throttle. You step a little closer, continue to scan the decks. And then you see her, there, standing along the safety rail, dark glasses hiding her eyes. She takes a cautious step forward.

There is someone behind her, helping her, guiding her hand to the rope railing. You do not see the face of this guardian, not right away. Your eyes are riveted on the face of this woman you have loved all of your adult life.

She starts down the gangplank. You take another step to meet her.

And then you see him: tall and broad and handsome, bigger than life. He blocks out the sun.

Your heart stops. Your eyes go cold. You feel nothing but anger and confusion. This person with her, this person who has accompanied her from the mainland, from Hyannis, from God knows where else, is your oldest friend, also your arch rival for this woman's affections, your collaborator and competitor, your ally and your adversary.

This is the person who more than once led you astray and who led your love astray as well, who wounded you and blinded her. So why the hell, you wonder almost out loud, is he here? Who invited him to this party? "Jesus Christ," you mumble to yourself, "I thought he was in Argentina or some such place, looking for his demons, searching for his destiny, digging up long forgotten Nazis who tortured and butchered his kin."

You stop not five feet from the bottom of the gangplank. You stop and wait for them to come to you, to utter the first words, to offer some kind of explanation. Of course, you know already there will be none, not from these two, not from Daniel and Rachel. No way. That's not their style. They won't say a word. They'll just stand there and suck in the power of the earth and the sky and those dark Nantucket waters.

So there it is. Now what do you say? What do you do? Do you get angry? Scream and stomp your feet? Or do you take it in stride? Roll with the punches.

Wait a second, don't answer, not yet. Let me give you a few more facts, fill in some of the background. Let me tell you my tale. And later, after I've finished, after you've read between the lines, then you can tell me what you would've said, what you would've done, had you been the idiot standing there on that wharf with your finger in your ear and your mouth hanging open.

You don't know me very well yet, but give us time. I think you'll find we have a lot in common.

July 15, 1990

RACHEL ANN FREDERICK, ALIAS MISTY GREY, *can feel him drawing closer. She knows he is coming. There have been vigorous signs over the past twenty-four hours: an extra heartbeat, the inspiration for a new painting, an evening thunderstorm, a dream wherein she finds his genitals floating on the sea, and, most telling of all, the onset of ovulation.*

Now she sits in the shade of the tall black walnut tree on the edge of Peapack's small park. Her sketch pad rests on her lap, but she has not drawn a line since arriving over an hour earlier. She watches the pair of black swans on the pond and waits.

Across the pond she sees an old man sitting on a bench reading a paperback book. His lips move as he reads.

On another bench a young man and a young woman hold hands. He says something to her. She laughs.

A dirt path winds around the pond. A young boy and his dog, a golden retriever, sit at the water's edge. The boy throws a stick. The dog retrieves it. The dog, not the boy, makes her think for a moment of Matthew.

Then she hears the familiar sound of the old VW's air-cooled engine. She turns and sees the van pull onto the shoulder of the road and stop. She smiles at her intuition, her innate understanding of the signs.

He steps slowly out of the van. Before she even sees his face she can tell by the tension in his shoulders that he is preoccupied, uneasy. And when he turns and begins to walk toward the pond, she sees his eyes wandering, looking for trouble.

He does not see her, has not seen her in over a year, and has absolutely no reason to think he will see her now. He begins to walk around the pond along the dirt path. She makes no sign to him. She knows the path will eventually lead him to her.

He passes the man reading the paperback book. The man looks up, nods, receives no reply.

He passes the couple holding hands. The young woman smiles at him. He does not see her smile.

He passes the boy and his dog sitting at the edge of the water.

"Hey, mister," she hears the boy say across the quiet of the pond, "my dog's got a tick on her ear."

She sees Daniel stop and consider the boy's words. Then he crosses to the dog, bends down, and examines the ear. He grabs the tick with his fingernails and pulls it loose.

"Thanks, mister," says the boy. "Red hates ticks."

Daniel flicks the tick into the water, pats the dog's head, and walks on.

She watches and sees the immediate future: he will express his astonishment at finding her here in Peapack, New Jersey. She will tell him she has been here all along, for the past year, since leaving Soho last September. He will scratch his head, say he had often felt her presence when he was in Mendham visiting his parents. Of course, she will say, you knew I was here, you just didn't believe what you knew. They will go back to her studio above the old red barn. She will put her scratchy recording of Billie Holiday's "Fine and Mellow" on the turntable. They'll dance, slowly. He'll kiss her. She'll resist, but not for long. They'll make love, wildly. Everything will change.

He walks into the shade of the black walnut tree. The warm summer breeze stirs the leaves overhead. Still he does not see her.

"Daniel," she says softly.

He wheels at the sound of his name. It takes him a moment to understand. "Rachel?"

"Misty, actually."

"Huh?"

She smiles. "Nothing."

He hesitates, takes a quick look around. "It's finished," he says. "I did what I had to do."

She studies his eyes, and then, after a moment, she nods. "You told me once the Gypsies have a saying."

"The Gypsies have a million sayings. Everything they say is a saying. Which saying are you thinking of?"

She smiles again. "Take a life, make a life."

His eyes soften. They embrace.

WE MIGHT AS WELL START AT THE BEGINNING.

Daniel and I arrived in the world just one day apart in late June of 1956. He was born on June 20, a full-fledged Gemini: intelligent, temperamental, as unpredictable as quicksilver. I came along several hours and a whole lifetime later, sometime after midnight but before dawn on June 21. I was born with Mercury in retrograde, on the cusp between Gemini and Cancer, a lost and wandering soul for all of eternity, a mixture of water and air with no clear notion of why I'd come or what I was supposed to do.

Our mothers arrived at Morristown Memorial Hospital in Morristown, New Jersey, at exactly the same moment. Actually Daniel's mother arrived first, by just a few seconds.

Both mamas-to-be had been through false labor a few days earlier, and both were anxious to successfully deliver their firstborns. For nine long months they had been competing silently to see who would deliver first. Our moms, you see, had known each other for years, since their own childhoods. They didn't like each other much, not really, never had; still don't.

They went to the same schools, played on the same teams, dated the same boys, belonged to the same clubs, sent each other invitations for dinner and cocktails. They spent time together not out of friendship, but because of the old adage that warns of keeping your enemy close at hand.

Enemies? A couple of smart, good-looking, well-to-do, middle-class white women? But why, you ask, would they be enemies?

Who knows? I don't know. Jealousy? Envy? Insecurity? The reasons reach beyond my ability to understand. The world is riddled with enemies, both real and perceived. I daresay most of the animosity between them originated with my mother. She has always been a small, petty woman.

My mother is a Whiting. Daniel's mother is a Hawthorn, just as Daniel was a Hawthorn. Maybe their conflict had its roots there. The Whitings were descended from one of New Jersey's oldest and most influential families. The Hawthorns were direct descendents of that nineteenth-century scribbler who you undoubtedly read but didn't quite understand back in high school. You know the gentleman I mean, the author of *The Scarlet Letter* and *The House of the Seven Gables* and *Young Goodman Brown*.

Anyway, the story of our birth goes like this: The Hawthorns, Victor and Carolyn, pulled up to the hospital in their '55 Ford station wagon. Victor hopped out from behind the steering wheel and dashed around the front of the car to open the door for his bulging wife. Half a minute later the Chandlers, my soon-to-be parents, pulled up in their '54 Dodge coupe with Hydro-Cruise.

They all made a mad dash for the front desk. The Hawthorns got there first, which meant they registered first, reached the maternity ward on the third floor first, saw the doctor first (both moms used the same obstetrician), and made it to the delivery room first. My parents brought up the rear. My mother had to wait, which meant I had to wait. Had the Dodge arrived ahead of the Ford, who knows? Maybe everything would've turned out different. But it happened the way it happened, and I haven't yet found a way to alter my own personal history, except, of course, through the ancient rites of denial and deception.

So Daniel got the jump on me right from the start. I hung around in the womb for several more hours, thinking things over, worrying about my future, wondering if the best thing might be to just lay low, stay put.

A couple of other interesting sidelights: Daniel's mother delivered Daniel naturally, without the aid of drugs or knives or forceps, a rarity in those days of overzealous doctor interference, whereas my mother, always scornful of pain either physical or emotional, opted for a cesarean section. They cut me loose from the womb, ripped me from my stranglehold on the umbilical cord, snatched me from the moist darkness, and held me up under a glaring white light.

Who knows what terrible traumas all this may have caused?

Also, I might as well mention that Daniel got the tit whereas I went straight to the rubber nipple. Bitch.

One of my earliest memories is lying there in the hospital nursery, right beside Daniel, surrounded by what seemed like thousands of other screaming infants, when all of a sudden my father appeared on the other side of the window. He pushed out his tongue, stuck his thumbs into his ears, wiggled his fingers. He pressed his lips and his nose against the glass. The old boy really got me going, really got me feeling pretty good about my future on the planet and my relationship with this guy who had donated his semen for a worthy cause.

But then this woman all dressed in white, either an angel or an RN, appeared next to my father. She shook her head and pointed not at me, but at the bassinet on my right. It was not my father at all; it was Daniel's father, Victor, who immediately moved down a few feet and performed the same silly faces for his own son.

My father came later, after work, while I was fast asleep, dreaming dreams of dark wet places I would never visit again no matter how hard I tried. I managed to open one eye and watch him for a few moments as he stood there looking kind of bored and bewildered. I didn't see him again until Mom and I arrived home a few days later.

Daniel's father came to the hospital every day, several times a day, in fact. Every time I woke up from a nap he stood out there clowning around with his kid, fogging up the glass with his breath. I didn't understand his enthusiasm. I mean, there were a hell of a lot of us in that nursery, more coming every hour, like cookies out of the oven; what made this one kid so damn special? Why did he get all the attention?

Well, maybe because Daniel's father had only been in America for a few years. Maybe his enthusiasm had something to do with the reality that his family had been virtually wiped off the face of the earth. That baby on my right was evidence, pure physical evidence, that Daniel's father's family's fortunes had survived the terrors of the Holocaust. Victor could look into that bassinet and see there would indeed be another generation of Gypsies.

Daniel's father was a Gypsy; at least he always claimed he was. He was a Gypsy and a magician and a Nazi hunter. He was also the best father in town, from a kid's point of view anyway. He was a big man, maybe six two, a hundred and ninety pounds, too big really for a full-blooded Gypsy.

Victor Hawthorn was tall and dark and handsome. He had wavy black hair and lots of it. Most of the fathers in town wore their hair very short, as if a stray strand or two might throw life itself into a tizzy. I cannot recall a single hair ever being out of place on my father's head. His crop weathered the storm like the man itself: steady and stiff and unwavering. Even after a full day under sail, his one and only passion, with the wind blowing and the sea washing over the gunwales, Charles Randolph Chandler (Chuckie, I called him behind his back) somehow remained perfectly coiffed.

I know for a fact he had his hair trimmed once a week because every Tuesday evening he walked through the front door bearing the evidence:

shiny white skin around the ears and along the back of his neck where a few rebel strands had tried to break loose. Chuckie had his hair cut at a barbershop on Wall Street, right around the corner from the offices of Chandler, Wright & MacPherson.

Daniel's father had gigantic hands. He had thick, muscular forearms and a broad, hairy chest. He also had the darkest tan even in the depths of winter. Only it wasn't so much a tan as his natural olive skin color. He stuck out in a crowd of fathers like a black sheep. Here were all these pale white guys with light brown or blond hair wearing either suits from Brooks Brothers or brown khakis from L. L. Bean, and standing there among them yucking it up with that big smile plastered on his face was Daniel's old man. He wore silk shirts and suede pants held up not by a staid leather belt but by a piece of rope containing all the colors of the rainbow. The other fathers hated his guts; they all wanted to kill him. But the women, the wives, they loved him. I'm sure they all secretly wanted to fuck his brains out.

Just as later on all the women wanted to fuck Daniel's brains out. Rachel, anyway.

If you think about it, Daniel was just like his old man, only more so, probably because of that Hawthorn blood circulating through his body. Half Gypsy and half Hawthorn, Jesus, what a mix.

THE FIRST MAGIC TRICK VICTOR PERFORMED for us was the one with the wooden box; first one I remember anyway. It was on our fifth birthday. Every year Daniel and I celebrated our birthdays with a joint party. The parties were always at his house, never at mine. His parents organized the parties, bought the favors, invited the other kids, baked the cake, grilled the burgers, provided the entertainment. They were the entertainment.

My parents didn't even show up for these parties, except to drop me off out front of the Hawthorn Compound on their way to the First Day of Summer Party over at Roxiticus Country Club. They wouldn't've missed that annual bash for the Second Coming of Christ. I can still see them standing out on the veranda of the clubhouse sipping gin and tonics and looking very smug about having been born white, wealthy, and Presbyterian.

My parents hated kids' parties; hated kids for that matter. If it hadn't been socially taboo to be married and living in the suburbs without children, Chuckie and Martha Chandler probably would've forgone the pleasure. But in those days, in the fifties, everyone liked Ike, everyone hated commies, and everyone had kids, usually several. Maybe it was an unconscious response to the nuclear threat: have many, and afterwards, maybe there'll be a few left.

Daniel's parents had three kids: him and his two sisters. Our buddy Leif Johnson had three sisters and a brother. Another kid we hung around with whose name I can't remember, Scott something or other, had four sisters and three brothers. Buckley had at least two brothers and two sisters. And so on and so forth.

I came from the smallest family in town: just my little sister, Margaret, and me. I called her Wanda. All she had to do was wave her invisible magic wand, and presto, the spoiled brat got whatever her beating heart desired.

Wanda's not so little anymore, twenty-nine years old she is, works down in Washington for some jerk-off congressman who combs his hair like he's definitely planning a run for the presidency early in the next century. Margaret says he's a reincarnation of Jefferson, a genuine environmentalist. Right. She's dating his son, who looks to me like he's stoned on Quaaludes and Coors Light most of the time. Rumor has it they're getting married next summer. I hope they don't invite me to the wedding—if, by chance, my ship is still in port.

The Hawthorn house, the most famous house in town, stood at the end of Thomas Lane, a narrow gravel cul-de-sac about a quarter of a mile long. There was no street sign; you just knew where it was. Thomas Lane might as well have been the Hawthorn's driveway since their house was one of only two on the entire street.

The house stood about a mile from the center of Mendham, New Jersey, the small town where Daniel and I grew up in the 1960s. The house rose off a fieldstone foundation a full three stories high. Cedar shingles protected the roof. Cedar shakes covered the sides. The years and the weather and the towering spruce trees had turned the cedar almost black.

Steeply pitched gables stuck out of the third floor like a host of twentieth-century American gargoyles. Massive brick chimneys, four of them, reached into the sky like so many smokestacks. In the winter and in the cool days of both autumn and spring, Victor often had smoke spewing from all four flues.

A wide, column-supported porch protected the house on all four sides. The porch hung covered but open on all but the back, the west end, where fine mesh screens had been installed to keep out the bugs, mosquitoes mostly, once New Jersey's state bird but now an endangered species after two and a half decades of chemical warfare against the bloodthirsty parasites.

The front door of the Hawthorn house was the largest regular house-type door I have ever seen. It must've been nine feet high and more than half as wide. Victor once drove the family station wagon through that front door after a group of local ladies came by looking for donations for their latest charity.

Daniel's mother had invited them in, offered them coffee and biscuits, listened to their tales of woe on the plight of our local American sycamores, which the ladies claimed were being decimated by some disease or other. Trouble was, Victor was out front with the car all packed up and ready to go off on some adventure when those ladies arrived. After maybe fifteen minutes he started to grow impatient. He rechecked the oil and water, messed with the fan belts, then got back into the car and slammed the door.

Daniel and I and Daniel's two sisters were in the back seat. Victor turned around and showed us a few card tricks but that didn't hold him for long. I forget where we were headed, some state park or battlefield, no doubt. Wherever it was, Victor wanted to roll. But the women inside, one of whom, thank God, was not my mother, had an agenda and they weren't leaving until Mrs. Hawthorn had heard their spiel. Victor tried the horn a few times but that didn't get the old girls moving.

So a few minutes later Victor turned the key and brought that big, powerful, sixties-style V-8 to life. That engine sounded like it had the fortitude to lift a C-130 transport plane off the ground and carry a couple thousand U.S. Marines all the way to Baghdad. A second later Daniel elbowed me in the ribs. "Hold on, Mac, we're going for a ride."

And sure enough, Victor put that station wagon into gear and drove directly toward the front porch. He rolled across the driveway and up onto the grass. Maybe fifteen feet from the house he stopped the car but left the engine running. He climbed out, went into the detached garage, and came back a minute later carrying two long wooden planks.

He laid the thick oak planks a few feet apart right over the top of the porch stairs, sort of built himself a ramp. Then he strode across the porch and swung open that massive front door. The women were still inside sipping java and crunching biscuits and talking a blue streak about the fate of the American sycamore. From the back seat I could see them through the living room windows.

Victor got back behind the wheel and put that station wagon into gear. We rolled forward nice and easy. Victor lined the front wheels up on the planks. Then he backed off a few feet and gave all of us in the back seat a wink. He hit the gas and we went screaming up that ramp, right across the front porch and through the front door. He slammed on the brakes just before we smashed into the carved wooden banister winding up the stairway to the second floor.

"Excuse me, Carolyn," he said, nice as can be, as though every husband picked up his wife in the family living room, "but I really think it's time we were leaving."

Well, dying sycamores or not, those women had been rendered speechless. Their lower jaws hung down around their ankles. Coffee spilled. Biscuits fell to the floor. Their faces looked flustered, horrified, even whiter than usual. With the exception that is, of Daniel's mother. Carolyn Hawthorn looked perfectly serene, as always. She finished her coffee, stood, and crossed the living room. She walked around the front of the station wagon, slipped easily between the front bumper and the banister, and opened the passenger side door.

"Would you ladies be so kind," she asked, "as to please close the front door on your way out? And thank you for coming. I'll send you a check."

And with that, we were off. Victor backed through the door and down those wooden planks. I remember turning around and looking out the window of the station wagon as we made our getaway down the gravel drive. Half a dozen of Mendham's most prominent ladies, most of them Daughters of the American Revolution, stood in that massive doorway, their mouths still hanging wide open. I knew right then that Victor's latest maneuver would be the talk of the town long before we got back from wherever we were going.

Victor's magic shows always took place in the small auditorium off the end of the living room. To get there you passed through a set of solid tiger maple doors. The auditorium had no windows, maybe twenty or twenty-five seats, and a pretty good-size stage. Daniel's mother's mother, Sarah Hawthorn, daughter of Madison Hargrove, the man who built the house with money made from manufacturing pistons and camshafts, had the auditorium built because among other things she was an amateur playwright and actress. She used to write plays and then perform them for her family and friends right in her own home.

A generation later Victor used the auditorium to perform his magic tricks. He used the wooden stage to cut his wife in half, make her disappear, suspend her in midair, even chop her head off every now and then. He also performed a few escape tricks. In one trick his wife would tie him up and lock him in one of those big steamship trunks. She'd offer a few words of hocus-pocus and then slip behind the curtain. Less than half a minute later Victor would be throwing open those tiger maple doors, running down the aisle between the seats, and opening that steamer trunk, where, of course, his wife would be waiting with a smile on her face. We'd watch him do these tricks over and over, but we could never figure them out.

"The reason you can't figure them out," he'd tell us, "is because they're not tricks at all. They're magic. Magic is not trickery. Magic is reality turned on its head. All you have to do is believe."

His wooden box trick, the one he performed at our fifth birthday party, that's the one that got the ball rolling. That trick was my introduction to the Hawthorn magic, to the Hawthorn mystique. I was captivated from that moment on. That house became my home away from home. Its occupants became my guardians, my mentors. With the transformation of that simple wooden box my obsession began.

Victor started the magic show that day with a couple of card tricks. Then he did some sleight of hand. He produced eggs out of thin air and little chicks from those eggs. He pulled so many rabbits out of his hat that I wondered for months how they had all fit.

But then he did something far more amazing. He disappeared behind the curtain, and when he returned he carried a small wooden box in both hands. The box was maybe twelve inches high by twelve inches long. There was nothing extraordinary about the box, no fancy design or inlay, simple dovetail joints held it together. It had a removable lid but nothing at all inside. He invited each of us up onto the stage to examine the box. I personally held the box in my hands. It weighed next to nothing, no more than a bag of peanuts.

We returned to our seats. There must've been about twenty of us in the audience, maybe a dozen kids and eight or ten parents. My own were nowhere in sight. They were over at the club discussing Jack and Jackie and sipping Beefeater's on the rocks.

Victor told us the box had belonged to his ancient ancestor nearly a thousand years ago when he had lived in the foothills of the Himalayas, within view of the Kanchenjunga. I had never heard of the Himalayas, didn't know Kanchenjunga from Katmandu, but none of that mattered; Victor's voice made it all as real as the throbbing hangnail on the end of my thumb.

"My ancient ancestor," he said, "now lives in this box. This box is his home. He has the power to make himself so small that the interior of this small box is to him like a giant fifty-room mansion."

The adults in the audience snickered. But none of us did. We held our breath and watched with wide-open eyes the man holding the ancient box.

"Even more incredible," he continued, "than his size is his weight. You might think that a man living in a box this small could not possibly weigh more than a few ounces, certainly no more than a package of gum. But here"—and Daniel's father looked deeply into each and every one of us—"here is where the mystery truly begins. For you see, my ancient ancestor has the power to make himself weigh as much as an elephant while still occupying a space no larger than this box."

He waited for out gasps to subside. And while he waited his voice rang in my ears. He always spoke in the same clear, modulated voice. English was Victor's third or maybe even fourth language. He spoke it carefully, enunciating every sound, accenting every syllable.

"Why, you might ask, would he want to make himself so heavy?" He waited for us to answer. No one did. "Because while he is asleep he does not want anyone disturbing his box, picking it up and carrying it off. This box, you see, is his home."

Victor again waited for our whispers to grow mute. "Because this is

THE GYPSY STORYTELLER 19

my son's fifth birthday, and because tomorrow is the fifth birthday of my son's best pal, little Matt Chandler there"—and he pointed to me while I got all red in the face—"my ancient ancestor has agreed to give you a demonstration of his powers. So without further ado, we will proceed."

Victor took a couple steps forward. He knelt down on one knee. "I will place the box here on the floor because if I were to hold the box during the transformation, I might be crushed by the tremendous increase of weight."

Even a few of the adults thought this sounded like a sensible idea.

Victor carefully placed the box on the floor in the center of the stage. Then he stood up, produced a silk cloth out of thin air, and covered the box with the cloth.

"*Evan doxy diem,*" he chanted, his eyes flickering and his hands circling over the box, "*consortium biem.* Flocks of angels and dens of panthers, ask us questions but demand no answers." Then more hocus-pocus under his breath. I couldn't quite hear it. I sat on the edge of my seat, mesmerized. Maybe a minute passed. No one in the audience drew a breath.

Suddenly Victor collapsed on the floor of the stage, right behind the box, almost right on top of the box. More than a few of us jumped to our feet. But Victor recovered. He held up a hand, motioned for us to sit, then brought himself up onto his knees. He whipped the silk cloth away from the box.

It sat there looking exactly the same as it had before.

"A volunteer, please," he whispered.

No one moved.

Daniel gave me a nudge. "Go ahead, Mac. This is your big chance."

I swallowed hard and slowly made my way up onto the stage. Victor looked like a giant. His eyes stared straight through me, burned holes in my chest. "Lift the box, son, lift it high over your head."

I swallowed hard again and bent down. I put my hands around the box. I tried to lift it but it wouldn't budge. It must've weighed a thousand pounds or more. I couldn't raise it even one inch off the floor.

"I can't," I said, "it's too heavy." And it was, far too heavy. It easily weighed as much as an elephant.

"Do not despair, son," Victor said to me in that clear and powerful voice, his massive hand on my bony shoulder, "you are not the first to fail to lift the box. Nor will you be the last."

In fact, many more failed that same afternoon. Every kid in the audience, plus several of the adults, tried to lift the box, but no one could. Four of us tried to lift it together, but even then it proved too heavy.

After our efforts had been exhausted, Victor again covered the box with the silk cloth. He chanted some more mumbo jumbo, then once again he invited me onto the stage to hoist the box off the floor.

"My ancestor," Victor announced, "has returned to a state of weightlessness."

And sure enough he had. I picked up that box as easily as I could pick up a peanut-butter-and-jelly sandwich. I turned and showed the box to the audience. I looked strong and confident standing there holding the box. But that was just on the outside. On the inside I felt weak and confused. I did not understand how the box had changed, how it had been so light and then so heavy and then so light again. The mystery of the box eluded me.

In my memory, anyway, it remains the first great mystery of my life, my first excursion into the unknown. There would be more to follow, more mysteries and illusions and aberrations. Daniel, and later Rachel, provided all the mysteries I would ever need. Without their acquaintance I might've stayed on the straight and narrow. But they became my devil's advocates, my tempter and temptress. If I was Faust, Daniel was Mephistopheles, Rachel his courtesan. If I was Samson, Rachel was Delilah, Daniel her Philistine.

But now they are both gone, murdered you might say, and I must go it alone, on my own. And yet, it's as though they're not gone at all but hiding in my shadow, taunting me to take another step, turn another corner, make another rash and impetuous decision. Which I have done. I have quit my job, dipped deep into my savings, ordered me a ship to carry me across the seven seas. I fear I am as far afield today as I have ever been in my entire life.

THE HAWTHORN BASEMENT WAS ONE OF THE CENTERS OF my youth. On days when we couldn't play outside you could almost always find us down in the cellar. The Hawthorns had built a rec room down there with all the amenities. There was a pool table, Ping-Pong table, foosball table, knock hockey board, darts, checkers, chess, and just about every board game ever invented.

But the rec room occupied only one side of the Hawthorn basement. There was another side, a forbidden side, a side where we were not allowed to go. The rec room side you reached via a stairway from the kitchen. But the forbidden side you could enter only from outside the house, through one of those louvered cellar doors. Victor kept this door locked. He had his tool room down there where he worked on his magic tricks. When Victor retreated to this room he was not to be disturbed.

On rainy days and wintry days, after we had worn out the rec room, we used to use the whole house for a game of hide-and-seek. In our version of hide-and-seek you had to not only see the person but you had to catch him. You had to catch him and hold him for three seconds before he was officially caught.

It was always tough to catch Daniel. He knew every hiding place in the house from the attic to the basement. You could spot him across the living room, and when you got there he'd be gone; he'd've vanished into thin air.

Many times I was the seeker when I'd spot Daniel in the kitchen. Always he'd head directly for the basement. I'd follow as fast as I could but by the time I reached the rec room he'd be nowhere in sight. I'd look everywhere: under the tables, in the closets, under the tables again. But no Daniel. Even as a kid he had the power to disappear, to make himself invisible.

"How do you do it?" I asked him more than once.

"Magic."

"No, really. Where do you go?"

"I don't go anywhere, Mac. I'm right there. Close enough to smell your salty breath. I can see you. You just can't see me."

"That's a lie."

"No it's not."

"Yes it is."

"No it's not."

"Prove it."

I don't have to prove it," he said, "it's true. You don't have to prove what's true."

I pushed him. He pushed me back. I pushed him again. He pushed me again. Pretty soon we were outside rolling around on the grass, wrestling, and maybe, if we got in a lucky elbow, giving each other a fat lip or a bloody nose. Daniel and I fought at least once a week, in the summer sometimes once a day.

One time, in the middle of a marathon game of hide-and-seek during a January snow day, I finally discovered how Daniel disappeared. Buckley was It. It was his job to find us. I went down in the basement and hid under the pool table. I waited more than fifteen minutes before I heard someone come racing down the basement stairs. Sure enough, it was Daniel. Buckley followed not far behind. But Daniel moved so fast that Buckley didn't have a chance. I mean the guy disappeared so quickly, it did seem like magic. If I'd blinked or turned my head, I would've missed it. He hopped up onto the pool table, pushed aside one of those fiber panels in the drop ceiling, and climbed through the narrow opening as fast as a squirrel up a tree. By the time Buckley entered the room Daniel had replaced the panel and grown silent. Buckley had no trouble finding me. I lay there on the floor staring up at the ceiling, my mouth practically unhinged.

Buckley took hold of me for three seconds. I didn't even try to resist. "You're caught, Chandler. Where's Hawk?" Hawk was Daniel's nickname, short for Hawthorn, I guess. He made it up himself. The guy had nicknames for everyone. I was Mac for Matthew Anderson Chandler. Buckley was Buckley because he supposedly looked like William F. Buckley. The fact that none of us even knew who William F. Buckley was made no difference. The nickname stuck. Before long even parents and teachers called him Buckley.

"Haven't seen him," I said. I knew Daniel was up in the ceiling listening, waiting.

"What do you mean you haven't seen him? I followed him down here."

No way would I divulge his secret. "Yeah, well, if you followed him down here, where is he?"

Buckley looked around. I could see how I must've looked all those times I'd chased Daniel into the basement only to come up empty.

A few days later I climbed up through the drop ceiling and replaced the panel. I sat up there for a few minutes and tried to imagine what it was like to be Daniel. I didn't do too well, not that time. But believe me, I'd try again in the future, many times.

After my eyes adjusted to the semidarkness, I realized I was inside some kind of an air vent, a heating duct or something. It took a while but I finally got up the courage to do some investigating. I barely had enough room to crawl on my hands and knees. But that wasn't much of a problem since we'd spent the summer and most of the fall building foxholes and tunnels out in the fields beyond the tennis court.

I quietly slithered through the vent, fearful at any moment I would encounter some evil prehistoric creature, maybe a giant python or some mutant cockroach. But nothing grabbed hold of me or chomped me in two with its bone-crushing mandibles. I made it safely to the end of the air duct, to the other side of the basement, the forbidden side where Victor had his tool room.

And there, below me, stood Victor, leaning over his workbench, drilling holes in a piece of wood. I caught my breath. He stopped, listened, looked around. After a few seconds he went back to work.

I rested almost directly over his head. I could easily have reached down and touched his wavy locks. But no way was I about to do that. I stayed perfectly still, barely drew a breath. Only my eyes moved.

The tool room had a concrete floor covered with sawdust. There were no windows, not even in the door. I saw a band saw and a drill press and a wood lathe. Hammers and chisels and screwdrivers hung on the wall over the bench.

Along the far wall stood a large wooden cabinet with glass doors. Inside the cabinet was a long row of guns. I saw a shotgun and some rifles, a pistol or two. My knowledge of firearms is only a little better now than it was then, but I can tell you the guy had quite an arsenal. No wonder he kept his side of the basement padlocked and off limits.

I hunkered there in the heating duct, my eyes as big as softballs, staring at all that firepower. I wondered why Victor had all those guns, what he did with them, where he used them. My brain was working through the possibilities when suddenly something grabbed my feet. I screamed. Thank God Victor had his drill press running at maximum R.P.M.s. Someone could've dropped a bomb on the house and he wouldn't've heard it.

But what of the creature? I couldn't turn to see; the space was too tight, too dark. The creature started to drag me backward through the vent—back to its lair, no doubt, where I would become its main meal of the day. I kicked at the creature but the creature easily overpowered me.

The creature dragged me all the way back to the fiber panel in the drop ceiling. The creature was Daniel. I finally got a look at him by the light filtering up through the missing panel. We lowered ourselves onto the pool table. Me first, Daniel right behind. I was his prisoner. We hopped off the table.

He wore a red bandanna over his face, like the one Jesse James wore when he went in to rob a bank. "Okay, kid," he began in a voice I had not heard before, "out with it. Who you working for?"

"What?"

"Don't play dumb with me, soldier. Who's the boss? Who pays your expenses? Hitler? Goering? Goebbels?"

"I don't know any of them," I insisted. "I'm not working for anyone."

"Don't feed me that crap. You've been caught red-handed spying on our most important nuclear scientist."

"No," I said, "I wasn't spying."

"You were."

"I wasn't."

"You were."

"But I wasn't, I promise, I wasn't." Make no mistake, he had me rattled. I was scared, ready to run.

"You'll have to face the consequences."

"What consequences?"

"The sentence for spying is death."

"What?"

"Death."

"No!"

"Yes. Tomorrow at sunrise you will be executed by firing squad. Do you have any last requests?"

I thought it over, but not for long. Instead I turned and bolted for the door. As I raced up the cellar stairs two at a time I could hear him laughing, that deep, mischievous laugh I still hear sometimes in the middle of the night when I can't sleep. But that laugh didn't make me stop, didn't keep me from sprinting full bore, not that day. That day I kept right on going, out the back door and across the lawn and all the way down Thomas Lane. I didn't stop running until I reached the relative safety of my bedroom, where for the rest of the day I daydreamed about Victor and his glass case full of armaments.

VICTOR ARRIVED IN AMERICA ON THE FOURTH OF JULY 1953. He was the only member of his family to make the trip. All the others—mother, father, brothers and sisters, grandmothers and grandfathers—had been slaughtered by the Nazis between 1939 and 1944. The Nazis thought Gypsies were even lower on the evolutionary ladder than Jews. They shot, gassed, hung, and beheaded Gypsies more easily and with less conscience than I stroll past the homeless people on Seventh Avenue. Four hundred thousand of them they murdered during their reign of terror, and several hundred of those were related in one way or another to my friend Daniel.

Daniel's mother's family came to America much earlier, the same year Cromwell won his great victory on Marston Moor, 1644. The Hawthorns came even before the Chandlers, and we came two full generations before the War for Economic Independence. The Hawthorns crossed the Atlantic for religious reasons; the Chandlers had money on their minds.

The first Hawthorns, originally spelled Hathorne, settled in and around Plymouth in the Massachusetts Bay Colony. They were prominent folk during the witchcraft hysteria of the early 1690s; one John Hathorne was even an influential judge during the trials, which ended in several women being hung and one man being pressed to death because of their purported dealings with the Devil.

More than a century later, the writer Nathaniel changed the spelling of the family name from Hathorne to Hawthorne supposedly to distance himself from those seventeenth-century religious fanatics. But it doesn't take a master's degree in psychology to see that old Nate never quite got over his family's legacy of actually sentencing human beings to death for casting spells and mixing potions. His writings are proof enough of that. The poor fellow was obsessed with evil, with its moral and spiritual implications.

Whatever their lineage, the Hawthorn clan (the final "e" was dropped a hundred or so years ago for reasons I've never fully understood) has cast into the New World over the past three and a half centuries a wide array of strange and vivid characters. Hawthorns have been not only judges and writers, but also warriors and adventurers, and now even Gypsies have been added to the family tree.

Chandlers have had no such lineage. Snobs have been our most plentiful contribution to the genealogical chart, generation after generation of boring, pompous snobs. We came to this country with money and with the sole aim of making more money. We've spent an inexcusable amount of time watching over our money, making our money grow, preserving the status quo so that the flow of our money would not be interrupted.

My ancestors, as our name implies, did once manufacture candles, had the contract for many years to light Hampton Court actually, but we ceased that vocation the moment something else became more profitable. Since then we Chandlers have been merchants and bankers and most recently lawyers. That's what I am, that's what my father is, that's what his father was. But make no mistake, Chandlers possess no fervent love of justice, except, clearly, where justice defines our own interests and objectives.

Victor had his own reasons for crossing the Atlantic, for leaving the Old World behind. His real name, however, was not Victor. I never knew his real given name, but his surname, I believe, was once Romankova.

"You listen to me, Chandler, you little scrap a liver," he'd growl at me when I was just a kid, "you quit calling me Mr. Hawthorn. I'm not Mr. Hawthorn, never have been, never will be, but even if I was, I wouldn't want you calling me that. You call me Victor, boy, and later, when you get older, if I still like you, maybe I'll let you buy me a whiskey and call me Vic."

"Yes sir, Mr. Haw— I mean, yes sir, Victor."

Victor took the name Victor after he married Carolyn Hawthorn in Paris in June of 1953. They got married just a few days after Carolyn had won the mixed doubles at the French championships on the slow red clay of Roland Garros. That championship, won at the age of twenty-two, was the crowning achievement of Daniel's mother's tennis career.

Carolyn and Victor got hitched in the first week of June and then went to England, where Carolyn competed in the Wimbledon championships. She lost in the first round of both the ladies' singles and the ladies' doubles, but she made it to the third round of the mixed doubles before being ousted. Victor cheered her every stroke from the friends' box. He cheered with such enthusiasm that several times those stuffy Englishmen asked him to please refrain from whistling and stamping his feet. Had they acted on impulse they probably would have thrown "that ill-mannered Latin in the Hawthorn camp," as the Fleet Street press called him, out on his ear. But they allowed him to stay, and to this day he still tells the story of how a great sigh of relief emanated from the royal box when the lovely young Carolyn Hawthorn was finally eliminated from the championships of '53.

I think Carolyn Hawthorn was almost as much of a Gypsy as her husband. From the age of fifteen to the age of twenty-five she traveled around the world from city to city, from tournament to tournament, from tennis club to tennis club, swatting overheads and forehands and backhands and fending off the advances of countless upper-crust bachelors. Family legend has it that she dined with royalty in both Monte Carlo and London and rejected proposals from an heir to the Daimler-Benz fortune and a member of the Rockefeller clan. These stories I heard not from her husband or her son, but from her daughters, who, like their father and brother, had a special artistry for exaggeration and yarn spinning.

Still, I think their stories had at least a kernel of truth, for in one of the many upstairs bedrooms of that huge house on Thomas Lane hung a photograph of Carolyn with then senator John F. Kennedy on the grounds of the Newport Tennis Club—the Newport Casino, as it is properly called. Jack, his white tennis sweater draped rakishly over his shoulder, had his arm around Carolyn's waist. Both wore suspicious-looking smiles.

No doubt about it, Daniel's mother knew her way around. That's why news of her elopement to a dark-skinned, Eastern European of dubious descent threw such shock waves not only through the Hawthorn family, but through the society pages and sports pages as well. To my knowledge Carolyn never offered a word of explanation to anyone about this man who refused even to give his real name at a press conference at Idlewild Airfield on Long Island the afternoon the couple arrived in the United States via Paris and London.

"Victor," he told them, "the name is Victor, as in victory." And then he rolled up the sleeve of his silk shirt and showed those reporters the number the Nazis had tattooed into his forearm years before at the concentration camp at Dachau.

Victor was the finest storyteller I ever heard. At least he was for the first ten years of my life. Then his son began to usurp that role. Daniel could tell a story just as smoothly and with just as much zing as his father, but his birthright had provided him with a bonus. He had that additional gene that had once belonged to his ancestor Nathaniel, one of the finest storytellers in American letters. The combination of the Gypsy blood and the Hawthorne blood blended in Daniel and turned out a guy who would've rivaled Homer for an audience in ancient Greece.

Daniel started out telling the stories he'd learned from his father, stories from the Old Country, old Gypsy tales that had been handed down from generation to generation for several hundred years, since the days when the first Gypsies had been driven out of India and the foothills of Afghanistan.

Before long Daniel could tell these stories better than Victor. I remember sitting up in our tree fort listening to Daniel tell us how the Gypsies, riding elephants and camels and saber-toothed tigers bareback, had crushed Attila the Hun and his armies at the Khyber Pass. We had no idea where the Khyber Pass was, Daniel probably didn't either, but that mattered not a hoot. He made us see it: the wide pass in the high mountains, covered with snow, the wind howling, the ice covering the beards and cloaks of the warriors, the hand-to-hand combat, the blood turning the snow red, the bodies dropping like flies, Attila's boys finally surrendering, raising their white flags, but the Gypsies taking no prisoners, slashing the heads off the defeated Huns and the heads rolling down the steep slopes into the valleys far below.

Daniel just used his mouth, formed some words, usually pretty simple words, but every last one of us could see the battle clearly, hear the cries of pain, smell the stench of blood. He held us captive with his tales long after most of us should've been home eating supper, cleaning our rooms, working through our multiplication tables and grammar lessons.

If we tried to beg off, attempted to escape so we would not have to once again bear our parents' wrath, Daniel would rip into us with his razor-sharp tongue. "Go ahead, Chandler, run home to Mommy. But tell me something before you go: How do you expect to grow into that gigantic head of yours with walnuts the size of flea eggs?"

Walnuts, that's what he always called the male reproductive organs. He never respected the size of mine. Never.

Sometimes, if the parental wrath had been overly severe in the past fortnight, I would indeed run home to Mommy. Not because I wanted to but because I feared her husband's fury even more than I feared Daniel's scorn. Often, however, I would just sit there and take Daniel's abuse, wait for him to finish and then get on with his tale. Running away not only brought on the ridicule of my peers the next day at school, but I wanted to hear, needed to hear, the rest of Daniel's story. Daniel was our Moses. His stories were the pillars of my education. I wanted to know how the good guys wiped out the bad guys. I wanted the blood and guts. I wanted to hear how in the end justice prevailed, how right won out over might.

Daniel never had to be home at any special time. It must've been an old Gypsy thing, part of their wandering nature. They gave their kids room to roam. Most of the parents in town didn't. You could hear the same angry screams all over town practically every night of the week. "I don't care if Danny Hawthorn is allowed to be home after dark! You are *not* allowed to be home after dark! I don't care what Danny Hawthorn's parents allow him to do! Danny Hawthorn's parents are eccentric and irresponsible, and I won't have you being led down the devil's path by that band of soothsayers!"

Take the time Daniel told us the story about Jesus and the Gypsy. That night I got home way after dark, caught all kinds of hell for that, got grounded for a week. But so what? Sometimes you have to take risks. You can't always walk the straight and narrow.

"The day before they nailed Jesus to the cross," Daniel told us, "that guy Pilate sent two Roman soldiers out to find some nails to do the job. The two soldiers walked around Jerusalem for a while before they found this Jew blacksmith. The blacksmith wanted to know what the nails were for. The soldiers told him. The blacksmith refused to forge any nails for the crucifixion. So the Roman soldiers lopped off the Jew's head."

"For that they cut off his head?" I asked.

Daniel nodded, made a chopping motion with his hand. "Lopped it right off. Right at the base of the neck. Then, a few minutes later, the soldiers found a Gypsy blacksmith. They ordered him to forge the nails. He forged three nails before the dead Jew came to him in a vision and told him about the wooden cross on the hill in Golgotha and about the man who would be nailed to the cross in the morning."

"Jesus?"

"That's right, Mac," said Daniel, "your old buddy Jesus."

I'd been going to Sunday school over at the First Presbyterian Church of Mendham for several years by this time. I'd never heard this story before.

"The Gypsy," Daniel continued, "refused to finish forging the fourth nail. He told the soldiers he would not take part in their crucifixion. The soldiers just laughed, grabbed the three finished nails, and marched off."

"They didn't lop off his head?"

"No, they didn't lop off his head. But the fourth nail still glowed red hot in the Gypsy's forge. The Gypsy poured water on the fire but he couldn't kill the flame. No matter what he did the nail continued to glow. So the Gypsy abandoned his forge, turned, and ran from the nail. He ran as fast as he could. But the nail followed. Everywhere the Gypsy went the nail showed up, always glowing red hot. The Gypsy moved from town to town, but always the nail found him, reappeared every time he tried to eat a meal or take a rest."

Daniel paused a moment to let us think it over.

"This is why," he then told us, "the Gypsies wander, why the Gypsies roam, why they cannot sit still, why they cannot stay for long in any one place. And this is also why Jesus of Nazareth was crucified with only three nails and his legs together instead of with four nails and his legs apart."

DANIEL ALWAYS CARRIED A KNIFE. Maybe it had something to do with the Gypsy in him, with some ancient need to have a weapon, to protect himself and his property from bandits and highwaymen.

I still remember the first time Daniel waved his knife in my face. It happened the same summer the U.S. government started bombing Hanoi for its persistent insolence. A bunch of us were camping out in our tree fort in the woods behind the Hawthorn house. I was there. Daniel was there. Buckley was there. A few of the other guys; not many. The tree fort club was a very exclusive one. You had to pass some pretty severe initiations to become a member.

It was a dark night, no moon, not many stars. We had some candles burning. Daniel started telling us how he'd seen his mother in the shower. He told us, in great detail, how she slipped off her robe, stepped into the tub, soaped up her breasts—every single one of us was as hard as a tree limb. After he had us all swimming in our Fruit of the Looms, he pulled out his blade, narrowed his eyes, and said, "If I ever catch you peckerheads sneaking around the house trying to catch the scent of my mama, I'll cut out your stinking gizzards and fry 'em up for breakfast."

We didn't know what gizzards were but we believed he'd do it, even then.

Daniel, you have to understand, was Head Honcho. Besides his verbal skills, his ability to hold us in rapt attention, he possessed the physical attributes so important for getting and holding power. He was the biggest, toughest, roughest kid around. He took lip from no one, King of the Jungle.

The tree fort club's a good example. We all helped build that tree fort, but Daniel told us where to build it and how to do it. He selected the tree (a big old white oak with a trunk as big as a VW Beetle), supplied the lumber (via Victor), drew up the plans, and acted as full-time labor foreman. And when we finished, Daniel decided who could join and who couldn't.

Although actually, anyone could join, as long as you had walnuts big enough to pass the initiation test. Daniel made up the test.

The lowest branch of that white oak must've been twenty feet off the ground. We didn't have a ladder running up the trunk, just a heavy piece of knotted rope that we'd pull up after us once all blood members had arrived for a meeting or an overnight. The last guy to leave the fort had to pull up the rope, then climb down using the special emergency exit. We did this so outsiders couldn't get in while we weren't there.

You couldn't become an official blood member of the club until you'd used this special emergency exit. To use the exit you had to pull up the rope, climb into the top branches of that old oak to where its skinny limbs extended out and mixed with the limbs of a shagbark hickory. Then you had to steady your nerves and catapult your body from one tree to the next. If you found the courage to do this (many of us didn't), then you climbed down through the branches of the shagbark hickory and dropped off to the ground. Simple.

The first guy into the tree fort each day had to take the same route in reverse: shinny up the trunk of the hickory, climb to its highest limbs, throw himself out into space, grab hold of the white oak, then climb down through the top hatch of the fort. No sweat, right?

Well, maybe not, but this midair free fall kept membership in the tree fort club pretty low. Daniel called it natural selection. We only had six or seven full-time members. As I said, he created the test, but I have to tell you, he was also the first to pass it. In fact, most days he was the first guy up the tree in the morning and the last guy down at night.

"You squaws wait here," he'd say, "while I go up and flush out the enemy."

He was a born leader. That was his role. Few of us ever argued about it. We knew he had the sharpest tongue, the fastest feet, the quickest hands, by far the largest walnuts.

He refused to admit some of our best buddies into the tree club because they didn't have the walnuts to make the midair crossing. "We're looking for a few good men," he told all potential recruits, "no crybabies or chickenshits accepted."

I passed the test, finally, after several weeks of putting it off, after endless taunts and accusations. But let me tell you, I did not enjoy the experience. As I let go of the upper branch of that old white oak and threw myself out into space, I saw my life pass before my eyes, I felt the long arm of death pull me toward the ground, invite me to splatter myself all over the forest floor. But my instincts took hold. I grabbed for that shagbark hickory, and luckily the branch I found held tight. I'd made it. I was in. I was a member, a full blood member with all the privileges after

Daniel sliced open my index finger with his knife and had me wipe my initials and the year onto the wall of the tree house: M.A.C./66.

The same night Daniel threatened to cut out our gizzards if he ever caught us gawking at his mother; I in fact spied her in the solarium. She stood there on a stepladder with her pruning shears, naked, naked as a jaybird.

Carolyn Hawthorn spent a lot of time in her solarium, a large glass room attached to the southeast side of the house. She grew orchids. She used to win prizes for them at all the local flower shows. The orchids hung off the ceiling on long wires and jutted out of the walls on wrought-iron brackets. They grew everywhere, a virtual jungle of orchids. There were big ones and small ones, white ones and purple ones, blood red ones and even black ones. They thrived in the solarium from the warmth and the humidity, even in the middle of winter.

If you had to find Daniel's mother, the first place you looked was the solarium. Even when not pruning and watering and transplanting, she liked to sit out there and read and write letters and talk on the telephone. She had friends all over the world, friends she'd made during her years as a globe-trotting tennis player.

Anyway, that night, after Daniel put away his knife, we started playing grab-ass up in the high branches of that white oak. We chased each other all over that tree like a bunch of New Jersey chimpanzees. Now I can't remember exactly what happened, but all of a sudden Buckley screamed out in pain. The game came to an abrupt halt. Someone got a candle and held it near Buckley's hand. The guy had driven a splinter the size of a toothpick way up underneath his fingernail. It looked plenty nasty.

I could see the jagged end sticking out from under the nail and the other end embedded beneath the little half-moon where the nail meets the cuticle. It hurt to look at.

Daniel tried to grab hold of it with his fingers and pull it out, but he couldn't get a decent grip. Buckley kept screaming, and even though he tried like a prizefighter to hold back, those tears started rolling down his cheeks. Daniel told him to take the pain like a man. He pulled out his knife and tried to cut the splinter loose, but all he could've done with that steel blade was amputate. So he ordered me to go get Victor. "Wake him up if you have to. Tell him to bring tweezers and iodine. Tell him what we got here, Mac."

I took off down the rope without uttering a word. Before I even hit the ground the fear had swelled up in me like a bruise. Why did I have to go? I wondered. Why couldn't someone else go get Victor?

I took one last look up at the tree house. I could hear Buckley screaming. I could hear Daniel telling him to view the pain as a challenge, as a way of increasing the size of his walnuts.

I turned into the darkness. I hadn't ever been alone in those woods before at night. I'd always had Daniel leading the way. He had the eyes of an animal in the darkness. He could see better at night than I could see in the middle of the afternoon.

But this time I was on my own, all alone. My walnuts had shrunk to the size of cherry pits. Something rattled in the brush. Probably just a coon or a groundhog, but I imagined hordes of Nazis wearing those helmets with the long points on top. I jumped, broke into a sprint. Then I slowed, fearing I might be moving in the wrong direction, maybe in circles. I looked for the lights of the house, didn't see any, figured everyone had gone to bed.

An owl hooted overhead. I just about jumped clear out of my PF Flyers. Then I saw it, through a break in the trees, a glimmer of light. I made for it. I got caught up in some brambles, tore a pretty fair gash in my cheek. The brambles drew blood but I kept going. Before long I came into the clearing behind the house. I made my way across the tennis court and around the swimming pool. I could see the silhouette of the big house against the night sky. It looked to me like a huge haunted mansion.

I headed directly for the light I'd seen from the woods. Cutting across the lawn, I realized it came from the solarium. Not a single light burned in the whole rest of the house. I climbed the stairs to the brick patio and walked right up to the door that led into the greenhouse.

And just as I was about to push open the door, I saw her. She stood on the top step of a small stepladder. She had her arms high over her head as she pruned one of her orchids. She was completely naked, not a stitch of clothing anywhere on her body. I just about fainted dead away. My breath ran right out of my chest. I could feel my heart smashing against my rib cage, partly from my adventure with the darkness, but mostly from this unexpected encounter with Daniel's mother and her small, perfect breasts.

I saw her in profile. I ran my eyes down the swell of her lower back and over the hard round ball of her buttocks. The muscles in her smooth thin legs tensed as she reached higher on the tips of her toes. I remember she had hair in her armpits, golden hair, the same color as the hair on her head and the perfect "V" of hair on her crotch.

I don't know how long I stood there staring at her, ten seconds, maybe ten minutes, maybe an hour. But too long, I guess, because suddenly someone threw me to the ground. I felt the cold steel of a razor-sharp blade against my Adam's apple. I feared Nazis but found Daniel instead. He had the injured Buckley at his side.

"We thought you were lost, Chandler," he whispered in my ear as he pressed that blade more firmly against my throat, "but now I see you're just standing around getting ready to make your underpants sticky."

"No," I lied in desperation, "I *was* lost, for hours. I just got here a second ago."

Daniel didn't buy it. "First we have to get Buckley patched up, but then, boy, out with your gizzard."

The blade tickled my throat.

"But but but," I stammered.

He pulled the blade away. I swallowed hard and sat up.

The two of them went quickly around the side of the house. I followed, without looking back. We went through the back door into the kitchen. Daniel went upstairs and got his father. We didn't bother his mother at all. So far as I know, she never knew what happened, never knew I'd spied her in the buff.

Victor performed the operation on Buckley's finger while Daniel and I stood around the kitchen table trying to stay out of the overhead light. Buckley bit down hard on a wooden spatula and managed not to scream as Victor grabbed that splinter with a pair of tweezers and slowly extracted it from under the fingernail.

I can still see the pain in Buckley's eyes.

That splinter was bloody and sharp and close to an inch long. Buckley saved it, used to show it to the kids in the neighborhood if they paid him a nickel. He kept it in his pocket, called it his lucky charm. For all I know he might still have it.

I haven't seen Buckley in a long, long time.

THEY CLIMB OUT OF THE SWIMMING POOL, *naked and dripping wet. It's just past dusk, hot and muggy. They cross the lawn to the back porch. They sit and sip whiskey with a splash of cold water.*

"You okay?" *Victor asks. He wears nothing but a towel draped across his lap.*

"Yeah, I'm okay."

The first few fireflies start their show.

"You did the right thing."

"You think so?"

"Damn right. It was something you had to do . . . something you needed to do."

Daniel stares out at the fireflies, then turns to his father. "It was definitely something I needed to do."

"For all of us."

"I don't feel bad, just strange. And maybe a little scared."

"Strange is good. So is scared. Keeps you on your toes."

Daniel shrugs, lifts an empty glass.

Victor pours another ounce of whiskey into each of their glasses. "I'm just not real sure about this Indian woman."

"The housekeeper?"

Victor nods.

"I wasn't about to kick—"

Victor holds up his hand. "Of course not. It's just that, well, you never know, that's all. You never know."

They watch the darkness settle in among the spruce trees. More fireflies begin their light show.

"So what should I do?"

"Do what any self-respecting Gypsy would do: celebrate."

They touch glasses, pour the whiskey down their throats.

"Now what?"

"So now you hit the road. See the country. Do what we've always done."

"And you think the heat'll pass?"

Victor shrugs. "I think so. There may not even be any heat. Probably nobody gives a damn anymore about that stinking Nazi. Probably not even his wife. We'll just have to wait and see."

Daniel hears his mother pass by the back door, pause, then her footsteps retreating into the kitchen. "She okay?"

"Hell, you know as well as me. Maybe better. You're half her. You know she doesn't buy this 'eye for an eye' stuff."

Daniel nods, stares into the bottom of his glass.

"So," Victor asks, "any place you want to go you haven't been?"

Daniel thinks about it. "Sure. There's always some place."

"Then go. It might be a good idea to disappear for a while. Come back in five or six weeks. We'll know by then if there's anything we need to do."

"Maybe I'll go to Canada."

"Great idea. Go to Canada. Go to the goddamn north country. Take your alias with you. Just in case. You've got a passport, visa, driver's license, the whole shebang. Do some fishing. Find some drunken fishermen who like to play poker. Take their money. Take every nickel they've got. Take their fishing poles and their fishing vests. Take their tackle and their nets. Take their clothes. Leave 'em out in the woods of Canada with nothing but a pair of rubber waders."

Daniel starts to laugh.

"It'll make a great story."

Daniel nods.

They have another drink, father and son.

"I'll go," Daniel says. "I'll go and see what happens."

"Exactly. Go and see what happens. That's the point, after all. And forget about Herr Heinrich. That cocksucker got what he deserved."

LET US BRIEFLY PONDER MY PRESENT PREDICAMENT. I sit here in my hovel on Seventeenth Street between Sixth and Seventh Avenues, a sort of transient nonneighborhood between midtown and downtown, between this river and that river, between the past and the future.

I make notes on yellow legal pads, pads I pilfered from the plush Wall Street offices of Chandler, Wright & MacPherson. I feel small pangs of guilt regarding this misdemeanor, this petty theft, but that guilt pales in comparison with the self-accusations I suffer concerning my possibly premeditated destruction of the trinity.

My hovel is like a ship carrying me through the treacherous waters of this dangerous borough. This is my sanctuary against the outside world, against the muggers and murderers and merchants settling their scores with the opposition. I have so many locks on my door I fear in case of fire I might not get out in time. The underclass and overclass will need chain saws, axes, and a good supply of surface-to-air missiles to reach me here in my inner sanctum.

I do, however, have a window on the world. Through the dusty pane in my closetlike galley I can watch the street below: Bentleys and Beamers in the Barney's department store parking lot; a crack deal on the stoop between a jive-talking black dude and a well-dressed white man; a little old lady with snow white hair pushing a damaged baby stroller filled not with her granddaughter, but with refuse she has recently pinched from overflowing garbage bins.

For nearly a decade I have lived in this city. Now, finally, in this hot and festering summer of '91, the hottest on record, the agony is fast coming to a close. As soon as Chuckie and Martha vacate the family house on Nantucket, on or shortly after Labor Day, I will pack up my few remaining possessions and blow this joint forever. Bye-bye Big Apple.

My ship has been ordered and outfitted and taken on more than one trial run through the reasonably calm waters of Nantucket Sound. It is a gaff-rigged catboat, just twenty-two feet from stem to stern. Some old salts will no doubt call me crazy for taking a vessel built mainly for coastal cruising on a voyage such as I propose, but I say screw 'em, from now on I'm doing things my way.

For years I've threatened to circumnavigate the globe, venture out solo upon the seven stormy seas. That was my plan, hatched in a moment of madness, but with Daniel no longer around to comment upon the size of my genitalia, I have decided a simple transatlantic voyage will fulfill my desires. I will sail across the Atlantic, west to east, then through the Strait of Gibraltar into the Mediterranean. Why bother sailing in circles if a straight line will do the trick? Why go all the way around only to wind up back in a place you want so much to escape?

What I want more than anything is to sail out far enough so that all I can see is water and sky. I want to get away from the huddled masses, away from all the noise and crap in the air, away from the endless stream of insults flowing from the mouths of the melting pot, away from the tempests blowing almost continuously now in the memory cells of my mind.

Slowly but surely I take care of business. I have finally put my affairs concerning Isaiah Jackson behind me. We lost, yes, they found Isaiah guilty, threw him to the wolves on Riker's Island for God knows how long.

The press and probably more than a few of my peers labeled me a naive bleeding heart liberal do-gooder with his heart on his sleeve and his head halfway up his ass. Perhaps they were right. Perhaps each of us is solely responsible for our actions here on earth. Perhaps the moment and the place of our birth, and whether we grow up in a five-bedroom colonial in the suburbs or a rat-infested tenement in the inner city have nothing whatsoever to do with who we are and what we become.

Summer now, nearly a year since all that dirty business out on Nantucket, the middle of August, the dog days, hot and gritty here in the big city. The smell of rotting garbage permeates the air even up high in my fifth-floor walk-up. The sanitation workers have gone out on strike again: more money, fewer hours, more benefits. Who can blame them? For their dirty work they deserve to earn at least as much as the bullpen ace for the Bronx Bombers.

Still, the foul stench of the three-day-old table scraps rises through the simmering heat and wafts through my open window. The smell is just another sign that this great metropolis is on the balls of its buttocks, reaching irreversibly toward its own urban apocalypse. The beginning of the end has long since passed. Abandon ship now, I say to all ye still aboard, before it's too late, before your bellies are ripped open by the savages, before your children are wounded by random gunfire, before some drug-crazed lunatic pushes you or your loved ones in front of the downtown express.

Aren't I in a cheery mood?

I suppose I could have lived in a finer apartment in a part of town more suitable to a man of position and means. After all, I was an attorney at a prestigious firm in the heart of our great country's financial center, our Mecca, if you will. I earned excessive wages, which would easily have paid for fancier digs on the Upper East Side or perhaps down in the luxury condos along the Battery. But I chose to remain here in this humble abode, partly, I guess, to impress Rachel with my display of poverty, with my offerings of great sums to this cause and that, to the rain forest and the whales and the starving children, but also because here I could save my nickels and dimes for the day when I would make my great escape, when I would, like Ishmael, sail about a little and see the watery parts of the world.

I handed in my resignation on June 22, my thirty-fifth birthday. Before I did I took these legal pads plus two boxes of number two pencils. Lawyers prefer lead to ink; so much the easier to erase when the truth starts to get murky.

I think Dear Old Dad and his stodgy colleagues were glad to see me go. I saved them the trouble of pushing me out the door. I'd embarrassed them long enough with my defense of that homeless black man accused of murdering one of our own. And I'd gained their wrath long before that with my endless ruminations on legal ethics and free service to the poor. Pro bono was not an expression that flowed easily from their lips.

They're telling all interested parties that Matthew is on sabbatical, but they know as well as I do that my days at Chandler, Wright & MacPherson have come to an end. I'll never step through those glass doors again.

"He's sailing around the world," they tell the thieves, liars, and manipulators who used to be my clients. "I'll be handling your affairs now."

Sure. You don't change the system, you just get pissed off at it and either join in or move on.

So I'm moving on, sailing off. But first I must tell my tale. I've always wanted to be a storyteller, a spinner of yarns. But I had to suppress my desire because my old man did not approve.

I suppose he was simply being a realist when he told me, "Don't waste your time on such nonsense, Matthew. The stories have all been told. There's nothing new under the sun."

How nice.

To be honest, my father was not the only one to suppress my storytelling ambitions. I inflicted suppression upon myself. You see, I had to compete with Daniel—no small chore considering his storytelling talents. It was like competing against Zeus for a spot on the very first Olympic storytelling team.

Maybe Chuckie did trample my desires and suppress my dreams, but I can say this about him: he taught me how to sail. He taught me not in the waters off Nantucket, but on the pond behind our house in Mendham.

We lived out on Cherry Street, about a mile from the Hawthorn compound on Thomas Lane. Even though we had a great place with a big house and an old barn and plenty of woods and fields, the guys in the gang rarely came to visit. They hung around the Hawthorn place, mostly. And I know why: Daniel's parents liked kids, welcomed us with open arms, whereas my parents viewed kids as pests, drove them off with fly swatters and bug spray.

Still, the old boy did give me my first experience with wind and water.

One summer morning he took my hand and led me down to the pond. There he kept a small sailboat with a wooden mast and a cloth sail. He pointed out the various parts of the boat. He showed me how to rig the sail, how the tiller moved the rudder, how to pull in the sheet to keep the sail filled with wind.

I listened closely because Chuckie loved to give quizzes and he hated with a passion to repeat himself. He likened his word to the Gospel, and who in his right mind would dare miss a word of that?

After the quiz he put me on board, secured a life preserver around my chest, and bade me bon voyage. The breeze must've been blowing just right. As soon as he let go, that sailboat raced across the calm waters of the pond. I screamed with joy, then promptly ran aground on the far bank.

The old boy did not rant and rave, not then, not yet; he gave me a few more chances before that part of the lesson began. Not many, however. He must've thought I had Viking blood in me, an instinctive feel for small craft navigation. But I was just a young American lad of English descent. I had never crossed a pond before, much less a mighty ocean.

Now do not think for a moment I enjoy portraying my father as a ghoul. Believe me, it hurts. I know the man suffered. I know he had conflicts, conflicts no doubt in many ways similar to my own. Nevertheless, a father is much more than just another human being to his son.

Before the sun reached its zenith that summer day, Chuckie boy lost his cool. First he grew impatient, then he began to bark in that raspy Anglo-Saxon voice. Things deteriorated quickly after that. I set sail across the pond. He shouted orders from the shore. I did my best to follow his orders, but under sail many things can go wrong. His shouts turned to screams. I grew nervous and slammed the boat into the cattails on the far bank. He called me an idiot. The boat sprang a leak. He called me a moron. I cried.

End of lesson.

MY FIRST SAILBOAT WAS A SUNFISH I CALLED *FREEDOM;* had it written right across the transom. I kept it moored out on Nantucket Harbor alongside my father's twenty-eight-foot sloop, *Bountiful.* Whenever we wanted to use our vessels we had to travel halfway across the island. The town of Siasconset, you see, has no harbor, no home port. Siasconset stands right on the edge of the Atlantic, one of the easternmost points in the United States. Our house, out on Baxter Road, also verges on the Atlantic, smack on top of a sheer cliff not a stone's throw from the mighty ocean.

In 1933, the year Prohibition cut its losses and FDR decided to drop the gold standard, my father's father bought two acres and a two-room bungalow from a destitute New York investment banker for a price so low that few Chandlers to this day talk openly about the Great Depression. Our family managed to prosper before, during, and after the country's worst economic disaster; we prospered while so many millions of others suffered. But you would never know this to hear us talk. I don't know if it's guilt or humility or the Chandler concept of cultured breeding, but I've never heard a member of the family tell anyone we snared our Nantucket real estate for not much more than two thousand dollars.

The bungalow came down in '37 to make way for the three-story tower now occupying that chunk of land. Glass and open space was the theme, with nearly every room staring out upon that vast and lonely sea. Once you enter the house you cannot even for a moment escape the watery route to the Old World. It's out there always, night and day, summer and winter, beckoning you, taunting you, daring you to venture beyond the breakers.

I'd estimate the value of that house, even now in '91 as the Northeast drones through another year of recession, at somewhere in excess of one and a half million dollars. That's a pretty fair return on the original investment. Better even than war bonds.

My father inherited the house from his father, and I will no doubt one day inherit it from mine. Chandlers believe in continuity.

Father rarely took us to Nantucket before the summer of '65. That's the year Grandfather Chandler died of a massive heart attack at an apartment over on Sutton Place that supposedly belonged to one of his wealthy clients but in fact, if you believe the rumors, belonged to Chandler and Wright, the name of the family law firm before Ian MacPherson finagled his name onto the letterhead. The rumor goes on to say that Grandpappy died in bed with his paramour while she performed fellatio on the old-timer's wrinkled wiener. I don't know if the scenario's true but I hope for our sake it is; this family could do with a little recreational therapy.

Anyway, we didn't go out to the island much until after my grandfather died because Chuckie disliked his pappy as much as I dislike mine. For years after he took possession, my father threatened to sell the house on Baxter Road and buy a place near the harbor so he could be closer to his boat. Of course he never did. He didn't have the guts; figured his old man would come back to haunt him. Not that the old geezer didn't do that every day anyway.

The same summer Daniel threatened to cut out my gizzard, the summer of '66, he came to Nantucket for his first visit. He came pretty much every summer after that. He never stayed long, usually just a week or so. He couldn't handle my parents any longer than that.

But I remember the summer of '66 because I earned my captain's bars that summer and could sail my Sunfish on my own. I rarely went far from shore, usually only as far as I thought I could swim if the boat swamped or the boom knocked me overboard. I'd sail back and forth across the harbor, first running with the wind, then beating against it. I loved the repetition. I'd do it for hours. Back and forth, back and forth. I did it well, very well. And rarely, if ever, did I have the urge to do anything different, to sail any faster or any farther.

But then Daniel came aboard. He did not enjoy repetition. After a single broad reach to Abrams Point and back, he was ready for open water. He'd had enough of the harbor; he wanted to try the Sound, maybe the sea.

He sat forward, his body golden brown after just a couple days in the sun, his T-shirt tied around his forehead. "To deep water, Mac," he commanded, "to where the big fish live!"

Well, after all these years, I have a confession to make. You see, I did not want to leave the safety of the harbor. I was afraid. I admit it. So what did I do? I started for Coatue Point, but halfway across, while Daniel studied something off the port bow, I pulled the pin holding the rudder and dropped that pin to the bottom of the harbor.

"Oh, shit!" I screamed.

Daniel turned. "What happened?"

"The pin holding the rudder to the transom must've come loose," I said, sounding both pissed off and disappointed. "We'll have to head for shore."

By the time we procured a new pin, the day was gone. No time left to sail. Foul weather and other activities kept us off the Sunfish the remainder of his week on the island. Each night in our room up on the third floor I breathed a sigh of relief that I had once again avoided sailing out into the Sound. Of course, I had only postponed the inevitable.

The major activity that week was tennis. We played every day at the Siasconset Casino, the tennis club in the center of town where Chandlers have been hitting bad serves and lousy ground strokes since before the Second World War.

Daniel beat me every time we played. Usually he had to give me a few games just to keep it interesting. He had inherited his mother's prowess on the tennis court.

One morning we sat on the clubhouse steps waiting for a court when Mr. Covington, an old friend of my father's, showed up looking for a game. "Matthew Chandler," he said in a voice loud enough for the whole town to hear, "top of the morning to you."

Mr. Covington was a great big man with a red nose and bushy eyebrows. He scared the bejesus out of me. "Good morning, sir," I mumbled.

"Who's your friend? Haven't seen him around town before." He said this while his eyes looked Daniel up and down. He was no doubt curious about Daniel's dark complexion, about the lad's family line. Siasconset was summer home to many a closet bigot.

Daniel stood up, looked Mr. Covington straight in the eye. "Name's Hawthorn, sir."

"Hawthorne," Covington wondered out loud, "Hawthorne. Any relation to the writer?"

"Direct descendent, sir."

"Excellent, Hawthorne, really fine. Bloodlines are everything. New on the island, are you?"

"Yes, sir," Daniel answered, "brand new. Just moved in."

Mr. Covington wasn't too sure he approved of that, his eyes told us as much, but he sighed and said, "Well, Hawthorne, welcome. And welcome also to your family."

"Thank you, sir. I'll be sure to pass on your kind words."

I wanted to tell Daniel to cool it, not to hang it on too thick, but Covington moved directly to the nitty-gritty: "So what line of work is your old man in? He in the writing game, too?"

That should've been the end of it. Daniel should've answered with some benign line of employ like banker or financial consultant or CEO of IBM and then shut his mouth. That's what I would've done. But not Daniel. "No, sir," he said, "Pop's a detective."

"A detective, huh?" Covington gave me a wink.

I squirmed.

"Yes," said Daniel, "a detective. He tracks down Nazis, old Nazis who got away when the Allies whipped the Krauts."

I thought for a moment that loudmouthed racist might not've heard, had perhaps not even been listening, but I knew he had when a single word tumbled out of his mouth. "Nazis?" he uttered the word as though he himself might've been a storm trooper on the run.

Daniel smiled and nodded. "That's right, sir, Nazis."

And then, before Covington could respond, Daniel said, "Mac here is not really much of a player, sir. Could I interest you in a game of singles?"

Well, I'll tell you, Mr. Maxwell Covington tried to find a way out; he had nothing to gain, everything to lose, but Daniel persisted, so finally they played. Daniel lost, but not by much. They played one set that day. If I recall correctly, the score was 7–5, maybe even 8–6.

Daniel played tenacious tennis, running down every ball and swatting it back, if not with great force, then with even greater consistency. More than once Covington voiced his frustration with a flurry of obscenities he would not normally have used in a public place.

I loved my buddy that day. Silently I cheered every single time he hit a winner.

A year passed. Another summer arrived. Johnson and Kosygin met in Glassboro, New Jersey, in June. They agreed, in theory, not to bomb each other's countries into oblivion. A couple of true statesmen. Heroes of the little people.

A few weeks later, one hundred and five years after Lincoln announced the Emancipation Proclamation, race riots broke out in Newark, New Jersey, prompting Dear Old Dad to exclaim, hopefully in jest, "We're gonna have to gas 'em or ship 'em back to Africa." This from a man with a bachelor's degree from Cornell and a law degree from Columbia.

Ah, to be a white man in the waning years of the twentieth century.

Anyway, while the riots raged, Daniel and Buckley came to the island for a week in early August. Right away they started bugging me to take them sailing. The inevitable had finally arrived. I had to raise my sail and go to sea.

I tacked well up into the harbor, hoping that would be enough to break their sailing fever. But when we came about and went practically wing and wing past Brant Point, they both started chanting, "Sound! Sound! Sound!"

I had no choice. My time had come. I pulled in the sail, set my course, and drove us beyond the Jetties, out into open water.

We sailed west in a light breeze along Dionis Beach. The fears I had imagined did not materialize. Sailing in the Sound was no more difficult from sailing in the harbor. I couldn't even recall what all my fear had been about. And then my first moment of madness fluttered past my eyes on the wings of a sea gull. I grabbed for it.

"I'm gonna sail around the world someday," I informed my mates.

They both laughed.

"Come on, Mac," said Daniel. "You don't have the walnuts to sail around the island, much less around the world."

"The hell I don't. We'll do it right now. We'll sail around the island this afternoon."

"Okay," he said, "let's do it."

Immediately I balked. The moment passed. My madness had gone the way of the gull, back to the harbor where the fishing was sweet and easy. "Well, maybe not today. It's late."

"Pussy," said Daniel.

"Pussy," said Buckley.

"We'll do it tomorrow," I shouted. "Tomorrow at dawn."

"No," said Daniel, "not tomorrow. We'll do it when I have my own boat. We'll race."

This time I laughed. "You're gonna race me around the island?"

"That's right. And I'll kick your butt because as soon as the going gets tough you'll panic and probably drown."

I laughed again. I was on my home turf out here on the water. This was the one thing I could do better than he could. "*I'll* drown? *You'll* be the one who drowns. You don't even know how to operate the tiller or rig the sail."

"Big deal. Lesser men have learned. So will I."

I felt pretty sure he would.

So that, you see, was when we first hatched our plan for an Around the Island Race. But the race didn't happen that summer, or the following summer, or the summer after that. It took us twenty-three years to finally launch that race. The Around the Island Race did not happen until last summer, until the summer of 1990.

Back out on the Sound, the wind shifted. It blew offshore, from the southeast. It blew the *Freedom* north and west, away from the island. We began to move farther and farther from land. I swung the Sunfish on a broad reach, back to the east but even farther north. The island disappeared, not a trace of land anywhere in sight, not even the spires of the church steeples.

And then the wind died.

Buckley and Daniel jumped for joy. They couldn't imagine a better adventure. We were dead on the water. The sea barely heaved. The sail could not even catch enough wind to luff or drag. We had hit dead calm. My mates immediately began inventing headlines.

"JERSEY BOYS LOST AT SEA."

"THREE BOYS AND A BOAT VANISH."

"SEVEN DAYS IN AN OPEN BOAT."

"WILL THEY EVER BE FOUND?"

I told them to shut up, to quiet down.

Daniel called me a lily-livered landlubber.

Buckley pulled his lucky splinter out of his pocket and asked me if I wanted to rub it for good luck.

I told him to stick his splinter up his nose.

They both laughed at me, heckled me, pointed their fingers at me and called me names I'd rather not repeat.

Soon after, with little else for us to do, we settled in for one of Daniel's stories. This one concerned the journey of the old wooden whaling schooner, *Essex*, and its deadly encounter with a giant sperm whale.

"My ancestor," Daniel began, "Mr. Jason Hawthorne, was aboard the *Essex* when the great leviathan struck her on the starboard bow."

"Leviathan?" I asked.

"That's a whale, you idiot," said Buckley.

Daniel nodded. "For hours the crew had been trying to land that sperm whale and its brood. The crew wanted to turn that beautiful creature into so much candle wax and lamp oil and scrimshaw. But the whale had other plans. The whale wanted to turn the *Essex* into driftwood, into fractured planks that would drift forever over the seven seas. He wanted to cast those small spear-throwing animals with little fur and less blubber into the cold and wild South Pacific. He wanted to watch them thrash and struggle on the surface before the sharks arrived and tore their fragile bodies into a zillion bloody pieces."

Buckley and I sat there mesmerized, our mouths wide open.

"The whale," he continued, "made a few passes under the boat. A couple times he even bumped the bottom with his gigantic head. The captain and crew went flying. Then he dove, deep, disappeared. Several minutes passed. The men on board figured the whale had made his escape. But then, suddenly, he reappeared a few hundred yards off the starboard bow. He came directly at the whaling schooner, full speed, like a torpedo."

Daniel paused, gave us a few seconds to think about the image, long enough for me to ask almost breathlessly, "So what happened?"

"The whale slammed directly into the schooner. He made a huge hole in the hull, a hole the size of a house. Water poured in. The ship began to founder. 'Abandon ship!' shouted the captain. 'Abandon ship!' So they did. But the swirling sea quickly swallowed up most of the flailing bodies. A few of the men escaped in the three harpoon boats. My ancestor, Jason Hawthorne, was one of them."

"He lived?"

Daniel nodded. "Jason was head harpooner on the *Essex*. He made his living thrusting long steel shafts into the bodies of enormous sea mammals. In those days that was considered a noble and fearless profession. His kind were hailed heroes and idolized in books and poems."

He gave us some more time to think about this.

And then, "The survivors of the whale attack spent months drifting across the Pacific Ocean. The sun burned away their skin, seared holes in their eyes. Slowly but surely they began to die from thirst and malnutrition. At first the living offered the dead bodies to the sea, threw them overboard with a prayer and a sigh. But after their rations ran out they changed their minds. With nothing left to eat, they turned to cannibalism."

"Cannibalism! You mean they ate each other?"

"That's right, Mac, they ate each other. They ate their dead mates. In my ancestor's boat they actually drew straws to see who would die next so the others might live. Jason lived because he pulled a long straw. Less than an hour after he pulled that straw he feasted on the loser's flesh, had all to himself the dead man's loins."

Sitting there as rigid as an oar, I nearly gagged.

"Hey," Daniel told me, "don't be grossed out by one guy eating another guy's bloody heart or fleshy thigh muscle. Men do what they have to do to survive. There was no sense everyone on board dying of starvation."

He paused. Buckley and I sat on the gunwales of our drifting Sunfish. We didn't say a word. Out of the corner of my eye I saw Buckley rubbing his lucky splinter between his thumb and index finger. I searched the sea for evidence of water spouts.

"If the time comes," said Daniel, "when we need to draw straws, we'll do it sooner than later, before all the fat and goodness has melted off our bodies."

Another silent moment passed before I sounded off. I couldn't take it anymore. "That's such bullshit. Total crap. We'll be home in time for supper."

I said it, but I'm not sure I believed it.

"What's the matter, Mac?" Daniel asked with a smile. "Reconsidering your voyage around the world already?"

"Shove it, Hawk."

"Feeling those first tingles of fear? Sharks and whales everywhere on the horizon?"

"Shut up."

He laughed. "No need to get hostile. It's all carved in stone anyway."

"What do you mean, carved in stone? What's carved in stone?"

Before he answered I saw a strange sparkle in his dark eyes. At first I thought the sun might've danced across his face, but no, he sat against the mast in the shadow of the sail.

"It means," he answered, "that what you said an hour or so ago was exactly right, one day you will set off on a voyage around the world."

"I will, huh?"

"Yeah, you will. But you'll never finish it. Along the way a storm will hit, a wave will wash over your boat, throw you overboard, you'll bob on the surface for a day or two, then, out of nowhere, a giant hammerhead will bite you in half, chomp you in two. And just like that"—and he snapped his finger—"you'll be shark soup, fish chowder."

I sat there staring at him for I don't know how long before Buckley started to laugh.

"What the hell's so funny?"

"Your face, for one thing," said Buckley.

And then Daniel started to laugh, too.

But not me. I didn't even crack a smile. I didn't see the humor. The guy had just told me how I would die, prophesied my death; no laughing matter in my book.

I sat there scowling at them and occasionally glancing up at the telltales on the sail in the hope of finding even a puff of wind.

"You about ready to head for home, Mac?" Daniel asked.

I nodded.

He drew in a big breath and blew on the sail. Almost at once the canvas billowed and cupped. He had brought back the wind.

I grabbed the tiller. We began to move forward. A moderate breeze, this time from the southwest, soon drove us on a slow but steady starboard tack for home.

We made it back to the harbor late in the afternoon, just in time to catch a ride out to Siasconset with Dear Old Dad.

I'VE DUG DEEP INTO MY PAST TO RESURRECT MY YOUTH; no small chore. I don't mean the easy stuff, the stuff that makes us smile. I mean the tough stuff, the stuff we've tried to forget, the stuff we've buried so far beneath the bullshit, we need a dredge to bring it up.

I've brought it up all right, washed it off and let it dry, then taken a good hard look at it. I've lopped off the fat, left only the tenderloin, the heart of the matter. Now only the essentials remain, just the stuff that has brought me to this particular point in time.

Right now I want to go back to the summer of 1967, to the days just after Daniel and Buckley and I returned home from Nantucket. It was August, a couple of weeks before school reopened. A heat wave had settled over New Jersey. The mercury reached into the nineties by midmorning every day for almost two weeks.

The gang spent most of its time hanging around the Hawthorn Compound, rarely straying far from the swimming pool, an old concrete hole in the ground shaped like a four-leaf clover. Daniel's mother's father had the pool built in that shape because he'd had a dream the night before construction began that it would bring his family good luck.

As good a reason as any to do most anything.

The swimming pool game we played for hours on end during that heat wave was blindman's buff. You've probably played it. One guy closes his eyes and swims around the pool, trying to tag someone while everyone else tries to avoid being tagged.

Normally, the players with their eyes open are required to make a certain amount of noise so the player with his eyes closed can have some idea where to search. But during the heat wave of '67, we abolished that rule. You were not required to make a sound. You were required, however, to keep your body, or at least some part of your body, in the water. Under no circumstances, or so I thought, were you allowed to get out of the pool.

Probably the reason I recall those days of blindman's buff so vividly is because after Rachel lost her vision, I went back into my past and tried to find any experience that might help me better understand her sightless point of view. Rachel, you see, was not born blind. She lost her vision when Daniel drove his Honda motorcycle head on into an ambulance on the Garden State Parkway on September 23, 1985, nearly six years ago.

In the weeks after the accident, as we began to realize her vision might never return, I spent countless hours trying to comprehend her darkness. I spent entire days with my eyes closed, pretending I was a blind man. Simple tasks like getting out of bed, making my way to the bathroom, brushing my teeth, washing my face—all these things took enormous amounts of time and energy. And often I would cheat. I would drop something on the floor, a comb or the toothpaste, something, anything, and for a while I would keep my eyes sealed, feel around on the floor for what I'd dropped. But if too much time passed, if I grew annoyed or frustrated, I'd simply open one eye just long enough to spot the missing item. Which leads me back to blindman's buff.

I enjoyed being the one with his eyes closed, except when the others cheated. Like the time the whole gang jumped up onto the deck the second I shut my lids. They kept their feet in the water and made plenty of splashing noises, but every time I got close to someone he'd lift his leg out of the pool until I'd pulled away.

This went on for about fifteen minutes, a heck of a long time for an eleven-year-old kid to keep his eyes closed. I started to feel a little crazy not being able to see. So finally, close to panic, I did what I had to do: I opened my eyes, an offense punishable by banishment.

I found them all sitting up on the deck laughing at me. Immediately I got ticked off, called them all a bunch of swine, liars, and cheaters. But my name calling did nothing to bring about justice. When I accused them of breaking the rules by getting out of the pool, they chanted, "Banishment! Banishment! Banishment!"

"What!?" I cried. "Banish me? You're the ones who cheated, not me. You're the ones who should be banished."

But there is power in numbers.

A court was quickly assembled and I was brought to trial. Daniel, of course, acted as judge. He always did. I had to defend myself. No one else would take my case. Buckley was the prosecutor. The others served as jury. The trial did not last long, a few minutes.

Each of the jurors took a turn on the witness chair, actually an old stump between the pool and the tennis court. Every last one of them said I had indeed opened my eyes. I objected that jurors acting as witnesses and vice versa was a violation of my constitutional rights.

The judge, seated high atop the umpire's chair normally used to call the lines during a tennis match, overruled my objection and ordered me to keep quiet or be held in contempt.

I kept quiet.

The prosecution rested. The defense took its turn. But I had no witnesses, only myself. And besides, I was guilty, I had opened my eyes. So what could I do? What could I say?

I hadn't been to law school yet. I hadn't learned that a jury trial has nothing whatsoever to do with the truth. I sat on the stump and admitted that I had opened my eyes, but for a very good reason, I explained, because an injustice had been perpetrated against me.

The judge listened from his perch and then told me the court was not interested in why I had opened my eyes, only in whether or not I had opened them. "You're either innocent or guilty," he proclaimed. "Not half and half."

I quickly saw the writing on the wall. I threw myself on the mercy of the court. It did no good. The jury found me guilty. The judge immediately passed sentence: banishment.

I tried to take it like a man. But I had seen others banished, and I knew it would not be easy. Before parting I had to ride the gauntlet. My brethren, bearing long, thin willow sticks, lined both sides of the driveway. I had to ride my bike through their fury. I got up as much speed as I could and started my run. They lashed at me with their whips while screaming like a band of bloodthirsty Iroquois. I sustained only minor physical damage, nothing but a few cuts and bruises.

All the way down Thomas Lane and all the way along Hilltop Road and all the way up Cherry Street, I cried. I cried so hard I slipped off my pedals and brought my walnuts to bear upon the crossbar of my bicycle. That made me cry even louder, although even then it was the emotional pain that forged the tears, not the physical pain.

The twenty-four hours that followed, the length of my banishment, was easily the longest day of my life. Those hours went on forever. I thought they would never end. I felt my whole life slipping away, passing me by; important events were unfolding without my knowledge or participation.

By the end of my banishment from the Hawthorn Compound, which was, quite frankly, the center of the known universe, I had learned a very important lesson: Never, under any circumstances, no matter what happens, open your eyes while playing blindman's buff.

History, however, as we all know, is destined to repeat itself.

Less than a week later, just a few days before school reopened, I found myself back in the swimming pool. I swam around and around, my eyes firmly closed. I kept begging my pals to make a sound, any sound at all, but those SOBs wouldn't raise a peep.

I threatened to open my eyes if they wouldn't at least make a splash. But really I knew I'd never open my eyes, no way, not again. I had learned my lesson.

I kept swimming. I think I must've worked my way around that pool fifty times. Twice I slammed my head into the concrete side. I rubbed away the pain and kept searching.

I knew we had to be down at the grammar school field for our first Pop Warner football practice of the season, but that wasn't until three o'clock. At least that's what Daniel had told me. Or Buckley. One of them. So I kept swimming. I refused to believe they weren't in the pool. They had to be in the pool. That was the rule. Rules were rules.

But so what? Maybe they'd broken the rules. Maybe they'd gone inside for lunch. No, no way. They were up on the deck with their feet in the water just waiting for me to open an eye. I wouldn't give them the satisfaction. I kept swimming, kept searching.

I stopped and listened. I heard nothing, not a sound. I didn't know what to do. I faced a moral dilemma. I wanted to abide by the rules. I wanted to cooperate. I wanted to be an upstanding member of society. And most of all, I didn't want to get caught with my eyes open and once again face banishment. On the other hand, I didn't want to look like a fool. I didn't want to swim around that stupid pool with my eyes closed for the rest of the afternoon if no one else was even there. So what to do? Which way to turn?

Well, here's another confession for you: I cheated. I worked my way into a corner and very carefully opened one eye, opened it no wider than an eyelash. I glanced around, didn't see anyone. So I closed my eye up tight and swam to the other side. Again I flicked open one eye, still didn't see anyone, not a soul.

I did this a few more times. Nothing, no one. So finally I just opened both eyes wide. And dammit, there wasn't a soul in the swimming pool. There wasn't a soul in sight. Those bastards had abandoned ship, the dirty rats. Every last one of them deserved banishment.

I looked all over for them: up in the tree fort, down in the basement, out in the garage. Finally I found them over at the grammar school. Football practice had started at two o'clock, not three o'clock. The coach was mad as hell. He dressed me down in front of the other players. "This won't do, Chandler. Forty-five minutes late. On the ground. Push-ups!"

I did as ordered. The coach counted off. "One, two, three, all the way down, Chandler, all the way down. I want that beak of yours touching the dirt. Four, five, six . . ."

All the while my pool pals snickered in the background.

The next day I filed a formal protest. I demanded banishment for every last one of them. But Daniel cited some obscure rule about formal sports involving coaches. He said these sports took precedence over informal sports like blindman's buff and British Bulldog.

I objected but he silenced me by pounding a tennis racket on the umpire's chair. "I therefore rule," he declared, "that all those who left the swimming pool in order to get to football practice on time were perfectly within their rights."

"Including yourself, I suppose?"

He nodded.

I ripped off a series of cuss words. "You could've told me it was time for practice!"

The judge shook his head. "Sorry, Mac," he said, "but the blindman's buff charter does not require a player to inform the other players when he exits for another athletic arena."

You have to understand here, there was no blindman's buff charter. Daniel was just making it up as he went along, just the way he always did.

"However," he continued, "the charter is very clear regarding the premature opening of eyes. And it appears to this court that you must have opened your eyes prematurely if in fact you came to the realization that no one was left in the pool other than yourself."

"What!?" I couldn't believe my ears. "That's such bullshit!"

But Buckley and the others in the courtroom saw the wound open. They immediately went for blood. "Banishment!" they shouted. "Banishment! Banishment! Banishment!"

The judge held up his hands, demanded quiet. He spent several minutes mulling over his decision. I wanted to further my protest but before I could I saw that sparkle in his eyes again, the same sparkle I'd seen out on the Sound a few weeks earlier.

"In this case," he said, finally, "banishment will not be enforced."

The courtroom exploded. My detractors demanded an explanation.

Daniel gave one. Actually he gave two. "None of us," he began, "were here when the accused opened his eyes."

"Wait a minute," I shouted, "I'm not the one on trial here."

Daniel ignored me. "None of us actually saw Mac open his eyes. It would be folly to pass judgement on something we did not see. This court does not rule on hearsay."

"He must've opened his eyes," shouted Buckley, "if he knew we were gone."

"Excellent point," answered the judge, "and one well taken. But other factors are at work here, factors beyond our control. The defendant, Matthew Anderson Chandler, sometimes known as Mac, has an important job to do later in life, once he enters adulthood. In order for him to do this job correctly, he has to have a clean record, no felonies or misdemeanors or banishments. Therefore, this case, as well as his banishment earlier this summer, will be stricken from the record, and from our memories. Today the issue is blindman's buff; tomorrow the issue might well be murder."

I stood there, my eyes and mouth wide open, his final word ringing in my ears. Was this another prophecy? Two in less than a month?

Daniel had transcended his position as judge, taken on the role of Supreme Deity. With a wave of his hand he'd wiped a smudge off my past, opened a window onto my future. Twenty years before the fact, he had foreseen my involvement with Isaiah Jackson.

Or had he actually anticipated what I would one day do to him?

Difficult to say.

Whatever rendering we give his words, his prophecy did nothing to squelch the uproar in the courtroom. Those maniacs wanted blood. They demanded a retrial. It took Daniel several minutes to restore order.

Finally court was adjourned. I was a free man with an untarnished record. The judge put his arm around my shoulder as we walked across the lawn on our way to the kitchen for some of his mother's homemade sticky buns. "Don't worry about these assholes, Mac," he told me, "every mob loves a lynching."

So I learned early, long before my first course in legal ethics, the weird and wicked ways in which justice works. A couple other things I've learned: justice is not blind; justice may wear a blindfold, but that woman holding the perfectly balanced scales, she sees as well as you and I. Maybe better.

RACHEL ANN FREDERICK, ALIAS MISTY GREY, *dips the tiny brush into the tin of blood red. She brings the brush to the canvas, hesitates, then dabs the coated bristles gently against the surface. The effect is immediate but not complete. She picks up an even smaller brush, a brush almost as fine as a pin, and dips it in a tin of pure black. Gently she brings the black to bear upon the canvas. The black blends and shadows the red.*

She steps back to study the painting. It changes before her eyes, takes on a life of its own, becomes a swirl of color and form. The painting is still in its infancy, barely beyond conception. Rachel has not even decided yet if it is a picture of the past or the future.

She covers her paints, places her brushes in a can of mineral spirits. Her thoughts have wandered; she needs a diversion. And no wonder. She has been at work on the canvas since before midnight. And now she sees the clock on the bureau closing in on four o'clock.

She crosses the creaky second floor of the old red barn where she lives, where she works, where she paints. She pulls off her paint-smeared smock and tosses it over the back of a chair. She wears baggy shorts and a light cotton sweatshirt that says MUSEUM OF MODERN ART *in large letters across the chest.*

She goes down the warped and rickety stairs and out into the dull gray darkness lingering before the dawn. The early morning is warm, and utterly quiet. She checks the tires on her bicycle, then climbs aboard and pedals down the driveway.

The old red barn stands just outside the town of Peapack, New Jersey. In a recurring dream Rachel had for several years prior to leaving New York City, an old red barn was the site where she did her best work, where she painted her finest paintings.

Misty rides up Willow Avenue through the dim light, away from town. She pedals easily over the rolling terrain. Her legs have grown strong and hard after nearly a year away from the city. She rides the bike everywhere: to the market and the library and the art supply, wherever she needs to go. But she especially enjoys these rides in the middle of the night before the small town has begun to stir. She can ride in peace, clear her thoughts, forget for a few minutes about the latest canvas demanding her attention.

She turns onto Hub Hollow Road and rides along the river. Never during all her years in New York did she feel safe out on the streets at this hour. Always there was a certain measure of fear. No longer. An artist, she finally realized, needs a safe haven, a place to work where she can feel secure.

She thinks for a moment of Daniel. He stopped by the barn earlier to say he was leaving for a few weeks, heading north, maybe for Canada. His ability to wander, to drift, more or less with the wind, has always thrilled and intrigued her. Quiescent and solitary by nature, she was long ago seduced by his reckless, nomadic ways.

She turns left on Mosle. The road rolls up and over several small hills. She shifts the derailleurs frequently to keep her legs moving smoothly and efficiently. At the top of the hill she shifts into high gear and begins the steep descent back to town. The rush of air blows her short blond locks straight back. Rachel cut and bleached her long dark hair just after she left the city, just before she took on the alias of Misty Grey.

At the Mendham-Peapack Road she turns left again, then right on Overlook to Main Street. The big old white house on the corner stands silhouetted against the emerging dawn. It is still for sale. It has been for sale for months. Every time Rachel rides by the house she thinks about owning it, about living in it, about painting in the big room on the second floor with the bay window gathering in the southern light.

She pauses for a few moments in front of the empty house, then continues along Main and through the town of Peapack: Clayton Amerman Dodge, the Copper Kettle, the U.S. Post Office, Bob's Flower Shop. She turns again onto Willow, and without having seen a soul, she is back in her apartment on the second floor of the old red barn.

She decides to rest for an hour before returning to the canvas. She lies on the sofa and watches through the window as the sky begins to brighten. It has been just over a week since they listened to Billie Holiday's "Fine and Mellow," since he kissed her, since they made love. It has been just ten days, but already she knows.

IN THE SUMMER OF 1968, THE SUMMER WE TURNED twelve, Victor took Daniel and me to Europe. It was no small chore getting permission to go on that trip. For months my parents absolutely refused. No way would they allow their boy to go tramping off with that lunatic Victor Hawthorn and his delinquent son. A weekend to Valley Forge or Sandy Hook or Stokes State Forest was one thing, but six weeks under Victor Hawthorn's tutelage in the Old Country? Forget it.

In my parents' eyes Victor was a ne'er-do-well, a bum, a freeloader who had never, so far as they knew, worked for gainful employment. He'd never been seen dressed in a business suit or making his way to the office, any office. He treated Sunday like any other day of the week and thought nothing of passing an entire afternoon sitting in the old wooden rocker on the porch outside Joe's Barbershop at the corner of Hilltop and Main.

My parents feared if I went off to the Old Country with this man, I might never come back. They had nightmares of me trashing my alligator shirts, cotton slacks, and tan bucks for a silk blouse, silk culottes, and leather thongs. They saw me wearing bells and dancing around a bonfire with hundreds of dirty no-good nomadic lowlifes. They feared I'd become a Gypsy, a pickpocket, a fortune-teller, a magician, an astrologer, a tarot card reader, a sorcerer.

But in the end, primarily because of Carolyn Hawthorn, they relented. She went to see them, if memory serves, on or about the same day Charlie Company swept into My Lai with their helicopters and M-16s and promptly executed several hundred unarmed South Vietnamese villagers. Of course, no one in the village of Mendham, or anywhere else in America, for that matter, knew a whit about the massacre. I'd be a year older and a year wiser before any news of the incident leaked out. And when it finally did leak out, well, I don't think I really thought much about it. Lately I've been thinking about it a lot.

Anyway, Carolyn sat down with Chuckie and Martha on the living room sofa, where we, as a family, rarely sat. She talked to them in her calm, quiet voice. She assured them Victor would take excellent care of me.

I listened to her appeal from behind the wall in the dining room. Her voice, as always, radiated confidence. I could not see her from my vantage point but I knew she sat forward, her legs crossed, her hands folded across her lap.

"Victor," she said, "has been wanting to take Daniel on this trip for years. As you know, he grew up there, in Czechoslovakia and Austria. And of course, we met in Europe, in Paris, in fifty-three. He wants to show Daniel where he lived, where he went to school, where—"

I thought she was going to say "where he spent four years in a Nazi concentration camp," but she decided to skip that particular point.

"—he went to church." Church? Jesus, she was pushing my luck now. I'd only ever seen Victor over at the Mendham Presbyterian a few times, usually with his head bent forward, his chin practically resting on his chest, his eyes blissfully closed. No, his wife was only using the "C" word to instill confidence in Ma and Pa Chandler. They were big churchgoers, rarely missed a service. They believed zealously that God was an American, a white Anglo-Saxon American, who showered his greatest gifts upon Ivy League professionals who drank expensive Scotch, wore tailor-made clothes, and practiced their leisure activities at elitist private clubs.

Carolyn knew all this and so tactfully left Dachau and the Gypsy life out of the big picture. Instead she concentrated on the finer points: the Eiffel Tower, the Mona Lisa, the Alps, the beautiful blue Danube. She painted a canvas of educational venues and spirited adventures. She made the whole thing sound like the experience of a young man's lifetime. And so it was.

And so, they let me go. I got my very own United States passport with my picture on the inside front flap. I remember I took it to school and showed it off like a slab of solid milk chocolate. The girls swooned. The boys frowned with envy. For a few days that spring I was a big man on campus.

On July Fourth we flew to Paris. Actually to London, but then directly on to Paris. At least that was the plan. The itinerary my parents had taped to the refrigerator said Paris. We would stay at a hotel on Montmartre not far from the Sacré Coeur, the same hotel where Carolyn and Victor had consummated their marriage. But at Heathrow Airport, just outside London, Victor grabbed each of us by the arm and hurried us through a thick crowd of fellow travelers.

"Hang on to your hat," Daniel warned me, even though I had no hat to hang on to, "the roller coaster ride's about to begin."

We never saw Paris, never laid eyes on the Eiffel Tower or that famous smile or the guillotine that had severed Marie Antoinette's long, lovely neck. Those things we missed. We flew instead to Frankfurt, West Germany, never part of our itinerary, where we spent two restless days in a fancy hotel with long dark hallways and a special channel on the TV where you could see men and woman stark naked frolicking in the shallow water of a blue sea. Daniel and I, when we weren't staring at those naked bodies, chased each other from one end of that hotel to the other while Victor talked on the telephone to mysterious persons.

My parents might just as well have torched that itinerary on the Frigidaire because I don't think we followed it much after that initial New York–London leg. Victor had other plans, other destinations, other objectives. Not that it mattered. When I finally arrived home a few days before the beginning of another school year, my parents barely said a word about my long absence. I could've been in some Buddhist monastery on the outskirts of Katmandu for all they knew.

I retired to my bedroom as soon as possible. In an old notebook I tried to record some of what had happened. It was my first real attempt at creative writing. I knew for sure I'd have the best stories of any kid in school when the teacher asked, "So what did you do on your summer vacation, Matthew?"

Of course, when the question came, it was Daniel, not I, who took center stage. He kept our classmates and our teacher on the edge of their seats for one whole afternoon. About all I could do was sit by and nod and feel proud just to have been part of it.

We left Frankfurt by car. It was a big car, probably a Mercedes. We incredibly fast along the autobahn. The speed made my head spin.

Victor told us stories about the Nazi war machine, about Hitler and Himmler and Goering and Goebbels. I had heard of Hitler. He had somehow worked his way into my mind as an evil warmonger and murderer, as despicable as Lucifer himself. The other men mean little to me, although just by the way Victor said their names they gave me the creeps.

"Look around, boys," Victor told us as we slowed slightly to pass through small towns and villages, "this is Germany. Never trust a German. They're like sheep. They're followers, people who need to be led. If their leaders tell them to cut your throat, watch out, because they'll cut it. They'll cut you from ear to ear and then stand there and watch you bleed to death without changing the expression on their face. They're oppressed, these stinking Germans, descendents of the Huns and the Goths, oppressed sexually and morally and religiously. Don't trust the sons of bitches, not for a second."

Victor rambled on like this most of the way to Munich. We checked into another fancy hotel late in the afternoon. Victor made some more telephone calls. He let us drink beer with our dinner.

In the morning we went to Dachau. We did not have to go far, less than half an hour from the hotel. Because of Daniel's stories over the years and Victor's ramblings the day before, I had expected something far more sinister and ominous than what we found.

The concentration camp at Dachau had been turned into a memorial museum. It stood in a not unpleasant setting surrounded by alfalfa fields and that day anyway under a clear, bright summer sky. The camp looked harmless enough except for its high chain-link fences topped with rolls of barbed wire.

We arrived early, before the crowds. There were few other visitors as we passed through the main gate. We crossed a large, open courtyard, grassy but dusty from lack of rain. Rows of wooden barracks lined the edges of the courtyard.

"This is where I lived when I was your age," Victor told us. "I came here when I was twelve and stayed until I was fifteen. It was the Germans who brought me here against my will, brought me and my mother and father and my sisters and brothers and my aunts and uncles here because we were Gypsies, because we were Jews.

"They rounded us up outside of Salzburg soon after the annexation of Austria in 1939. We were on our way from Vienna to Innsbruck, stopping in many small villages to perform for the townspeople. We danced and played music and performed magic tricks and told fortunes. Our Gypsy blood had two or three generations before been cut with the blood of Jews, poor Jews, wandering Jews, Jews who'd been subjugated over the centuries just as we had.

"Word had spread from Warsaw to Prague to Heidelberg that the Nazis were on the loose, kicking down doors, arresting and even beating all those who had the audacity to think the Bible ended with the book of Malachi and the words 'And he shall turn the heart of the fathers to the children, and the heart of the children to their fathers, lest I come and smite the earth with a curse.' Well, the curse was loose, brought not by God, but by this psychotic little Bavarian with the pencil-thin moustache and the fetish for high, shiny black boots.

"So we decided, actually my elders decided, that our Jewishness would be suppressed until the Nazi terror had passed. We would hide away our Torahs and our skullcaps until a new day dawned. We did not think the Nazis were interested in a band of wandering Gypsies. We bothered no one, stole nothing, earned our pennies through music and magic. But little did we know that these new demons who had swept into power in central Europe feared practically everything, and hated everything they feared.

"They arrested us in Bergheim on the morning of October 27, 1939. They beat my grandfather senseless because he demanded an explanation for our incarceration. 'Shut your filthy mouth,' growled the SS lieutenant after he spit in my grandfather's face. 'Dirty Gypsy scum does not deserve an explanation from the Fatherland.'

"'Damn the Fatherland!' shouted my grandfather, an almost mythical figure in my life who had once lifted off the ground the back of a fully loaded pickup truck after the jack had given way while my father was underneath greasing the axle, 'damn the Führer! To hell with your Third Reich. I belong to no man. I belong to no country. I am a Gypsy, as free and as clean as the wind in my hair.'

"For this they beat him with their rifle butts and their high black boots. My grandfather died in my grandmother's arms during the train ride across southern Germany."

I stood there next to Daniel in the middle of that dusty courtyard with my mouth hanging wide open and my eyes riveted on this Gypsy storyteller who had lived to tell his tale. I was mesmerized with all this talk of torture and death and heroism.

We crossed the courtyard and entered one of the barracks. It looked clean and orderly, like a cabin you might find at any summer camp for kids from Maine to Montana. There were lines of wooden bunkbeds against the walls and long wooden tables with benches running down the center of the building.

"You see this," said Victor, "this is not the way it was. This was the barracks for male children under the age of sixteen. There were at least two of us in every bunk, sometimes three. The place was infested with lice and rats. They fed us food we wouldn't feed to pigs. They worked us from sunrise to sunset. If we didn't work, they beat us. Grown men and women, men and women with children of their own, pushed us face-down into the mud and kicked us between the legs if we grew too weary to work. German men and German women. Devils. Barbarians. They brought us food, but before setting it on the tables they would gobble up the few choice morsels and then sometimes just toss the rest onto the floor. We would throw ourselves at the food like a pack of starving dogs while the Nazis laughed and laughed."

I stood there wondering if the story was true when a large woman in a gray dress and an official-looking badge over her right breast walked into the barracks. First in German and then in English she asked, "May I help you, answer any of your questions?" She did not smile, but she seemed pleasant enough in a stern, maternal way.

Victor looked at her, studied her, fixed his eyes on her face, seemed almost to burn holes through her flesh. At least a minute passed. Then he spit on the ground at her feet and walked out into the sunlight.

Another minute passed. The woman did not move. She looked stunned, paralyzed.

"You gotta understand," said Daniel, finally, "your father killed his father. He hasn't quite gotten over it yet. Maybe in time he will. He's not usually pissed off like this. Usually he's a pretty happy-go-lucky guy."

Then he spit on the floor as well, not quite so close to her shoes as Victor had, but close enough. He then stepped out the door. I dropped my head and followed close behind.

Our tour continued.

We made our way past the barracks, through another gate, across another courtyard. In the distance I saw several low-slung, squatty-looking buildings. They were made of block and mortar. None of them had any windows. They all had a single smokestack sticking up out of the center.

We stopped and stared at those buildings, just stood there right out in the open and stared. I can't remember how long we stood and stared; long enough for me to grow uneasy. I could hardly believe Victor had actually lived here, that here he had spent a significant part of his childhood. It seemed impossible. It seemed more like just a story, like something that might've happened, but probably not.

I glanced at Daniel. He looked straight ahead. I could not read the expression on his face. We both knew what had gone on inside the buildings. I knew because he had told me. He knew because so many members of his family had been victims of the gas. The gas was part of the family history. It could not be denied. It could not be buried in the past.

We must face up to who we are and how we got here. Victor believed that, and so did his son. And so now do I.

Then the father and the son did something quite remarkable, something I will never forget as long as I live. Probably Victor went first and Daniel followed, but in my memory of the event they both began to disrobe simultaneously, at exactly the same moment.

The camp at Dachau was no longer deserted. Quite a few other visitors had arrived for a tour of the death camp. They, like us, wandered around the courtyards, strolled in and out of the barracks and some of the administration buildings. I saw parents taking pictures and young lovers holding hands and two little girls playing hopscotch on a pattern they had drawn in the dust. At least fifty people were in view, most of them solemnly going about the business of touring a Nazi concentration camp.

The shirts of my companions came off first. They did not unbutton the fronts but simply drew the blouses over their heads and tossed them on the dry grass. Then came the shoes and the socks. They did not hurry but rather took their time now as though savoring the moment.

I think I took a step or two backward as though that cowardly ploy would somehow separate me from them. Others were watching now, stopping in their tracks and gawking at this man and this boy as they shed their civilized skins. I saw one or two people actually point.

Victor pulled off his khakis, Daniel his dungarees. They both stood there in their underwear, but not much time passed before these concealments came off as well. Father and son then stood there totally naked, not a strip of clothing between them. Their peckers dangled between their legs, the elder uncircumcised, the younger well sculpted to a fine, fleshy point. Victor removed his wedding ring and the beaded leather band he wore around his neck. He dropped these items onto the ground beside his shirt.

Quite a crowd had gathered by this time. But they didn't get too close. They kept their distance. So did I. I took another step back.

Victor and Daniel took a few steps forward. They stopped on the threshold of the gas chamber and turned around. "Long live the Gypsies!" Victor shouted, and then he and his son ducked their heads and stepped through the low, narrow doorway.

I don't know how much time the universe used up before the two uniformed guards came sprinting through the crowd and across the courtyard. A minute or two, at least. Plenty of time for the Zylon B to take effect, had it still been exterminating the lives of innocent men, women, and children. But as it happened, the gas had been turned off, and this time the guards were forced to remove Gypsies from the chambers rather than shove them inside.

I do not think the irony of this was lost on any of us, not even the young.

The guards literally had to drag Victor and Daniel from the gas chamber. Once they had forced the Hawthorns out through the door, they ordered the father and the son to put on their clothes and leave the camp, immediately. It seems if they did not obey, they would be arrested for indecent exposure and disturbing the peace.

Victor laughed in their faces. "But the last time I was here," he shouted, "you butchers ordered me to take off my clothes. You ordered me into the gas chamber. I don't understand. I'm confused. Why don't you get your story straight! Why don't you make up your minds! Do you want us robed and alive or naked and dead? Which is it? What'll it be!?"

The guards looked trapped and angry, and absolutely capable of inflicting violence on this rabble-rouser if only someone would give them the order. But the order never came, for the Reich had been crushed, pinched into submission by the commies and the capitalists. There would be no more deaths at Dachau.

Slowly the Hawthorns dressed, but not before Victor had recalled in a loud and clear voice the name of every member of his extended family whom the Nazis had exterminated. It was quite a show. There must've been close to a hundred names, maybe more. I found myself moving closer to him both as the names flowed from his lips and as the clothes began once again to cover his thick, muscular body.

The guards, with two new comrades for support, led us across the courtyard in the direction of the main gate. They wanted us, Victor anyway, on the other side of the fence, off the grounds of their dominion. But halfway between the gas chambers and the barracks Victor stopped. The guards grabbed his arms and tried to keep him moving, but he broke free merely by flexing his biceps. They did not dare use further force. Tourists were snapping photos like crazy.

"Here, Daniel," he said, "right here where I stand at this moment. This is where they did it. This is where those two bastards, kids really, not more than twenty years old, clubbed my father, your grandfather, to death because he asked them if he might have some ointment to treat a wound on his son's leg. That son was me, Daniel, I was the son. I'd been stung by a bee and the bite had swelled. It was red and angry. I stood at his side, as close as you stand to me now. He begged them for assistance. They ordered him to shut up, to keep quiet, to return to his barracks. He refused. He demanded they do something to help me. They raised their clubs high over their heads. I screamed. His arms went up in defense. But his arms did no good. In no time at all he lay on the ground, right here at this spot, in a widening pool of his own blood. His head had been split open in several places. I bent down to him, but their pointy black boots kicked me away. Right before my eyes they killed my father and then they did not even have the decency to give me a moment to kiss him good-bye."

Good God.

"Until that moment," he added, "I do not think I had spent even one full day away from my father. He believed, as I believe, that a son's place is at his father's side."

Victor grew quiet then. Daniel went to him and put his arms around the big man's waist and squeezed. Victor squeezed back. After a few moments they separated. Daniel took his father's hand. The three of us walked slowly across the courtyard and out through the open gate.

WE LEFT DACHAU AND DROVE SOUTH. We crossed the German-Austrian border at Lake Bodensee. We spent our first night in Austria in the town of Bregenz. Most of the time I had no idea where we were. I was a stranger in a strange land. The language, the money, the food, the people, were all foreign to me.

In Bregenz we stayed with a family that had an old house on a hillside overlooking the town and the lake. We stayed three days. I think the man who owned the house was related to Victor, a third cousin or something; I never knew for sure. As with most things during those weeks, I was usually in the dark. I spoke not a word of German, and very rarely was anything translated for my benefit.

Daniel and I spent our time in Bregenz with the family's fourteen-year-old daughter. She had a pretty face but absolutely no interest in me. Maybe she disliked Americans. She definitely did not like being our tour guide while the adults spent hours drinking ouzo and discussing who knows what in the peach orchard behind the house. Karin led us on long walks through the old parts of town and along the lakeshore and up through the green, rolling hills with the still snow-covered Alpine peaks shining white in the distance.

On one of those hillsides we stopped to eat a picnic lunch her mother had packed for us. After eating we lay on our backs and stared up at the sky. I fell asleep. When I awoke, Daniel and his cousin were gone. I called out but received no reply. Immediately I began to panic. I felt sure they had deserted me, left me there to fend for myself. But a few minutes later I saw them come out of the trees and across the hillside. They held hands. At least they did until they saw me watching. Then they fell apart, him ahead and her behind.

Had they been off doing the dastardly deed, fiddling each other's young diddles? I don't know. It's certainly possible. That might've been the afternoon Daniel lost his virginity. If so, he never confided in me.

*   *   *

The next day we left Bregenz. We drove south and east through the Alps. We did not drive for long. Victor rarely drove more than an hour before stopping. "The idea," he liked to say, "is never to get somewhere, but to assume you're already there."

I didn't know then and I don't know now exactly where we were; surrounded by high mountains is all I can tell you. Without saying a word, Victor drove the car into a narrow parking lot just off the highway and shut down the engine. We threw some light packs on our backs and started up a trail. Victor led the way. Then me. Daniel brought up the rear. We hiked uphill most of the day.

We stopped for a while early in the afternoon and ate some sandwiches and waded into a cold, fast-moving stream where you could see the trout straining against the current in a constant search for food. Then back on the trail and another two or three hours high into the hills. Most of the time we hiked out in the open, beneath a scorching sun and a bright blue alpine sky. I asked Daniel if he knew how far we might go. He just shook his head.

I didn't bother to ask Victor. I knew from our many weekend adventures together that he didn't like questions about destination. He considered youth a privileged time when destination did not matter, when the journey was the only important thing. He told us we were lucky not to have to think about where we were going or why.

Victor set a slow but steady pace, one our young legs could handle without too much strain. And then, with the sun no longer quite so high or hot, we stopped. "We'll camp here," he said.

As far as I could tell we stood on top of the world. I could look out and see a million miles away. The valley where we had started loomed below, so far below that the highway looked as thin as a shoelace thrown in the grass. The mountains and their snow-covered summits encircled us. The tops of the highest mountains appeared to reach right up into the sky, right up into the heavens. I had never been in a place like that before. I had never been so high.

We spread our blankets beneath some tall pines. We gathered wood for a fire. We found another stream, and I watched while Daniel and Victor took turns catching trout with a fly line attached to the end of a long, thin stick. I learned to gut and clean a fish right there on the banks of that stream. We took a dozen. "Four for each of us," I said.

"Three for each of us," Victor replied.

We got back to camp and started a fire. The sun began to slide behind the mountains in the west. Right away the temperature began to dip. I pulled on a sweatshirt and stayed close to the fire. Victor made a pot of coffee and sliced a loaf of bread. He had everything he needed in his leather rucksack. He even had a skillet and a folding grill, which he placed over the fire and held steady with several fist-size rocks. Darkness came quickly, the sky turning from blue to black while I stared into the fire and tried not to shiver.

Victor threw some grease into the skillet. When the grease began to bubble he carefully placed two fresh fillets end to end. I stared into the skillet, watching those fish fry, and so taken was I by the sight and the smell of the trout that I did not see or hear the man enter our camp.

Three of the fish were his. He also shared our bread and our coffee. After the meal he gave Daniel and me thick bars of Swiss chocolate wrapped in foil. I could not make out his face very well in the flickering light of the fire, but he had a long, thick beard and a bushy mustache and hair that grew almost to his shoulders beneath a wool hat.

He and Victor spoke in a language that did not sound like German. I couldn't understand a word they said. They continued to talk long after Daniel and I had wrapped ourselves in our blankets. We lay so close I could smell the coffee and the chocolate on his breath.

"You wanna hear something, Mac?" he asked.

"Yeah. What?"

"We're pretty good pals, right?"

"Right. The best."

"Blood buddies and all that stuff, right?"

"Right. So?"

"So we're gonna have to be careful."

"Why? Whattaya mean?"

And that's when he hit me with another prophecy. Up there on top of that mountain, up there on top of the world, he got that sparkle in his eye and went to forecasting. I could just barely see that sparkle as the flames of the fire danced through the darkness.

"Someone's gonna come between us."

"What? Who?"

"I don't know. Probably a woman."

"No way. Never."

"Yeah, it'll be a woman all right. A beautiful one with long dark hair and wild eyes."

"You're crazy."

"Maybe."

I thought about it. "So when's all this gonna happen?"

"Hard to say. Not for a while."

"Well," I said after a pretty good pause, "I think you're full a shit."

"Hey, you two," said Victor. "Shut up and go to sleep."

So we did. We closed our eyes, and in no time we were both fast asleep beside the fire.

When I opened my eyes in the morning the man was gone. Daniel slept on my left, Victor on my right. A thick fog hung over our camp. The damp cold seeped right through my blanket, right through my skin, right down to my bones. I tried for a while to warm myself but knew the only way was to crawl out from underneath that blanket and start moving.

I stood up, pulled on every stitch of clothing I had. I ran in place, did a few jumping jacks. Then I stirred the fire. Only a few hot embers remained. I added some fresh kindling, blew on those coals until I was blue in the face. Finally a small flame appeared. It sprang up and did a little dance across the dry pine. I had that fire roaring by the time Victor and Daniel opened their eyes.

"Well, I'll be a horse's ass," bellowed Victor, "young Chandler has actually taken some initiative! Praise the day! The young lad's not entirely useless after all."

I turned redder than a ripe tomato. But inside I beamed. Inside my happiness and pride exploded like a Roman candle.

After breakfast we climbed off the mountain, down through the fog. Victor didn't offer to explain why we'd climbed up in the first place. That part was up to us.

Over the next few days we traveled to Innsbruck and Kitzbühel and Salzburg. We always stayed at someone's home, never in hotels. Victor knew people everywhere, and after an hour or so of eating and drinking and toasting, the adults always withdrew to a private room.

"Business," Daniel told me.

On our last day in Salzburg we drove out to Bergheim on the German border. We stood in the middle of the town square. Local farmers, their wagons forming a wide circle, were busy selling produce, fresh fruits and vegetables.

"On a warm October morning thirty years ago," Victor told us, "this square was filled with Gypsies. We came into the square to entertain the townspeople. For twenty years our people had been stopping in Bergheim to dance and sing and play music and perform magic. I assumed then that I would stop in Bergheim every autumn for the rest of my life."

Victor paused, took a long look around at the old wooden houses and the colorful shop windows. "But late that morning the Nazis swept into the square. They had us surrounded before anyone knew what had happened. They came with tanks and trucks and enough men to battle an armored division. It happened right here, right here where we stand."

He paused again, turned to his son. "This is where they beat your great-grandfather, Daniel, where they began their extermination of nearly one whole side of your family."

"But why," Daniel asked, "why did they do it?"

"Because we scared them," Victor answered. "They feared our freedom. A caged animal cannot stand a wild animal. If given the opportunity, the caged animal will kill the wild animal every time. This is why wild animals like us must stay alert and stick together."

Daniel nodded, and so did I. I nodded, but I had no idea why.

On the morning of August 18 we arrived in Vienna. We checked into a large hotel, the Stephansplatz. I remember the name because our room was on the top floor and when I pulled open the drapes I saw this incredible cathedral tower, so close I thought I could open the window, reach out, and grab hold of the spire.

The tower was attached to St. Stephen's Cathedral, where I spent most of the rest of that day and a good deal of the next. I wandered around the cathedral for several hours, never afraid of getting lost or being alone. Somehow I felt safe there.

I wandered from the catacombs deep beneath the chapels to the top of the belfry towering high above the city. Daniel and I ran to the top of the belfry, nearly two hundred and fifty steps if memory serves me right. When we reached the top, panting and gasping for breath, I asked Daniel, "Are we in heaven?"

He assured me no such thing existed, except maybe in my imagination.

The second day I mostly just sat in various nooks and crannies of that great cathedral, sometimes with my eyes open, often with them closed. I had never been in a cathedral before. The only religious place I had ever been was the Mendham Presbyterian Church.

I was in awe of what God had created. I sat perfectly still while a man dressed in black robes strode past me. He did not stop until he had reached the top of the high altar at the far end of the church. When his mouth opened his voice exploded off the walls. He did not speak loudly, but the force of his voice filled the cathedral. All visitors stopped in their tracks and did not move again until the man in black had finished. He spoke first in Latin, then in German, and finally, briefly, in English.

I do not know why the clergyman spoke in English; I like to think it's because he knew I was seated in the nave and what he had to say he knew I needed to hear.

"Many centuries have passed since the last Crusade," he said. "Now each of us, in our own way and for our own reasons, must undertake our own Crusade. Our salvation lies in Palestine, in the Holy Land, in the

Old City of Jerusalem. I want you to go there. I want you to stand on the hill of Golgotha. I want you to stroll lightly but boldly down the Walk of Sorrows. I want you to cast rose petals into the wind. And I want you to enter in peace the Church of the Holy Sepulchre. If you make this simple pilgrimage for the Holy Trinity, for the Father and the Son and the Holy Ghost, God will bless you and those around you forever and ever. Amen."

EARLY THE NEXT MORNING, LONG BEFORE DAWN, we left Vienna. I was dreaming of a great sailing ship carrying me through the Strait of Gibraltar and across the Mediterranean bound for Jerusalem when Victor rattled me awake and ordered me to dress.

We left Vienna in a car I had not seen before. Daniel and I sat in back, Victor up front with the driver, the bearded man who had been with us on the mountain many days earlier, the same man who would point a .357 Magnum at my chest in my father's house on Nantucket a dozen or so years later. I suppose it's like Rachel says: everything is somehow in some way connected, even when you don't realize it, especially when you don't realize it.

We drove out of the city, out into the darkness of the countryside.

"The commies are getting ready to invade," Daniel whispered in my ear.

"What?"

"The commies are invading Czechoslovakia. We gotta get there before they do."

And so we did. We arrived about twelve hours before the tanks.

An hour or two after leaving Vienna we reached the border. It was still dark when the car stopped. A man in uniform approached the car. The driver handed him some papers. They exchanged words I could not understand. They spoke softly. The man in uniform glanced over his shoulder at the small wooden guardhouse where another man sat reading a newspaper.

Victor handed the uniformed man our passports. I could see a thick wad of American money sticking out of the bottom of the bundle. The guard opened the passports and quickly stuffed the greenbacks into his breast pocket. Not long after, the gate opened and we drove into Czechoslovakia.

By the time we reached Prague the sun had risen into the morning sky. I knew it was Prague because just before we arrived Victor turned to Daniel and said, "We're going to Prague to convince your aunt and

uncle the time has come to get out of the country, to go to the
west."

The aunt and uncle, I learned later, were not really Daniel's aunt
and uncle at all. They were Victor's godparents, not blood relations, but
nevertheless kin, especially as far as the Gypsies were concerned.

The aunt, an old lady with deep wrinkles and a few wisps of white
hair, had helped Victor clear the womb. She had severed the umbilical
cord. The uncle, an old man with even deeper wrinkles and hair as gray
as a battleship, shook my hand when I held it out and nearly crushed it.
He smiled with his few remaining teeth when he saw me grimace.

They lived not far from the center of the city, near the wide bend in
the Vltava River, upstream from the Charles Bridge. Their apartment had
a small living room and a kitchenette and a bathroom the size of a closet.
My hovel here on Seventeenth Street is vast in comparison.

Old plaster hung off the ceilings and walls. Large chunks of plaster
fell to the floor and shattered several times during our thirty-six hours in
the dreary flat.

The old couple owned no lamps. Each room had a fixture in the
ceiling, but they had only one light bulb they moved from room to room.
The old man would stand on a rickety chair and unscrew the hot bulb by
grabbing it with a rag. There were no rugs on the floor, few pictures on
the walls, little food in the cupboards. The aunt and uncle, you see, were
dissidents. They disagreed with the government, so the government made
them suffer.

They believed the communists were being driven from power. They
believed in the Prague Spring, even now in the late summer. They believed democracy was right around the corner. They did not believe the
Russians were getting ready to invade.

I picked up bits and pieces of the conversation whenever Victor took
the time to translate the mix of Romany and Slavic into English. At first
the conversation maintained a steady calm, the three of them taking
turns, making their points, listening while the others made theirs. But
within an hour tempers started to rise. They began to shout, one louder
than the next.

"They won't listen to reason," Victor told us. "They're as stubborn
as mules. They think all this talk about a Russian invasion is a ploy by
the secret police to bring the subversives out of hiding. They won't
leave."

As morning rolled into afternoon and afternoon into evening, their
discussion rolled on. The aunt made us tea and something to eat, canned
peaches and dark brown bread covered with marmalade. That was it, that
was all they had.

I looked out the window. On the street below I saw the bearded man leaning against the car smoking a cigarette. Across the street I saw the river and the Charles Bridge with its tall steel towers.

Daniel asked me if I wanted to go out and take a walk around. I said no. He called me a chickenshit and went by himself. I saw him stop and say something to the bearded man and then walk away, down the street, and across the bridge.

I spent the rest of the day in that apartment except for a brief excursion when Victor and I went down the street to buy some food. Victor did not even ask after Daniel, only wondered aloud if the boy had any crowns so he could buy himself something to eat.

We bought fruit and bread and meat. The bearded man came upstairs with us to eat. During the meal the arguing stopped. The uncle wanted to know who I was and where I was from. Victor told him. He stared at me with icy eyes and said America had no soul and had long ago become the dominion of the devil. At least this was the translation Victor offered. I felt scared and confused, so I didn't say much, not a word.

Daniel returned just as the meal ended. He told us a crowd of thousands had gathered in the public square to protest Russian aggression. Someone in the crowd who spoke English told him the Prague Spring was being crushed by petty men with paranoid minds. Victor translated this for the aunt and uncle. They threw up their hands. The debate continued.

The bearded man returned to the street. Daniel produced a deck of cards from his pocket and showed me a new trick or two. The sky grew dark. We played War on the floor under the dim light of that single bulb while Victor and the old people ranted and raved.

We all slept together in the living room. The sofa opened into a bed where the aunt and uncle slept. Victor slept on the armchair where he'd been sitting most of the day. Daniel and I curled up on the floor on top of some spare blankets. I did not sleep well. I dreamed again of that great sailing ship crossing the Mediterranean, but this time I found myself below deck, down in the darkness, one leg chained to an iron bar, the other leg chained to the leg of an enormous black man with a shaved head and the cross of Jesus tattooed into his broad chest.

The dream drove me from my light sleep. I opened my eyes. Right away I heard the low rumble in the distance. I stood and crossed to the window. I drew back the curtain. What I saw made my heart skip a beat, maybe more than one. I know for sure I gasped.

"What is it, Matthew?" I heard Victor ask.

It took me a moment to answer. "Ta-ta-ta-ta-tanks," I stuttered.
"What?"

Before I could say it again he stood beside me. He wore nothing but
a pair of boxer shorts. He was enormous, like the black man in my
dream, a giant before my eyes. Together we stared out that dusty window
at a long line of tanks as they rumbled slowly but surely across the
Charles Bridge. The Russians had arrived. I, Matthew Anderson Chandler, was in a city under siege.

All day we holed up in the apartment. Victor would not let us go
out, not that I would've anyway. The bearded man brought news. Others
came with news as well. We listened to the radio. Of course, I couldn't
understand a word the announcer said, but I listened very carefully. I
remember he sounded calm and under control. I learned a few facts that
day, not many: The Russians along with the East Germans and a few
other communist countries had invaded Czechoslovakia. There had been
few shots fired. Casualties were low, practically nil. The Czechs, aware of
their vulnerable position, had decided not to fight.

"But what it means," Victor told us, "is another era of suppression.
There will be arrests, beatings, prison terms, assassinations. Czechoslovakia, like all of Eastern Europe, will once again be turned into a giant
prison camp."

From the window we saw the camp taking shape. More and more
tanks, accompanied by thousands of soldiers, took up positions around
the city. The aunt and uncle watched all this with narrowed eyes. I had
the feeling they had seen such things before.

Late in the afternoon the bearded man came to the door. He held a
brief conversation with Victor. As soon as it ended the bearded man left.
Victor turned to his godparents. I could tell by the tension in their voices
that something had happened, something had changed.

Victor pointed to Daniel and me and ordered us to follow him. We
did so without a word. Victor hugged and kissed his aunt and uncle, then
led us out of the apartment, down the hallway, and up several flights of
stairs.

"The police are coming," he explained briefly as we passed through
a narrow doorway and out onto the roof. "We cannot be found without
visas."

We crossed from that rooftop to another rooftop, where a young
woman met us and led us across several more rooftops. Below we could
see clearly the occupation of the city. I will never forget those tanks. They
looked like prehistoric insects crawling along those old cobbled streets,
their long gray muzzles pointing the way, just itching to blow apart some
walls, blast away some lives.

We followed the woman into another apartment building. She led us to an empty room, gave us bread and cheese and wine. Victor encouraged us to drink, not too much but two or three glasses each during the several hours we sat in that room lit only by a single candle.

Finally, long after it had grown dark, we heard a knock on the door. It was the bearded man. We followed him down the stairs and out into a back alley. Daniel and I got into the back seat of a car, a different car from the one we had arrived in the day before.

We drove slowly out of the city. Several times we had to back up and turn around. The tanks were everywhere. Roadblocks had been set up at practically every intersection. But the bearded man knew the city well. Before long we had left the city and the soldiers behind. We drove for several hours, to where or in what direction I had no idea. Daniel didn't know, either. He told me so, then fell asleep.

But I couldn't sleep. I couldn't even close my eyes. I stared straight ahead at the narrow road. We made a million turns that night, never seemed to stay on any one road for more than a few miles. Occasionally we saw troops and tanks, but as soon as we did we made a beeline in the opposite direction.

Sometime in the middle of the night, the car stopped. The bearded man shut down the engine and turned off the lights. I shook Daniel awake. We all got out. It felt somehow as though we were in the middle of nowhere. It was a black night; not a single star showed through the cloud cover.

The bearded man opened the trunk. He handed Victor a long length of rope and several small plastic bags. Then he and Victor embraced before he stepped back into the car and drove off. We watched until the taillights disappeared.

"Follow me," Victor ordered.

We followed him across the road and into a field. On the far side of the field we entered a stand of tall trees. We held hands as we made our way slowly through the dark forest. After maybe fifteen minutes we came out along the bank of a wide river. It was too dark even to see the other side.

"The Danube," Victor said very softly, as though that explained everything.

He ordered us not to say a word, not a single word no matter what happened. We put into the plastic bags our passports and the few other possessions we had been allowed to bring. We sealed the bags and stuffed them into Victor's leather rucksack. Then Victor tied the rope around my waist and around Daniel's waist.

"We're going into the river," he whispered. "Don't panic and don't fight the current. And don't, under any circumstances, let go of the rope."

Let me assure you, I was already close to panic, scared shitless, more scared than I had ever been in my entire life. But I said not a word, uttered not a single sound in protest. About all I remember thinking is how incredibly far we had strayed from the itinerary taped to my parents' Frigidaire. I doubted very much if they would have allowed me to go on this trip had they known of my midnight swim across the blue Danube.

It was a warm night, the water as warm as the air. We waded in until the river rose over our heads. Then we started to swim, slowly, cautiously. We tried not to disturb the surface of the water. All went well for the first hundred yards or so. But then we hit the current. Right away it felt like a whirlpool sucking me under, pulling me downstream. I fought against it. I began to kick and splash. Victor ordered me to stop. But I couldn't. I had already panicked. I let go of the rope. My body spun. My head went under the water. I swallowed some of the Danube. The rope around my waist came loose. Like an astronaut on a space walk severed from his ship, I floated off, into the darkness, farther and farther from my link to reality, from my family and friends. I thrashed at the water but it did no good. I was all alone on the river Danube a million miles from home.

The darkness hung over the river like a shroud. I could just barely make out my hand in front of my face. I may as well have been blind.

But then some deep-rooted instinct I did not know I had rose to the surface and cleared my thoughts. It reduced all my fear to one simple message: Get to the other side!

I washed up on the far bank. Black muck covered me from head to toe. I did the best I could to cleanse my body, then I tried to get my bearings. I knew only that I had crossed the river, I had not gone back to the Czech side.

I wanted in the worse way to call out to my companions, but Victor had ordered us to maintain silence, and so I did. I sat there huddled on the bank, shivering but proud of myself for getting off the river, for surviving, for keeping silent. I crouched in a tight ball, my arms wrapped around my legs, and waited for something like morning to happen.

It did not take long. The first faint traces of dawn crept over the river before my clothes had dried. Soon I could see the forest on the other side. Curls of mist rose off the water. I looked up and down the river. Several more minutes passed before I saw them. They sat together on the embankment maybe a hundred yards upstream. They saw me at the same moment I saw them. I stood and started to wave my arms, but Victor shook his head, pressed his hands in a downward motion. He wanted me to sit still, to stay quiet. We were not yet out of danger.

I watched them very closely. Never for a moment that whole day did my eyes wander. I barely blinked.

They moved a few yards downriver to a small clump of brambles, where they would be less visible from out on the water and from the embankment above. I did the same. All that day I squatted behind a thorn bush that pricked me every time I moved. That was easily the longest day of my life, longer even than the day I had been banished. It was like a day on acid, every second lasted a million years, an eternity. I learned more about myself that day than on any hundred days up until then. I found I could go without food or water. I realized I could stay calm if I just concentrated on breathing in and out, in and out. I discovered I could endure and that I had courage.

Boats and barges plied up and down the Danube all day long. Some of the boats carried soldiers. The soldiers studied the riverbanks with their binoculars. More than once I felt sure we would be seen. I made myself so small I think I could've fit inside that box where Victor's ancestor lived.

Behind me and overhead I could hear trucks and cars and an occasional motorcycle passing. I decided it must be a secondary highway because the traffic ran steadily but not heavily and not too fast.

Slowly the day passed. The sun circled across the sky. I knew we were waiting for the sun to set, for night to return. I knew partly because it made sense and partly because I had seen my share of war movies.

Night fell completely before Daniel and Victor waded back into the river and down to where I sat concealed from all those who might want to shackle and torture me. Victor hugged me and kissed my cheeks, called me a man, and told me if given half a chance I'd probably make a damn fine Gypsy. I was glad darkness had fallen so they could not see me wiping the tears from my eyes.

We scrambled up and over the embankment. We crossed the highway after all the headlights had cleared. Safely away from the river, we rested on the edge of a woods. "We're in Hungary," Victor told us, "not far from the Austrian border."

We walked maybe a mile along the edge of the woods. Twice we stopped and hid while convoys of trucks worked their way along the road. Finally we entered a small town. I believe it was the town of Rajka in the northwest corner of Hungary, but I can't say for sure. Wherever we were we did not let anyone see us. We crept along the sidewalks, ducking down alleys and behind walls whenever someone approached. On the far side of town we knocked on the back door of a small farmhouse. A woman answered. She saw Victor, and immediately her face broke into a smile. She had been expecting us. She feared we had been captured.

Her husband entered from another room. He greeted us with smiles and hugs. They brought us into their kitchen, gave us food, water for a bath, clean clothes, a bed in which to rest. I fell asleep before my head hit that soft feather pillow.

Morning came in a flash. I didn't even have time to dream. We ate again, eggs and some kind of blood sausage. Then we said good-bye to the woman and went out the back door with her husband. We climbed into the bed of an old truck with wooden sides. The truck was loaded full of apples. Apple trees covered the earth for as far as I could see.

"The plant where they make the cider is just over the border," said Victor, "not more than fifteen kilometers from here. So get comfortable, try to relax, and make sure you can breathe. And when we get to the crossing don't make a sound, don't even take a deep breath."

We burrowed our way deep into the load of apples. The man who had given us food and shelter climbed into the cab of the old truck and started the engine.

Well, it might've been only fifteen kilometers, but that truck couldn't go more than ten or twelve miles an hour. I thought I would be crushed under all those apples, and if not crushed then massacred by honey bees and yellow jackets. They swarmed all around me. Several times the pests landed on the bridge of my nose. But my arms were trapped at my sides, so I could do nothing to swat them away, nothing but endure.

We crossed from Hungary into Austria without fanfare. The truck barely stopped before the border guard waved us through. The men at the cider plant were shocked when suddenly a man and two boys rose from the pile of apples, jumped out of the truck, and kissed the ground.

"I never thought I'd be so happy," Victor shouted, "to be in Austria again."

The bearded man waited for us. I have no idea how he got back across the border.

He drove us to Vienna. Soon we were back at our room in the Stephansplatz. Victor took us out to the fanciest restaurant in the whole city. We ate steak and schnitzel and every kind of dessert on the menu. We drank two bottles of wine and grew so loud and giddy that twice the maître d' came to our table and asked us to please be aware of the other guests. Victor stuffed American dollars into the pocket of the maître d's jacket and told him to go away.

"I think we've done all we can do here, boys," he told us after the second bottle of wine had been emptied. "We've seen all we can see."

There was sadness in his voice. He no doubt felt elated over our escape and safe return, but also on his mind was the plight of his godparents and the country where he had been born.

In the morning we checked out of the hotel and drove to the airport. By early afternoon we were airborne, heading west, heading home.

THE OLD VW CAMPER-VAN PULLS OFF INTERSTATE 95 *onto Exit 47 just west of Bangor, Maine. Daniel Hawthorn, alias Daniel Romankova, shifts the van down into third gear as the VW winds through the exit ramp. The sound of Charlie Parker's alto sax blowing "Slow Boat to China" echoes through the van as Daniel slows to a stop at the red light at the end of the ramp. Off to his left he sees an Exxon gasoline station. When the light turns green he accelerates through the gears while the Bird blows "East of the Sun."*

The afternoon sun hangs high in the western sky. He has driven out of the west, along Route 15, from Moosehead Lake. More than ten days out of Jersey and still he has not reached Canada. "Slow and easy," Victor always told him, "there's too much to miss."

He drove north through Massachusetts and Vermont, spent a few days in the Northeast Kingdom, then swung east through Dixville Notch in New Hampshire before entering Maine. He passed a couple days in Jackman, then headed over to Moosehead, where he camped along the eastern shore for most of a week.

The weather was good: dry and warm, not too hot. He did some fishing, saw his share of moose, lived pretty much off the fish he caught and what he could scrounge up in the woods. Victor had taught him long ago how to survive on berries and boiled bark and wild greens.

In the past ten days he has seen virtually no one, uttered barely a word. Now, as he swings the van into the Exxon station, he grows anxious with the possibilities of the present. In less time than he needs to lower the volume on the stereo, he takes in the scene at Bob's Bangor Exxon. It looks like hundreds of other Exxon stations across the country: the red, white, and blue sign, the line of pumps with the Regular, Plus, and Extra priced accordingly, and beyond the pumps the garage with two bays and on the end an office with a door and a large plate-glass window advertising the price of oil changes and brake jobs and new rubber.

A long black Cadillac occupies the outside bay. It hangs in midair atop a glistening steel shaft. Oil drips from its engine into a large, pole-mounted pan. A 1972 Chevelle Super Sport, probably with a 427 V-8, occupies the inside bay. It rests on the concrete floor, its hood open wide. Three bumper stickers have been plastered on the back window of the Chevelle: GRATEFUL DEAD SUMMER TOUR 1990 . . . SLOW DOWN, DUDE, YOU'RE BEHIND A DEAD HEAD . . . THE ONLY HOPE IS DOPE!

Daniel pulls up to the regular pump, turns off the jazz, and shuts down the engine. Immediately he hears music coming from the garage. He knows right away it's the Grateful Dead but it takes him a moment to place the song. Definitely an oldie, from the early '70s, from his high school days, probably off American Beauty *or* Workingman's Dead. *Then he sees and hears a man, probably Bob, behind the desk in the office.*

"Turn down that goddamn music," *Bob shouts,* "and get your butt outside! We gotta customer." *Bob picks up a thick deli sandwich, shoves it into his mouth, and tears off a large chunk of bread and bloody roast beef.*

A body slides out from under the Chevelle on a mechanic's dolly. Daniel watches as a young man, not more than eighteen or nineteen, skinny and pale, a cluster of picked-over pimples on his chin, stands and wipes the grease off his hands. He reaches in through the open window of the Chevelle and turns down the music. He comes out of the garage, his eyes squinting in the bright sunlight.

"What can I getcha?" *He wears grimy overalls, an old Boston Red Sox cap, and a dirty T-shirt that says the same thing as one of the bumper stickers:* THE ONLY HOPE IS DOPE!

"Five bucks of regular, please."

"Gotcha."

Daniel pushes open the door and steps out of the van. He reaches his arms up over his head and stretches. "So where am I, anyway?"

"Huh?"

"What town is this? Where am I?"

The gas station attendant glances at Daniel. His eyes are glassy and bloodshot. "Yer in Bangor, mister."

"Bangor. Right."

The attendant pulls the nozzle out of the pump and resets the gauge. "Nice van. She looks like she goes back a few years."

Daniel rubs a smudge off the window. "Over twenty years," *he answers.* "A 1969. Everything original, except of course the wear items and the rebuilt engine."

The attendant unscrews the gas cap and shoves the nozzle into the tank. "Ya don't see 'em like this anymore, not in this good a shape and not with the straight-up pop-top roof like this one's got."

Daniel leans against the side of the van. He figures he has a pretty good shot at getting the kid going. "This one's been around all right. But how 'bout that Chevelle in the garage over there. That one goes back a few years."

"Yeah." *The attendant's eyes light up.* "That's a seventy-two. Mint condition. Just sticking on a new exhaust."

"That one yours, is it?"

"Yup. Restored the sucker myself. Bitch goes like a bat outta hell." *The attendant grasps the hand of the nozzle and the gasoline begins to flow into the tank.*

"I'll bet. Buddy of mine had one like that once."

"Yeah? A seventy-two?"

Daniel takes the time to think about it. "Might've been a seventy-four."

"Coulda been. To the untrained eye they looked pretty much the same."

Daniel decides that sounds like the perfect cue. He turns away, wipes another smudge off the window. He doesn't say a word, just waits patiently.

"So yer van," *asks the attendant, after a moment,* "had her long?"

Daniel smiles, then turns to face his mark. "A few years. My uncle gave her to me."

"Jesus, that was awful nice of him."

"He's a pretty generous guy."

"Must be."

"Maybe you're heard of him. He's a rock and roller. Used to be big time, but I don't think the young guys listen to him much anymore."

"I'll bet I do. I listen to nothing but classic rock. The new stuff's a lotta crap."

"Yeah."

"So what's your uncle's name?"

"Garcia, Jerry Garcia."

The attendant's eyes grow wide. "You're shittin' me? Jerry Garcia? Of the Grateful Dead?"

"You've heard of him?"

"Whattaya, crazy? He's my goddamn rock 'n' roll hero, my main man, the guy who drags me outta bed in the morning, gets me through the day."

Daniel cracks a smile. "That's amazing. I really didn't think you young guys listened to the Dead."

The attendant stands there grinning and shaking his head. "Are you kidding? Jesus, I can't believe this. He's really your uncle?"

The gasoline continues to rush into the tank.

"He's my mother's brother."

"And this was his van?"

Daniel nods as he watches the counter click off the gallons. "Yeah, he used to cruise the Big Sur in it with Kesey and Moon Mullins. At least that's the story I used to hear when he came around to visit."

"Unbelievable. Can you imagine the coke and weed and the booze they must've snorted and smoked and drank in this old buggy?"

"Hey, listen," says Daniel, "I don't want to disillusion you or anything, but reports of Uncle Jerry's substance abuse have been greatly exaggerated. It was mostly a publicity ploy."

"What?"

"I'm serious."

"Come on, you can't tell me Jerry hasn't done a few lines in his day, rolled his share of reefers."

"Probably he has. But not many and not for a long time. Don't kid yourself, these rock and roll guys are smart. They're not a bunch of morons. Not only do they know drugs will kill you, but they also know the drug image sells records." Daniel steals a glance at the gasoline pump out of the corner of his eye. "That's all they care about, selling records. Sales is the bottom line. That's the only reason they grow their hair long and pretend to be whacked out on chemicals all the time."

The attendant takes all this in, wipes a greasy finger on his pimply chin as he thinks it over.

Daniel points at the gauge. "You best watch that pump, son. I said I wanted five bucks' worth. You're up close to fifteen."

The attendant releases his grip on the nozzle. "Oh, shit! Goddammit!"

"You have to watch what you're doing in life, kid."

The attendant mumbles a few obscenities. "Sorry about that."

"You might be sorry, but what am I going to do with all that extra fuel?"

The attendant removes the nozzle and screws the cap back onto the tank. "Hell. I guess just pay me the five and we'll call it even."

Daniel considered handing over a fin and being satisfied with the extra free gallons. That was his original plan, a simple matter of deception and distraction. But he decides to push a little further, a little harder, just for the hell of it, just because he's been out in the woods by himself too long. "That's fine, except you see, I asked you for five bucks' worth for a very specific reason."

"Come on, man, I know you wanted five but gimme a break. What's the difference?"

"The difference is a lot of excess fuel that my tank can't handle. When

I pulled in here I checked my gas gauge. I knew five bucks was the max I could take."

"What're you talkin' about?"

"I'm talking about the hole I've got in my gas tank, and I know damn well as soon as I start driving down the road, all that extra petrol is going to start leaking out."

"Son of a mothering bitch." The attendant glances at the guy in the office hunched over his sandwich, then at the two other cars waiting to get fuel. Before he turns back to Daniel a third car pulls into the station. The attendant looks both confused and annoyed. He pulls off his Bosox cap, rubs his forehead with greasy fingers. "So whattaya want me to do?"

"I want you to get those excess gallons out of my tank."

"What!? You can't be serious. How am I going to do that?"

"Look, pal, I don't want to be a hard-on, but I can't be driving down the interstate leaking eighty-seven octane all over the state of Maine. The cops will throw me in jail. This is the nineties, friend, decade of the environment. People don't take kindly to polluters."

Bob is on his feet now, still munching on his deli sandwich but wondering why the line at the pumps has suddenly come to a standstill. The attendant sees him out of the corner of his eyes. "Look, forget the five. Call it good and we both go about our business."

Daniel thinks that sounds reasonable, more than reasonable. A nearly full tank of gas for nothing. More than enough gas to push him up to Canada. But he has swindled a free tank of gas many times before. He needs something more to happen, something fresh.

"I'm afraid you miss the point here, friend. I'm gonna have gasoline leaking from my van all the way north to the border. I'll be leaving a trail a blind cat could follow."

The guy in the car behind the van blows his horn. The attendant pulls a thick wad of cash from his pocket. He rips off a ten. "Here's a tenner to forget the whole thing."

Daniel glances at it, shakes his head. "Cops'll fine me a lot more than ten bucks, pal."

Bob puts down his sandwich, stands, marches out of the office, and starts across the macadam.

The attendant spots him. He rips off another ten and thrusts both tens into Daniel's hand. "Come on, man, from one Dead Head to another, take the twenty and split. Nobody's gonna give a damn about a few gallons leaking out of your van. It ain't like it's another Exxon Valdez, fer chrissakes."

Daniel scratches his chin, considers the Valdez angle, then closes his fist around the money and stuffs it into his pocket. "Okay, pal, I'll let it slide this time, but believe me, I ain't happy about it. And if the cops stop me, I'll be back."

"Screw the cops."

Daniel climbs back into the van just as Bob arrives on the scene. Bob has a paunch the size of a truck tire. He also has a piece of roast beef and a dab of mayo stuck to his cheek. "What's goin' on here, Stinky? Can't ya see we got people waitin', for cryin' out loud?"

The attendant rushes to the window of the next car in line.

Daniel turns the key. The engine fires immediately. "Real fine young man you've got working for you there, mister. Helped me out considerable with some much needed directions."

Bob kicks at something invisible on the oily asphalt. "You let that stupid son of a bitch Stinky give you directions? That pothead has a hard time finding his asshole. You'll be lost sure as shit before you get half a mile from the station. Where you headed?"

"Never-Never Land," says Daniel, "the Land of Make Believe." He pushes in the clutch, shoves the gearshift into first, turns on the jazz, lets out the clutch, and pulls away from the pumps. Even before he has accelerated away from the station, Charlie Parker, with a little help from Flip Phillips and Max Roach, fills the van with his smooth, powerful rendition of "How High the Moon."

THE SUMMER AFTER OUR ESCAPE ACROSS THE DANUBE, Daniel and I boarded our first freight. The whole thing was his idea. He masterminded the plan, set the plan in motion, took care of the details. I just went along for the ride, for the adventure.

I was not his first choice. He wanted Buckley to go, but Buckley's parents had already committed him to summer camp up in the Poconos. So with Buckley out of the picture Daniel asked me. What was I going to do? Refuse to go because I hadn't made the first team? No way. Being selected was an honor. Every guy in the gang wanted to go hoboing with Daniel.

I had to lie to my parents so I could make the trip. No problem, I'd been lying to them for years. Like a lot of kids, I lied to my parents to protect myself from their wrath, but also to shield them from things I did that would've upset them. Almost every day of my youth, usually because of Daniel, I did something that would've made my mother hysterical.

So you could say I lied to protect her. Sure. If I had told Mom that in the morning I was leaving for a few days on a westbound freight, she would've locked me in my room. And there I would've stayed until my flight of fantasy faded. But I wanted to make that flight, my position among my peers depended upon my making that flight; so I protected my mama from the truth: I lied.

I told her Victor was taking us camping up on Bear Mountain and that we'd be gone for two or three days. She nodded but barely looked away from the afternoon soaps while the fib fell from my mouth.

"Have a nice time, dear. Take plenty of warm clothes and a rain jacket. And don't let that Victor Hawthorn keep you up all night with his ghastly ghost stories."

I assured her I would and I wouldn't, and then I slipped away to pack my gear. I wasn't sure what to take on a freight train trip. Daniel had told me to keep it light, "nothing but the clothes on your back and a few bucks in your pocket."

I thought about packing my stuff in a large handkerchief and tying

the handkerchief to a stick, like the hobos of old, but in the end I settled
for my plastic Mendham Middle School gym bag. I stuffed into the bag
an extra pair of underwear, an extra pair of socks, my rain jacket, a pocket
flashlight, my Swiss Army knife, and my transistor radio.

Then I broke into my piggy bank, actually a large metal globe of the
world with a slot in the top for money. I pilfered five dollars in bills and
change. "This money's for your college education, son," Chuckie told
me each time he came into my room to shove a dollar bill or a couple of
quarters into the bank. "Save this money and someday you'll be a smart
man."

Well, I might not've been going off to college in the morning but I
justified the heist by assuring myself that this trip was definitely part of my
education.

All night I lay in bed, unable to sleep. I kept looking out the
window, hoping it would stay dark forever. You might've thought I was
getting ready to ship out to Tangiers with the French Foreign Legion. I
found a hundred reasons why I couldn't make the trip: the grass needed
cutting, weeds needed picking, driveway needed raking. I had the
mumps, the chicken pox, a broken leg. My father was dying of cancer,
my mother of encephalitis; you name it and I thought it up in bed that
night. But all for naught.

Very early in the morning, during the gray hours before dawn, my
eyes fell closed and I nodded off. Instantly I found myself aboard an old
locomotive, like the one on the TV sitcom "Petticoat Junction," only this
locomotive wasn't on the tracks but on the launch pad and pointed
straight up into the heavens. A voice kept singing over and over, "Here's
Uncle Joe, he's a-movin' kinda slow at the Junction." And there I was,
strapped in between Daniel and Uncle Joe. Only I knew as well as every
other kid in America knew that the real guys taking off this very morning
weren't Matthew and Daniel and Uncle Joe, but Neil and Buzz and
Mike, the guys of Apollo 11, the guys on their way to the moon!

"Five, four, three, two, one," announced the voice of mission
control. "Lift-off, lift-off! We have lift-off!" Slowly but surely that locomotive rose off the launch pad and began its ascent into the clear blue
yonder. But we didn't get very far before our ship began to tumble out of
control. I opened my eyes, and there was Daniel hovering over me,
shaking my shoulder. "Wake up, Mac. What's all this crap about a
lift-off?"

"Huh?"

"Never mind. Let's roll, we're burnin' daylight."

I looked out the window. "Burnin' daylight? It's still dark outside."

As always he came straight to the point. "You faggin' out or what?"

My excuses rolled through my head. "Hell no."

"Then let's go."

I slipped out from between the sheets. "Be right back," I said. "I gotta pee."

"Do it out in the grass, Mac. We're outside guys now."

I sighed and pulled on my dungarees and my undershirt and my gray zip-up sweatshirt with the hood. I looked around my room, figured I'd probably never see it again.

"You ready or what?"

What I said next I never should've said because for years, whenever Daniel told about our freight train adventure, he always started out by telling his audience how we almost missed our train because Chandler here had to brush his teeth. "Hang on a second," I said, "I gotta get my toothbrush."

"You don't use a toothbrush when you ride the rails, Mac. You just snap a twig off a willow as you're rollin' through the swamps and scrub your teeth with that. No hobo worth his walkin' shoes would be caught dead carrying a toothbrush."

As I followed him across the bedroom and out the window, I wondered what he'd say when he saw my pocket flashlight and my transistor radio.

We slipped out the window onto the porch roof. We crept across the roof, right past my parents' bedroom window, and then over the side, half supported by the drainpipe and half supported by the thick vines of ivy growing up the walls. We dropped to the ground and ran across the lawn wet with dew.

We rode our bikes, gear strapped to the handlebars, to the train station in Morristown. It must've been eight or ten miles. Dawn broke as we pedaled our Sting-rays frantically along Tempe Wick Road and then through Jockey Hollow to Route 24. I tried but failed to keep pace, especially on the steeper hills. Daniel had to wait for me at the intersections.

At every intersection I reminded him we had to avoid the 7:26 express to Hoboken. That was the train my father took. I certainly did not want to meet him so early in the morning. He rode the train to Hoboken, then the tubes under the Hudson to the financial district, then he walked across town to the offices of Chandler & Wright on Trinity Place.

We just made the 7:05. We chained our bikes to a fence post and climbed aboard just as that commuter train prepared to pull out of the station. Daniel paid the conductor for our tickets, two one-ways to Hoboken.

"So what do we do once we reach Hoboken?" I asked.

"Don't sweat the details, Mac," came the reply. "Just sit back and enjoy the ride."

Sure. It was just like the year before in Europe when I never knew where we were going or how we were getting there or when we were coming back. Only this time it was Daniel leading me into battle instead of Victor.

We arrived at Hoboken station and followed the crowd down the stairs to the tubes. The New York–bound commuters slipped quarters into the turnstiles. Daniel had a different plan for us. "Just slip under the bar, Mac. We gotta save our dough."

I watched him go first. He walked right up to the turnstile and slipped underneath the bar as though he'd been doing it for years. No one noticed. Then it was my turn. My first real test of this new adventure. I screwed it up. I looked guilty even before I ducked under the turnstile and got the handle of my plastic gym bag caught on the metal bar.

"Oh, shit," I heard Daniel mumble through the drone of hard-soled shoes marching across the concrete floor, like cattle to the slaughter.

I worked the bag loose eventually and slipped back into the crowd. Several commuters eyed me critically, but only one guy, the spitting image of Dear Old Dad, said a word. "Don't break the law, son," he said, "to save money. Break the law to make money."

I filed away his pearls of wisdom and then melted into the crowd. I couldn't find Daniel, but he found me. "Very smooth, Mac. Like silk through a weaver's loom."

"Screw you," I said, ready to head for home, where maybe Mom would fix me some pancakes with real Vermont maple syrup, "I could've been arrested."

He laughed. We got on the train. The doors closed. The train pulled out of the station, into the tunnel, into the darkness. No sooner did it start than it stopped. "Pavonia," crackled the voice on the loudspeaker, "Pavonia station."

"Let's go," said Daniel, and he steered me for the doors.

"Where?"

"Follow me."

I could see it was going to be a long day.

We came up out of the underground station and immediately saw a huge red sun rising between the skyscrapers across the river. For maybe half a minute we just stood there and stared. Neither of us said a word.

We started walking. Daniel led the way. We cut across a vacant lot.

Stuff that looked like the tumbleweeds you see in old westerns blew across our path in the light summer breeze.

We reached the end of the vacant lot and walked along a sidewalk beside a road littered with potholes the size of swimming pools. Gigantic dump trucks and huge tractor trailers rumbled up and down the road, shaking the earth and digging those potholes even deeper. They made so much noise, I had to cover my ears.

At the first corner we turned left. We walked through an area of tall buildings. "Jersey City," was all Daniel said.

I saw a guy selling coffee and doughnuts out of the back of his van. "I'm hungry," I told Daniel. "Let's get something to eat."

"Not from that roach coach," he told me. He opened his rucksack, the rucksack Victor had carried the year before in Austria, the magic rucksack, the one with the endless supply of matériel. Daniel handed me a hard roll wrapped in wax paper. Inside the roll was a thick slab of homemade sausage covered with ketchup and a slice of raw red onion, absolutely my favorite sandwich whenever I ate at the Hawthorn Compound. I sank my teeth into that sandwich as we strolled along the sidewalk beside the businessmen carrying their leather briefcases and folded newspapers. The ketchup squirted out the side of my mouth. I smiled. That might've been the greatest sandwich I've ever eaten.

"Hey, Hawk," I said after the last bite, "thanks."

"No sweat, Mac. A hobo's gotta eat, too."

I looked around. Everything looked pretty good, pretty clear. I felt like I had a handle on the situation. So I decided not to go home, not for a while, anyway.

I can't remember exactly where that giant freight yard was, somewhere on the south side of Jersey City, not far from the river. There must've been a thousand train cars in that freight yard. They stood perfectly still in long straight rows. A chain-link fence topped with barbed wire, much higher even than the one surrounding Dachau, enclosed the railroad yard. But that fence didn't stop us, not the Hobos from Mendham, as Daniel had dubbed us.

I didn't know it then, but in those days, in the summer of '69, the Penn Central Railroad was on the balls of its ass. The company was about to go broke, declare bankruptcy, and the federal government was preparing to move in and bring the entire railway system under public control. For us, for Daniel and me, this meant very few security guards in the freight yard. We pretty much had the run of the place. The tricky part was figuring out which line of cars might be preparing to head west. We roamed around most of the morning looking for the right train.

I can't recall exactly how we decided, but I can tell you for sure Daniel made the decision. There must've been a hundred, maybe a hundred and fifty cars attached to this enormous diesel locomotive that stood idling and spewing black smoke from its exhaust stacks. We went about three-quarters of the way back, past boxcars and flattops and tankers. Daniel pulled open the wooden door of a box that said PENN-SYLVANIA RAILROAD in large, faded letters across its side. "Here's home, Mac. Gimme a boost."

I helped him up. He slipped through the open door and into the boxcar. "Hang on a second," he said, "lemme take a look around."

I stood there for what seemed like half an hour waiting for some giant railroad cop to come up behind me and crack me over the head with his billy club, then drag me off to the caboose, where he and his buddies would put me to work stoking the fire and making strong black coffee. But that didn't happen. Nothing happened.

Daniel returned. "Looks good. Nothing in here but a couple empty crates."

"See any rats?" I had rat paranoia.

"No rats, Mac. Throw up your bag."

I did as ordered. And then, with Daniel's help, I climbed into the boxcar. After some hesitation about what he might say, I got out my pocket flashlight and took a look around. The car looked pretty clean, not a bad place at all to spend some time.

"Good idea bringing a flashlight," he said. "What else you got in that bag?"

I decided not to push it. "Oh, nothing much. Some socks and stuff." I figured I'd save the transistor radio for later.

We pushed the two large wooden crates, they were the size of small rooms, all the way to the back of the boxcar. We left them just far enough away from the wall for us to hide in case someone came snooping around. Then Daniel took up his position near the sliding door on the right side of the car and I took up my position on the left side of the car. We kept the doors open a few inches so we could keep an eye out for railroad cops and scoundrels. We settled down to wait for the train to roll out of the freight yard, to take us on our journey west.

Several times I complained about the lack of action. Daniel told me to take it easy, told me hobos never complain. "Hangin' around smokin' and jawbonin', that's the job of a hobo. It doesn't matter when we get goin' because we don't know where we're goin' anyway. We're just goin' somewhere for the sake of goin'. Makes no difference when we get there."

Just thirteen years old, babes in the woods, kiddies in the freight yard, but already my buddy could sit there in full possession of the wisdom that life should be lived as a journey, not as a destination. Then he said to me, "You know, Mac, Victor rode in a car just like this when the Nazis arrested him and his family and dragged them off to Dachau."

I thought about that for a while. And then, late in the afternoon, the steel wheels of that boxcar creaked and moaned and started to roll forward. At first we moved slower than I could crawl, but little by little, minute by minute, our train began to gain momentum. I felt both scared and excited. My ticker seemed to pound harder as our boxcar traveled faster. Daniel ordered me to close the door, to leave it open only a crack. I obeyed.

For a few minutes I saw nothing but more freight cars sitting idle in the yard. But then, suddenly, we broke free of the train yard and rolled out into open country. The open country quickly gave way to industrial sprawl. We passed warehouses and factories and a generating station with a tall smokestack that spewed black smoke into a dusty blue sky. Then we were on a high bridge, the train rumbling forward, out over a body of water, "Newark Bay," shouted Daniel, and heading west for somewhere, for anywhere.

We rolled through Jersey on a southwest line: Elizabeth, New Brunswick, Princeton Junction, Trenton. The train never stopped. Safe now from the freight yard cops, we threw open the doors and watched the Garden State turn from an ugly urban corridor into stretches of small towns surrounded by green fields and orchards teeming with the fruits and vegetables we'd be eating later in the summer.

For a time we sat on one side of the train, and when that got boring we moved to the other side of the train. Daniel sat with his legs dangling over the side, his sneakers just a few feet above the gravel of the railroad bed. I preferred to keep my legs inside the boxcar.

We each ate another sausage sandwich. Then we smoked cigars, big fat stogies that smelled like damp newspaper burning. But we smoked 'em anyway, smoked 'em right down to the nub, smoked 'em until they burned our fingers. We were hobos all right, hobos riding the rails, hobos as free as the wind whistling past that open door.

SOMETIME AFTER DUSK, OUR FREIGHT TRAIN STOPPED. Daniel reckoned we were in Philadelphia because the train had rumbled slowly over the Delaware just before it coasted to a stop in a yard almost as big as the one in Jersey City.

"So what do we do now?" I wanted to know.

"Nothing," he said, "just hang out."

"What about dinner?"

He tossed me another sausage sandwich. They seemed to be reproducing themselves in his rucksack.

I ate it in a hurry. As soon as I finished he tossed me a Hershey bar. I gobbled that up and he tossed me a banana, still a little green and tough to peel, but it tasted great to me.

"You satisfied yet?"

I started to shake my head but that's when the train bucked for the first time. It didn't last long, just a second or two, a tremor. "What was that?"

"I don't know," Daniel answered. "They're messing with the train. Either getting rid of some cars or coupling on some new ones."

"Whatever it was scared the crap outta me."

"Good," he said, "that means you're alive."

The coupling and uncoupling went on all night. We slipped out of our boxcar for a while and watched the train crews work. They took out a tanker here and stuck in a flattop there. The long line of cars kept moving back and forth in the night. We heard men shouting, giving orders, cussing, laughing. Later we saw a group of them standing in a circle beneath a bright overhead light, drinking coffee and passing a bottle of whiskey.

"God," I said, "I hope I'm not like them when I grow up."

"You'll be just like them, Mac," Daniel said, "except instead of hangin' around the train yards with the boys you'll be shootin' the shit out on the golf links and over to the yacht club."

"No way."

My friend just laughed.

We went back to our boxcar. I asked Daniel where were going to sleep.

"Right here."

"Where? Here?"

"Yup."

We passed that endless night inside one of those huge wooden crates. First Daniel cut the heavy nylon straps holding the crate closed with his brand-new Bowie knife with the six-inch blade. He carried that knife on his waist, secure inside its leather sheath. After he cut the straps we pried loose the steel pins holding the corners together. I stood there half expecting a lion or a gorilla to come charging out and rip my arm off. But the crate was empty except for a pile of Styrofoam packaging. We spread the packaging out, made it as smooth as possible, then settled down to get some rest.

"This is living, hey, Mac?"

"Yeah," I said, wishing more than anything that I was home sitting in front of the TV with a big pile of chocolate-chip cookies and a tall glass of ice-cold milk. The second half of "Batman" was on tonight and I wanted to find out if Robin and the Caped Crusader would solve the Riddler's latest puzzle. Of course, I knew they would. They always did. "Batman," like all the other shows I watched on TV, never failed me. The good guys always won.

The train lurched again. "I'll never get to sleep with all this racket."

But Daniel didn't hear me. He was already sound asleep, the son of a bitch. I wanted to wake him up, maybe blast my transistor radio in his ear. But what difference would it make? He'd just deal with me, with my radio, then roll over and nod off again.

I've always been a lousy sleeper, even as a kid. I thrash around in bed, sometimes waking up at three o'clock in the morning drenched in sweat, my heart pounding a million miles an hour. It's like I run marathons in my sleep.

But Daniel, he slept like the dead. Actually, he slept more like a cat. You could wake him up and he'd be instantly alert, ready for action. But just as quickly he'd be asleep again. He could relax and fall asleep at will. The guy could sleep anywhere, anytime. It was a gift. It must've been in his blood, part of his Gypsy heritage.

Me, I didn't sleep at all that night. My Anglo-Saxon blood boiled for clean, soft, cotton sheets. Every time I'd start to nod off, the lunatics out in the train yard would slam another boxcar or another flattop onto the back of our line. The train would lurch. Our crate would shift, slide a little ways across that smooth steel floor. I'd jump up, startled, no idea where I was, slam my head on the top of the crate, then need another half hour to bring myself even close to slumber.

Once I woke Daniel up and asked him what we'd do if they uncoupled our car.

"Ain't no use speculatin', Mac," he told me. "Only keep you up nights." Then he turned on his side and went back to sleep.

Sometime before the first light our train rolled out of Philadelphia for points west. I crawled out of that crate and went over to sit by the door to get some air. The day before had been a hot and humid one, and the night hadn't done much to cool things off.

Still, I felt better as soon as I saw the sun rising. The first light of a new day always clears me out, makes me wonder why I'd been up all night worrying. Anyone who's ever suffered insomnia knows what I mean. You lie there in the dark, convinced everything's totally screwed up, then you spend several hours tossing and turning, getting everything straightened out, put away nice and neat. But then dawn breaks and you can't remember why the hell you weren't fast asleep dreaming sweet dreams.

I got out my transistor radio and turned it on. I worked through the dial until I got a live report from Cape Kennedy: Apollo 11 had broken free of the earth's gravitational pull and was speeding successfully toward a rendezvous with the moon!

I looked up and thought for just a moment that I saw that spaceship sizzle across the sky. It appeared as nothing but a blur, but I knew right then that after I sailed my ship around the world, I wanted to fly deep into space and drive that special car NASA had built, the Lunar Rover, across the surface of the moon. I told Daniel as much as soon as he crawled out of the crate.

"You think you got the walnuts to go all the way to the moon, Mac?"

I thought about it. "Yeah, I think so."

"How 'bout California? You got the walnuts to go to California?"

"Why California?"

"Because that's where we're headed."

A twinge of panic rumbled in my chest. "No way."

"What do you mean, no way? Every hobo's destination is California."

"California's clear across the country. Three thousand miles. I ain't goin' all the way to California." My jigsaw puzzle of the U.S.A. popped up in the back of my head. You know the puzzle I mean. Every American kid has one. You dump the pieces on the floor, then see who can put them back together faster. Sitting there in that boxcar I saw the little cutouts of Ohio and Illinois and Kansas and Colorado and Utah and Nevada expand into these gigantic pieces a thousand miles from end to end. "No way," I said, "not California."

"All right," he said calmly, "then you hop off at the next station and make your way back. I'm going until I see the Pacific Ocean."

I had to think quick. No way was I letting Daniel out of my sight. I didn't even want to think about riding the rails solo. The whole idea of it gave me the willies. "But I told my mother I'd be back tomorrow, day after at the latest."

"So we'll call her, tell her you might not be back till fall."

I had to laugh at that one. "Yeah, that'll go over big."

"What's she gonna do? No way she can find you."

I took a moment, then tried a flanking maneuver. "Why do we have to go all the way to California?"

"Why not go all the way to California?"

"Because," I said, the litigator in me beginning to develop, to take shape, "California's just a destination. All you want to do is see the Pacific Ocean. That's no reason to go. That's no reason to do anything. Hell, yesterday we looked out across New York harbor and saw the Atlantic. Why go three thousand miles just to see the Pacific?"

He thought about this. At least a minute went by. "You know, Mac," he said, "you got a point there, a damn good point. We'll just go west till we're sick of goin' west and then we'll go in some other direction."

I was already sick of goin' west, already ready to go in some other direction, maybe east toward home, but I decided not to push my luck. "Yeah, okay, that sounds sensible."

"So that's how we'll do it," he said. A moment later he added, "But don't think for a second I don't see through all your talk about destinations. I know your talk's just a cover-up for the fact that your walnuts are so shriveled up in your BVDs that we'd have a tough time finding them even under a high-powered microscope."

With no judge or jury in sight I decided not to retaliate.

"Here," he said, tossing me another banana, "better make it last. The food bag's empty and it's a long way to the moon."

All morning long the train rolled through lush Pennsylvania farmland. We saw farmers in their fields riding tractors pulling plows. We saw Amish farmers in their fields walking behind teams of horses and oxen.

The train paralleled a country road. For at least a mile our boxcar rode alongside an Amish family in their buggy. The man and the woman sitting up front never even glanced over at us. But their two young sons sitting in back kept waving and smiling. I waved back. Daniel made funny faces at them. They kept snickering, trying not to laugh, hiding their faces in their hands. Their mother must've heard because she turned and reprimanded them.

"What's the matter with her?" I wanted to know.

"Nothing," said Daniel. "She thinks there's something the matter with us."

Sometime in the middle of the morning the train pulled into Lancaster. We didn't stay long, maybe an hour. Daniel and I spent the better part of that hour arguing about whether or not we should get off the train and find something to eat.

Now I'd love to tell you I hopped out of that boxcar in Lancaster, Pennsylvania, sprinted across the freight yard, slipped under a fence, and disappeared down a dark alley. That I came back maybe ten minutes later, after that train had already started to roll for points farther west. That I had to run as fast as I could to catch up with the boxcar, where my buddy sat cheering me on, shouting at me to run faster. That I got neck and neck with the boxcar, tossed the bag of fresh muffins and the carton of orange juice up to my buddy, and then, a split second before the boxcar cleared the fence and left the yard, I grabbed hold of the handle on the sliding door and swung myself up into the car, somersaulting across the car and very nearly rolling out the other side. I'd love to tell you all this, but in good faith I can't.

I can't because Daniel was the one, not I. I ate half those muffins (blueberry) and drank half that orange juice, but believe me, I didn't enjoy any of it, not a single mouthful.

In Harrisburg I had the chance to redeem myself. The train pulled into the state capital in the middle of the afternoon. We lay low waiting to see what would happen. The railroad yard workers started tearing the train apart again and putting it back together.

An hour passed. A yard cop approached our boxcar. We hid inside the wooden crate. He climbed up into our car and took a walk around. We buried ourselves as best we could in the Styrofoam packaging. He walked right by the open end of our crate but didn't see us.

We didn't move for at least fifteen minutes. Then, finally, we crept out of that crate like a couple of moles. He was gone. We had the boxcar to ourselves again.

Daniel carefully pushed open one of the sliding doors, just an inch or two, just far enough to see straight ahead into the railroad yard. Then he opened it a little farther, stuck his head out, took a look around.

"Coast is clear," he said. "I'm goin' out for vittles."

"No," I said, "I'll go." And believe it or not, I did.

I slipped out of that boxcar and hit the ground running. I never looked back. Actually I did, several times. But I never saw anyone. So with the sweat pouring off my face, I stopped running. I started walking. I had the usual stuff on my mind: What would I do if I got caught? Would I be able to find the boxcar again? What if the train took off for points west before I got back? How would I get home without Daniel?

I thought about sneaking back to the boxcar, hiding just outside it, then hopping aboard as soon as the train started to roll. Sort of re-create what had happened back in Lancaster. Only I wouldn't make it quite so dramatic. But then I realized I'd be returning without the bacon. So I kept walking.

I managed to procure our afternoon supplies without much trouble. I reached the end of the train yard, crawled through a hole in the rusty fence, and walked a block or two through a neighborhood of small dirty houses, dry cleaning shops, and pizzerias. But I didn't want pizza, so I kept going until I found a sandwich shop, where I spent almost my whole five dollars on two roast beef hoagies, a big bag of barbecue potato chips, and a giant bottle of root beer.

The woman behind the counter, an old lady with gray hair and glasses, said to me as she put my stuff into a paper bag, "I've never seen you in here, young man. You look like one of the Rossis. You related to Anthony Rossi? A nephew or something?"

"No, ma'am," I said. "The name's Mac. Mac Beaumont. I'm off the freight, heading for points west, California. Then on to the Orient via merchant steamer."

She looked at me as though I spoke some foreign language.

I smiled, grabbed my bag, and walked out of that store like a man six feet tall. The world looked different to me as I walked back through that neighborhood and crawled through the hole in the fence. I felt like I had power, like I had courage. I crossed the railroad yard like I owned the place. I held my head high, stared straight ahead. I found the boxcar no problem, walked straight to it as though I'd made that trip a thousand times.

Daniel waited for me. "That was quick, Mac. How did it go?"

I climbed aboard. "A couple yard guys chased me right after I left, but I outran 'em."

"No shit?"

"Yeah, a couple fat guys. One of 'em with a harelip. Then there were a couple of rough guys at the sandwich shop, Italians, who gave me a hard time."

"You're full of it."

"Like hell," I said. "The Rossi brothers."

"The Rossi brothers?"

"That's right."

"Yeah? And what did they do?"

"They tried to get my bag away from me but I kicked one 'em in the walnuts and started runnin'. They couldn't catch me."

"First the fat train guys, then the Italians. You're a goddamn superman, Mac."

"Yeah, well, you know I had my adrenaline pumping." I broke out the hoagies and the chips and the root beer. We sat there and ate and listened to the reports on my transistor radio coming out of Cape Kennedy. Neil and Buzz and Mike were all doing good and feeling fine, looking forward to the days ahead, looking forward to landing on the moon.

We looked out of that boxcar, up at that hazy blue summer sky.

"That's something," said Daniel, "thinking of them up there."

"Yeah," I said, still feeling ballsy and courageous from my solo jaunt, "it's something all right." A little, I thought, like riding the rails cross-country and wandering all alone into some working-class neighborhood in Harrisburg, Pennsylvania.

The train rolled out of Harrisburg not long after we finished our lunch. It traveled slowly north along the Susquehanna. Huge boulders littered the river like small islands. I sat next to Daniel with my legs dangling over the side.

"I'm just about outta money," I told him.

"Good," he said, "a hobo oughta run outta money."

"You got money?"

"A couple bucks."

"What are we gonna do when we run out?"

"We'll figure on something. We'll rob a bank. Or we'll finger some rich guy. Rub him out and steal his wallet and his gold pocket watch."

"Like hell."

"Like hell nothing," he said. "You'll do the killin', I'll do the stealin'."

My courage slipped behind my backbone. "Forget it, I ain't doin' either one."

"Then we'll go hungry."

"Fine, we'll go hungry."

We looked out at the river for a while. I got to thinking about something.

"Hey, Daniel."

"Yeah?"

"I got something I want to ask you."

"So go ahead and ask." He was slightly pissed off at me for backing off on his scheme to do some killin' and stealin'.

"How did Victor get out of that concentration camp?"

"Dachau?"

"Yeah."

"He didn't tell us last summer?"

"He didn't tell me."

Daniel swung his feet back up into the boxcar and leaned against the wall. He put on his storytelling face. "Then I'll tell you."

I was all ears.

"Beyond the barbed-wire fences," he began, "there were fields where the Nazis grew corn and wheat and vegetables. They used the prisoners to tend the fields. Victor was always ordered to help with the harvest because he had a strong back.

"In the fall of forty-three he was taken out to the fields every day to help bring in the corn. Then, for the whole next year, he planned his escape. During that year he managed to get hold of a map and he stole a knife from the mess, which he honed to a razor-sharp edge.

"For three days in the fall of forty-four he cut and carried those ss of corn before he decided to make his move. On the fourth morning he slipped his knife into his shoe and his map as fas far up his asshole as he could push it.

"He worked the edge of the field that morning, more than a mile from the camp, on the edge of a forest. Two Nazi guards patrolled the area between the field and the woods. They marched back and forth in opposite directions, meeting momentarily at the halfway point.

"For a couple hours Victor cut corn while keeping a close eye on those Nazis. No one else was around. The rest of the harvest went on beyond a low rise in the land. He knew this was his chance, maybe his only chance to escape. The rest of the family had pretty much been wiped out by this time."

I sat there with my mouth open, listening. I could see Victor perfectly out in that corn field, not much older than us, that knife in his shoe, that map up his a-hole. I felt my walnuts start to tingle.

"Victor carried his burden, a full fifty ears, to the edge of the field. The guards barely took notice of him. He stacked the ears carefully, then retreated to the cover of the uncut stalks. But instead of returning to his labor he crouched in a swell on the edge of the field. He waited and watched. He reminded himself what the Nazis had done to his father, to his mother, to his grandfather and grandmother, to his brothers and sisters.

"The guards passed and began walking in opposite directions. Victor waited for the guard to march by his hiding place. Then he crept forward. He came up behind the guard as quiet and invisible as a ghost. He raised his knife and sliced through that Nazi's neck right down to the bone from earlobe to earlobe. The bastard didn't even have time to say so long to God or Hitler or his sweetheart back in Berlin."

Instinctively I reached up and touched my throat.

"That stinking Nazi fell back against him. Victor stepped aside and let the body slide to the ground. He was not yet dead, but very close. His eyes bulged and his hands twitched as he tried to stop the blood from spurting out of his terrible wound. Victor thrust the blade through his rib cage and into his heart as far as it would go. Then he pulled it out, wiped it on the Nazi's uniform, and fled without looking back, into those thick dark woods."

Daniel paused. I saw the dead Nazi lying on the floor of the boxcar. I saw his blood running along the floor and out the door. "So he made it?" I managed to ask. "I mean, he got away?"

Daniel nodded. "It took him most of a month. He could only travel at night. But finally he reached the Swiss border and safety."

And I thought I had guts for getting off that train and going into town to buy a crummy hoagie and a bottle of root beer.

I crawled over to the wooden crate to rest my eyes, to think things over, especially my own life. Before long lack of sleep and the steady rhythm of the boxcar riding the rails drew me into a deep sleep. So far as I can remember, I didn't even dream.

IT SEEMED LIKE I HADN'T BEEN ASLEEP A MINUTE when I felt Daniel's hand upon my shoulder. "Wake up, Mac," he said, "we're pulling into another station."

And so we were. The freight train rumbled slowly across the Juniata River and into the small town of Huntingdon, Pennsylvania.

I rubbed my eyes. "How long I been asleep?"

"A few hours."

The day was just about spent. The light was fading fast. The brakes squealed and the long train ground to a halt.

Huntingdon didn't look like much. There wasn't even a railroad yard to speak of, just some switches and sidings running along either side of the depot. Out the southbound door we could see the river and beyond the river some hills. Out the northbound door we could see a tall brick building with lots of broken windows, five or six stories high, looked to be the tallest building in town. In big, worn letters printed across the top of the building it said JC BLAIR & COMPANY, HUNTINGDON, PENNSYLVANIA.

"Wonder why we're stopping here?"

"Beats me," said Daniel. "Probably won't stay long. Better sit tight."

So we sat tight, and while we sat dusk fell and another group of railroad workers started ripping apart our train. The coupling and uncoupling sounded closer than ever, almost right outside the door. Men kept walking back and forth along the tracks, so we stayed back by the crates, out of the way.

It grew dark. Moonlight flooded through the open door. I wanted in the worst way to turn on the transistor radio and get a progress report on Apollo 11, but Daniel wouldn't let me, told me we had to worry about our own mission first. "Something's up," he added, "and I don't like the sound of it."

Not long after, we felt the tracks start to rumble. That rumble had grown familiar. We knew that big diesel locomotive had started to hum, ready to roll, ready to pull that long line of freight cars farther west. But this time something changed. This time we heard the rumble but didn't feel our own boxcar grab the track and secure its place in line. This time our boxcar stayed perfectly still, didn't move an inch. For a long while we sat there, not really knowing what to do or say, listening to that powerful rumble fade in the distance. Finally we slipped out from behind those crates and crossed to the door. Our boxcar stood all by itself in front of that tall brick building. We'd been uncoupled, left behind.

I felt nervous, panicky, uptight. "Now what are we gonna do?"

Daniel took it in stride. "We're gonna go get something to eat. Then we're gonna come back here and get a good night's sleep. In the morning, we'll make a plan."

We stowed our gear, including my transistor radio, under some Styrofoam packaging in one of the crates, then we slipped out of the boxcar into the night. We walked back along the tracks for a few hundred yards until we came to a cross street. We followed that street for a block or two and then turned right on what I think was Allegheny Street. There weren't many folks about: a woman walking her dog, a guy carrying a six-pack of Iron City beer, a couple holding hands, an old lady with a cane. We must've walked a mile or two through that town, up one street and down another, before we finally found a place to eat.

The place we found was one of those all-purpose joints: open twenty-four hours a day, you could gas up your car or get an oil change, buy a gallon of milk or a tin of chewing tobacco, order a deli sandwich or, like us, two hot dogs with onions and mustard for sixty-nine cents. We ate four dogs each, long scrawny things sitting for God knows how long on those steel spits that run the dogs around and around. They came on these doughy semistale buns, but we ate 'em anyway, ate 'em as fast as the guy behind the counter could bring 'em up.

After the dogs and some more sugar water we each ate a pretty good size shoo-fly pie and a bag of ginger snaps. We walked out of that place stuffed to the gills. All the way back to the boxcar I kept thinking I would surely puke at any moment. I kept burping and blowing gas, my stomach rumbling, preparing to explode.

Old Iron Stomach Hawthorn, he just walked along laughing at me, trying to get me to take a pinch from his brand-new tin of snuff, stick a wad between my teeth and gum. One whiff of that crap and those hot dogs retreated halfway up my esophagus. I swore off hot dogs that night forever, and except for the game or two I attend each year up in the Bronx, I've pretty much kept my pledge.

My digestive complaints were in full swing as we cut through the railroad yard. Our boxcar stood in the middle of two other boxcars, half a dozen empty flattops, and as many fuel haulers. We got to within twenty yards of our boxcar when Daniel stopped me, put his finger to his lips, and pointed at the open door of our car.

Sitting there in the doorway, silhouetted against the moonlight, my pocket flashlight stuck in his mouth and his hands occupied by the dials of my transistor radio, was a man old enough to be my father. He had long scraggly hair and a ratty-looking beard.

I backed off, just a step or two. Daniel went right on forward.

"Hey," I whispered, "slow down. He looks like some kind of madman."

But Daniel didn't slow down, kept moving forward until he drew right up close to the side of that boxcar. "Hey, mister," he demanded, "what're you doin'?"

The bum raised his head. He had on boots with no laces, worn-out corduroy pants, and a flannel shirt you could practically see right through. His face, bruised and bumpy, looked as though a fist or two had made solid contact. My pocket flashlight, still sticking out of his mouth, shone straight in Daniel's face. "Huh?"

"I said, what're you doin'? That ain't your radio."

"This radio here," the bum slurred, that flashlight rolling around between his dry white lips, "this radio here belongs to Gawd. Gawd All Mighty."

I came up behind Daniel. Nothing played on the radio but static. A half-empty quart bottle of no-name gin stood like a sentinel at the bum's side.

"God, huh?"

"That's right," he mumbled, his teeth cracked and his eyes all buggered out and the size of golf balls, "Gaawwddd." Then he belched, a horrible-sounding thing that I thought for sure might lead to his immediate demise. But he rallied, spit my flashlight into his lap, and in one deft motion he hoisted that bottle to his lips and took a long hard swallow. When he brought the bottle away from his face we saw his lips curl up into a small satisfied smile as a tiny bit of gin dribbled down his chin.

"Okay," said Daniel, "now put the radio and the flashlight down and get the fuck outta that boxcar."

The bum belched again (his breath had that dead fishy smell you get at the beach at low tide), and then, to my astonishment, he obeyed Daniel's order. Very carefully he set aside the radio. He turned off the flashlight after no small struggle and set it on the bed of the boxcar. He didn't really have it in him to stand, so he just kind of pushed himself toward the door, making sure to bring his bottle along for the ride. When he got to the edge he belched once again, exclaiming in midbelch,

"Gawd loves thee!" and then he rolled out the door onto the hard brown earth.

Instinctively I moved to help him but he came up like a spring, made sure his bottle had not suffered in transit, and then he smiled as a filthy foam dribbled out of his mouth, across his cheek, and onto his shirt.

"Jesus Christ," I said, "we gotta do something to help this guy."

"Yeah," said Daniel, "maybe shoot him. Put him out of his misery."

"That's not what I had in mind."

The drunken bum raised his head. "Sorry," he slurred, "to have disturbed your domestic bliss." Then he fell back against the ground, thumping his head solidly on a large rock.

Daniel went over to him and bent down. I expected him to check the poor bastard's head, maybe his pulse, but instead he shoved his hand into the bum's pocket.

"Jesus, what are you doing?"

"We're about busted," he answered. "Maybe this poor bugger has some cash or—"

"You'd take money from him?"

"—or maybe he has a fancy red Swiss Army knife, maybe somebody else's fancy red Swiss Army knife."

When he pulled his hand out of the bum's pocket, Daniel did indeed hold a Swiss Army knife, my Swiss Army knife, the one I'd hidden in the crate along with my flashlight and my transistor radio. "How did you know?"

He tossed it to me. "Just a feeling, Mac, just a feeling." He showed me his own knife then, that six-inch Bowie, hanging from his belt in its own leather sheath. "It's better to keep your tools close at hand when you're on unfamiliar turf."

I caught the knife, nodded, and shoved it in my pocket.

"Now," he said, "I think we best get some shut-eye. No telling what tomorrow might bring."

So we left the bum lying there under the moonlight and retreated to our crate. It took some time, maybe an hour or more, but finally I dozed off. I had this weird dream about being asleep on a bed of knives.

Sometime in the middle of the night I awoke, my bladder near to bursting. I crept over to the door of the boxcar and pulled out my relief valve. The bum hadn't moved. But Daniel's windbreaker lay across his chest and shoulders, and Victor's rucksack lay under his head. I looked over at the crate. Daniel lay there, snoring lightly. I knew he must've covered up the hobo, given him a pillow. But when? I hadn't heard him stir. I didn't understand. Earlier he had been so brutal, so rough. He'd treated the bum like a worthless pile of junk.

I shook my head, made my puddle, and went back to bed.

It seemed no sooner had I rested my head against that Styrofoam packaging than I felt Daniel shaking my shoulder and shouting in my ear, "Mac! Get up! We gotta move. We gotta move. We gotta roll! Now!"

"What!? Why?" I tried to remember where I was. "What's the matter?"

"There's an eastbound freight rolling through town."

"Eastbound?"

"Yeah. Eastbound."

I sat up, brushed aside the Styrofoam, rubbed my eyes. I could see the early morning light flooding in through the door of the boxcar. I crawled out of the crate, stood. And there he was, the bum, I swear to God, lying on the floor of the boxcar, halfway between the door and the crate, with Daniel's six-inch Bowie knife sticking out of his chest. I screamed.

"I had to do it, Mac. I had to kill him."

"What!?"

"I had to kill him. There was no other way. He was coming after us. See the bottle in his hand?"

Damn right I saw the bottle. I saw the gin bottle broken in half. I saw its jagged edge glistening in the morning sunlight. I saw the neck of the bottle still resting in the dead bum's right hand.

"Son of a bitch was gonna steal our stuff and cut our throats. Little did he know I sleep like a panther, ready to pounce. I was on him before he had time to remember his name."

"But but but—" I kept shaking my head, thinking it was a dream.

"Easy, Mac. Just get your stuff together, right now, and let's get the hell out of here before that train passes through. We gotta get on that train."

I don't really remember grabbing my plastic gym bag and my pocket flashlight and my transistor radio, but later, on the eastbound freight, once I'd started to think straight again, I had everything, all my stuff, hadn't left anything behind—except maybe my innocence, although I think even that had been usurped before I saw Daniel's Bowie knife sticking out of that bum's rib cage.

We jumped out of that boxcar together, Daniel first, then me right behind him. We started across the railroad yard, really just an empty lot overgrown with weeds. The eastbound freight rolled slowly along the tracks, maybe a hundred yards distant.

All of a sudden Daniel stopped. "Hey, Mac," he said, "hang on a second. I forgot something."

I told him to leave it, to forget about it. I told him we had to get moving, we had to make our getaway before it was too late. But he ignored me. He turned and started running back toward the boxcar.

I watched him climb inside, disappear for maybe fifteen seconds, then reappear and jump down onto the ground. He sprinted back to where I stood and together we raced across that dusty lot.

The eastbound freight moved so slowly that we had no trouble climbing aboard. Once safely inside an empty boxcar I caught my breath and asked, "So what the hell was that all about? What was so important you had to go back?"

"This," he answered, and held up his Bowie knife for all the world to see.

I DIDN'T SEE EVEN A SPOT OF BLOOD on Daniel's Bowie knife. But later, after we'd settled into that empty boxcar on an eastbound freight, after we'd caught our breath and cleared out thoughts, Daniel told me how he'd pulled the blade out of the hobo's chest and wiped it clean on the dead man's worn-out flannel shirt.

After that we didn't talk much. We rode all the way across Pennsylvania without hardly uttering a word. Daniel played the harmonica. Pretty well, too. By the time we reached Jersey he could play "Dixie" well enough for me to recognize the tune. He never said so but I knew he'd pilfered that mouth organ from the hobo's pocket. No place else he could've gotten it.

We didn't get back to the train station in Morristown until late in the afternoon the day after Daniel had done in the hobo. Our bikes stood where we had left them but both tires on my bike were flat as pancakes. Daniel threatened to ride off without me but I threatened to spill the beans about the dead hobo back in Huntingdon, so Daniel called Victor, who came and picked us up. We loaded our bikes into the back of the Hawthorn family station wagon. And no sooner had we pulled away from the station than I knew something had gone wrong.

"Sorry, kid," Victor told me, "I would've covered for you but my loving wife took the call and she had no idea what was simmering on the stove."

The call! I could see Victor looking at me in the rearview mirror. He didn't have to say another word. I understood all about the call. I understood the proverbial cat had been let out of the proverbial bag.

"In the dark," said Victor as we drove west along Route 24, "she spilled the coffee and kicked the can and stubbed her toe all at the same time."

Ma and Pa Chandler did everything but spill their only son's blood. They were waiting for me at the kitchen table, fire in their eyes. After a savage flurry of verbal attacks, they made a frontal assault wherein I was battered into submission before being reduced to the world's rottenest and most pernicious child. After this assault they flanked me with the heavy silent treatment. I was then banished to my bedroom and ordered to remain there until further notice. I went willingly to my solitary confinement, happy as a lark to escape their scowling faces and accusing eyes.

The way they treated me you might've thought I'd slipped away for a few days and done in one of the Kennedy clan. Perhaps Teddy. Or Rose. They were about the only ones left by the summer of '69. In the twisted minds of my parents I belonged in the same cell as Sirhan Sirhan. Remember that guy? Jesus. Can you imagine how his parents must've felt?

Anyway, I stayed in my room without making a peep all that night and right through the following morning. I didn't even go down the hall to take a leak. I just hung my hose out the window and peed in the rhododendron bushes far below.

Now I can't remember the exact time, late morning, I think, maybe early afternoon, that the knock came on my door. I thought about ignoring the knock but decided that might lead to a renewed fury from my jailers. "I'm still here," I whispered.

"Report to the TV room," squeaked my little sister's voice, followed by one of her cute little giggles that never failed to arouse in me the desire to barf.

I reported as ordered. I walked into the TV room and found Ma, Pa, and Sis huddled around the RCA ColorTrak. No one glanced my way.

"Sit down," Chuckie demanded. "There's something on the television we think you should see."

Right away a bolt of lightning raced down my spine. I fully expected to glance at the television screen and see mug shots of Daniel and me in connection with the murder of that dead hobo. "If you have any information," I waited to hear a Jack Webb look-alike say, "regarding the whereabouts of these two fugitives, please call your local police department immediately. Use caution. These young hoods are armed and dangerous."

"Sit!"

So I sat. I dropped silently to the carpet, long woolly stuff that always felt to me as though it belonged on some shivering mountain mammal rather than on our rec room floor. No one said a word. I could not even hear my family breathing. Were they all dead? I wondered, eyes open and hearts a-poundin', but nevertheless dead?

I stared at the screen. And what did thirteen-year-old Matthew Anderson Chandler see when he looked into that strange, flickering box?

He saw the moon. Not a long-range, telephoto shot of the great white orb, either, but a close-up—so close he could have reached out and grabbed a handful of moon dust. And then an astronaut, my hero that summer, Neil Alden Armstrong, dressed in a wonderful silver suit of space armor, stepped out of the lunar module, slowly descended a rickety-looking ladder (I'm sure you remember the one), and announced, "One small step for man, one giant leap for mankind."

His words rocketed through the heavens, all the way back to Mother Earth. Those ten simple words somehow traveled across a million empty miles of space, slammed into our home planet, echoed into and out of our TV set, slipped into my ears, rammed up against the walls of my brain, and sent all kinds of wild signals through my young and still impressionable psyche.

I began to shake and tingle. A wide smile broke across my face. And then Neil stepped off that ladder and planted his gigantic silver space boot right smack down in the moon dust. Momentarily I stopped breathing; I feared Neil might suddenly vanish, simply disintegrate on contact with the moon's surface.

But he didn't. No, he still stood there. Right before my wide-open eyes he stood there grinning inside his space helmet. And why not? The surface of the moon was as solid and secure as the baseball field over behind the Foodtown.

Neil took that step and then another. And another. He walked away from the lunar module like a commuter leaving behind the evening train. I laughed. I laughed right out loud. I laughed so loud my laughter echoed all the way to the moon. I felt free, lighter than air, like I could've run all the way to California, all the way to the Pacific Ocean right alongside the rails, jumping easily from tie to wooden tie.

But then I looked around at the faces of the other people in the room: my family, my blood relations, the humans who purportedly had the same genetic makeup as I did. They sat there and stared at the screen the same way they sat there and stared when Kirk and Spock beamed down to the planet Spiros to rescue Bones from the evil Deltoids.

I didn't get it. I felt confused, beguiled, cheated. And then, after Neil and Buzz, their space helmets the size of asteroids, planted Old Glory firmly on the lunar surface, Dear Old Dad ordered me back to my cell.

THAT FALL FOR MY SINS, MA AND PA sent me, their heretic, to private school. Cruel despots.

Maybe they had justification, I don't know. In their hearts they no doubt felt they were doing the right thing for their only son. But in my mind then, and still today (a child's scorn fades so slowly), Chuckie and Martha were shackling my spirit. They did nothing to instill in me, as Daniel's parents daily instilled in him, a sense of freedom, of yearning to see beyond the borders of our suburban spread. From me they demanded submission. Upon me they imposed suppression.

I hated private school. I don't really even want to talk about it. But I suppose I must briefly anyway. You see, no matter what reasons they gave, and oh, they gave many, the main reason my parents forced me to go to the Peck School on South Street in Morristown was because they wanted to sever my daily lifeline to Daniel.

It was not enough to strictly forbid me from seeing him, to abolish my right to enter the Hawthorn Compound; no, they had to go a step farther, they had to go to extremes. They had to send me to a whole other school where the only person I knew was Tommy Wagner, the kid whose baseball mitt Daniel and I had buried under the pitching mound the previous summer after we'd beaten his team in the local Little League championship.

So on my very first day of eighth grade, Tommy Wagner was the only familiar face in the crowd. He scowled at me. He had not forgotten about the mitt, had not allowed bygones to be bygones. Tommy'd been at the Peck School for a few years. He had allies there, kids he considered friends. I stayed out of his way. Even though he was a nerd, the kind of kid who always got mocked out and spit on at public school, at private school he'd found his niche. So I gave him plenty of room. See, I was all alone, a satellite adrift in the cosmos.

Peck was full of nerds and dorks and losers. I guess if you come right down to it, Peck was full of kids like me. Of course, I never for a moment thought I belonged there. No way. I belonged back in Mendham with my old buddies. I'd had the same friends, Daniel and Buckley and the other guys in the gang, since kindergarten and even before. I didn't want any new friends. I didn't even know how to make new friends. And believe me, I was mighty pissed off about it. I blamed Chuckie and Martha. Every single day I hated their guts a little more.

They sent me to the Peck School to save me, to make sure I developed into their image of a proper young man. They believed an individual's responsibility was to tow the line and prepare for the future. And they made me pay the price for their superstitions.

Still, I survived my year at Peck. Seems now like just a speck on the anthill of time. I even learned some stuff I probably wouldn't've learned had I stayed at Mendham Middle School. The teachers at the Peck School handed out homework like grandparents hand out cakes and cookies. And if you dared come to class the next day unprepared, look out, they really broke your balls.

A couple of the old-timers still believed in corporal punishment, a slap across the wrist with a ruler or a shot across the shins with a stick. Discipline, discipline, discipline—that was the name of the game at Peck. I never got hit, not old Tow-the-Line-Chandler. I always came prepared. Got all A's that year, too, except for B's in math and music. My favorite subject was history, something I hadn't paid much attention to up until then. I liked learning about what had already happened and how what had happened might affect what would happen next. Four years later, when I entered Cornell, I decided to major in history, which I did, even though my old man told me every chance he got that I'd never get into law school studying the causes of the Civil War and the reasons for the rise of the Third Reich.

In early June of 1970 I graduated from Peck, and that summer something very interesting happened. Actually, what was interesting was what didn't happen. You see, my parents did nothing to prepare for my freshman year of high school. Perhaps it was the parties at the club or the long stints at the house in Siasconset playing golf and drinking vodka gimlets on the veranda—I can't recall. They assumed, I suppose, that their boy would be going back to Peck. But that, you see, was impossible, unless they wanted me to repeat the eighth grade. That was as far as one could go at the Peck School.

When they uncovered this fact, in late August, chaos swept through the Chandler house on Cherry Street. First they blamed their ignorance on yours truly, then they tried to enroll me in this school and that school, but already the students had started to arrive and I hadn't even taken the entrance exams. It was too late. So unless they wanted to teach me algebra, earth science, and *The Great Gatsby* at home, God forbid, there was only one alternative: Mendham High!

I must've been the happiest kid in school on opening day. I smiled in homeroom. I smiled in the hallways. I smiled in English class and math class and during study hall. I smiled during freshman football practice. And I kept smiling even after that stupid fat geek, Marty Sutton, stuck his elbow through my face mask and just about busted my nose.

Daniel was, of course, the star of the freshman football team, star of the freshman basketball team, too. But he didn't star on the freshman tennis team; he was too busy going undefeated as the number one singles player on the varsity squad. I don't think he lost a match until he got to the semifinals of the New Jersey high school state championships.

We didn't lose many games on the gridiron with him at the helm either. He played quarterback, led the team in yards rushing. He would've played halfback but the coach didn't want to chance a screw-up during the hand-off, so about three plays out of four the center would snap the ball to Daniel and he'd either run around the left or run around the right with the rest of us blocking and shouting obscenities.

Our coach had some American Indian in him. He believed firmly in verbal intimidation. So we'd sweep right and all along the line our tackles and guards and ends would be screaming, "Kill the fucking morons! Kill! Kill!" Daniel would slice into the line, stiff-arm some poor kid who probably wished he'd tried out for the chess club, break a tackle, get to the outside, and romp for eight, ten, twelve yards before half the defense ran him out of bounds.

But the best part of those games was in the huddle when the coach would send in a play and Daniel would say, "Screw that," and we'd all laugh and then Daniel would diagram his own play on Marty Sutton's fat back. Marty was the center, and when Daniel told him to bark, he barked. So Marty'd turn around and Daniel would diagram a play. "Mac," he'd say to me, "split right, all the way out to the sideline. Buckley, you line up in the slot. Mac, you go down about fifteen yards, break in, and knock that cornerback flat on his butt. Buckley, you break off Mac's heel and go deep on a flag. If the rest of you pork bellies can block long enough, we'll get a touchdown."

Well, sometimes we did and sometimes we didn't. More often than not I'd get penalized for an illegal block and the coach would pull me out of the game and give me a pretty good tongue-whipping. But if the ref had his eyes elsewhere, Buckley would break free down the right sideline and Daniel would loft the ball high over everyone's heads, right into Buckley's outstretched arms: touchdown, six points Mendham Frosh!

We had a pretty lousy hoop team, nobody who could really get the ball consistently in the basket. Daniel could handle the ball pretty well, dribble and pass, but, incredibly, he wasn't much of a shooter. He didn't even like to shoot. He'd bring the ball up to the top of the key, pass off, then pretty much hand back, ready to play defense. The coach used to try to get him to move under the boards, drive to the basket, give and go. He'd do it a time or two, usually with success, but then he'd back off, leave the offense to the rest of us.

You have to understand, Daniel played these games, these athletics, effortlessly. He never had to think about running with the football or dribbling the basketball or slicing his backhand down the line. The guy was a natural.

I've thought about it a lot, why he excelled in competitive situations. It's been a lifelong study of mine. He had the essentials: a strong, lean body, perfect hand-eye coordination, total confidence in his abilities. But he had something else as well; he had perspective. He knew games were bullshit, measures of nothing but winning and losing. Still, he loved games, loved to play games. He lived to play games. He died playing a game.

So why didn't he dominate the hoop court the way he dominated the tennis court? Well, I've thought on that some, too, and as with most things, I have a theory. See, I think Daniel wanted me to have the glory on the basketball court. I think he wanted me to be the star, score the points. I think he knew I faded into the background as soon as he stepped forward and took charge. A week or two into that freshman season, he and I stood in the showers, soaping up after a pretty good beating at the hands of Bernards High.

"See the way the water flows out of the shower head, Mac?" he said to me. "See the way it just keeps coming, nice and steady?"

"Yeah," I said, "I see it."

"Now do you see this?" And he turned the water off and on, off and on, off and on.

"Yeah, I see it. So?"

"So that's the way you play hoops. Like this." And again he turned the water off and on, off and on, off and on. "But you can't play hoops that way. You gotta play hoops like this." And he turned the water on full blast, left it on, grabbed his towel, and went back to his locker.

My first lesson in Zen and the Art of Basketball.

He never said another word about my hoop game, but from that day on I looked at the sport in a whole different way. I can't say I came out for our next game fully able to flow around the court like running water, but at least I had the concept in mind. I kept moving, offense to defense, defense to offense, making the transitions, passing, shooting, guarding my man, grabbing rebounds. I tried to concentrate on these things as I kept my feet moving. The game became more fun. I became a better player.

A few months later, near the end of our losing season, the team had a meeting. The coach lectured us on our most recent pitiful performance. "You guys get out on the court and start running around like a bunch of chickens with your heads cut off. You can't play the game that way. You have to think out there on the court. You have to be thinking all the time."

Daniel, spinning a ball on his right index finger and keeping it spinning by slapping it lightly with his left hand, cleared his throat and asked the coach if he could speak.

"What is it, Hawthorn?"

"I don't think the problem is our lack of thinking out on the court, Coach. The problem is we think too much. All we do out there is think think think. And since most of us are pretty insecure about our basketball skills, our thinking tends to get negative, and as soon as we get negative we screw up. We throw the ball away, double dribble, forget to box out. This game happens too fast to think. Watch Clyde and Pearl and Willis. They just do it."

My second lesson in Zen.

Coach, of course, dismissed Daniel's theory as a crock, told him he was entitled to his opinion, but we'd do things the coach's way or get off the ship. Personally, I thought Daniel had bounced the basketball firmly on the floor. Most of the other guys did too. But Coach was Coach, so we did things his way and wound up with like three victories and fourteen defeats.

Still, that was some year, that freshman year. I saw Daniel and Buckley every day. We were the Three Musketeers of Mendham High. We rode the bus together, hung around together in homeroom, had world history and Spanish together, ate lunch together in the cafeteria, went to practice together, won and lost together. Little did I know that behind the scenes plots were unfolding to bring down our triumvirate, our most unholy trinity.

These plots began, I learned later, even before the first day of school. Ma and Pa were secretly in communications with the headmaster at Mercersburg Academy, a gentleman who had been a classmate of Chuckie's back in the late forties. Without my knowledge or my consent, the threesome was in deep discussion about my fate.

Well, it turned out I couldn't enter the academy before January, so for the time being, anyway, my sentence was postponed. Then, and this also I learned later, my mother actually intervened in my behalf, said I shouldn't be sent packing until the following September. She felt a midyear change, right in the middle of basketball season, might emotionally damage her precious son. Three cheers for Mom, a real heart of gold.

So for a while I was off the hook. But they set the hook firmly and irrevocably the day the mailman delivered my grades for the first marking period. I'd hacked off, you see, put my studies on the back burner. In the eyes of some parents that first-quarter report card might not have looked too bad. But to Ma and Pa Chandler that C in algebra leapt off the paper and smacked them right between the eyes like a giant flying horseshoe. Knocked them silly.

They were waiting for me in the kitchen when I came home from football practice. I got the evil eye (actually four of 'em) for a minute or so, and then the old boy stirred. He pointed at the evidence lying on the kitchen table. "What's this, young man?"

I took a look. It looked to me like a flimsy piece of paper with some stupid letters printed on it. But I was not a smart-aleck kid, especially not with my old man. "My report card?"

"Exactly. And not a particularly impressive one at that."

Two A's, three B's, and a C; didn't look too bad to me; not for a first-semester freshman in a new school with football practice five days a week, girls starting to look pretty good in their miniskirts and tight sweaters, parties on weekends; no, not too bad at all. Nevertheless, I hung my head. "I'm having a little trouble with algebra."

"I'll say."

"It's pretty tough, those equations and all, but I'm starting to get the hang of it."

"You'd better start getting the hang of it, buster. Do you think the Ivy League schools will even glance at your application if you show them grades like this?"

"I can do better."

"Damn right you can do better. You will do better."

And then my dad the lawyer, who wanted so desperately to be a judge, announced, in his very next breath, my sentence. "Next year you'll go to boarding school."

I gasped. "What!"

"In the fall you'll go to Mercersburg Academy, where I went and where your grandfather went. Enough of this public school nonsense. Hanging around with these ruffians and these immigrants who don't give a damn about their futures. I won't have it." Then the old boy slammed his fist down on the kitchen table, stood up, and marched out of the room.

Mom and I watched him go: the Provider, the Enforcer. After a minute or two Mom sighed. "Really, Matthew, I think it's for the best. You'll see."

"But I don't wanna go away to school, Mom. All my friends are here."

Her eyes grew almost compassionate. "It's nice there, Matthew. You'll see. And it's coed now, too."

Big deal, I thought, but after a couple days I shrugged off the sentence. September seemed an eternity away. When you're fourteen, ten months is close to forever. All kinds of stuff could happen in ten months to alter the course of history. There could be an earthquake or train wreck or even a world war. This boarding school thing, I assured myself, was no way written in stone.

But Christmas came and went, and so did Easter and Memorial Day and our fifteenth birthdays and the Fourth of July. We spent most of that summer hanging around the swimming pool or lifting weights or running wind sprints over at the high school gym in preparation for the upcoming football season. All the guys knew I wouldn't be out there with them on the gridiron come fall, but no one ever said a word about it. Not even Daniel. Kids, at least the ones with hoses between their legs, are like that—about as sentimental as water buffalo.

July wound into August, and I started to feel the moment of truth bearing down on me. I might not've been the first kid to ever get sent away to boarding school, but I'll tell you what, I must've been the most miserable. No way did I want to go. A few days before my scheduled departure I actually went into my parents' bedroom while the old boy was at work and begged my mother to let me stay home. I got down on my hands and knees. I promised her I'd get all A's in school, would keep my room clean, help with the dishes, take out the garbage, even be nice to my sister.

The bitch wouldn't budge.

We packed up the car on the night of August 31. I'd seen the guys earlier, before dinner, but they hadn't made much of a fuss, just pounded me on the back and told me to hang in there, keep a stiff upper lip, see you at Thanksgiving and all that crap. Thanksgiving, Jesus, that was on the whole other side of football season.

After the old man and I finished packing the car with my suitcases and sports equipment, I went up to my room for one last sulk. I don't really know how long I sat there; it grew dark outside, but I didn't bother to turn on any lights. I just sat around and moped and thought up ways to bring on a quick and painless death.

That's when I heard a tapping on the window. At first I thought it was just the wind blowing the branches of that old maple against the side of the house. But the tapping grew louder and more insistent, so I went over and opened the window. And there they were, down on the front lawn: Daniel and Buckley and three or four of the other guys.

"Let's roll, Mac," whispered Daniel, "we haven't got all night."

I slipped out the window and down the drainpipe. Before I even hit the ground my buddies were off and running. We ran all the way down Cherry Street, cut across Freeman's alfalfa field, out onto Hilltop Road, then down Thomas Lane to the Hawthorn Compound. We went up to our clubhouse in the top of the garage. Sitting on the old wooden table in the middle of the room were two six-packs of beer and an almost empty bottle of bourbon.

"This is your farewell party, Mac," said Daniel. "Drink up."

We drank down those twelve beers and those four or five ounces of Kentucky sour mash in no time at all. The only thing that slowed us down were the toasts the guys kept making to yours truly.

"To Mac, a real horse's ass."

"To Mac, a pretty good guy, when he's asleep."

"To Mac, may he return without having turned into a complete preppie asshole."

And so it went until the booze ran dry. But as soon as it did, Daniel pulled a small plastic bag filled with green stuff out of his hip pocket. "Marijuana," he announced, "the real thing, our first bag."

And so it was. A couple of the guys chickened out and went home but the rest of us watched intently as Daniel spread the grass out on the table and removed all the little brown seeds and twigs. He brought out some rolling papers and prepared to roll his first reefer. He carefully placed a small quantity of marijuana in the fold of the rolling paper. Then he grasped the ends of the paper and slowly began to twirl the thing closed. To me it looked like he had done it before, like he'd pretty much mastered the art of rolling doobies, but so far as I knew, that was his very first one. He licked the edge of the paper and sealed the thin cigarette.

He took a slow look around the table. "You boys ready?"

A bit reluctantly, we nodded.

"We're smoking this inaugural reefer," Daniel said in his best toastmaster's voice, "on the night before our buddy Mac Chandler goes off to boarding school because this is a special occasion. He's the first of us to leave the coop, to face the world without his pals. We smoke this herb to celebrate his going and to wish him Godspeed. He's scared shitless about going, but within a couple days, once he gets away from us deadbeats, he'll feel like a new man. Mac's going down there to—where is it you're going, Mac?"

"Mercersburg."

"Right. Mac's going down to Mercersburg to kick some butt and tell some stories, and so what if most of 'em won't be entirely true. He'll know he's been on a few adventures, tipped a few beers, smoked himself some reefer. You're a man of the world now, Mac. You're gonna do important stuff."

"Like what?" I asked, and then held my breath for another prophecy.

But none was forthcoming. "Hell, I don't know. Maybe you'll get laid."

Everyone laughed and Daniel lit up. The reefer caught fire, glowed orange in the dim light of the clubhouse. The smoke swirled slowly up toward the ceiling. Daniel took a hit and passed the reefer to his left. None of us really knew what to do. We choked some trying to inhale but after the cigarette had gone around a time or two we started to catch on. Not much happened; I mean, we didn't freak out or jump out the windows or start hallucinating, so Daniel rolled up another one. I tried rolling one, too, ripped the paper the first time but finally managed to get one licked and ready to burn.

Pretty soon we had three or four reefers going at once. We began to lean back in our chairs, play it cool and loose. The room was dense with marijuana smoke. We smoked the whole bag, about a quarter of an ounce, maybe eight or ten joints.

It's difficult to describe those first few times you get high on marijuana. Those first times are definitely the best times, the most memorable. You turn into a kid again. Sure, I was only fifteen at the time, still just a kid, but the weed turned me into a five-year-old. We laughed even when nothing was funny. We played grab-ass and yucked it up pretty good that night, enough for me to forget all about what would happen come the dawn.

After we'd emptied the bag, Daniel took us on an adventure. He told us we were an elite underwater commando unit with orders from the top brass to infiltrate and secure the Hawthorn Compound swimming pool. He started out of the clubhouse and down the stairs. As always, we followed without a word.

We slipped out of the garage, darted across the driveway, and hit the dirt. We slithered across the lawn on our bellies, careful not to raise our heads for fear of having our eyes shot out by Vietcong snipers lurking at the edge of the wood. The grass was long and thick and wet with dew. I remember I licked the dew off several blades of grass. Buckley saw me.

"Survival strategy," I told him.

"Like hell," he said. "You're stoned, Chandler."

Finally we made it to the pool. Without getting off our bellies we pulled off our clothes and flopped silently over the edge into the water. We swam around in single file, all of us following Daniel, to where or for what reason none of us knew, none of us cared.

I don't know how long we circled that four-leaf-clover swimming pool before Daniel's mother came; long enough for me to conclude that marijuana was pretty neat stuff.

Then, suddenly, the lights snapped on, both the underwater lights and the patio lights surrounding the pool. And standing in the light, wearing a thin white cotton robe wrapped tightly around her waist, was Daniel's mother.

"Daniel?" she asked. "Is that you?"

The guys were all trying to hide their naked bodies in the shadows. A couple of them even had their hands crossed over their crotches. But not me, not old Mac Chandler; he floated there in the middle of the pool, like some bull rhino awaiting a cow in heat.

"Yeah, Mom," answered Daniel. "We're just having a little farewell party for Mac."

"Oh, yes," she said, and looked directly at me. "You're leaving us tomorrow morning, right, Matthew?"

"Yes, ma'am."

"Well, take care of yourself. And have a good time."

"Okay, Mrs. Hawthorn, I'll try." At that moment I felt completely ready to whisk that woman off her feet, carry her up to one of the empty bedrooms, and ravage her. I felt, for the first time in my life, like a man.

"Good night, boys." She turned and went back to the house.

I sighed and took a look at what lived between my legs. It stuck up out of the water like some nuclear-powered periscope.

"PLEASE TURN OFF YOU ENGINE, SIR, and step out of the car."

Daniel Hawthorn, alias Daniel Romankova, listens to a few more notes from the horn of Dizzy Gillespie, then he does as ordered. He shuts down the engine and steps out of his VW camper-van.

Two Canadian border guards climb into the van and begin a lengthy and thorough search of its contents. A large black German shepherd is brought from the guardhouse to sniff for illegal contraband.

"Please," says Daniel, his Czech accent honed to perfection, "I would like dog not to go in van." He touches the tip of his nose. "Allergies, you know."

The border guards encourage the shepherd to jump into the back of the van.

"Thank you," says Daniel. "Is not this maybe a violation of my Bill of Rights?"

One of the guards leads him into the customs house. They are on the north side of the St. Croix River, in St. Stephen, New Brunswick, just across the border from Calais, Maine.

"More questions?" Daniel asks.

The guard nods.

He is seated across the desk from an official he had not seen before. The man has a thin, stern face. He has Daniel's passport, visa, and international driver's license spread out on his desk.

"You are Mr. Daniel Romankova, of Four Purkynova Street, Prague, Czechoslovakia?"

Daniel nods. "I am. And just for me to say, I am used to this treatment of violation. Until very recently in my country we had no, how do you say? liberties. I thought maybe here was different. I thought maybe here I could travel without harassment."

"What is your business in Canada?"

"I have no business here. I come purely for pleasure. I come because all my life I hear how beautiful and friendly is here."

"How long do you expect to stay in Canada?"

"I suppose one week or two."

"And you have money?"

Daniel throws up his arms. "No, I have no money, not a silver dollar. I come all this way for my own good looks alone."

The official does not smile. "I can easily deny you permission to enter the country, Mr. Romankova."

Daniel considers this, narrows his eyes, grows indignant. "Worse things they have done to me."

The official sighs. "Please, Mr. Romankova, cooperate."

"Yes, cooperate. The favorite word of all fascists."

"Your occupation?"

"I am an oculist."

"Occultist?"

Daniel smiles. "No, no. Oculist. I make eyeglasses. Spectacles. For the eyes."

The official writes it down. He pauses over his paper for several moments. "I am going to ask you to sign something, Mr. Romankova." He pushes a piece of paper and a pen across the desk.

"And this is what that I will sign?"

"This is a declaration that you will not, during your visit here, seek political asylum in Canada."

Daniel studies the form. He picks up the pen and draws a large X across the page. "You have much nerve," he says. "Political asylum. Do you not know Czechoslovakia is democracy now? Do you not know Mr. Václav Havel is president elected by the people? Do you know Czechoslovakia is birthplace of my father, and his father, and many of our fathers before that?"

"Do you refuse to sign, Mr. Romankova?"

Daniel stands. "I refuse to sign. I refuse any more insult." He turns and marches out of the customs house and across the parking lot to his van.

The guards have finished their search. They stand near the van, the German shepherd at their feet.

"Do you find any Czechoslovakians," Daniel asks, "or maybe Levi blue jeans, hiding in van?"

The border guards say nothing. The customs official comes out of the customs house. But not before Daniel climbs into the van and drives back across the river, back into Maine, back to America.

I DIDN'T GET HOME UNTIL AFTER MIDNIGHT, didn't get to sleep until after three, what with my brain all wound up with marijuana and alcohol and thoughts of leaving home. Then Chuckie woke me at six twenty-five, had me out the door a little after seven, and by seven-fifteen we were in the car and driving past the Mendham town line. So long. Farewell. I kept hoping the car would break down. It didn't happen.

But something did happen that day, something I think demonstrates the tiny twists and turns our lives take, sometimes when we're not even watching, not even paying attention, when we absolutely least expect it.

At seven o'clock on that, I believe it was a Tuesday morning, I felt low and depressed, a morose and tired teenager with a dry mouth and red eyes. But by noon of that same day, just five hours later, I felt energized and intoxicated. By noon my gloom had lifted, been swept aside, replaced by a kind of exhilaration I have never felt before. By noon I wore a huge smile on my face. By noon my entire life had changed. By noon, you see, I'd seen and even said hello to Rachel for the very first time. By noon, friends, I'd fallen in love.

I knew it was noon because while I stood there outside the chapel on our tour of the Mercersburg campus with several other soon-to-be prep school students and their parents, the chapel bells began to ring. We stopped to listen. Something made me turn around. I have no idea what, some cunning and mysterious force. When I turned around I saw her sitting cross-legged on the grass in the shade of an enormous white oak. The thick limbs of that old tree framed her perfectly, as though she'd been placed there by some magazine photographer who'd been hired to sell perfume or blue jeans or the soul of every fifteen-year-old American boy who turned the page.

She had a long, thin pencil in her right hand and a large sketch pad resting against her left forearm. She wore faded cutoffs and a tie-dyed T-shirt, no shoes or socks. She had a leather band around her right ankle, bright red paint on her toenails and fingernails. I knew right away I'd never forget that image of her sitting there sketching on that lush green lawn. And I knew right away I wanted to kiss her, hold her, marry her, be with her forever.

Sickening, isn't it?

The bells continued to toll. I continued to stare. She must've felt my eyes, for she looked up from her sketch pad. She looked directly at me. I glanced quickly away but not before our eyes met, not before I saw her smile.

The bells stopped ringing after a dozen blows. The campus tour continued. But that same mysterious force that had caused me to turn around in the first place now pulled me off the sidewalk and pushed me in her direction. This force even managed to pry open my mouth, a mouth usually silent in the presence of females, especially young pretty ones. "Hi, uhh, I'm Matthew, uhh, Matthew, uhh, Chandler." I babbled like an idiot.

"Hello, Matthew Chandler." Her voice sounded like her face looked, perfect: calm and smooth and collected. She had very long dark brown hair that ran all the way down her back and actually rested on the grass. The hair got my attention but the eyes blew me away: huge round eyes of mountain-sky blue. "I'm Rachel."

Rachel, I said to myself, Rachel Rachel Rachel. I knew I was staring at those eyes but I couldn't help myself. They had me mesmerized. They put me in a trance. Those were the first eyes I had ever seen, maybe the only eyes I have ever seen, which looked both happy and sad at the same time. You couldn't read Rachel's mood by her eyes, could not tell her thoughts or be sure if what you saw was a smile or a moment of melancholy. Her eyes told you everything and nothing all at once.

She blinked. Some infinitesimal amount of time passed. But enough time for my mystery force to fade. My cool gave way to that hot and humid late summer afternoon. I started to sweat. "W-w-weel," I stuttered, "I-I-I guess I better get ba-ba-ba-back to the group."

She laughed, but not really at me, not maliciously, more to let me know it was all right. "Okay, Matthew. I'm sure I'll see you around."

"I-I-I hope so," I mumbled, and then I pretty much sprinted off to find the others.

Rachel was right. I did see her around. I saw her every day. She was a tenth-grader, same as me. We had American history together, and never in my life was I so glad to possess a wide and otherwise useless array of facts and figures. The Peck School had taught me well.

On the first day of class, with Rachel sitting right beside me (I'd arrived first, and she'd actually chosen that seat of her own accord), the teacher, a kindly woman named Mrs. Stover who'd been teaching for a hundred years, asked us if we knew the location of the first European settlement in the thirteen colonies. I shot up my hand. She pointed in my direction.

"Jamestown," I answered proudly, and then glanced out of the corner of my eye to make sure Rachel was paying attention. She was. Boldly I went on. "It was settled in 1607 by Englishmen of the London Company headed by Captain Christopher Newport."

"Very good, Mr. ? . . ."

"Hawthorn," I answered. "I mean Chandler, Matthew Chandler."

"Very good, Mr. Chandler. Excellent. Now can someone else tell me where Jamestown was located?"

Mrs. Stover called for someone else, but I didn't want to give up the glory. I wanted to answer myself. I wanted to answer all the questions for the rest of the year, every single one.

But before I could blurt out the answer, another voice, softer and more soothing than my own, rose to the occasion. "Jamestown stood near the mouth of the James River on a swampy peninsula in eastern Virginia. And although Mr. Chandler is correct, Captain Newport did bring the first settlers to Jamestown, it was Mr. John Rolfe who made the community a successful settlement."

"Excellent, Rachel," said Mrs. Stover, "very good."

So, I thought, they know each other. Buddy buddy. I sat there frowning and staring at those big blue eyes. Rachel glanced over at me, smiled, and then suddenly she winked. I just about fainted dead away.

I would like to report that my friendship with Rachel blossomed immediately upon my arrival on campus and from that first day on I gave up all thoughts of home. I would like to tell you I grabbed the academy by the walnuts and held it tight until it became my own. I would love to give the impression that I did in my first few months on campus what Daniel did in his first few months on campus a year later—namely, become famous among both students and faculty alike. But this narrative is at least partly about the truth, about uncovering and dealing with events and emotions as they really happened, not as I would have liked them to happen.

My roommate's name was David Surry. I called him David Scurvy. He was a pale, skinny kid who only went outside when absolutely necessary. He rarely spoke, never initiated a conversation. When you asked him a question he just sort of mumbled under his breath. I lived with Scurvy for nine months but I doubt I could fill half a page of biographical information on the guy. I knew Scurvy was troubled, knew he probably needed a pal more than anything else in the world, but he gave me the creeps. I wanted nothing to do with him. I avoided him like I avoid poison sumac. About all I did in that room was sleep. I even started keeping my clothes over at the gym, and at first, anyway, I did my studying in the library.

Football practice started a couple days after I arrived on campus. The team had a new coach. His name was Mr. Frederick but he told us to call him Coach or Tom. I called him Coach. Coach Frederick had never been a football coach before, nor had it ever been his ambition to be a football coach. You see, at Mercersburg Academy in the early seventies they had a tough time finding a coach, so Tom Frederick, also the school's art instructor, agreed to do the job until they could find a real coach. I think he ended up being the interim coach until 1985, the year Rachel lost her sight in that motorcycle accident.

Those first few days out on the practice field moved a little slow. Coach Frederick didn't have a real good grasp of the game. He'd watched it on TV like practically every other American male over the age of seven, but he'd never played the game, never been in a huddle or on the line of scrimmage. He asked us what position we wanted to play. That simple question took several days to work itself out since most of us wanted to play quarterback on offense and free safety on defense. But since football is mostly a game of attrition, our natural positions on the field soon became evident. I wound up at flanker because I was quick off the snap and had reasonably good hands. The fact that we threw only about six passes a game severely hindered my desire to be a star, but I felt fortunate to start on the varsity as just a sophomore.

We lost our first game 30–6 and our second game 42–0. Our third game we actually led at half-time but eventually lost 18–12. Coach Frederick stood on the sideline and cheered no matter how poorly we performed. He believed fully in positive reinforcement. During my three years playing under him I never heard him swear at or chastise one of his players. When the going got tough, either on or off the gridiron, Coach Frederick liked to quote Plato: "No human thing," he would say in his quiet voice, "is of serious importance." And then he'd add, "So give it your all, and then let it slip gently from your grasp."

I enjoyed practice. It got me outside, away from my books, away from David Scurvy. And I enjoyed being part of a team. I didn't know my teammates very well but that didn't matter. They had on helmets and pads and jerseys, and first they'd take a lick at me and then I'd take a lick at them. Call it primitive male bonding.

But mostly I enjoyed practice because almost every day Rachel came to watch. Just about every afternoon that fall, and I remember those afternoons as being warm and dry with just a hint of autumn in the air and huge fluffy white clouds in the sky, Rachel walked down from campus and sat about halfway up in the bleachers on the home side. I used to stare up at her all the time, daydreaming that she had come to watch me catch passes and run wind sprints. More than once I got hit right smack in the head with the ball as I stared stupidly up into the bleachers where she sat sketching or reading or just looking off into the distance.

We were well into October and had even won our first game before I found out why Rachel really came out and sat in the bleachers every afternoon. Coach Frederick was Rachel's father, and Rachel came to practice to be near him. That may seem and sound unlikely but that's the way they were. Rachel hated football, found the game slow and boring and barbaric. But she loved her father and found his close proximity reassuring.

As I came to know them better, I realized just how close a kid could be to his or her parent. It was a real revelation for me. They actually liked each other.

Of course, Daniel and Victor were close, they liked and respected one another. But I don't know, there was something strange, something cryptic, something obscure about those two. They had stuff going on between them that no one else could understand, that no one else could touch.

But Rachel and Coach Frederick, they just loved one another, nothing strange or cryptic about it. Their love no doubt had a lot to do with Rachel's mother dying when Rachel was still a child, but whatever the reasons, Rachel's relationship with her father was something I envied. I can't really say how early in our friendship I felt this, but at some point I concluded that if she could have such a sound and positive relationship with her father, then certainly she had it in her to have a similar kind of relationship with a young man who loved her and cared about her and wanted to spend the rest of his life with her.

Alas, few things in life prove so simple or turn out the way you first envision them.

Nevertheless, when I found out Coach Frederick was Rachel's father, I started watching him very closely. Soon I was emulating him, even taking on his mannerisms right down to the way he walked and talked and stroked his chin with his left hand. Coach smoked a pipe, so I smoked a pipe, too. Actually I didn't smoke it, I just carried it around in my breast pocket.

Right around that time, mid-October, I asked Rachel out on a date. It took me a while to get up the nerve but finally I found the courage to do it. At the end of history class one day, as we collected our books and started out of the room, I just sort of nonchalantly, as though I did this kind of thing all the time, but with my heart popping and firing like a machine gun, asked her if she wanted to go to the movies on Friday night.

"Sure, Matthew," she said, just like that. "What's playing?"

I thought hard about that one but couldn't come up with an answer. I didn't even know if there was a movie playing on Friday night. I didn't even know if there was a movie theater in town or on campus.

"Oh, well," she said, "it doesn't matter."

"It doesn't?"

"No. Why don't you just drop by our house around six-thirty? The movie usually starts at seven."

"Your house?"

"Yeah. Do you know where we live?"

Of course I knew. I knew exactly. I even knew which room she slept in (middle room, second floor, southeast side), but I didn't want to let on, you know. "Sure, I think so."

"The big white house with the porch just beyond the main gate."

"Right."

Now I can't tell you what movie we saw, probably couldn't've told you an hour after it ended, but I can report that our date was a rousing success. At least I thought so. During the movie I sat there nervous and uncertain of what to do. Should I talk, I wondered, or should I just stay quiet? Should I offer to get her some popcorn, or should I just sit still? It was all very complex.

I thought about holding her hand, but my own hand felt sweaty and clammy. I wanted in the worst way to lean over and kiss her full on the lips, but no way did I have the walnuts to do that. So I just sat there, kind of clenched, and watched her out of the corner of my eye while I tried to keep my palms dry by wiping them covertly on my khaki trousers.

After the movie we took a walk. It was kind of chilly, I remember, not cold, but you could feel the bite in the air, now and then see your breath. Rachel had on a big wool sweater, a cardigan with a wide collar. I figured it probably belonged to Coach Frederick. Someday, I told myself, I wanted to see Rachel wearing my sweater.

All I had on were my khakis and a blue button-down oxford, standard issue at the academy. I hadn't worn a jacket, thinking it might look uncool. I even kept my sleeves rolled up because I thought they looked best that way, you know, casual, laid back, slightly roguish. The pipe rested in my pocket.

We strolled through the campus, out past the chapel and the old library, along the winding, tree-lined road to the east gate. There was a sliver of moon, I remember, but it was still pretty dark under those tall maples with their giant leaves beginning to turn red. I did my best not to shiver.

We talked about all kinds of stuff. Actually, Rachel did most of the talking. At least at first. I'd never really talked to a girl my own age before, not for any length of time, anyway. Sure, I'd sat around the lunch room at Mendham High with Betsy Gallagher or Irene Sullivan talking about the upcoming geography test or next Saturday's football game, but always the guys had been there on the periphery, ready to cut me if I said too much, went too far. But here I was, out in the dark, no one else around, Daniel a million miles away, and the most beautiful girl I had ever seen right at my side, practically up against my shoulder.

She talked about everything all at once. In her mind, even then, it was all connected, all part of the same package. Before we even reached the east gate she'd talk about painting and her father and the Civil War and the headmaster and Vietnam and Tricky Dick Nixon. I did all I could just to keep up. She asked me if I thought there'd be more Kent States and more My Lais before the industrial-military complex finally pulled out of Southeast Asia. I swallowed hard and said I hoped not but only because the sound of her voice had indicated that more Kent States and more My Lais might not be such a good thing.

I walked along and tried to think what Daniel would do, what Daniel would say. I knew he'd find some way to turn the tables, gain control of the situation. And that's when I realized he'd probably tell her one of his tales. So I decided to do the same.

We reached the east gate, crossed Main Street, Highway 16, and started back into town along the brick sidewalk. I told her the story of our trip to Europe. I told her about Dachau and the tanks in Prague and how Victor and Daniel and I had escaped across the Danube. I did the best I could, tried to hit all the high points, exaggerated a bit here and a bit there whenever the story started to drag. In that particular version, for instance, I took off my clothes and entered the gas chamber right along with Victor and Daniel. No way was I going to tell this young beauty that I'd stayed outside fully clothed, not even part of the demonstration.

Rachel didn't say much, definitely didn't swoon or anything (that was never her style), really just said enough to let me know she was listening. When I'd finished she said, "Boy, Matthew, that's some story."

I smiled into the darkness and made a triumphant fist. Believe it or not, that was the first time I'd told that story. Always before it had been

Daniel who did the telling. I guess I'd told a few bits and pieces of it but never before had the audience been all mine.

I wanted to keep going. I wanted to tell her everything. I wanted to tell her every single one of my adventures right then. I especially wanted to tell her about the trip across country by freight train. That's right, all the way across, all the way to the blue Pacific, no use stopping in that hick town of Huntingdon, Pennsylvania. But just as I was about to launch into how I'd recruited Daniel for that particular adventure, we walked under a streetlight and I saw again those sky blue eyes. They smiled at me but told me nothing about her thoughts. I had the impression she could see right inside me, right inside my head, right inside my soul. She knew better than I when I spoke the truth and when my words were nothing but lies.

So I kept my mouth shut and we kept walking, and pretty soon we stood outside the front door of their big white house. "Do you want to come in?" She asked. "Maybe have a cup of hot chocolate? You were shivering earlier."

Indeed I was. I'd hoped she hadn't noticed.

We went inside, and for the first time in my life I sat in the Fredericks' large white kitchen with the ten-foot ceilings and the picture window looking out across the backyard to the black wrought-iron fence and beyond the fence the manicured grounds of the academy bathed in a shower of spotlights and waning moonlight. I sat there tapping my pipe on the wooden table and feeling warm and secure and happy.

Rachel heated up some milk. As she poured the milk into two cups, Coach Frederick came down the front stairs and into the kitchen. I stood up. "Hello, sir."

"Chandler. Yes. Hello." Coach Frederick looked preoccupied, slightly disheveled. He had kind of a weird, faraway glint in his eyes and paint smeared across the right side of his face. He crossed to his daughter, kissed her on the cheek. "Have a good time?"

"I did," she answered. "I don't know about Matthew. He was half-frozen walking home."

"No, I wasn't," I lied. "I like the cold. Makes me feel like a . . . like a Gypsy."

"Like a what?" asked Rachel.

But I didn't have to answer because Coach Frederick was already on his way out. "I, uhh, just wanted to say, uhh, good night, so good night, and uhh, I'll see you in the morning, Rachel. And Matthew, I guess I'll see you in the locker room before the game."

"Yes, sir," I said.

He started into the hallway, then stopped. "By the way, who are we playing?"

I told him. He nodded absently, then retreated quickly up the steps.

Rachel brought over the mugs of steaming hot chocolate and set them on the table.

"Is he okay?" I asked.

"He's fine," she asked, "just gets a little spacey when he's painting."

"Oh, I thought maybe he was up there working on strategy for tomorrow's game."

Rachel laughed. She loved a witty remark, the more sarcastic and facetious the better. I decided not to tell her my comment had been made with complete sincerity. I didn't have a witty bone in my body.

I FOUND A SPACE, AND I MADE THAT SPACE MY OWN. I have always needed a sanctuary, someplace where I feel safe and secure. The Fredericks' kitchen became that space, my home away from home. I spent more and more time there as autumn waned and the first blasts of cold arctic air roared out of Canada and over the Alleghenies.

Rachel and I became pals. I, of course, longed to become more than pals. My feelings toward our relationship were far more complicated than that even in the beginning. I was in love, after all, whatever that meant. I think I defined love then as that rumbling in my loins, a quickening of my pulse, a longing in the middle of the night when I awoke and found myself already thinking about her.

Beyond my instinctual desire to have her, to inflict my manness—or I suppose I should say my boyness—upon her, there arose inside my head this overwhelming need to know how she felt about me.

Rachel, however, had her sights on the stars. Her needs were very different from mine. I didn't fully understand it then, but she had already discovered the love of her life.

Several evenings a week we studied together in the kitchen at the old cherry drop-leaf table in front of the picture window. And at least once a week Rachel would invite me for dinner. "We can't have you eating that cafeteria food all the time, Matthew," she'd say, "it's nothing but sugar and salt and fat."

Rachel and Coach always prepared the evening meal together. It wasn't like at my house, where Mom fixed the food and then called us into the kitchen just as the steaming plates of meat and potatoes and canned peas were heading for the table, where I sat only long enough to gobble down my protein and carbos before racing back to my bedroom or the TV set. At the Frederick house Rachel and her father met in the kitchen at a preset time and made the preparation of the meal part of the overall enterprise. It gave the food a whole different flavor.

They ate mostly fresh vegetables and whole grains, sometimes fish, and once in a while chicken they bought from a friend who owned a small farm south of town. No matter what they ate, they didn't eat much. Minuscule portions compared with what I was used to getting back home or over at the cafeteria. Later, on the way back to my dorm room, I usually had to slip over to the snack bar and chow down on some cookies and candy bars just to keep my belly from rumbling through the night.

Still, I never refused an invitation to dinner. No way. From one invitation to the next I'd do little else but wait for Rachel to ask me again. Had she asked, I would've eaten there every single night.

The Fredericks drank wine at dinner. The first time I ate over, Coach poured me a glass without even asking me if I wanted it. I looked at the glass, glanced at Coach, then over at Rachel. Neither of them paid me any mind. I figured they figured everyone drank wine at dinner. So I settled back in my chair and took my cues from Coach. When he drank, I drank. When he ate, I ate. When he rested, I rested.

Coach didn't drink much, rarely more than one glass at a meal. And he drank it slowly, in small sips, usually between foods. He never gulped anything. He'd eat some rice, then, before eating some carrots, he'd take a sip of wine. I did the same. And I'll tell you something: I still eat that way to this day, especially when I dine alone. There's something rather soothing about the deliberateness of eating every bite as though it might be your last.

A meal with the Fredericks was the complete opposite of a meal back at the Hawthorn Compound. Where Rachel and her father ate quietly and spoke of their own activities that day, the Hawthorns descended upon the dinner table like a band of, well, like a band of wild Gypsies. There was nothing quiet or subdued about a meal at their house. Even a simple midweek meal of spaghetti and meatballs was cause for boisterous celebration. Victor of course led the charge, hosted the feast. He served the main course, always in heaping platefuls, and he dominated the conversation with talk of anything that came to mind. Arguing was absolutely permissible around the Hawthorn table, sometimes even encouraged.

"You got a beef, Chandler, my boy," Victor would shout, "let it out! Don't hold it in for the rats to find. They'll chew up your insides till you're nothing but compost for the bean field."

Not that Coach Frederick ever held anything in; he was as open and honest an adult as I ever came across as a kid. He just liked to eat his dinner calmly and with a very subtle smile on his face. He chewed and swallowed practically in slow motion.

After the meal ended the Fredericks had another unusual ritual— unusual, at least, from my limited point of view. They'd sit at the table once the plates and glasses were empty, and for a few minutes no one would say a word. Eventually one of them, usually Coach, would hear some voice I couldn't hear; his muse, I suspect. He'd push back his chair, stand, and excuse himself. Often you would not see him again for the rest of the evening.

He'd retreat to his studio on the third floor, where he painted paintings often seen by no one but himself. I knew nothing about painting then, very little now, only what Rachel and her father have taught me, but one look at his work and I knew he was a great painter. It would be difficult for me to classify or categorize his work. He painted everything he could see: portraits and landscapes and bowls of fruit and rooms filled with the clutter of daily life.

An air of surrealism hung over many of his paintings, as though painted by an angel floating on one of those huge white summer clouds. A certain childlike quality existed in his colors and shapes. There was something joyful, and yet profoundly powerful, about Coach Frederick's paintings.

He did, however, have a peculiar habit. After he finished a painting, he often began a new painting right over the old. He'd let the canvas dry, then whitewash it and begin again. If you didn't catch him in the right frame of mind, you might miss one of his creations entirely as though it had never existed.

"Once a painting is finished, there is nothing but pain or praise for the painter," he used to tell his daughter, "and neither is constructive for making the next painting better."

Rachel had a disappearing act as well. Her studio was on the second floor, right next to her bedroom. Occasionally she invited me to visit, but usually she retired there alone.

Unlike her father, Rachel never painted over or threw away anything. Even at that early age she had a sense of destiny. She believed absolutely in her skills and felt even then that someday people would want to study her development as an artist. She had pencil drawings done before her fourth birthday.

In time she showed me virtually all of her work. I was, after all, her greatest fan. She would solicit my opinion often, and in great detail. It was never enough for me simply to say I loved it. No, much more was expected. I understood: her work was by far her favorite topic of conversation. I might go so far as to say the primary reason she favored our friendship was because my praise for her paintings was unending and always unwavering.

But let me go back for a moment to those early pictures. There is one in particular I remember very well. She handed it to me one evening after supper and said, "I painted this when I was seven. I didn't know it at the time, but it is the first picture I ever made from a past life."

"Past life?"

She nodded. "Yes."

I studied the painting. It was a watercolor of a large brown field with a bright red stream running through the middle of it. Men, scrawny and naked, were scattered across the field, many of them flat on their backs. At first glance it looked like a simple picture, like something you would expect from a seven-year-old. But then I began to see the violence and the misery in the picture. The men had no faces, the stream ran red with blood.

"Is it a battlefield?" I asked.

"Sort of," Rachel answered, "a prison camp, actually." She pointed to one of the men lying on his back. "That is my great-great-grandfather. He died in that camp of starvation and malnutrition. He left behind a wife and two sons, one of them my father's grandfather."

I nodded, and for most of a minute I continued to stare at the painting.

"You don't understand?"

I shrugged my shoulders. "Not really."

"I made this picture," she explained, "before I had any knowledge of my great-great-grandfather living and dying in that terrible prison. I somehow knew what had happened to him in that awful place, even though no one had ever told me his story."

That is how I learned of Rachel's belief in reincarnation. And let me tell you: at first it sort of freaked me out. I wasn't real sure what to say or how to handle it. I remember thinking maybe Rachel was slightly off her rocker, a little crazy. But that attitude passed in a flash. I very soon came to believe that Rachel and her father were the coolest and most intelligent people I had ever known, maybe even cooler and more intelligent than Victor and Daniel.

So I settled in to learn all I could. When the Fredericks retired upstairs to their private domains, I would sit all alone and stare out that picture window at the cold dark winter night. I would drink my wine, perhaps even pour myself another glass.

And then, once the last drops of wine had been consumed, I'd go to work: I'd clear the table and do the dishes. Then I would feed the cats. The Fredericks had beautiful cats with thick, rich fur, who loved vegetables cooked in cayenne pepper. Percy, named after Rachel's favorite poet, was the size of a small panther and almost the same color. Half

Siamese and half alley cat, Percy stalked through that house as though prey lurked behind every shadow. Cocoa was Percy's mother, a long, thin Siamese, who, when in the mood, could scream as loudly as any infant. I'd scrape the leftovers into their bowls. I did this partly out of kindness, but mostly I had an ulterior motive. Rachel, you see, loved those cats, lavished endless attention upon them, held them and stroked them and allowed them to sleep on her bed. It was in my interest to have those cats like me. So I fed them. And often they'd jump into my lap and lie there purring as though I were the greatest cat lover in the world. The sight of those cats in my lap never failed to bring a smile to Rachel's face.

Oh, what wicked demons we mortals be. . . .

And while I tidied up the kitchen I always listened to jazz. On his way to the third floor Coach always slipped into the living room to pile a thick stack of LPs onto the record changer. He had long ago placed speakers in almost every room of the house. Each set of speakers had its own volume control. I liked to turn the jazz up loud so I could hear the horns and the piano and the percussion over the sound of water rushing from the faucet.

Before those dinners at the Fredericks' house on Main Street, I'd never heard a note of jazz. I'd heard the names of some of the more famous players, men like Louis Armstrong and Dizzy Gillespie, but during those evenings in the Fredericks' kitchen I heard everything from ragtime to bebop to new wave fusion. I heard Billie Holiday and Huddie Ledbetter sing the blues. I listened to the big bands of Count Basie and Duke Ellington. I heard scratchy recordings of Mr. Armstrong and Jelly Roll Morton and King Oliver recorded live on Bourbon Street.

"This is American music," Coach would tell me when he came down from his studio on the third floor for one last glass of wine before bed. "Music as much or maybe even more than painting and literature is the purest definition of a culture as you can find. Most of what you see and read about America, Matthew, is a lie, a distortion at best. But not this stuff." And he'd pause to listen to a sax riff or a bass line. "This stuff's as clean and pure as it gets."

That was about as far as Coach would go on the subject. Jazz was not something he cared to intellectualize; he just liked to listen. And so did I. Sometimes all I want to do is drive down to Mercersburg and sit in the kitchen with Coach and sip some wine and listen to Charlie Parker live at the Roost.

That's what I'd like to do, but I can't. Not now. Maybe not ever.

THE REAL ESTATE AGENT OPENS THE BACK DOOR of the big white house on the corner of Main and Overlook. Tom Frederick and his daughter walk through the doorway into the kitchen. The room is large and airy, lots of light.

Rachel holds her father's hand. "Come on, Papa, I want to show you the room I'll turn into a studio if I actually go ahead and buy this place."

Tom Frederick follows his daughter out of the kitchen, down the hallway, and up a wide set of wooden stairs to the second floor.

"I'll wait for you here," the real estate agent calls from the front foyer. She is a small, perky woman with tidy gray hair.

Rachel and her father enter a large room on the south side of the house. Wide pine planks cover the floor. The ceiling is at least ten feet high. An enormous bay window juts off the end of the room.

"I can set up my easel here," Rachel says, standing near the window. "The light is wonderful."

Tom Frederick takes a long look around the room. "You're right, it'll make a great place to work. Reminds me of your room back home."

"It's almost exactly the same," says Rachel. "The whole house is almost exactly the same. That's why I love it. It even has the same address: Thirty-six Main Street."

They take a leisurely walk through the house. Tom asks the real estate agent all the pertinent questions: cost, taxes, heating system, sewage system, water supply, and so on.

"And how long has the house been on the market?"

"About a year now," answers the agent. "A young couple bought it, had plans to fix it up, but then he got transferred so they didn't really have time to get much done."

"The place does need work," says Tom Frederick, "plastering, paint-

ing, carpentry. And it looks to me like the plumbing in that upstairs bathroom is about shot. Same might be said for that oil burner in the basement. I hope the price is negotiable."

"I'm sure it is," agrees the agent, beaming from the mere possibility of her first sale in months. "The market's been atrocious. I'm sure you can get it for a steal."

Tom and Rachel stand on the sidewalk in front of the house. The real estate agent has locked up and driven off in her small Mercedes sedan.

"So, Papa, do you like it?"

"I do, yes. But it sounds like a lot of money considering the shape it's in. You'll spend twenty thousand on repairs before you stretch your first canvas."

"So what? I like this town. I love this house. This is where I want to live."

Tom Frederick lets his eyes wander over the house. "It's an awful big place."

"Enormous. That's one of the things I love about it."

"And for just one person."

Rachel puts her arm around her father's waist. "You never know."

"What does that mean?"

"Come on, Papa, let's go back to the barn and get some lunch."

They walk along Main Street, past the Peapack-Gladstone Bank and the pond with the new fountains shooting water high into the steamy summer air.

A young woman pushing a baby stroller waves from across the street. "Hello, Misty."

Misty waves back. "Hi, Lynn. How's Ted?"

The woman glances at the stroller, shakes her head. "Hungry and cranky, as usual."

Both women laugh.

The Fredericks keep walking. "I can see why you like this town," says Tom. "People are friendly."

"Maybe not as friendly and open as they are back home, but after all those years in the city, this town is like paradise. A perfect place to work."

"I still don't like this Misty business."

Rachel manages a laugh. "Hey, I wish I'd started with a better name myself, something normal like Mary or Jennifer. But I'm stuck with it now. I'll just have to live with it."

"I don't mean the name," says Tom Frederick. "I mean this whole business of you using an alias."

✳   ✳   ✳

They sit at the kitchen table in the old red barn. They eat salads with the season's first tomatoes from Rachel's garden. In the background Sarah Vaughan sings "Lover Boy."

"So you're sure you want to make an offer?" Tom asks.

"Absolutely."

"Then I think we should have the house checked out. We'll get someone in there, a professional, to have a look at the foundation and the roof and whatever else. Then we'll know better where we stand."

Rachel smiles. "This is why I waited for you to come before I made a move. I knew you'd know what to do."

They finish their salads. Rachel pulls a fresh blueberry pie from the refrigerator. She cuts two pieces and sets them on the table. They eat in silence.

After he finishes Tom asks, "Any chance of you teaching in the fall?"

Rachel shrugs. "I don't know. I'd like to. I miss it. There's a prep school not too far from here. Gill-St. Bernard's. But even if a position opens up, I have this problem with credentials. Misty Grey didn't graduate from Cooper Union. She didn't teach there for three years, either. Misty Grey doesn't even have a Social Security number or a driver's license."

"See where lies lead you."

"It's been a trade-off, Papa."

Tom shakes his head. "Sorry, I don't buy that, not for a second." He hesitates, then smiles. "But I won't push it, not on this beautiful summer day."

PROBABLY THE MOST INTERESTING THING TO HAPPEN when I went home for Thanksgiving in late November was what didn't happen: I didn't tell anyone, not even Daniel, especially not Daniel, about Rachel; never once did I even mention her name.

He and Buckley showed up outside my window just before midnight on Wednesday, the day before Thanksgiving. I'd arrived home only a few hours earlier, been picked up by Dear Old Dad, who'd come early in the afternoon to the academy so he could have a chat with his ex-classmate, the headmaster. Chuckie forked over some endowment dollars that day and then no doubt inquired about the academic well-being of his son.

I threw open the window and let in my buddies. We shook hands and hugged and whispered in excited voices.

"Jesus, what're you guys doing here?"

"Just wanted to find out if you were still alive."

"See if you had metamorphosed into a preppie or not."

We laughed and punched each other on the shoulder. I felt like I'd been away for years.

"I'm doing good," I said, "doing okay."

"You get laid yet?" Daniel wanted to know.

I looked away, down at the floor. "A couple times."

"Bullshit a couple times," said Daniel. "Have you even talked to a girl yet? Touched any titties?"

"Shut up," I pushed him.

"Hey, Buckley," he asked, "you see that? Mac got pissed. He must've talked to one, it's got him all riled up. What did she do, Mac, smile at you, throw you a kiss?"

"Fuck you," I mumbled. I wanted to punch him in the head but knew it would only lead to more needling. Then I wanted to defend myself, tell him I'd talked to one all right. I wanted to tell him all about Rachel. But I knew he'd never get it, he'd just cut me, slice me up into little pieces. I knew I'd get all knotted up inside and my voice would crack and Daniel and Buckley would immediately know their old buddy

Mac had fallen head over heels for some prissy prep school babe. At least that's the way they'd see it. They'd turn the whole thing inside out. So I decided to just keep my mouth shut. Besides, I wanted Rachel all to myself; didn't want to share her with anyone, especially not with Daniel.

And to hell with Daniel's prophecy that night on that mountain in Austria when he said someday some female would come between us. To hell with prophecies. Prophecies were just more bullshit that once in a while proved true and got everybody all excited.

The next morning I watched Daniel run for three touchdowns and almost two hundred yards in the annual Thanksgiving Day game between Mendham High and Chester Borough. He ran like a guy destined for the Football Hall of Fame in Canton, Ohio.

For the first time in my life I had negative thoughts about his performance. I wanted him to fumble. I wanted him to lose yardage. I wanted him to get hurt. I wanted him to blow the game in the final seconds. I wanted him to walk off the field in defeat. I wanted him to fail.

When I got back to the academy late Sunday afternoon I went straight to the Fredericks' house. I climbed the stairs to the front porch. Through the window I saw Rachel curled up on the sofa in the living room. Cocoa and Percy had their heads resting on her lap. A fire roared in the fireplace. I looked at Rachel more closely. She had tears in her eyes. I could see the tears on her cheeks glistening in the firelight.

I froze. I didn't know what to do. At first I felt like I should turn and walk away, not intrude upon her privacy. But then I thought I should go in and make sure she was all right, find out if everything was okay. Maybe something bad had happened; maybe her father had been killed in a car crash. Maybe I'd have to step in and take care of her. Maybe I'd move into that big old white house on Main Street before another night fell.

I don't know how long I stood out there in the cold, shivering, probably not long, only a minute or two; however long, a thousand emotions tugged at my sleeve. This was all new to me: girls, tears, love, lust, confusion.

And then I saw Rachel smile. And then she started to laugh, right out loud. I glanced around the room, figured someone else must be in there with her. But no, she was all alone.

I knocked on the front door.

"Yes," said her soft feminine voice, "come in."

I pushed open the door and stepped cautiously into the front foyer, then through the tall archway between the foyer and the living room.

"Matthew!" She smiled, shooed the cats away, stood up.

"You okay?" I asked. "I thought I saw you crying." As I said the words I thought they were surely the wrong words but Rachel didn't seem to mind.

"Yes," she said, "for a moment. But the story had a happy ending, a funny ending."

"The story? What story?"

"Yes, well, I'd been reading something for English, Faulkner, but it grew so boring and tedious that I tossed the book aside and began to tell myself a story. . . ."

There on the floor lay a paperback copy of As I Lay Dying.

"It became quite involved, and there was an accident—"

"An accident?"

"Yes, an accident. One of those giant motor homes slammed into a VW Beetle, and both vehicles went over this canyon wall and—"

"Jesus," I said, fully aware that Coach Frederick drove a VW Beetle.

Rachel laughed. "But everyone survived, you see. Nothing but a few bumps and bruises. And then they all collected these big settlements from the insurance company and went off to Cannes together, where they made a picture about the accident and won first prize at the film festival."

"Huh?" I was totally lost.

"Nothing, Matthew," she said, "forget it. It's just a story." And then she passed in front of the fire and stood closer to me than she had ever stood before. Maybe three inches shorter than I then, she pushed herself up onto her toes and kissed me lightly on the mouth.

She had the sweetest breath, like something from the inside of a wildflower. For just a moment, I'll have to admit, while her lips touched mine, I trembled. I know this is not the kind of thing a guy should confess; I should tell you her kiss meant nothing or that I swooped her up into my arms the moment her kiss ended and carried her upstairs, where I made passionate love to her in the doorway between her bedroom and her studio. But no, not me; I trembled ever so slightly. That kiss took my breath away.

She stepped back then, not far, I could still smell the sweetness on her breath. "I'm glad you're back," she said. "Did you have a good time at home? See all your friends?"

For the remainder of that school year I never once mentioned Daniel to her. She knew he existed because he had played an important role in many of the stories I had told her up until then. But from Thanksgiving on he ceased to exist. The adventures of my youth began to take shape in a different way.

As I told my tales to Rachel I found myself taking on more and more the personality of Daniel. Whatever role he had played in reality became the role I played in my fictional accounts. I became the boy with the steel walnuts, willing to do anything, go anywhere, take on any challenge. I became the leader, the Head Honcho, the one who initiated and controlled our boyhood adventures. Daniel became just another nameless, faceless member of my gang.

This total revamping of my childhood took place over the course of several months. I didn't just unload it all at once. I built myself up slowly, modestly, one story at a time. It was inconceivable to me then that Rachel and Daniel would ever meet. I certainly had no intention of introducing them, and if not me, then who? So far as I was concerned the distance between them was vast, insurmountable. I could tell Rachel anything and Daniel would never be there to contradict me, to set the record straight.

I made the varsity basketball team that winter. I thought I should've been a starter, but the coach, a tall bald guy who had played a season with the Baltimore Bullets, preferred to start seniors. "Patience, Chandler," he told me more than once, "you'll get your chance."

Good soldier and puritan that I was (and probably still am even though I'm trying to break the mold), I practiced hard every day and only rarely complained about my lack of playing time. We had an average team that year, won a few, lost a few. I didn't really care if we won or lost. I was far more interested in the juniors and sophomores on the team who would be back the following year. I used to try to get the younger guys together for extra practice on weekends so we could hone our skills, learn to play as a team.

See, not only was I taking on Daniel's character when I told Rachel the stories from my youth, I was also taking on his character in other, more immediate ways. If Daniel had been there, he would've organized those weekend practices, pushed the younger guys on the team to prepare for next season. But with him so far away, it was left to me. I relished the role. And I performed it admirably. After all, for fifteen years I'd had the perfect mentor.

This preparation for the future earmarked another interesting facet of my development. Upon first arriving at Mercersburg, I had spent an inordinate amount of time thinking up ways to wind up back at Mendham High for my junior year. No way did I plan on spending the rest of my high school days at prep school. But by Christmas, mostly because of Rachel, almost entirely because of Rachel, I had changed my tune. My parents would've needed a team of wild horses to drag me away from those ivy-covered buildings. So those weekend practice sessions were for me a kind of declaration of independence. Come hell or high water, I'd be back.

Hoop season ended and spring came to that Pennsylvania valley on the very same day. I walked out of the gym after cleaning out my locker, and immediately I smelled spring in the air. The breeze had lost its bite. The snow was long gone, and everything, the grass and the trees and the bushes, held that hint of green you see before the explosion of new growth.

Rachel appeared at my side and asked me if I wanted to go for a walk. She might as well have asked a dog if he wanted to fetch a stick. I fell right into line.

We walked out through the back of campus, across playing fields filled with the boys' baseball team and the girls' field hockey team and the coed softball team. Spring sports were under way but I'd already decided to take the season off.

A barbed-wire fence, just three rusty strands not more than three feet high, marked the end of the academy's property. A farmer had installed the barbed wire not to keep out students but to keep in his cows and sheep. I held down the top strand of wire so Rachel could climb over. She did the same for me.

Rachel did not participate in organized athletics but she was athletic nevertheless. Thin and agile, she loved to run through the fields and climb trees. She could walk for miles without tiring. We must've walked five miles that day across just plowed fields, up steep hills, through stands of oaks and maples just waiting for the air to warm so they could throw out their leaves.

We walked for at least an hour without hardly saying a word. I had the urge to talk, to tell her how I felt, to tell her a story, to build myself up, to tell her anything and everything. But just as she would do for the next, well, really for the next eighteen years, Rachel controlled me, dominated me emotionally and even physically.

That day she just wanted to walk, to look at nature, to feel the earth awakening after the winter freeze. She didn't want to hear words coming out of our mouths. Winter had been full of words, so many words during those gray days and dark nights. Now she wanted us just to listen. She communicated this desire to me without saying a word, without even bringing her finger to her lips. In this way she was very much like Daniel. They were both such strong, stubborn individuals. Neither of them ever gave an inch. Their way was the only way.

On the way back we did talk some. Rachel talked about Nixon's trip to China. I knew all about his trip because I'd listened to her and Coach talk about it at dinner. I'd even gone to the library and read the newspaper so I could add a few details to the conversation. But out there in those fields, under a bright blue, late March sky, Rachel at my side, I didn't want to talk about Tricky Dick Nixon or Chairman Mao or Henry Kissinger or that little guy with the tight collar, what was his name? Chou En-Lai. I wanted to talk about us. I wanted to tell her I loved her, just stop and hold her tight and look her in the eye and say, "Rachel, I love you."

But before I could she moved on. "As soon as the wildflowers begin to bloom," she said, "I'll set up my easel right here. This'll be perfect."

We stood on high ground at the edge of a wide meadow, a stand of oaks at our backs. Looking east toward the campus, we could see fields and hedgerows and the tall white steeple of the Mercersburg Chapel.

"I've painted this before," she said, "but I feel as though I'm ready to paint it now in a whole different way, in a whole new light."

I wanted to say something about getting married someday in that chapel, but instead I just nodded and smiled and said nothing. On the way back, for a while, we held hands.

Many times that spring we took long walks together. Rachel usually brought along her sketch pad, and while she sat on the grass working with her pencils I would stretch out nearby and watch the sky. I enjoyed doing nothing. For the first time in my life I became aware of relaxation and reflection. I'd just lie there and let my mind wander.

Sometimes, if everything was just right, I'd actually forget all about stuff I'd left undone and stuff I had to do. "Couldn't we just lie here forever?" I said to Rachel one afternoon.

"That would be fine with me," she said, her pencil moving quickly and skillfully across the white paper.

"You say that now," I said, "but as soon as you ran out of paper, or your pencils grew dull, you'd head back to town for more supplies."

"You're right," she said after a moment, "I probably would."

"So you wouldn't want to just lie here forever?"

Her hand had already gone back to work. "I guess not."

"So I guess that's the difference between us."

A minute passed. She said nothing. I decided she hadn't heard my remark. I was about to repeat myself when she said, "No, the difference between you and me, Matthew, is I already know what I want to do whereas you're still searching."

That pretty much shut me up for the rest of the afternoon. At first I felt hurt, as though Rachel had shot an arrow through my heart. But then I decided she hadn't meant her remark in a mean or insulting way. She had merely stated a fact. And so I lay there in the grass and tried to figure out what I wanted to do with my life, what I wanted to be when I grew up.

A few days later, back out in those fields, I said, "I wonder if there's anything creative I can do."

"What do you mean?" she asked.

I'd been thinking about it a lot. "Well, I mean like painting. You and your father paint. Painting's creative. Like music or literature. I wonder if I can do anything like that."

"Of course you can." She said it without even looking away from her sketch.

"I don't think so," I said.

"Why do you say that? Have you ever tried?"

"Not really."

"Then how do you know you can't?"

"Just because I don't think I can. I have no talent."

She looked up at me. "That's ridiculous, Matthew. Creativity isn't talent, it's desire."

That bit of profundity blew me away for a minute or two. I had to stop and think about that one. "But you're good at what you do," I said long after she'd gone back to her sketch.

"Says who?"

"It's obvious."

"Maybe, maybe not. You're talking about something completely different now. Good and bad have nothing at all to do with creativity. I think some of the most famous paintings ever made stink. Some of the most famous books as well. So what? Good and bad are nothing but subjective. Creativity's just doing it, that's all. The rest is crap."

Like Daniel, Rachel, in some ways, was wise beyond her years.

In late May, just a few weeks before school ended, Rachel and I spent an entire Saturday out in the fields. We packed a picnic lunch. I carried that while Rachel carried her portable easel and a box of watercolors. We hiked to that place on the edge of the meadow where we had stopped almost two months earlier. The sun was high and warm. The occasional breeze blew from the south. High, stark white clouds drifted across the sky.

The meadow was alive with wildflowers. Millions of different colors danced across that field every time the breeze fluttered.

"Who says you can't see the wind?" I asked.

Rachel looked at me, a hint of surprise crossed her face; she did not often hear me say things so . . . so wistful, so impractical.

While she set up her easel I spread out the blanket. While she painted I read. Actually I only pretended to read, *The Sun Also Rises*, I think it was. Inside the pages of that novel I had a pad, and in my hand I held a pen. While Rachel painted I wrote. I wrote poetry, at least what I thought was poetry. And from Rachel's definition of creativity it was poetry.

I will not reprint here what I wrote there. Better to save both of us the embarrassment. Let it be enough to say I wrote about those wildflowers, about the breeze stirring them invisibly, about the clouds and the color of Rachel's eyes, about the way my heart roared in her presence.

Deep in thought, I heard her ask, "What are you writing, Matthew?"

I slammed Hemingway's novel closed. "Nothing. Just some English notes."

She seemed satisfied with that. She crossed to the blanket, sat down. "Should we have something to eat?"

I nodded while discreetly slipping the novel and its contents into my book bag.

We had sandwiches and fruit and pie, even a bottle of wine. I had a corkscrew on my Swiss Army knife, the same knife I'd had on our freight train trip. That trip seemed like it had happened a million years ago. I peeled off the cap and twisted the screw down into the cork. I did it all with a manner of nonchalance, as though I drank wine with my woman out there in the fields several times a week.

"So," I heard Rachel say, "it finally looks like we're all set."

"What's that?" I asked, the cork now ready to be withdrawn.

"Our trip to Europe. Looks like everything's finally fallen into place. Father's going to order the tickets from the travel agent today."

"Huh?" I pulled too hard on the cork. Several ounces of cool white wine splashed out of the bottle onto my shirt. I tried to act as though it hadn't happened. "What trip to Europe? When?" My nonchalance had turned to vinegar.

"Come on, Matthew, I must've told you that Father has been thinking about taking me to Italy and France and Belgium this summer."

"You might've thought you told me," I said, "but you didn't."

That was my first encounter with a particularly annoying facet of Rachel's personality. She did not deem it necessary to explain herself in any way. "Well," she said, "I thought I did, but if I didn't, well, I guess I'm telling you now."

Well well well.

I do not think she intended to sound cold or impertinent. Rachel was neither of those things. But she was self-absorbed. In the years to come her emotional independence would more than once drive me nearly out of my mind.

If I raised even the slightest objection to her autonomous, free-wheeling ways, she'd look at me as though I were some kind of prehistoric creature, some monster or madman recently escaped from the insane asylum. You see, she made no demands, so quite naturally she expected no demands from others.

"Yeah," I said, averting my eyes, "I guess you are."

And that was that. She spent the rest of our picnic telling me about all the great cities she would visit, all the fantastic artists whose work she would see: Rome and Florence and Paris; Raphael and Michelangelo and Van Gogh.

I sat there and listened, but I didn't gave a damn for any of those foreign cities or any of those long dead artists. I felt only hollow inside and a little bit afraid. Rachel sat right next to me, close enough to touch, but soon, I knew, she'd be gone. I freely admit it: I missed her already.

On the last day of school, after our exams had been taken and our books put away, we said good-bye. It happened on the Fredericks' front porch. An early morning walk into the fields had been planned but rain and thunder and lightning had washed those plans away. Soon my parents would arrive to haul me back to Jersey.

I stood there on the porch, soaking wet, an envelope folded in half and stuffed into my back pocket. In the envelope were four poems: the one I'd written while pretending to read *The Sun Also Rises* and three new ones I'd written late at night when I couldn't sleep. Scurvy complained when I flipped on the light, but I had no patience for fools. "Shut up, Scurvy, you little twit. Just shut the fuck up."

Now, the moment of truth, but I couldn't seem to pull that envelope out of my pocket. I wouldn't see Rachel until September, nearly two and a half months. I had to make my move, and pronto. But you would've thought I had a gold brick in my pocket the way I just couldn't seem to lift it out and hand it over.

The next day being my sixteenth birthday, Rachel sang "Happy Birthday" to me. She gave me a chocolate cupcake with a single candle, one of those kinds you can't blow out no matter how hard you try. I blew and blew until finally I just pulled it out of the cupcake and threw it out into the rain. Rachel laughed and said it would probably still be burning when we got back in the fall.

"I hope so," I said.

Coach came out onto the porch and looked around as if he weren't real sure where he was or what he wanted to say. "Well, Matt," he said finally, "have a good summer." Then he shook my hand and went back inside.

Rachel talked about this and that: Nixon in Moscow, the Louvre, *Starry Night*. I just stood there looking stupid and trying to find the gumption to hand over the envelope.

Then I heard her say, "Well, Matthew, I guess I better get going. We have to drive up to Harrisburg to get our passports."

"Passports, right," I mumbled, and I remembered the excitement I'd felt four years earlier when I'd gotten my passport for our trip to Germany and Austria and Czechoslovakia.

She kissed me hard on the mouth then, harder than she had ever kissed me before. I put my arms around her waist and drew her close. I pressed our bodies together. And then I kissed her back. I kissed her with everything I had. During that kiss tears came to my eyes. I felt those tears beneath my lids. I felt them roll out and over my lashes and down my cheeks.

So when we parted, because I did not want her to see my tears, I turned away. "Have a good time," I managed to mumble, and then, that envelope still filling my pocket, I practically jumped off the Fredericks' front porch and sprinted across the lawn through the rain.

BY THE TIME WE REACHED MENDHAM, late that afternoon, the rain had slowed to a drizzle under a heavy gray sky. I kept busy unloading the car and putting away my gear. Chuckie and Martha hung around only long enough to change their clothes, then off they went to the Opening Day of Summer Party over at the club. Bully for them.

It was Daniel's birthday, and I wondered if there might be a party. I thought about riding my bike down to the Compound, but after mulling it over for an hour or so I decided I didn't really feel like seeing anyone. So instead I called Rachel. No answer.

I took the poems out of that still damp envelope and spread them across the top of my bureau. Some of the ink had started to run but you could still read the words without much trouble. I lay down on the bed and stared up at the ceiling.

I thought the guys might come over, welcome me home, maybe throw me a party the way they'd done back in the fall. But that longest day of the year, the summer solstice, faded into darkness and no one came. Our house on Cherry Street stood silent and empty. I kind of hoped it might stay that way until September.

I woke up early the next morning, my birthday, and the first thing I did was creep downstairs and pilfer an envelope from my mother's desk. I took the envelope back up to my room and addressed it to Rachel Ann Frederick on Main Street in Mercersburg, Pennsylvania. Then I carefully folded the four poems in thirds and stuffed them into the envelope. All this took a lot of time. At least it seemed to take a lot of time. I was aware of every second passing, ticking off the clock.

I went back downstairs and out into the garage. My bike had a flat tire. I pumped it up and climbed aboard, my envelope secure in the pocket of my gray academy sweatshirt. Outside, I found the sky had finally started to clear. On the way downtown I thought about riding all the way to Mercersburg but I knew I'd never make it, at least not before Rachel flew off to Rome.

I reached the post office before it opened. I had to hang around outside for fifteen or twenty minutes before Mrs. Smithers, the woman who sold the stamps and knew the most intimate business of everyone in town, unlocked those glass doors and let me inside.

"Well, Matthew Chandler, you're a sight for sore eyes. Haven't seen you in quite some time. Been away at school, have you?"

"Yes, ma'am."

She went behind the counter and asked after my parents. I told her they were fine and dandy, the most wonderful parents in the world.

This just made her smile. "So what brings you out so early this morning?"

"I'd like to mail this." Confident now in my course of action, I pulled the envelope from my pocket and handed it over.

Mrs. Smithers took it without even glancing at it, as though the envelope might contain nothing more than payment for that month's electric bill. She dropped it on the scale. "You'll need one first-class stamp to mail that off, Matthew."

I handed her the money. In those days I think it cost twelve cents, maybe fifteen. I figured she'd give me a stamp and let me stick it on myself. That's what I wanted her to do. I wanted to handle this myself, make sure that stamp was properly secured, maybe reinforce it with some glue and a piece of Scotch tape. No way did I want that envelope returned to sender.

But Mrs. Smithers licked and stuck on the stamp herself, kind of haphazardly, I thought, as though she didn't give a damn about its destiny, and then she announced for all the world to hear, "Rachel Ann Frederick, Mercersburg, Pennsylvania. . . . Writing to your sweetheart, are you, Matthew?"

I wanted to grab that envelope out of her hand and disappear from the post office. But instead, my skin as red as blood, I said, "Sweetheart? No, just someone I knew at school. I took some of her papers by accident, and"—and I knew Mrs. Smithers knew the truth, the whole truth—"and, well, I just thought I'd better send them back to her."

Mrs. Smithers gave me a look that just about sent me down on the floor. Then she tossed that envelope practically over her shoulder into a great pile of other envelopes. "We'll make sure it gets there, Matthew. Don't you worry."

I crept out of the post office feeling completely naked, as though I wore not a stitch of clothing anywhere on my body. Once outside I thought about going back in and asking Mrs. Smithers, maybe even begging Mrs. Smithers, not to mention the envelope to my mother. But in what may have been my first adultlike twinge of paranoia, I decided if I asked her not to tell my mother, she would make a point of telling her.

So I went home and waited all day for Daniel to come. He never did. None of the other guys came, either.

I moped around all day. My mother asked me what was wrong. I told her I had a stomachache. She gave me some syrupy concoction that I threw down the drain when she turned her back.

Once or twice I called Rachel, but no one answered. I imagined her out in the fields sketching some muscular stud with massive biceps and nothing on but a Day-Glo orange jock strap. More paranoia.

I picked on my little sister for a while but that grew boring so I went out in the backyard, out by the pond, and sat in the grass. I stared at the water, then, later, I stared at the sky. I squeezed the life out of a tiny red ant and then felt bad about it. I kept trying to feel like I'd felt when I wandered around out in the fields with Rachel. But it was no good. Not only was the guy wearing the orange Day-Glo out there with us, but I felt different, strange. I felt like a dead tree trunk, hollow inside, crawling with bugs. It was my heart, not my stomach, that ached.

The next day they still didn't come. Had my old buddies forgotten about me, their old pal Mac Chandler? Had I ceased to exist?

Finally, late in the afternoon, I climbed aboard my bike and rode over to the compound at the end of Thomas Lane. I leaned my bike against the garage and walked around back to the swimming pool. It was a warm bright summer day. The water in the pool sparkled, absolutely crystal clear. But the place was deserted, no one around.

I went to the back door and knocked. No answer. I went around to the front door and rang the bell. No one came. I went around the side, to the greenhouse. I climbed up onto the brick patio and peered through the glass. Memories of Daniel's mother's naked body flashed through my mind. I fantasized I would find her there that way once again. And this time we would make love among the orchids, the sweet smell of nectar floating in the air above our naked, sweating bodies. And afterward we would run through the grass and plunge together into the deep end of that four-leaf-clover-shaped swimming pool. . . .

"Matthew, is that you?"

My fantasy faded as the real thing appeared at the door of the greenhouse. Only this time Daniel's mother wore shorts and shirt and old tennis sneakers. Her hair was pulled back, and she had dirt on her face where she had wiped her soiled hands across her cheek. She held a small towel in one hand and a beautiful purple orchid in the other. From the orchid sprang a long white pistil that looked to me very much like a penis.

The whole scene struck me like a dream or maybe a movie. "Hello, Mrs. Hawthorn." I wanted to step right up to her and wipe the dirt gently off her face. She would smile and I would kiss her and she would kiss me back and one thing would lead to another...

"Did you just get home from school?"

I practically had to punch myself in the side of the head. "Oh, yes, ma'am. Just got back the other day, yesterday, the day before yesterday."

She either ignored or didn't notice my stammering. Men had probably been stammering around her most of her life. What a queer gender we are.

"Did you get to see Daniel before he left?"

Left!? Left for where? I wondered. "No," I said, "I haven't seen him. Where did he go?"

And that's when she hit me with the news. She told me as casually as Rachel had announced her trip to the Old World. "He's gone off with his father."

I felt my chest tighten. "For the weekend?"

"You mean he never told you?"

I wasn't sure what she meant. "I guess not."

"He's gone away for the summer."

"For the summer? The whole summer!"

She had turned away from me by this time, retreated to her potting bench, where she very carefully placed that purple orchid with the long white pecker in a clay pot filled with rich black soil. "Can't let the roots dry out," she explained.

I nodded to no one as I followed her across the tile floor, my fantasy struggling with this latest barrage of reality. "So, where did he go?"

"He and Victor went to Europe."

"Europe!" Thoughts of him and Rachel meeting at some Parisian cafe and falling in love while the bombs dropped all around them, à la Bogie and Bergman in *Casablanca*, sprang into my mind. Yet more paranoia.

"Yes," she answered, "but I can't understand why he wouldn't have told you."

I was having a tough time understanding that myself.

Carolyn Hawthorn wiped her hands on her shirt and turned back to me. "You see, Matthew, it's an old Gypsy tradition. When a boy turns sixteen he and his father go off together, just the two of them. The focus of their relationship changes. The emphasis shifts from father and son to man and man. These weeks they spend together are the beginning of Daniel's initiation into manhood."

I stood there listening, my mouth partway open, the fingers of my left hand scratching the few strands of stubble on my chin. Goddamn Gypsies, I thought. And then I wondered when I would spend time alone with my father, when I would become a man.

I must've stood there quite a while looking perplexed because the next thing I knew she asked, "Can I get you something? A Coke or maybe a glass of lemonade?"

I thought about it, shook my head. I wanted to get out of there, fast. But I had one more question. "So when'll he be back?"

"Well, they weren't sure. Probably August. Certainly before school starts."

In that moment the longest summer of my life grew considerably longer.

I thanked her, and while I thanked her I backed out of the greenhouse.

"Come and see us," she said as I backed through the doorway. "Don't be a stranger."

I assured her I wouldn't be, and then I was gone. Across the lawn, back on my bike, and pedaling nowhere a million miles an hour.

You might say I was a lost and wandering soul that summer. No way was I as lost and wandering a soul as I am today, but that's only because I was younger and far more innocent then. In those days loneliness and melancholy were the limits of my emotional distress.

Sometimes I hung around with Buckley and the other guys, but they seemed even more disoriented than I without their leader. They argued all the time about what to do and where to go. So as July slowly slipped away in a haze of oppressive New Jersey heat and humidity, I found myself spending more and more time alone. I'd go for long bike rides, then spend hours just sitting somewhere under a tree with a book that usually went unread.

The highlight of the summer came on the last day of July. I walked into the kitchen after a long ride, sweating and breathing hard and needing a glass of water. My mother stood at the sink washing something, a cup or maybe a cucumber. "There's a letter for you, Matthew."

I figured it was probably something stupid, a piece of junk mail or maybe a reminder from Mercersburg telling me when to report for fall classes.

"Postmarked Paris," my mother added, a certain satiric lilt to her voice. Or was that just my imagination?

I stopped dead in my tracks, felt my heart skip a beat. I glanced over at the table where she always put the pile of mail. I had my back to her, but I could feel her looking over her shoulder at me. "From Paris, huh?" Very casual, as though I got mail from Paris all the time.

"Yes," she said, and believe me, she didn't have to say anything else, "Paris."

I took my time, quenched my thirst, brought my breathing under control. And then, before too much more time passed, I had that letter in my hand and was in the hallway, out of sight, and sprinting up the front stairs to the safety and security of my bedroom. I closed and locked the door.

I still have that letter. In fact, I have every letter Rachel ever wrote me. I've thought about reprinting that first letter, that letter from Paris, right here, in full, but have decided it would be a breach of trust. Rachel intended that letter for me and me alone, so I'll do no more than hit the highlights.

It seems my poems did not reach Mercersburg until after the Fredericks had flown off to Rome; an erroneous zip code might have been the culprit. So my precious envelope, along with certain other important pieces of mail, had been forwarded. My poems had reached Rome a day late, Florence three days late, Venice nearly a week late, but had finally caught up with the Fredericks at some small but fashionable Parisian hotel in the old Latin Quarter just off the Quai d'Orsay.

Rachel read the poems over and over, as many as a dozen times, she claimed, and then, the next day, after she had given them time to settle, she wrote back.

I would like to report her letter contained a vow of eternal love, a commitment to be mine forever. But read between the lines though I tried, I could find no such vow or commitment. She praised my poems, called them the most beautiful things she had ever read, claimed that in no way did she deserve to have such things written for or about herself. She went on this way for most of a page in her beautiful, swirling penwomanship.

But by page two she had shifted gears. Her prose moved on to lengthy descriptions of the Sistine Chapel ceiling and the statue of David in the Academy at Florence and Van Gogh's painting hanging in the Louvre of the church at Auvers, which reminded her very much of the chapel at Mercersburg. And then she went on to ask, this sixteen-year-old girl, "How do we see the world, Matthew? And how does the world see us?"

She signed her letter "Love, Rachel," and for me, then, that was more than enough.

☩   ☩   ☩

August passed at a dirgelike pace. My parents went to Nantucket but I refused to go. I said if I could survive on my own at boarding school for nine months, I could certainly survive for a few weeks on my own at 367 Cherry Lane in Mendham. Quite a struggle ensued but in the end they relented. They did so mainly because they knew I'd be a pain in the butt out on the island if they forced me to go. So I stayed home alone, although not really. The old man, busy on some important case, spent at least two or three nights a week in the house with me. We nevertheless avoided each other with incredible precision; our paths rarely crossed.

So much for time together, for Chandler tradition, for the whole father-son thing, for my passage into the heady realm of manhood.

Look, I don't put all the blame on Chuckie. I'm not that spiteful. I accept my fair share. In fact, I suppose every word I utter about my parents should be taken with a grain of salt. People far wiser than I actually think Chuckie and Martha Chandler are a couple of fine and upstanding citizens. Who am I to argue?

Daniel returned in late August. Word of his arrival spread through our tiny burg like the Second Coming of the Messiah. I tried to stay away, to hold myself in reserve, but soon after dinner I boarded my bike and steered straight for the compound.

I was not the first to arrive. Buckley was already there, as were several other members of the old gang. It was a warm night, as humid as it had been all summer. I heard them out by the pool. I could hear him storytelling even before I could see him. For a moment I stopped in the shadows to listen. I heard something about Nazis. Something about a flight from Zurich to Buenos Aires. I would have continued to listen but another member of the old gang, in a rush to reach the inner circle, came up behind me.

"Hey, Mac," he said, and slapped me across the back, "can you believe it? He's finally home." Then he moved off, across the damp grass and into the light surrounding the swimming pool. I followed.

Later, after the stories had been told and the gang had gone away, I finally had a moment alone with my old buddy. He gave me a long, hard hug, told me he'd missed me. I could see in his eyes he meant it. Then came the news that would change everything, news that almost from the moment he broadcast it caused within me feelings of profound ambiguity.

"So when do we report?" he asked.

"Report where?" I wanted to know.

"To practice."

"What practice?"

"Football practice."

"Huh?"

He laughed. "We're gonna be on the same team again, Mac. Me and you, fightin' for yards, fightin' for victory."

"What are you talking about?"

"You mean no one told you?"

"Told me what?"

"I'm comin' to the academy, Mac. I'm gonna be a preppie. We're gonna be preppies together."

HE THINKS THE BLACK SEDAN HAS FOLLOWED HIM INTO
TOWN. *Town this time is Kennebunkport, Maine, summer home for the
forty-first U.S. president.*

*Daniel Hawthorn, alias Daniel Romankova, has made his way
slowly south after his run-in with Canadian border officials. News reports
on his car radio that President Bush was at his Kennebunkport retreat
coordinating efforts to drive Saddam Hussein from Kuwait caused Daniel
to alter his course and head for the coast.*

*But the black sedan bothers him. He reassures himself it is only his
imagination; the sedan is not occupied by people trailing him in connection with the death of Herr Heinrich in Buenos Aires.*

*The small seaside town is jammed with cars and pedestrians. Daniel
senses a carnival atmosphere, or perhaps it's war fever. Everyone moves in
a great hurry. Almost everyone carries either a camera or a notebook. He
sees the woman from TV who reports on the White House for one of the
networks. Everywhere he looks he sees pockets bulging with excess cash. He
decides to try for his small piece of the action.*

*On the east side of town he stops the VW camper-van along the edge
of a small park. A sign says two-hour parking but he figures he'll be lucky
to last that long.*

*He climbs out of the van, stretches, takes a look around. The black
sedan is nowhere in sight.*

*The afternoon is hot and sunny. A stiff breeze blows off the ocean. To
provide some shade for his show, Daniel puts up the canvas canopy that
attaches to the side of the van. Under the canopy he sets up a folding card
table and two chairs. In front of the table he leans a wooden sign:* MAGIC
TRICKS, FORTUNE-TELLING, PALM READING.

*He climbs into the back of the van and dresses in his costume. And
quite a costume it is. The pants are made of velvet, tight at the waist and*

ankles, but loose and baggy through the thighs and calves. A band of fine mohair, looped casually just below the navel, holds the pants in place just above the hips. The shirt, a pullover with a deep neck and a wide collar, is pure silk of blood red.

He wears nothing on his feet, leather straps with tiny bells around his ankles. He wears similar leather straps around his wrists. He wears a gold earring in his left ear. On his right ear he wears a long silver earring that hangs down almost to his shoulder. He combs his hair straight back over his head and slicks it down with bear grease.

Outside, a few people have gathered around the van: an elderly couple looking puzzled and cross, a woman with a camera around her neck and a notebook in her hand, two young bucks on bikes with punk haircuts. Daniel takes a look, then steps out of the van under the canvas canopy. He says nothing. In his left hand he holds a long piece of nylon rope, in his right hand a pair of scissors. He smiles broadly at his audience, then proceeds to cut the rope into several small pieces. Then, too fast for the eye to see, he pulls the pieces this way and that, and presto, the rope becomes whole again.

The two young bucks elbow each other in the ribs. "You see that?"

"How did he do that?"

"Do that again, mister."

But Daniel is not ready to do that again. He has something else in mind. He produces a pack of playing cards from thin air and opens them up with a flick of his fingers into a perfect fan. He holds the cards out to the audience. The woman with the camera takes one from the middle of the deck. Daniel closes his eyes. The woman shows the card, the ace of diamonds, to the others. Daniel holds out the fan again, and the woman reinserts the card into the deck.

He rubs the cards lightly with the tips of his fingers. Then he pulls out the waist of his velvet pants, drops the entire deck of cards inside, and pauses just long enough to let the cards settle. He then reaches down and grabs a card out from under the ankle strap of his right pant leg. He straightens up, slowly raises the card over his head. And when he turns the card toward his audience . . . sure enough, it is the ace of diamonds.

The crowd grows larger. Soon a dozen or more people stand just outside the canvas canopy. A couple members of the audience point video cameras at the performer.

Still Daniel says nothing. He sits on one of the folding chairs and pulls it up to the card table. From somewhere he produces four silver dollars. He spreads them out across the top of the table. Slowly he waves his hands over the silver dollars. He pauses, holds up his left hand so the audience can see it is empty. Then, suddenly and forcefully, he makes a fist with his right hand and slams it down on one of the coins. At the same instant he slips his left hand under the table. When he lifts his right hand off the table the silver dollar has disappeared. But when he brings his left hand out from under the table, he holds the silver dollar between his thumb and index finger. He holds up the coin for the audience to see. Cameras roll and click. Pens scribble across notepads.

Daniel smiles. One by one he pounds the other three silver dollars through the table.

And still the crowd continues to grow. He repeats the rope trick and the playing-cards-down-the-pants trick. Then he passes the hat, an old well-worn straw Panama he wears when he sits in the sun. Some members of his audience ignore the hat, a few even turn away, but the majority toss in some loose change or a dollar bill. He sees at least two fives and a ten fall into the hat.

When the hat returns he speaks for the first time. "You, I thank," he says, and bows. "And now I read palms. Come forward. Do not be afraid."

The accent is the same one he used at the border, straight out of Eastern Europe. He speaks slowly, each word chosen only after deliberation. He seems to have to struggle with the language, as though this might be his very first day in the New World.

The old lady who earlier looked so stern smiles shyly and steps forward. Daniel smiles back at her and pulls out the second chair. "Please. Thank you. Sit."

She sits. Daniel places the Panama hat in the far corner of the table and sits down beside her. Gently he takes her right hand into his hands and turns it palm up. Slowly he spreads her fingers. Her hand is old and withered, the fingers bent with arthritis. He massages them until the hand begins to relax. All the while he smiles and studies the lines in her palm.

"You have lived long," he says, "seen much. But not everything. Surprises, you still will have surprises. Pleasant surprises." He traces a long, deep line running from her wrist diagonally all the way up to the base of her index finger. "You have wanted to go somewhere for very long time, somewhere far away."

The old lady turns and glances at her husband.

"You must go," Daniel tells her. "Very important you go and see what you find."

The old lady puts money in the Panama hat. So do several others *after Daniel massages their palms and tells them the obvious. "Money, mystery, and longevity," Victor taught him long ago,"those are the big three for successful fortune-telling and palmistry." Like the simple magic tricks he can perform in his sleep, it is nothing but a matter of deception, of showing and telling people what they already know.*

His Panama hat practically runneth over by the time he sees the patrol car and the black sedan pull up to the edge of the park. So as not to arouse too much attention, he eases the hat off the table and slips it into the back of the van.

No one steps out of the sedan but two of Kennebunkport's finest exit their patrol car and make their way through the crowd. People move aside reluctantly. Daniel ignores the men in blue for as long as possible. He continues to study a young man's palm. But when the young man sees the two officers he pulls his hand away, stands, and backs into the crowd as though he has been participating in something unsavory, perhaps something illegal.

One of the officers, a tall, ramrod-straight type with a square jaw, does the talking. He looks at the van and its contents disdainfully. "What's all this?"

Daniel smiles. "You like for me to read palm?"

The crowd laughs. The officer doesn't. "You got a permit?"

"Permit?"

"That's right, a permit. You need a permit in this town to do what you're doing."

"I just do some magic tricks." Daniel holds up his piece of nylon rope and begins snipping it into small pieces.

"I don't care what you're doing," says the cop, "you still need a permit. And if you're soliciting these people for money, you not only need a permit, you need a vendor's license."

"Solicit? I no understand solicit."

The officer turns to his partner. "Who the hell is this joker?"

His partner shrugs. "You got me." The cop turns his head and glances in the direction of the black sedan. "We're supposed to move him out. That's the word I got. Just move him along and disperse the crowd."

Daniel figures it probably has something to do with the president. National security and all that. A foreign national in an old hippie van. They no doubt see him as some kind of threat, maybe an assassin or an antiwar demonstrator.

The square-jawed officer has a few more questions. "You taking money from these people?"

Daniel nods. "Some give a little money, yes, for what I do. For the magic."

"What about a driver's license? A vehicle registration? You got some identification?"

"Driver's license! Yes." Daniel makes a show of going into the van and pulling out a pile of papers. The audience watches as closely as when he pounded the silver dollars through the card table. Finally he presents the officer with an international driver's license.

The cop takes a long look at the document. "Daniel Romankova. That you?"

Daniel nods.

"You live in Prague, Czechoslovakia?"

"Yes. Prague. Very beautiful city. You come sometime. I show you around."

The crowd loves it. The cop scowls.

Daniel produces more documents: registration, passport, visa.

"This is all fine and dandy," says the cop, "but you're still operating illegally within the town limits. You'll have to pull up and get out."

"I can no even do magic?"

"That's right, pal, no more magic."

"But magic is what I do."

"Tough luck, friend. The law's the law. Now break down this circus and scram, or we'll take you down to the station and give you something special to write home about."

"Circus? Scram? Station? I no understand."

The crowd bustles. "Hey," someone wants to know, "why are you hassling him? He didn't do anything."

"Yeah, leave him alone."

"Damn cops."

"Back off!" shouts the officer with the square jaw. "Move along."

Daniel sees a tall man in a dark suit wearing sunglasses step out of the black sedan. The man signals the officer's partner with a quick wave of his hand.

The partner nods. "Come on, Hank, let's roll. We got work to do."

"What about moving him out?"

The cop rolls his eyes toward the sedan. "We gave him the word. He'll go."

The officer hesitates but then follows his partner through the crowd.

Daniel knows the deal; they don't want any trouble; too many media people around. It wouldn't look good on TV, a police brutality thing just a stone's throw from where the prez is trying to keep the world safe for democracy.

Still, he decides not to push it. He doesn't need anyone checking up on this Romankova character. So, much to the crowd's displeasure, he folds up his table and rolls away the canvas canopy.

Back in the van, back in his civilian clothes, he counts the cash piled high in the Panama hat: $93.17. Not bad for a couple hours' work. More than enough for a hot meal and a couple of cold beers.

He decides it's in his own best interest to blow Kennebunkport. So he drives south out of town on Route 9, Art Blakey and the Jazz Messengers pounding out the hot rhythms of "A Night in Tunisia." He drums his fingers on the steering wheel. From time to time he glances in the rearview mirror. No sign of that black sedan.

IT WAS TRUE: Daniel had enrolled at the academy. Just a few days after his return from Europe and points south, we set off together. His parents drove us. Mine were busy, had some important legal dinner at the Waldorf-Astoria. So my mom asked his mom if they might have room for me. Of course they did. Plenty of room. The Hawthorns always had room.

I found out sitting there in the back seat of the Hawthorn family station wagon, as we sped west through Pennsylvania, that Daniel's enrollment at Mercersburg was, like his trip abroad with Victor, part of the Gypsy tradition. A boy, upon reaching his sixteenth birthday, spends twenty-four hours a day seven days a week for six or eight weeks with his father. But then, after they've fully integrated their personalities, after they've become like one, they must separate. The son must leave his father. For a period of one year the boy, who is now almost a man, cannot talk to or even lay eyes on his father. This is why Daniel was on his way to Mercersburg Academy.

And how did I, Matthew Anderson Chandler, feel about this part of the Gypsy tradition? Well, I'll tell you, I didn't feel real easy about it. You might say I had mixed emotions.

The second we drove through the east gate I had my eye out for Rachel. I'd been waiting two and a half months to see her. All summer I'd been hoping to see her standing there outside my dorm when I pulled up to the curb. But now, as Victor drove slowly along the winding macadam road and Carolyn commented on the natural beauty of the campus, I hoped to see neither hide nor hair of Miss Frederick.

For the first time in my life I told Victor where to go. "Turn here," I said. "Turn there. Pull up right in front of that building." He did exactly as I ordered.

All the while Daniel remained uncharacteristically quiet and subdued. I wasn't sure why, but I wanted to think he felt sort of like I had felt a year earlier: nervous, scared, intimidated. I couldn't wait to see him on the campus tour.

We parked in front of our dorm. I took a quick look around. No sign of Rachel. I breathed a sigh of relief. I saw a familiar face or two. I greeted these faces with great fanfare. I called their names, slapped them on the back, shook their hands. These were people, students, whom I had barely shared a word with the year before. They looked at me as if I were some kind of sicko, just back to the academy after some treatments at the crazy clinic. I didn't care. I wanted to show the Hawthorns that Mac Chandler knew his way around campus.

We unloaded the station wagon, carried our gear up to our second-floor dorm room. Every time I walked out through the front door I looked for Rachel. I had to suppress a desire to bust loose, to sprint across campus to the Fredericks' big old white house on Main Street.

Subtle power plays, indications that things had not changed much between Daniel and me, took place in that small, seemingly benign dormitory room. At first glance the two sides of the room looked like mirror images of each other. But such was not the case. One side had a bigger closet, a shelf over the bed, and a window in front of the desk. Daniel took that side, the good side. I didn't say a word.

Carolyn unpacked Daniel's clothes and carefully put them away in the bureau while he and Victor and I finished unloading the car. She asked me if I wanted her to put my stuff away also, but I told her I could do it myself. She looked a little hurt. I felt bad.

Someone came down the hall and announced the formation of a campus tour for all new arrivals. The Hawthorns paid no attention. I waited a few seconds, then said, "You might want to go on that. It's a good way to get your bearings, to find out what's where."

They looked at me like I was nuts. Maybe I was.

Daniel shrugged. "I got you for that, Mac."

Right.

Some more time passed there in that dorm room while I got more and more anxious. I feared at any moment Rachel would appear in the doorway. Then what would I say? I had to make my move. I had to get out of there before she arrived.

Victor finally provided my opening. "Well, Carolyn," he said, "we best be heading out. Give these guys a chance to breathe. They don't need us hanging around their necks."

I took the opportunity to make my escape. I thanked them for driving me, then excused myself by saying they would probably like to say their good-byes in private. Daniel gave me a look like he knew exactly where I was going and why.

I didn't disappoint. Less than three minutes after ducking through our dorm room door, I bounded up the front steps of that old white house on Main Street. And there, sitting on the front porch, sipping iced tea, were the headmaster, Mrs. Stover, Coach Frederick, and the love of my life. I came to an abrupt halt.

"Matthew!"

I tried to calm my breathing.

Coach Frederick stood up and shook my hand. So did the headmaster. Mrs. Stover gave me a smile. They all welcomed me back.

I thanked them, and then, remembering my image as the young man with impeccable manners, I asked how they had been and if they had enjoyed a pleasant summer.

It took some time but finally Rachel grabbed my arm and led me off the porch—"I want to show you the garden"—and around the side of the house. When we were alone she said, "I thought you weren't coming back till tomorrow."

She was right, I wasn't due back for another day. But new student orientation was in the morning, so we had come a day early. "I couldn't wait any longer to see you."

She put her arms around me and kissed me hard on the lips. "I missed you," she said, "I missed you a lot."

I took a real good deep breath, then broke into this big stupid grin. The muscles in my neck and back relaxed for the first time in two and a half months.

That night, that first night, we lay in bed, lights out. I could tell I wouldn't be able to sleep, maybe not for weeks, months, maybe not ever again. "So you never told me," I asked, "where did you and Victor go this summer?"

"Here and there, you know."

"No," I said, "I don't know."

"We went to some of the same places the three of us went."

"Prague?"

"Prague, yeah, we went to Prague."

"Where else? The night you got home I heard you say something about Buenos Aires."

"Yeah," he said, "we went there, too. On our way back."

"How come?" I asked. I knew Buenos Aires was in Argentina, the capital, way down in South America. I'd looked it up in my old man's atlas the night Daniel got home.

"Victor was looking for this guy."

"What guy?"

"Some old Nazi."

"A Nazi! Really? Are you shittin' me?"

"I wouldn't shit you, Mac."

I waited for him to say more, but he didn't. "So, what happened? Did you find him?"

"No, we didn't find him."

"How come?"

"I don't know how come. We just didn't find him. You don't always find what you're looking for. At least not right away."

I thought about that. Then, "So how come you were looking for him?"

"Victor wanted to talk to him."

"About what?"

"You ask too many questions, Mac. Time for you to back off."

I argued with him for a few more minutes but he was having none of it.

"So who's the football coach?" he asked. "Is he a good guy? Does he know his ass from his elbow?"

"Coach Frederick?" I hesitated. "Yeah, he's a real good guy. The best. Doesn't know much about the game, but he doesn't try to act like he does, either."

"What about the backfield?"

"You should get any job you want."

I thought he'd want to know more about the team, but his next question came from a whole different angle. "So where'd you get to this afternoon, Mac? You disappeared."

I needed a couple seconds to find an answer. Did I still harbor the belief that he and Rachel would never meet? "Yeah, well, I wanted to give you and Victor a chance to say so long. I know you won't see him for a whole year."

"They left ten minutes after you did. You didn't come back for like three hours."

I must've hesitated a little too long because all of a sudden he hit me over the head with this one: "Got yourself a squeeze, hey, Mac?"

I didn't say anything but we both heard me almost swallow my tongue.

Then he laughed. "Glad to hear it," he said next. "I was beginning to think you were a monk or a homo or something."

And that was it, that was all he said. He didn't ask me her name. He didn't ask me if she was good-looking. He didn't want to know if she put out or if she had big tits or curly pussy hair or any of that other stuff I'd been anticipating for the past nine or ten months.

"Sleep well, Mac," he said after a few silent minutes. "See you in the morning." And then he turned over and went to sleep.

He was right, of course. I had been gone most of the afternoon. Rachel and I had gone for a walk across the fields. She told me all about Rome and Venice and Paris. She said she'd seen stuff so beautiful, so incredible, that as soon as possible she wanted to take me there so I could see everything for myself.

I told her I wanted to go. I told her I'd pack my bag and we'd leave right away, we wouldn't waste another second, we'd go and we'd never come back. She laughed and kissed me again on the mouth. I kissed her back. We kept walking. We held hands. My feet didn't even touch the ground. I was the happiest guy in the world.

I didn't say a word to her about Daniel, not one word.

When I got back to the dorm just before dinner I found a large throng of students in the hallway outside our room. I knew right away my old buddy had made his move, opened his bag of tricks. Nervous? Scared? Intimidated? Who had I been kidding?

They were pitching pennies. You remember that old game. You stand or kneel a few feet from a wall, a penny balanced on your thumbnail. You flip the penny toward the wall, and the one who lands his penny closest gets to keep all the pennies that had been flipped.

Although actually, by the time I arrived on the scene, the players had put away their pennies and moved up to dimes, even quarters. They pitched the coins against our dorm room door. As many as a dozen students pitched at once. Daniel ran the show. He'd taken on the role of croupier. He placed and held all the bets, never failing to take a percentage of any winnings.

He also did his share of pitching. I could tell right away he'd been practicing, told me later he'd learned his technique from the Gypsy street kids in Vienna and Budapest.

He didn't win every time; that would've been too obvious, too obnoxious. He just won a hell of a lot more often than anyone else. His pockets bulged with copper and silver.

After I'd been there for a few minutes he looked up and spotted me. "Hey, Mac, old buddy. Got any money you wanna lose?"

AND SO IT WENT. It didn't take him long. By the end of September the guy had pretty much taken over the campus. Everyone knew him. Or at least of him. Including Rachel.

The penny-pitching episode was only the beginning. Next came his exploits out on the gridiron. We won our first three games, mostly behind his running. There didn't seem to be a prep school in the state with a defense that could stop him.

He ran out of the halfback position. We had a guy on the team named Roy Stevens who played quarterback. Roy's job was to take the snap from center and either hand off or pitch out to Daniel. He did an excellent job.

But in the locker room, after our third victory, Daniel wanted to know why no one came to watch the games. He was right, of course; not many people did come. Maybe a hundred if you included students, parents, the water boy, the equipment manager, and the two first aid guys who had to be there with their ambulance in case one of us busted a bone or got knocked unconscious.

He stood up on the bench in front of his locker, stark naked and dripping wet, and said, "This is bullshit, boys. We gotta do something about this. I don't wanna practice all week just to play for the ambulance driver and his sidekick."

Monday morning I found the first sign of what he had in mind. A large poster hung on the door of the cafeteria: PUBLIC HANGING, SATURDAY MORNING, ON THE FIFTY-YARD LINE JUST PRIOR TO KICKOFF. BE THERE!

What did it mean? Everyone wanted to know. More signs sprang up as the week wore on. By Tuesday it was the only thing anyone on campus talked about. On Thursday afternoon the headmaster even called a special assembly to demand an explanation. None was offered.

Friday night after dinner Daniel disappeared. So did several of the other guys on the team. I went looking for them but didn't look for long because I had a date with Rachel.

When I got back to the room around eleven he still hadn't returned. And when I woke up at seven-thirty Saturday morning he was already gone. I knew he'd been back sometime during the night because his bed was all messed up.

At eight o'clock we had our team breakfast. Coach sat at the head of the table. His eyes wandering, he told us to play hard and play fair and not worry about victory or defeat. As soon as they finished eating, Daniel and Roy Stevens and a couple of the offensive linemen bolted from the cafeteria. I wanted in the worst way to follow, but I hadn't been invited.

After breakfast the whole team walked across campus to the field house behind the west bleachers. This was one of my favorite parts of game day. We spent a couple hours playing grab-ass, getting ourselves psyched up, butting heads, putting on our gear. It always took at least an hour to get dressed. It was like getting ready to go into combat. Everything from your socks to your cup to your shoulder pads had to be put on and adjusted several times. You had to wait for the trainer to tape your wrist or your ankle. you had to put that black stuff under your eyes even though you weren't sure why. You had to stand in front of the mirror and put on your game face. You had to shout every cuss word you had ever learned. It all took time.

About half an hour before kickoff Coach Frederick came in, gave us another little pep talk, then led us out onto the gridiron. We always went out early to loosen up, do a few calistenics, give the opposition the evil eye. Usually the only people in the stands at this time were Mr. Wattington, the math instructor, who kept the stats and supposedly hadn't missed a home game since 1947, and maybe some kid's parents who'd driven all the way down from Philadelphia to watch their son ride the bench for a couple hours.

But this Saturday was different. This Saturday, as we emerged from under the bleachers and jogged out onto the field, the stands were packed, practically filled to capacity. Everyone had come: students, faculty, town folks, the press from as far away as Harrisburg, someone even said they saw one of the state's ex-governors.

Had they come to see the game? Nope. They'd come to see the hanging. But they stayed for the game, most of them, anyway. We put on quite a show that Saturday, crushed the opposition 42–6 (Daniel ran for four touchdowns). The fans enjoyed the massacre. Most of them came back for the next home game. By the end of the season, the academy's first undefeated season in two decades, we had a loyal following.

Ah, but what about the hanging? Yes, the hanging.

Midway through calistenics, Daniel and his cohorts (of whom I was not one) jogged off the south end of the field. Maybe five minutes later they returned, pushing and pulling this large wooden contraption that did indeed look like a gallows. They pushed and pulled it right out onto the field, right out onto the fifty-yard line.

Everyone stopped to watch, even the opposing team and the guys in the concession stand selling hot dogs and bellywash. For the next couple minutes I don't think anyone in the stadium even took a breath.

Daniel and his three executioners climbed up onto the platform; there were no stairs. The gallows was just a large plywood box with a platform and two upright supports connecting a thick wooden beam. From the beam hung a rope. On the end of the rope was a noose.

All four of them had on their academy football uniforms. The two offensive linemen, big beefy kids who opened up the holes so Daniel could scamper through, stood on the edge of the platform like a couple of knights. All they needed were some swords and maybe a ball and chain.

Roy Stevens, our QB, slipped the noose around Daniel's neck.

I fully expected someone, Coach Frederick or the headmaster or even Mr. Wattington, to come running onto the field and put an end to this insanity. But no one came. No one made a move. The execution proceeded.

"Any last words?" Roy Stevens shouted.

Daniel nodded. "Just one," he said. "Victory!"

"Any last requests?"

Daniel thought about it. "A blow job would be nice," he said, and smiled, but he said it just loudly enough for his teammates to hear. Collectively we laughed and cheered.

Roy Stevens held up his right hand. The stadium grew perfectly silent. I saw Daniel smile. Then Roy kicked loose a block of wood on the platform. There was a split second when nothing happened, and then, suddenly, a trapdoor under Daniel's feet sprang open, and just like that, Daniel fell through, his legs disappeared. His neck snapped, at least it sounded to me like it snapped. He hung there with his tongue hanging out of his mouth and his eyes rolling around in his head.

The crowd gasped. More than one person screamed, me included.

I don't know how much time passed. Ten seconds. Thirty seconds. Maybe a minute. No longer than that. It seemed like an hour. No one moved or made a peep.

"Cut him down!" ordered Roy Stevens.

One of the offensive linemen produced a machete from inside his uniform. In one sharp blow he cut through the rope. Daniel's body fell through the trapdoor, out of sight.

The crowd gasped again, then caught its breath and grew silent. That stadium was as quiet as a cathedral.

Then the three executioners jumped off the platform, and with a mighty effort they began to push and pull the gallows off the field. They moved the killing machine as far as the end zone before he reappeared. He came back up through the trapdoor. The crowd cheered. He held his arms high over his head, the finger of both hands forming V for victory signs. The crowd roared its approval. Daniel held the pose a moment longer, then he jumped off the platform and helped his assistants remove the gallows from the playing field.

"So how did you do it?"

"That's a secret, Mac. Can't divulge the tricks of the trade."

We lay on our beds, side by side, lights out, windows wide open. He always insisted on having the windows open, even in the middle of winter. I used to freeze my ass off.

"So it was a trick?"

"What the hell did you think it was?"

"Where did you learn it?"

"Bucharest."

"This summer?"

"Yeah."

"From Victor?"

"No, this old Gypsy with no eyes and rope burns seared into his neck."

"No eyes?"

"That's right, Mac, no eyes. Just empty sockets. Black holes."

I just about retched. "So how did you do it?"

For the last twelve hours everyone had been asking him the same question. They all wanted to know how he'd done it. "I flexed my neck muscles till they cut me down," was his first response. "I hung there and begged God Almighty for another chance," came his next offering. "Danglin' from the end of a rope is like fornicatin'," was the answer he finally settled on. "You just got to hang on till she cuts you loose."

However he'd done it, by that one act lasting less than a minute, he had turned himself into a living legend. They still celebrate Hanging Day down at the academy to commemorate the Saturday morning Daniel Hawthorn hung from the gallows on the fifty-yard line and lived to tell about it.

A whole slew of stories grew up around the legend. One said he'd been hung for killing off all the instructors in the math department. Another said he'd swung for impregnating the headmaster's daughter. Still another claimed he'd committed sacrilege by running naked through the chapel during Sunday service.

"How many times you gonna ask me how I did it?"

"Till you tell me."

"I ain't ever gonna tell you. Now shut up, Mac, I'm going to sleep."

I heard him turn over. "Wait a second, Hawk," I said. "I want to ask you something else."

"What?"

"How come when you were planning this thing you didn't include me?"

"Hey, Mac, I would've, but you were too busy with your squeeze."

"What the hell does that mean?"

"I think it means you were too busy with your squeeze. I didn't want to cut in on your squeeze time. This operation took planning and organization, commitment. I needed guys I could count on, Mac, guys willing to get up in the middle of the night and man power tools and pound nails. Guys willing to go the extra mile. I didn't think you could take the added duty right now, old buddy, so I made the decision to leave you on the sideline."

"Yeah?"

"Yeah."

"Yeah," I said, "well fuck you too, old buddy." But I waited too long to say it; he was already sound asleep, purring like a kitten.

"Don't you see, Matthew? He just said it to upset you, to hurt you. I think he's jealous, jealous that you spend so much of your time with me. He came here to Mercersburg to be with his old boyhood friend. But when he got here he found out that you'd moved on, that you had a whole new life separate from him. Excluding you from this stupid, childish prank was just a juvenile way of expressing his anger and his resentment."

This was Rachel's explanation for why Daniel had invited Roy Stevens to participate in his public hanging instead of me. And that's exactly what she called it, the hanging, I mean: a stupid, childish prank. Maybe the single greatest stunt ever performed by a student in the long and distinguished history of the academy, and she reduced it to a stupid, childish prank.

I felt all tingly inside. Daniel had somehow always remained beyond criticism, above reproof. His words and actions had always been like something from the Scriptures. But here was Rachel taking a good, clean swipe at his omnipotence. I could hardly believe my ears. But was it true, I wondered, was it possible? Was his derring-do out on the fifty-yard line really nothing more than a stupid, childish prank?

We sat in the Fredericks' kitchen after dinner, trying to study but mostly talking about him, about the hanging. Rachel had brought it up, not me. I wouldn't've said a word, no way. I backed off from the subject of Daniel whenever possible.

For a year I had led Rachel to believe that I'd been the Head Honcho back in Mendham, the leader of the pack; Daniel had merely been one of my lieutenants. But now his massive shadow was beginning to swallow me up, just the way it always had.

Rachel had started the conversation by pushing aside her history book and asking, "So, did he tell you how he did it?"

I tried to act nonchalant. "How who did what?"

"How your friend Daniel did the hanging thing."

"Oh, yeah, sure, he told me."

"Well, how did he do it?"

"He made me swear not to tell anyone."

"Come on, you can tell me."

Believe me, I would've, if only I'd known. "It was a trick. His father's a magician."

"Really?"

I nodded "Just an amateur. Birthday parties and stuff." The last thing I wanted was to get started on Victor and Daniel.

"So Daniel learned the trick from his father?"

I tried to pretend like I was studying. "I guess." I wanted to tell her how I felt. I wanted to tell her how he'd left me out of the hanging, his old buddy, Mac. I wanted to tell her what he'd said the night before in bed before rolling over and falling asleep. I wanted to tell her but I couldn't because I'd created this image for myself and I was afraid if I cracked any part of that image, Rachel would see inside and find the real me.

"Does he know any other tricks?"

I shrugged my shoulders. "A few, yeah."

"So did you know he was going to hang himself?"

"Of course, sure, I knew."

"You never told me. All week long, everyone talking about it, and you never said a single word to me."

I could feel myself getting ready to break down. "Well, you know, he . . . I . . . we wanted everyone to be surprised."

She looked at me with those eyes, looked right inside me, she did, and I knew she knew the truth. "You didn't know, did you?"

I shook my head. "No, I didn't know." And then I told her everything. Well, maybe not everything. But I told her plenty. I told her how he'd cut me out of his scheme. I told her everything he'd told me the night before, including the part about her being my squeeze. That riled her up pretty good, sort of slammed the hammer right on the head. See, even at that age Rachel didn't much like being considered some guy's squeeze.

She launched directly into her tirade against my old buddy, the tirade that peaked when she referred to the hanging as a stupid, childish prank.

"I guess it was just a stupid, childish prank," I said after she'd finished her spiel. "Pretty damn silly if you stop and think about it."

"Absolutely," she agreed. "The display of a megalomaniac if you ask me."

"A megalo what?"

"Megalomaniac. Someone who thinks he's better and smarter and more powerful than everyone else. An egotist. An exhibitionist."

I wasn't sure about all that, but I wholeheartedly agreed with every word. If she wanted to rake Daniel over the coals, I'd get myself a rake as well. I figured the deeper we drove a stake into his chest, the closer the two of us would become. Pretty good logic, huh?

"He probably didn't get enough attention as a child."

I thought about Carolyn and Victor and the compound. Without much enthusiasm, I nodded. "Probably not."

"I mean really, to simulate a hanging before a high school football game, that's pretty bizarre behavior. There's something almost pathological about it."

I wasn't sure about the pathological stuff but it sounded good so I said, "He's always been kind of a show-off, always needed to be the center of attention."

"Well, he's certainly that now. Every girl in our class is in love with him."

That crossed me up. "What? Really?"

"Are you kidding? He's all they talk about."

"But why? Because of this hanging thing?"

"That, and some other stuff. It's been growing ever since he got here. The hanging will just make it worse."

"But why?" I asked again. "I don't get it."

"It's just the way he is, the way he moves, the way he smiles. Personally, I think it's all an act."

All this stuff was going on and I hadn't even noticed, didn't have a clue. I wondered if he knew. Of course he knew.

"I mean," Rachel continued, "he's great looking, and he moves like a wild animal, like a lion out on the plain, but still, there's something about him that's not quite right." She looked across the table at me, fixed her beautiful blue eyes on mine. "You can't really trust him, can you?"

I wanted to disappear, but there was nowhere to go, nowhere to hide. "No," I said very softly, "you can't. You never could."

IT BECAME SORT OF AN "US AGAINST HIM" THING. Only he didn't know about it. Or if he did, he didn't let on. He never showed the slightest interest in our nasty little game.

Rachel and I discussed him only in private, always out of earshot. We found fault with virtually everything he did, every move he made. And he made plenty. As I mentioned earlier, he led the team to an undefeated season. Rachel simply shook her head at this achievement, calling football "a mean and brutal game, of no consequence to the human spirit whatsoever." I think I may have defended the sport for a moment or two, certainly not for long or with any great tenacity. I found it much easier to go along with my love.

We verbally castrated him after he put on a magic show in the school auditorium. He performed most of the tricks I had seen Victor perform during my youth. He cut a coed in half, made another coed disappear, even did the trick with the wooden box where his ancient ancestor lived. And believe it or not, Daniel did these tricks with even more flair and imagination than Victor. Only I never said as much to Rachel.

"Tricks," she said when it was all over and we were safely back in the Fredericks' kitchen, "nothing but a bunch of stupid tricks."

"Exactly," I said, "just like the hanging."

"Exactly," she said, "just like the hanging."

Then there were the coeds he conquered. There were three we knew of for sure, a few other maybes. I think it's best to withhold their names. True identities are of no consequence to this part of our story; the deed itself is enough.

Daniel never mentioned his sexual exploits to me, nor to anyone else, as far as I know. That wasn't his style. But nevertheless, word got around. On a campus that small everyone knew everyone else's most intimate secrets.

And then there was the time I actually caught him doing the deed, walked straight into our dorm room right in the middle of the action.

There they were, the two of them, the football star and the cheerleader, flesh on flesh, pounding away in all their youth and glory. I instantly grew a most intimidating erection. But I kept the boner out of the tale I told Rachel.

"You actually caught them doing it?" Rachel asked after I practically ran over to her house to make a full and detailed report. "You'd think he'd have the decency to lock the door."

Actually, the door had been locked. But that didn't stop me. I fished my key out of my pocket, drew back the lock, and marched right in without knocking. It was, after all, my room, too.

"Whores," she called Daniel's coeds, "sluts in search of a cheap thrill."

It may simply be the way I remember it, but word of Daniel's sexual conquests caused Rachel's blood to boil faster and harder than all the other stuff combined.

I didn't say much during these particular verbal attacks, partly, I think, because I didn't really understand why she was so pissed off at him for getting laid. What did she care? What difference did it make to her?

Much more important to me at the time was the fire burning in my own loins. I wanted in the worst way to make love to Rachel. Day in and day out I thought of little else. My lust became almost unbearable. But the really weird part: Rachel never rebuffed my advances. If anything, she encouraged me; she wanted me as much as I wanted her. But whenever things started to heat up, get out of control, yours truly backed off. I don't know why except to say I was a coward, a real chickenshit.

With all this behind-the-scenes stuff going on, you might wonder how Daniel and I got along during our junior year at Mercersburg. Pretty well, actually. On the surface, anyway, about the same as always. I learned how easy it is to talk behind someone's back and still look him in the eye. Because really, that's exactly what Rachel and I were doing. I'm amazed now, thinking back, how we would tear him apart, criticize everything he did, and then, just minutes later, back in our room, I would laugh at his jokes just the way I always had during our younger and more innocent years, the years before the sweet smell of pussy wafted through the air.

What's really interesting about that year is why Rachel and I acted this way in the first place. Why did we spend a significant amount of our time ridiculing him? Putting him down? Why did we resent him so much?

I suppose the answers aren't that difficult to figure out.

Rachel was intensely ambitious. Before she made a name for herself as an artist, she rarely if ever had anything good to say about anyone, especially anyone living. Oh, she could praise the work of Michelangelo or Vinnie Van Gogh or Louis Armstrong, they no longer posed a threat, but mention the work of some modern artist or musician, and she'd almost without exception find fault with their creative efforts.

Daniel stole her thunder. She couldn't handle how easily he strolled onto campus and took charge. It was nothing personal. She didn't really even know him. She was just jealous, and probably envious, of his style, his savoir faire.

And what about Mac Chandler? What was his excuse? Why did he take part in these petty character assassinations?

I think we know the answer. All my life I'd taken a back seat to Daniel. All my life I'd played second fiddle. But now here was someone questioning his stature, his motives. I'd never been around anyone before with the walnuts to do that. Rachel offered me a whole new way of looking at the world.

There was, of course, another answer as well. If Rachel wanted to go on the attack, no way would I preach pacifism. I wanted her to be my ally, not my enemy. I was in love, after all, and a fool in love doesn't much give a damn about anything or anyone else. So just as I had long been Daniel's pawn, now I became Rachel's pawn. I cannot for a moment blame her. I went along of my own accord. I went along because I wanted her to love me. I wanted her to wrap her long legs around my back and press her firm breasts against my face.

Other more positive events did take place that year. We had a pretty successful basketball team. We didn't make it to any postseason tournaments but we managed a winning record. I led the team in scoring and rebounding. Rachel, not a real big hoop fan, never missed a home game. Neither did Daniel, and he always brought along a large cheering section. Whenever I scored a basket or grabbed a rebound, his voice rose above all the others.

In the spring Daniel took to the tennis courts. The academy had never had a player of his caliber before. He easily defeated his opponents. On weekends he usually took off for points north and east to play in junior tournaments in Maryland or New York. And when he returned Sunday evening or Monday morning, he frequently had a first- or second-place trophy in hand. He stuffed those trophies away in a bag under his bed, but everyone, including me, especially me, knew they were there.

While Daniel hit backhands and forehands and serves, Rachel and I resumed our walks in the fields beyond campus. Rachel always brought along her sketch pad. I carried a small, thin notebook. While she painted

I wrote a few new poems. Occasionally I even gave her one to read. She praised them endlessly. I know now she did so because she did not perceive me as a threat.

That spring may not have been quite as soft and mesmerizing as our first spring together, but I still remember well those long afternoons with the warm breezes and the apple blossoms and the purple lilacs and the sketch Rachel made of me stretched out in a field of wild violets.

Out there in the fields we didn't even talk about Daniel. He was a million miles away. Everything was a million miles away. For a while.

In the middle of June Daniel and I went home. We celebrated our seventeenth birthdays by getting our driving permits. A few days later we passed the proper tests and became two more licensed New Jersey drivers. It all happened on the same day Johnny Dean, with his wife, Mo, looking on, squealed on Tricky Dick, insisted under oath his former boss knew all about the cover-up. Oh, the vagaries of history.

Daniel's parents bought a new station wagon and gave him the old one. He used it that summer to drive all over the northeast to compete in various tennis tournaments. I didn't see him much, just a day here or a day there.

My parents told me I was too young to have my own car. They told me I didn't need my own car. Idiots. Of course I needed my own car.

"Where are you going?" they'd ask every time I wanted to borrow the keys.

"Out," I'd answer.

"When will you be back?"

"Later."

Sometimes I got the keys, sometimes not. But in late July, when they flew off for a long weekend on Nantucket, I swiped my mother's car and drove to Mercersburg. I say swiped, but I had permission to use the car, as long as I didn't venture too far from Mendham.

I spent three days and two glorious nights in the Fredericks' big old white house on Main Street. I was made to feel like a most welcome guest. They gave me the bedroom across the hall from Rachel. During my first night under their roof, after all the lights had been turned out and everyone had gone to bed, I lay there between the sheets and struggled with my desire to slip across the hall and enter her dark and sensual bedchamber.

It took me over an hour to get up the nerve. I almost didn't go. I feared running into Coach Frederick in the hallway.

"Where are you going, son?"

"To have sex with your, uhh, I mean, to get, uhh, a drink of water, sir."

But finally I made my move. As quiet as a cat burglar I slipped out from between those sheets and started across the wooden floor. Every board squeaked. No matter how slowly I moved, no matter how lightly I stepped, the entire house seemed to settle every time I planted my foot.

It seemed to take an hour to reach the door, even longer to get it open. The damn hinges sounded as though they hadn't received a drop of oil in a hundred years. I told myself to remedy that situation in the morning. Then I took my first cautious step into the hallway. It was dark, very dark. I reached out my hand to help me find the far wall. But instead of the wall I found a body. A shadowy figure loomed before me. I almost screamed. "Coach Frederick?" I said in a voice as tight as a clenched fist. "I-I-I-I was just going to the to the to the bath—"

"Quiet, Matthew," whispered a soft and familiar voice, "you want to wake up the whole neighborhood?"

"Rachel!?"

She took my hand. We retreated to my bedroom. She closed the door. It didn't make a sound. We crossed to the bed. The floorboards behaved.

What else can I say? What more dare I tell you? We broke virgin soil that sweet summer night, entered a virgin forest of tall and mighty hardwoods. Things most assuredly went more smoothly the second night; experience is a wonderful thing. But the sheer exhilaration at that moment when our young and naked bodies touched from head to toe for the first time—that moment will never be duplicated.

As I pressed myself against her and felt her warm, wet mouth against mine, I imagined it as the moment of conception. And when, after a long and patient struggle, we actually became one, I felt myself being born all over again. And afterward, as I suckled her small, firm breast, I felt so happy I cried.

TOM FREDERICK READS THE ENGINEER'S REPORT.

"You didn't have to rush back, Papa. I could have mailed it to you."

Tom smiles at his daughter and sips his glass of cool white wine. "It was a good excuse to come up and see you again before the fall term starts."

Tom sits at the kitchen table in the loft of the old red barn. Rachel scrubs her paintbrushes at the kitchen sink. For several minutes Tom reads over the report on the condition of the house at the corner of Main and Overlook.

Finally he says, "This guy seems to think that old house is in pretty good shape."

"That's what I gathered after I read it, but I still wanted you to have a look."

Tom closes the report and pushes it across the table. "So I suppose the next step is to make an offer."

"The sooner the better."

"And you're sure this is how you want to invest your money?"

"Absolutely."

"Then I guess we should call the realtor."

But the afternoon has grown late. They will have to wait until morning. Tom pours them each another glass of wine. Rachel puts away her brushes and turns on the stereo. Very softly Wynton Marsalis plays "The Majesty of the Blues."

"Papa, do you remember the night I got my sight back?"

"Hmm, let me think, the night you got your sight back? When was that?"

"Don't be sarcastic, I'm serious."

"Oh, I see. Then how 'bout November 18, 1986. At let us say

approximately eight-fifteen in the evening. At the Museum of Modern Art at precisely that moment when you took the podium to thank all concerned for hanging your first blind painting, Sudden Storm, in the contemporary gallery on the second floor."

Rachel laughs. "So, you do remember?"

"Vaguely."

"I think about that night a lot. And about that painting also. You made it possible, Papa. All your patience. I would've kicked me in the butt if I'd been you."

Tom smiles. "Don't think I didn't want to."

"But you didn't. Instead you convinced me that I could still see even though I was blind. You organized my palette and showed me how I could still put paint to canvas if I just had the guts to try."

"I appreciate the kudos, sweetie, but why so sentimental all of a sudden?"

Rachel shrugs and sips her wine. "I don't know. Why not? A little sentimentality never killed anyone."

"Not yet, anyway."

"I still remember your face after we got back to the hotel room. I hadn't told you yet, hadn't told anyone. You thought I was still blind as a bat."

Tom nods.

"You took off your suit, hung it in the closet, then paraded naked across the room right in front of your full-grown daughter—"

"Only because I didn't think you could see."

"Excuses, excuses. I commented upon the size of your manliness. I thought you'd faint dead away. You turned fifty shades of red."

Tom accepts the kidding. "Yeah, and then what happened?"

"We drank a bottle of champagne to celebrate."

"We did, you're right. And then what?"

Rachel takes a moment, then answers softly, "I told you I wanted it to be our secret."

"That's right. You didn't want to tell anyone else your vision had returned."

"I know, Papa. I know you didn't approve. I know you still don't approve. I know you think I've handled myself badly through all this. But—"

"You weren't even going to tell Matthew and Daniel."

"Of course I was. I told Daniel within just a few weeks. I would've told him sooner but the morning after the ceremony at the museum he flew off to South America or some such place. Of course I was going to tell him.

I wouldn't have kept something like that from him. I know how he suffered, how he blamed himself for the accident."

"And what about Matthew? You kept the truth from him for months. For over a year, wasn't it?"

"Three months, Papa. Not quite three months."

The room grows quiet. Dusk begins to fall. The room could use a bit of light. The silence lasts several minutes.

"I'm sorry, sweetie. I didn't mean to turn this on you."

Rachel shakes her head. "No, you're absolutely right. About all of it. I deserve your scorn. I should've told Matthew the very next day, but I didn't. I didn't tell him. I don't know why. I can't justify it or explain it away."

Tom stands and crosses to the window. He stares out at the approaching darkness.

After a moment Rachel says softly, "I am meeting him on Nantucket in a few weeks."

"Matthew?"

"Yes."

"That's good. I'm sure he's looking forward to that. All this hide-and-seek business has no doubt been driving him crazy."

"I'm sure it has."

Tom turns away from the window and faces his daughter. "Does he know yet where you live?"

Rachel shakes her head. "No, but he'll know soon enough. And I can't wait to tell him about the house."

Tom pauses a moment, then asks, "What about Daniel? Have you seen him?"

Rachel almost nods but stops. "No, I haven't, not since I moved out here last year."

"That's good, too," *says Tom Frederick.* "And I don't mean that in a bad way. You know how I feel about Daniel. It's just that, well, you know..."

"Yes, Papa, I know."

OUR ANTI-DANIEL CLUB HELD TOGETHER until early in our senior year. And when it fell apart, it did so quickly and completely.

Daniel and I returned to the academy in his station wagon in early September. Once again we shared a room. I'd tried the previous spring to line up a single but there were none available.

We settled in, and the cycle began anew. Football practice started, classes got under way, Rachel and I did our thing. It looked as though it would be the year before all over again. Just add some intercourse to the mix. But never, ever, take anything for granted.

The beginning of the end came during the second week of October, just a few days after Spiro T. Agnew resigned the vice presidency under a cloud of tax evasion and corruption. Nice work, Spiro.

Rachel had been aiming her verbal assaults that fall at various members of the Nixon administration, including the "Trickster" himself. She couldn't believe the highest and most powerful office in the land had been taken over by a bunch of crooks and thugs. Those two Germans, Haldeman and Ehrlichman, had resigned over Watergate, and it was now clear that the White House had given the Air Force the okay to secretly bomb Cambodia back into the Stone Age. These events kept Rachel very busy. She had little time left for Daniel.

On a Saturday morning in the middle of October the academy football team posted its twelfth win in a row. We tied a school record that day for most consecutive victories. And that night we celebrated, threw ourselves a party. We held it outside on the practice field behind the west bleachers. The headmaster and several members of the faculty showed up for the bash. They even overlooked the small amounts of alcohol, mostly beer, being consumed, and I doubt if they even knew what marijuana smelled like. Had they been so inclined, they easily could have found out that night.

Rachel and I went to the party together. We arrived late, as befitted the school's most beautiful and creative coed and her beau, one of the academy's most decorated athletes. I'd even caught the winning touchdown pass that day.

We stayed close, arm in arm, for an hour or so, making the rounds, pounding the flesh, sharing a Budweiser. We first got separated because one of the offensive linemen grabbed my arm and demanded a reenactment of the winning catch. I had to play along, had to give the masses what they wanted. So I let go of Rachel's arm and turned away.

And when I turned back, the reenactment complete, she was gone. I saw her drifting through the crowd, stopping, chatting with someone from her art class. I decided to let her roam. My teammates dragged me back to the huddle.

For half an hour I didn't think much about her. I yucked it up with the guys, predicting boldly over another Bud that we would not lose a single game all season.

Then they wanted Daniel. "Where is he?" they demanded. "Anyone seen the Hawk? Where's the Hawkster?"

No one knew. He hadn't made his appearance yet. So while they searched I took the opportunity to slip away and reclaim my woman. But, like Daniel, she was nowhere in sight.

So what did I do? I went looking. First I walked across campus to her house, thinking maybe she'd headed home. Parties, especially large, noisy ones, were never her favorite pastime. But no one was home. The house was dark. So I walked over to the art studio next to the gym. The door was locked, the building dark. I went back to the party, took another look around. No sign of Rachel anywhere, and still no sign of Daniel, either.

I walked, actually marched, back across the campus to our dorm. Why did I think they might be there, together? Who knows? I'd never seen them exchange more than a few words at one time. But keep in mind, paranoia is a daft and deadly vice.

I took the stairs two at a time. I pushed open the door without bothering to knock. But unlike the previous winter when I'd burst in on Daniel and his naked cheerleader, this time I found only an empty room. I stood there for a few seconds, my heart pounding. I felt like an asshole. I reminded myself that she hated him, despised everything about him. I slammed the door and went back to the party.

As I approached the broad circle of activity and light, I heard one of my teammates shout, "Hey, guys, there he is!"

I immediately put on my game face, erased my scowl and drew a smile.

But it wasn't me my teammate had spotted; it was him. I looked across the crowd, and there he was, bigger than life. And right beside him: Rachel! They were across the field from me, coming in the direction of the chapel. They walked together, not touching but damn close.

I can't quite tell you how I felt. I wanted to spit fire and throw up and scream all at once. They they separated. He fell in with the boys; she moved away. I crashed through the crowd; some of them no doubt figured I was drunk.

By the time I reached her I had myself under control, sort of. "Where you been?"

She looked at me like I was crazy. "What?" She didn't so much want me to repeat the question as possibly rephrase it or just drop it all together.

Too bad I couldn't. "Where were you? Where've you been?"

I think I probably lost her as a serious lifelong soul-mate right then and there. She saw something in me at that moment she had never seen before. Maybe the real me. It was not a pretty sight. "If you have to know," she announced, "I went for a walk with Daniel."

"With who? What? You did? Where?"

She ignored my babbling. "You never told me he was a Gypsy."

Oh, my God! I just about screamed. "I didn't?" I think I mumbled. "No."

I knew right then he'd had her. It was written all over her face. She'd come under his spell, something I had foolishly assumed impossible. "So he's a Gypsy," I said in a voice both cruel and cold, "so what? Big deal. Big fucking deal!"

The rest of the night did not go well. Rachel got pissed off at me for acting like such a jerk-off and marched off for home. I followed close at her heels, one second begging her to forgive me, the next second insinuating that some kind of tryst had taken place between her and Daniel. This went on until we reached the front porch, where she stomped up the stairs, pulled open the door, and slammed it in my face.

Coach Frederick and two or three members of the faculty observed our entrance from their rocking chairs on the porch. "Trouble, Matthew?" Coach Frederick asked calmly between sips of wine.

"Oh, uhh, no sir," I stammered, "no trouble at all. We were just, uhh, disagreeing on, uhh, whether Nixon knew or not."

They all gave a little laugh. "Of course he knew," said Coach. "You think he didn't know?"

I shrugged my shoulders and hurried off, to where I did not know.

Eventually, after a long walk and several tepid brews with the last of the revelers, I made it back to our room. The lights were out. Daniel lay in bed, his breathing steady and calm. I sat down practically right on his head. "Wake up," I growled, "wake up!"

"What's the matter, Mac?"

"Nuthin'."

"Too many beers?"

My eyes rolled from the alcohol and the rage. "You did her, didn't you?"

"What?"

"I know you did. Just tell me."

"What are you talking about?"

"You bopped her. I know you bopped her, you son of a bitch."

"Don't be an ass, Mac."

I grabbed him by the throat. "She's my girl."

He easily pushed my arms away. "Right, Mac, she's your girl."

"But you bopped her. You did, didn't you, you bastard?"

"Not a chance, pal. No way."

I looked at him. He was tough to see in the darkness. "You didn't bop her?"

"I didn't bop her. Now go to bed. Sleep it off."

I went to bed, I went straight to bed, clothes and all, didn't even bother to take off my Bass Weejuns. As soon as my head hit the pillow I drifted into this dream, a dream that lasted all that night, a dream I occasionally still have, like maybe two or three times a week. In the dream, you got it, he's bopping her and she's loving it and I'm standing in the corner wearing the fool's cap and a red T-shirt that says KICK ME across the chest.

It got worse, much worse. Although, first, I must say, it got better. It was an up and down kind of year.

Rachel and I did not break up over her walk in the dark with Daniel. On the contrary, we kissed and made up and for a while lived happily ever after.

My invitations to dinner continued unchanged. Two or three times a week the Fredericks shared their table with me. But now, occasionally, we had an additional diner as well. Coach Frederick invited him the first time, and much to my displeasure, Rachel offered no protest.

The Gypsy lad, of course, stole the show on opening night. Halfway through the meal he launched into one of his stories. At first I thought he would go too far and never be invited back. Coach Frederick liked a quiet table, and I assumed Daniel's rambunctiousness would not be appreciated. Assume nothing.

Before long my old buddy had both father and daughter practically in tears, they were laughing so hard. And let me not forget to tell you that his storytelling went on for so long that neither father nor daughter bothered to make a painting that night. Another bottle of wine was opened, the jazz was brought to bear, and we passed that evening, the four of us, without even bothering to clear the dishes off the table.

"But I thought you hated him?" I asked her the next time we were alone. "I thought you thought he was a phony and a shyster."

"So now I don't think so," was her one and only reply.

Where not all that long ago she had snubbed and ridiculed him, she now encouraged him. She laughed at his jokes, listened intently to his stories. She even sat beside him in the stands all through basketball season. They cheered me on together, both of them shouting my name every time I scored a hoop. "Mac! Mac! Mac!"

And I scored my share of hoops; broke the school record in our next-to-last game.

Too bad it was a season of discontent. Every day at practice I'd think about Daniel and Rachel out there, somewhere, beyond the walls of the gymnasium, free and possibly frolicking in the fields beyond the barbed-wire fence. At these times I would often catch the basketball with my face or trip over my own feet.

I had other things to worry about as well—namely, my future. Rachel had already been accepted to Cooper Union in Manhattan, one of the most prestigious art colleges in the country. She'd been admitted to the fine arts program after submitting a portfolio of her work and going into the city for an interview. So she knew exactly where she would be and what she would be doing come September. But me, I didn't have any idea, not a clue. I just wanted to be near her.

Chuckie, of course, had a few ideas regarding my future. He called me several times a week to make sure I'd completed and mailed my application for admission to Cornell University in Ithaca, New York, his alma mater. Dear Old Dad had no doubts whatsoever where I would be and what I would be doing come September. I would be up in Big Red country enrolled in Cornell's prelaw program, paving my path for the hallowed halls of Chandler, Wright & MacPherson.

He told me not to bother sending off any other applications. "You're in, Matthew," he assured me, "I've got people all over the country working on this thing."

"But Dad," I finally found the walnuts to tell him one night on the telephone, "I've been thinking I might want to go to Columbia."

"Columbia!" He became instantly furious. "Over my dead body. No son of mine will go to Columbia!"

"But why not, Dad? It's Ivy League."

"Columbia is the enemy, Matthew. Don't you know anything? Going to Columbia would be almost as bad as going to Yale."

"But you went to Columbia, Dad." I only wanted to go there so I could be closer to Rachel. I decided not to mention that.

"That was different, son. That was law school."

"So how's it different?"

"It's entirely different. If you don't see that, you're a fool. . . . Here, talk to your mother."

Mom was sympathetic to my plight but nevertheless sided with her Chuckie. "You'll be happy at Cornell, dear, you'll see."

Maybe so, but I secretly applied to Columbia anyway. To hell with Chuckie Chandler's competitive Ivy League bullshit, I thought, I'll go to college where I want to go to college.

Okay, Mac, sure thing, anything you say.

Now you might not believe this, but the old boy found out about my application. Don't ask me how. Spies are everywhere.

He drove all the way down to the academy to disembowel me in person. "You will not be going to Columbia, Matthew," he announced the moment he marched through my dorm room door. "Columbia is non sequitur."

I stared at him blankly "Huh?"

"You will, however, be going to Cornell." In his blue-veined hand he held an offer of acceptance from the Cornell University admissions board. He tossed it on my bed, turned, and headed for the door. He added over his shoulder, "You'll be hearing from that *other* school shortly." And with that, he departed.

Nice to see you, too.

And indeed I did hear, just a few days later. It was a letter of rejection; you've probably received one or two yourself. In that calm and condescending tone, they thank you for applying and then more or less call you a piece of crap not worthy of their lofty institution.

"Fuck you!" I screamed at the piece of paper.

"Who are you talking to, Mac?" It was Daniel. He stood in the doorway crunching on a piece of peanut brittle. Peanut brittle! Rachel loved peanut brittle, made it herself from scratch.

I scowled at him. "Oh, go to hell, Hawk!" I shoved past him and went quickly down the hallway. For once, he let me have the last word.

We graduated in June. Most of my classmates couldn't wait to graduate. They viewed commencement day as just that: the commencing of a bold, new adventure. They snared their diploma from the headmaster as though it were their own personal Emancipation Proclamation.

Not so yours truly. I would've remained a senior at Mercersburg Academy forever had I had my druthers. I've always resisted change, feared the breaking of new ground. I felt something die in me at that moment when our entire graduation class took off those ridiculous black caps and tossed them into the warm spring air.

An hour or so later I realized what part of me had died. It was at the postgraduation bash, attended by graduates, faculty, and parents, mine included. I avoided them like a couple of lepers. Not only did I despise the sight of them, especially him, but I knew also they were anxious to herd me into the family sedan and drive me away from there. My minutes at the academy, you see, were numbered.

I finally got a moment alone with Rachel. I shouldn't've bothered. She crushed me with the inevitable. I had seen it coming for weeks but had ducked and dodged it like a prizefighter every time she swung in that direction.

"Will I see you this summer?" I asked.

"Sure," she answered, and I knew right away that meant probably not.

"This sucks," I said after we stood there for a while not saying anything in my almost empty dorm room.

"Yeah," she said, and I knew from that one word that she didn't really think it sucked at all. Oh, she no doubt felt a twinge of regret at the passing of our time together at the academy; she was, after all, an artist and a romantic. But she couldn't wait to get out of that small town and try her luck in the big city.

"I'll miss you," I said, and I had to try real hard not to cry.

"I'll miss you, too, Matthew," she said, "but it's not like we're saying good-bye; we're just saying fare thee well for a little while."

"Fare thee well. Sure." I nodded but had my doubts.

"We're buddies, Matthew. Pals. Friends. . . . Friends never say good-bye."

Friends. Right.

"You don't have to look so glum."

I nodded again. I felt bad, but a few seconds later I felt even worse.

"You have to go your way," she said, "and I have to go mine."

I stared at her, my eyebrows all knotted up.

"But whenever we find something new, we'll share it with each other, tell each other all about it. And then she looked at me with those big, bright, shining eyes. "We'll always share everything. Right, Matthew?"

I felt the tears in my eyes explode and run down my face. "Yes," I muttered, "always."

IT WAS NOT THE FIRST TIME WE SAID FARE THEE WELL. Nor would it be the last. Over the next fifteen years we said fare thee well more times than I care to remember.

And the thing is: I rarely did, fare thee well, I mean. Oh, I suppose I did if you want to be difficult about it. I never wanted for food or shelter. I always had a full stomach and a warm place to sleep. I had the Declaration of Independence and the Bill of Rights and a newly elected executive both in the State House and the White House every four years. I didn't have anyone, other than myself, torturing me or forcing me to fight in some holy war or world war or any other war, for that matter. Relatively speaking, I guess I did fare pretty well.

I sit here in my apartment, this fifth-floor sweat box with nothing left between these walls but an old table, a wooden chair, my yellow legal pads, a sheetless mattress, some cans of chicken soup, an electric razor, a toothbrush, some paperback books I bought uptown, books on sailing and seamanship, stacks of nautical maps, and finally, still hanging on the wall on either side of my living room window, two original oil paintings by Ms. Rachel Ann Frederick.

Some days I want to take those paintings off the wall and punch my fist right through the canvas. Other days I stare at them and think they are my most prized possessions, possessions I will have even after everything else is long gone.

Most of the stuff I once owned is long gone already. I have discarded my vast array of material possessions, either tossed the crap on the garbage heap or given it away to homeless men down in the subway or bag ladies wandering the wide boulevards of this great, decaying metropolis. I've given away my color TV, my stereo with CD, my laptop PC, my telephone by AT&T, my answering machine from ABC . . . or was that XYZ? Who the hell knows? Who the hell cares?

My lease expires at the end of next month, at the end of September, September '91. By then I'll be gone, outta here. I wonder who will be the next lucky occupant of this humble abode. Some new arrival in the big city, no doubt. Someone with dreams of fame and fortune. Someone who will procure a subway map and find his or her way to Wall Street or Rockefeller Center or Broadway. They have my blessing. Also my pity.

All of my savings, almost all of my savings, anyway, I have thrown into a twenty-two-foot Marshall catboat that'll probably swamp the first time even a small storm hits me out on the Atlantic. People who know about these things cannot believe I bought a catboat for a solo transatlantic voyage. What an idiot, they think to themselves, secretly happy there is someone in the world more stupid and feeble than they. What do I say to them? I say fuck 'em. Fuck 'em all. I am forever more my own captain.

In the summer of '74 Tricky Dick was forced out of the political citadel, and a few weeks later I went off to college. College, "the best years of my life," Dear Old Dad always claimed whenever that four-year hitch of excessive drinking and illicit sex popped up in conversation.

I can't honestly agree with his assessment. Not that my four years at Cornell were all that bad. But looking back, I'd have to say my overriding concern while an undergraduate was earning my diploma so I could get on with the rest of my life. Funny, though, I turned thirty-five a couple months ago, and on my birthday I found myself wondering when my real life would begin. I keep telling myself it'll begin when I raise the jib of my catboat and head to sea, when I sail beyond the horizon. Although I have my doubts that'll do it either. I'll probably chase my goddamn tail forever.

Anyway, I went up to Cornell and Rachel moved here to Manhattan to begin classes at Cooper Union. And Daniel, well, he went off to make a name for himself as a professional tennis player. Several college coaches had tried to recruit him to play football, including Joe Paterno of Penn State University, but Daniel had decided to hang up his shoulder pads. I think his decision had more to do with his dislike of the classroom than with anything else. He'd never been much of a student. He was like a caged bull sitting there at one of those little desks, listening to some teacher deliver his or her tiny pearls of wisdom. So he broke free, went off with nothing but a duffel bag and half a dozen brand-new tennis rackets.

Most of the time I didn't know where he was. He never wrote, rarely called. Then every once in a while he'd show up at my door. He never let me know ahead of time, just popped in and made himself at home. Freshman year, when I lived in the dorm, he'd sleep right on the floor. It didn't bother him; he slept like a baby. I used to lie awake for hours listening to his steady breathing.

He might only stay the night or he might stay as long as a week. On one of his first visits he befriended the varsity tennis coach, and for the next four years, whenever he came to town, he worked out with the team. The guy knew how to operate.

And what about Rachel? Did I ever see her? Not a hell of a lot, I can tell you that, not nearly as often as I would've liked. She came up to Ithaca for a weekend a few times, but usually I had to make the effort. I'd take the bus home on a Friday afternoon and then go into the city by train on Saturday morning. Her first year at Cooper Union she shared a room with an NYU student, so we never had much privacy. We'd just walk around the Village, maybe listen to some music in Washington Square Park, have some lunch at this place she liked down in Little Italy, take in a movie or a museum.

Right from the start Rachel loved New York. I hated it. I found it noisy and dirty and threatening. I spent as much time as I could get away with degrading it, putting it down, calling it a hellhole, a place practically unfit for human habitation. Rachel ignored my petty posturing. She was too busy sucking in the city, devouring it.

I can't say exactly where our relationship stood during that year. I continuously tried to push us into an arena of commitment. If it had to be a long-distance love affair for the time being, so what? That didn't bother me. I would've held up my end even if she'd been studying primitive African art in Tanzania or Mauritania.

We spoke on the phone at least once a week, usually for an hour or more. It was a constant source of conflict with Martha and Chuckie. You see, I charged the calls to their number, so when the phone bill arrived they'd call me up and demand an explanation. Their wrath did not deter me from calling Rachel. As far as I was concerned they were forcing me to go to Cornell, so a few phone calls every month seemed like a small price to pay.

These phone calls and our brief weekend rendezvous were not dominated by romance. We did not often weep or whisper those words so often heard as you walked by the public phone in the dorm: "I miss you. I want you. I love you." No, Rachel and I, except on rare occasions, did not bother with the mushy parts. I easily could have been moved to tears and romantic pronouncements, but Rachel was far more interested in telling me everything that had happened since our last conversation. The city for her was like a perpetual-motion machine. On every corner, behind every window, she found something she wanted to paint. She could not often be distracted by my melancholy.

Oh, every once in a while I'd catch her on a bad day. She'd be very quiet at first, and I would have to ask her many times what was wrong.

"Nothing," she'd insist, "nothing, nothing, nothing." But eventually nothing would turn to something, to everything. She would spit in the eye of the city, call it a cruel and vile place, "the devil's domicile." She'd weep and tell me she loved me and ask me to take her away to some clean and quiet place in the country. I'd be on the next bus. She would weep some more when I got there. We would make love. Maybe we'd take the train out to Mendham and go for a long walk in the woods out behind the pond. In a day or two she would recover.

"You're my greatest and dearest friend, Matthew."

That was my clue that the crisis had passed. I hated when she called me her friend. I knew a friend was the most important thing in the world to her, almost as important as her painting, but still I cringed when she referred to me as such. I didn't want to be her friend, you understand. I wanted to be her man, her lover, her protector, her provider.

Was she seeing Daniel at this time? Excellent question. Too bad I can't give you an accurate or unbiased answer. I suspect they saw each other from time to time. To what extent or for exactly what reasons, I don't know. I felt sure he popped in on her whenever he was in New York, just as he popped in on me whenever he came to Cornell. And God knows the guy must've passed through the Big Apple a lot more often than he passed through Ithaca. But when or even if these, what should I call them? these visits took place, I never heard about them. These little get-togethers occurred, if they occurred, behind my back.

I can only remember a couple of times when I knew for sure they were together without my being part of the party. The first time was in the spring of my sophomore year. That was the year I lived in the frat house (that's right, I was a frat rat, although I'd rather not say which one, would prefer to forget the whole damn business).

One Friday afternoon I sat on the front steps outside the fraternity house when this white VW van pulled up to the curb. It looked like the kind of van you might want to drive cross-country while smoking doobies and listening to rock and roll music turned up real loud. I sat there focusing on this fantasy when the doors opened and out stepped Daniel and Rachel.

"Mac!" Daniel shouted. "I told Rachel you'd be waiting for us."

He was right, of course, I had been waiting for them. I just hadn't known it.

I was glad to see them, but at the same time I felt pissed off. You know what I mean. You know how I felt. They pull up, unannounced, out of nowhere, in this hippie-drug van, the two of them, smiling and waving and giving me the big hello. Fine. But they'd been together, alone, in that van for at least five hours. And who would ever know how long they'd been together or what they'd been doing before that? Certainly not I. And of course they offered not a word of explanation.

Still, I wasn't at all surprised to see them together. They were friends, after all; I guess that's what you'd call them.

Rachel looked great, beautiful with her long dark hair braided and hanging down across her neck and back. She looked like some Indian princess. Pocahontas. She glowed. But somehow I didn't want her to look that good, not after five hours on the road with him.

But as the weekend progressed, she began to look even better, even happier. She loved being with both of us, I could see that. On Saturday the weather turned warm and sunny. We went for long hikes at Treman State Park and Buttermilk Falls. Sometimes she held my hand, sometimes she put her arm through Daniel's arm. Once, while he scaled a rock wall below the falls, we stood in the sun and kissed.

"This is wonderful," she said, "this is perfect."

Daniel slept in his van. He assured me that's where he wanted to sleep. I asked him about the van. His answer was vague, something about winning it in a tennis tournament. I doubted that but didn't pursue it. I knew him well enough to know I'd never get a straight answer. Which is the same reason I didn't bother to ask him about Rachel. I knew he'd just tell me what I wanted to hear: "She's your girl, Mac. I just brought her up to see you."

Rachel slept in the frat's guest room, a bedroom reserved for occasions just like this. On Friday night, after everyone had gone to bed, I slipped down the hall and tried her door. It was locked. I knocked softly but Rachel didn't answer. Miffed, I headed back to my own room. But halfway there I detoured down the stairs and out the front door. I saw a light on inside Daniel's van. I approached cautiously. My mind was on fire with what I might find. But when I peered in through the back window I found Daniel stretched out on the fold-away bed reading a copy of *Tennis* magazine. I didn't think he could see me out there in the dark, but all of a sudden he flashed that grin of his and gave me the V for victory sign.

Saturday night I found Rachel's door closed but unlocked. She was happy to see me. I slipped between the sheets and in no time at all forgot about that VW camper-van parked just outside. We made love that night, and afterward I told her I wanted us to be together always, forever. But she didn't hear; she was already fast asleep, her head against my chest.

Sunday, after lunch, I stood on the front steps and waved good-bye.

They had arrived together; it was quite natural they would depart together. Still, my paranoia flared. What would happen when they got back to the city? How long would he stay? Where would he stay? No way would he sleep in the van parked there along Eleventh Street. Would he sleep in the apartment? On the sofa? Or would he sleep with her? In her bed? Would they be wrapped in a delirium of sexual frenzy before the night was over? My brain worked overtime on the problem for the next several hours.

I called her almost exactly five hours after they left. No answer. I tried again an hour later. Still no answer. An hour later.

"Hello?"

"Hi. It's me. I just wanted to make sure you got back okay."

"I got back okay."

"How long did it take?"

"About five hours."

"So you've been back a while?" What a prick.

"For a while, yeah. But we went out for something to eat right after we got back."

"Oh. Where did you go?"

"That little Italian place I like."

That pissed me off. I thought she went there only with me. "Was it good?"

"Kind of crowded. And Daniel was in a hurry."

"How come?"

"He had a plane to catch. I think there's a tournament starting tomorrow in Houston or some place in Texas."

"So he's gone already?"

"Left right after we ate."

Yes! My heart quit racing. I relaxed, took a deep breath. A little smile even broke across my face.

We talked about this and that, about what a wonderful weekend it had been, about how we should do it again soon.

Before we got off the phone she told me she loved me, and then she said, "Don't be jealous, Matthew, it's such an ugly and demeaning emotion. For both of us."

Jealous? Me? Mac Chandler? No way. I told her I didn't know what she was talking about, didn't have a clue.

I EASILY COULD'VE BECOME A MURDERER the next time I found out about Rachel and Daniel spending time together without me. It happened the following winter, right around the time a Utah firing squad blew away Gary Gilmore. Remember that guy? He wanted to die. He begged his executioners to pull their triggers, dared them even.

Anyway, a little background: I was halfway through my junior year that winter. During my first two and a half years at Cornell, Daniel, as I mentioned earlier, had called me only a handful of times. Usually when he wanted something. Usually when he wanted to use the house on Nantucket. I'd told him back during our days at the academy that he was welcome to use the house whenever he wanted. Of course, had Chuckie and Martha known about my offer they would've freaked out. They still referred to Daniel as "that Hawthorn boy."

Still, I'd given him his own key. I knew he liked the island best in the off season when the village of Siasconset became practically deserted. I encouraged him to go, to use the house, to make himself at home. And every now and then he would. He'd call me up at Cornell, I'd give him my blessing, and off he'd go.

I think I enjoyed knowing he was out there. At least in the beginning. Somewhere in my twisted mind I viewed that house as a cell, the island as a vast prison. Without really admitting it or understanding why, I enjoyed the idea of him being out there, cooped up in that cell, especially in the winter when the winds blowing off the Atlantic, rattling the windows and whistling through the gutters and leaders, were enough to drive you mad.

There's nothing to do in Siasconset in the off season: no tennis, no swimming, no golf, no cocktails on the veranda; nothing to do but read and walk on the beach and watch the sea. I had a tough time imagining Daniel out there all by himself with only these things to do, with nothing going on, no one to con, no one to listen to his stories. But if he wanted to go, fine with me, I wasn't about to stop him.

By the middle of my junior year he'd ventured out there maybe three or four times. I'd never even thought about joining him on the island. It just seemed too damn far. But when he called me that night in late January, my curiosity got the best of me. I decided to have a look-see for myself. He said he wanted to use the house for a few days. I said sure, no problem, the parents won't go near the place until Memorial Day or later.

Early the next morning, before dawn, I packed an overnight bag and headed out the door. In those days I drove an old Triumph TR6, my first car. I'd bought it a few months earlier with money I'd been bequeathed when my mother's mother died. That was the best car I've ever owned, except for a couple of annoying idiosyncrasies: the headlights used to blink on and off, and the starter often refused to function when the temperature fell below freezing.

Still, for all its English eccentricities, I loved that car, looked forward to getting in behind the wheel, pulling out the choke, bringing that engine to life. It smoked like a wet wood fire and it made more noise than an old diesel bus, but I didn't care. That car made you feel like you were in an old Hitchcock movie, zipping through Rio or Monte Carlo with Bergman or Kelly at your side, the roof pulled back, the wind blowing but never messing your hair.

I didn't have the roof pulled back that January morning. It was damn near zero in Ithaca when I stepped out of my Buffalo Street apartment. I had a tough time convincing the engine to turn over. For a while I thought I'd have to bag the trip and go back to bed. Too bad I didn't.

I finally got her going. She ran pretty well all the way out to the Cape. It took almost eight hours. I reached Hyannis in the middle of the afternoon. I decided to fly out to the island; didn't feel like a two-and-a-half-hour ferry ride. The flight from Barnstable Airport to Nantucket takes less than ten minutes. Up and down, that's all it is. Just a quick skip over the Sound.

When I reached the island I called the house but was informed that our number had been temporarily disconnected. The old boy did that to save money; a very frugal barrister, Chuckie Chandler.

So I rented a car. Actually I rented a four-wheel-drive Jeep with the idea that in the morning Daniel and I might drive out to Great Point, a long and desolate spit of land on the island's northeast shore. You could drive around on Great Point for hours, even in the middle of summer, and not see another soul.

I drove east on the Nantucket-Siasconset Road—Milestone Road, local folks call it. It's not far from the airport out to the house, five or six miles. The whole island's only about a dozen miles from east to west, less than half that from north to south.

Late that January afternoon, the shadows of the few barren trees stretching far out to the east, I pulled into Siasconset. The town was dead, not another human in sight. The general store looked open for business but I didn't see anyone around. The tennis club was all locked up, the nets and lines stowed away till spring.

Most of the houses I passed along Baxter Road were boarded up and battened down against another long and windy winter. A few old salts lived in Siasconset all year round in those days, mostly drunks and would-be writers and artists and disgruntled mainstream types looking for the far ends of the earth not too many air miles from Boston or New York. But pretty much the town stopped being a town during the winter months and instead turned into this beachfront fortress of abandoned homes.

My father always winterized our house before he left in September. So every time Daniel came he had to open the house, turn on the water, remove the boards from the windows and doors. He must've done a good job, both before and after, because during all the years he used the house I never once heard my old man complain about trespassers or interlopers.

I pulled into our sand-and-pea-stone driveway and shut down the Jeep's engine. There was another Jeep parked in the driveway. I figured maybe Daniel had come up with the same idea about a drive to Great Point.

I stepped out and stretched. An icy easterly practically blew me over. I sucked in the salty air and tried to loosen the kinks in my neck. The front of the house, the side facing away from the sea, looked as though no one were inside. Plywood covered the doors and windows.

I followed the brick path around the south side of the house, past the rosebushes all wrapped in burlap. When I reached the southeast corner of the house and stepped away from its protective cover, the wind hit me full force. It came off the sea steady and cold, almost a gale. The ocean looked black and wild. Far below, the surf exploded on the beach.

I covered my eyes from the blowing sand and started up the half-dozen cedar steps to the back porch. The porch runs the length of the house. It is long and wide and where, in the summer, most people spend the better part of their day lying about the chaise longues and wooden rockers sipping daiquiris or gin and tonics or ice-cold bottles of beer. But on that January afternoon the porch furniture had all been put away. Anything left out during the winter would either be stolen or blown clear over to Surfside by spring.

Most of the boards had been removed from the windows on the back of the house. The plywood had been taken off the two sliding glass doors connecting the living room to the porch. I took another quick look at the sea and then approached one of the sliders, eager now to get inside away from that biting wind. I couldn't wait to see Daniel's face when I suddenly popped in unannounced. Just the kind of thing he liked to do.

My hand reached out for the door handle. I grabbed it, started to slide it open. And that's when I saw them, the two of them. I remember I gasped. My hand let go of the handle. My arm dropped dead at my side. My mouth fell open. My instincts told me to turn away, not to watch for even one second longer. But I froze. I didn't move. I didn't turn away.

They were on the floor, on top of a thick pile of blankets and down comforters. They were turned away from me, away from the sea, before a mighty fire roaring and crackling in the fireplace. She rested on her knees and elbows. He knelt behind her, his hands on her hips, his swollen member no doubt deep inside her body. They did not move a muscle. If they spoke or merely moaned, I could not hear, not over the howling of the wind. I could not see her face but I knew it was she. Of course I knew. I could tell by the long dark hair spread out on the floor in front of the fire. I could tell by those long slender legs, bent double now as he pressed against her.

I did not know what to do. My anger and jealousy ordered me to barge in, to make my presence known. Hadn't I just spoken to her on the telephone a few days ago? Had she said a word about a trip to Nantucket? No, not one damn word.

I wanted to crash in there and rip them apart, throw boiling water on their bodies as though they were a pair of mongrel mutts who had no right to a sexual liaison. But I could not bring myself to open the door. Nor could I bring myself to turn away, to leave, to come back another day, or at least in another hour.

I do not know how much time passed. Probably not more than half a minute but it seemed like much longer; it seemed like forever. I stood out there in the wind and the cold, shivering, my teeth chattering, my heart practically pounding against the glass, and I watched them make love. They both seemed caught in some kind of trance, as though under the spell of some demonic sex goddess.

But then, in a movement so swift I almost missed it, he lifted her off the floor and turned her over. Suddenly she sat in his lap, her legs wrapped tightly around his waist. I saw her face then, flushed but beautiful, every muscle tense, her lips quivering, her eyes wide open. I feared for a moment she saw me. I turned quickly away from the door, pressed my back against the weathered clapboards. The wind plastered me there as though I'd been nailed to the cross.

More time passed. More wind blew through my soul. My heart

roared. I could hear it screaming. I could hear it slamming against the fragile walls of my chest.

And then I heard her scream. It broke through the wind and the pounding of the surf. And then another scream, even louder this time, as though, at that very moment, he might have been torturing her the way the Nazis had tortured his grandmother. I could not help myself. As terrible and sick as it sounds, I peeked around the edge of the door for another look. But I could not stand to look for long. They were flat out on the floor before the fire now, Daniel on top and Rachel spread out willingly below. No quiet, soothing love scene this. That part had passed. They pounded away now with a fury matched only by the wind. I could not bear to watch. I fled.

I drove back to the airport. I returned the Jeep, told the man behind the counter I had come simply to check on the condition of our house. Don't ask me why I even bothered to explain; it's something I've always done and will no doubt always do. It's definitely a Chandler trait, this almost psychotic desire to keep up appearances, to make certain others always perceive me as normal and under control.

But really, think about it, what was I going to say to the guy? "My best friend and the woman I love and hope one day to marry are lying naked on my living room floor fucking each other's brains out and I don't want to bother them so I won't need your miserable, stinking, motherfucking Jeep anymore?"

No way. I made my false explanations, dropped the key into his open palm, and slunk away. I had to wait all alone next to the out-of-order vending machines for two hours before the next flight out. I flew back to Hyannis, arrived well after dark. My mood was not good. I felt depressed and gloomy. I thought about getting a room but feared if I did I would probably masturbate a few times and then commit suicide by beating my brains out with the Holy Bible left by the Gideons.

So I climbed into my TR6 and began the long ride back to Ithaca, back to Cornell. I had car trouble along the way, somewhere in western Massachusetts, right outside Stockbridge, if I remember right. I stopped for gas and didn't get going again for hours, not till some mechanic who'd been trained on go-carts pushed and probed at my delicate British racing machine.

I finally reached my apartment on Buffalo Street late the following morning, nearly thirty hours after my departure. Thirty hours of pure hell.

I called Rachel several times a day for the next three days. Her phone just rang and rang and rang.

Finally, around midnight, more than seventy-two hours after I had last seen her, naked and climaxing, she picked up the phone. "Hello?"

I could hardly believe it. A moment slipped away before I could speak. "It's me."

"Hi you."

"I've been calling... trying to reach you." I was all balled up inside, vibrating on the outside like a jackhammer, desperately suppressing my desire to become a mass murderer.

"Anything the matter?" she asked so calmly that I wanted to reach through the phone and grab her by the neck.

Instead, "I was wondering the same thing. You haven't been around for a few days."

"No, I haven't."

I had the feeling, probably having to do with guilt more than reality, that she had seen me through the sliding glass door. She still had her sight in those days, perfect vision, twenty-twenty. So like a flaming, full-fledged jackass, I asked, "Did you go to visit your dad?"

"Of course not, Matthew. I just saw him at Christmas."

"Right, I forgot." I waited. I wanted to say something nasty, like "Where the hell were you?" Or "So how many times did you fuck him?" But instead, nicely, "So did you have a good time?" Jesus, what a jerk-off!

"Yes," she answered, "I did."

The blood vessels in my neck stood out like water-filled balloons ready to burst. My blood pressure must've been three hundred over two hundred. "So, what did you do? Where did you go?" I stood there next to my bed shaking and sweating and preparing for the lie, the Big Lie. But something far worse struck me on the side of the head.

"Actually, I spent a few days up on the island with Daniel."

Oh, my God! "What!? Really?"

"Yes," she answered calmly. "The weather was wonderful: stormy and cold with high seas and a strong breeze blowing out of the northeast."

Tell me about it. "I knew *he* was going," I said. "He called me last week to make sure it was okay. But I had no idea *you* were going."

"I didn't either until the day before I went. When Daniel showed up here and asked me to go, I didn't have to think twice. It was exactly what I needed. I've been working like ten or twelve hours a day. There's no time for creativity. All I do is work work work...."

I wanted to tell her to shut up. I wanted to scream. "So, you had a good time?"

"A really good time."

Yeah, right, of course you did, I could see that for myself, but who

the hell does that son of a bitch think he is inviting you to my house?
"Do any painting?"

"Some, not much. Really I just wanted to relax. This morning, before we started back, I made a few pencil sketches of the sea and the bluffs."

You didn't have the time to do any goddamn painting, I wanted to scream but of course I didn't. You were too busy pounding that bastard Hawthorn. "So, how is he? I haven't seen him"—actually I'd just seen him over the holidays—"for a while."

"He's good. Playing some indoor tournaments this winter. Although I have the feeling he's getting a little sick of the grind."

"Really? How so?"

And so it went for the next several minutes. She went on quite happily about what they had done and where they had gone, tactfully leaving out the more sordid and intimate details.

All the while she spoke I wanted to tell her I'd been there, I'd been outside the window, I'd seen them doing the deed. But of course, I held my tongue. I knew enough not to cross that line. She wasn't my property. I couldn't dictate what she did and with whom. Not only was it not my place but Rachel never would have stood for it. She needed and demanded an enormous amount of space. She had her own way of doing things, and if you didn't like it, well, tough luck, pal.

We had been friends for almost six years. For six years we had trusted one another with our thoughts and our feelings. We had spent endless hours talking deep into the night about every subject under the moon: art, law, politics, Daniel, sex, you name it and we'd talked about it. Rachel was my friend. She gave herself to me unconditionally. But she was not my wife, not even my fiancée or my girlfriend, for chrissake, just my friend. We made love, but she had never made a vow of faithfulness or fidelity to me. No, she had only ever offered me her friendship. But for me, then, that was not enough. It would never be enough.

THE OLD VW CAMPER-VAN COMES OUT OF THE DARKNESS
of the Queens-Midtown Tunnel into the bright morning light of Manhat-
tan. Daniel Hawthorn, alias Daniel Romankova, drives the van west
along East Thirty-fourth Street. At the Empire State Building he turns
south onto Fifth Avenue. The traffic at ten o'clock on this summer
Saturday morning is relatively sane: no horns blasting or caravans or taxis
accelerating full throttle from one red light to the next.

Daniel has the window open. Scott Joplin plays on the stereo. The
great turn-of-the-century composer plays "Pine Apple Rag," "Maple Leaf
Rag," "Wall Street Rag," "The Entertainer," and other ragtime classics.
Daniel taps his feet on the pedals and drums his fingers on the steering
wheel.

At Seventeenth Street he turns west. He parallel parks the van across
the street from the Xavier Parochial School. He shuts down the engine,
closes the windows, steps out, and locks the door.

As has become his habit, he takes a quick look up and down the street
for suspicious-looking cars and characters. He finds none, crosses the street,
and goes down the block.

He reaches the old brick apartment building just as a young man
carrying a guitar comes out the front door. Daniel holds the door open for
the guitarist, then slips through into the entrance foyer.

He takes the stairs to the fifth floor two at a time. He knocks firmly
three times on the door of 5-C. Several seconds pass. No one comes. He
tries again.

"Hold on to your hat," says a familiar voice from inside, "I'm
coming."

Daniel smiles and waits.

Finally, half a minute later, the door opens. "Daniel! Jesus." It is his
old pal Matthew Anderson Chandler. "What the hell are you doing here?

How did you get through the front door? I thought it was the Mexican woman down the hall looking to borrow some flour."

They stand there for a moment staring at one another, one of them inside and one of them outside.

"You going to invite me in or what?"

Matthew glances out into the hallway. Then he smiles, laughs. "Yeah, yeah, of course. Come in."

Daniel steps forward, puts his arms around his old friend, holds him tight. "Good to see you, Mac. It's been a while."

"It sure has." They retreat into the small apartment. Matthew closes the door. "You want something to eat? Something to drink?"

Daniel shakes his head. "Maybe later." He looks around the apartment, fixes his eyes for a few moments on the two oil paintings by Rachel Ann Frederick hanging on either side of the living room window.

"So," asks Matthew, "how's it going? Everything okay?"

Daniel shrugs. "Yeah, sure, everything's great. You know." He begins to pace. He takes a few steps in one direction, then a few steps in the other direction. In the small flat it is difficult to walk very far.

They talk it over, shoot the breeze. After thirty-four years they both know it takes time to say what needs to be said.

"So," asks Daniel, "how's the job?"

"It sucks. I hate it."

They both laugh.

"Why don't you quit? Sail around the world?"

"I'm thinking about it."

"You've been thinking about it for twenty years."

"You know me, Hawk, I don't like to rush into anything."

Daniel nods, paces. He stops, stares again at the two paintings on the wall.

Matthew takes a deep breath. "You seen her?"

Daniel turns around quickly, faces his friend. Then he pauses before slowly shaking his head. "Not for a while, no."

They look at one another, study each other's eyes.

Daniel blinks first. "How 'bout you? You seen her?"

Matthew nods. "For a few days last spring. Out in Mercersburg."

Another pause. "How was she?"

"Pretty well."

"That's good."

"We made plans to meet out in Siasconset next month, actually in just a couple weeks."

"Great."

"Yeah."

"It's nice out on the island in September."

"Best time of the year. It's not too crowded."

"Water's still plenty warm for swimming."

"And sailing."

Daniel nods. Most of a minute passes.

"So," asks Matthew, "you sure you don't want something to eat?"

"Yeah, thanks, I'm sure." More pacing, and then, "Listen, Mac, I was wondering . . ."

"What?"

"You're a lawyer."

"That's what they keep telling me."

"You know, I'm thirty-four years old and I've never needed a lawyer."

"That's why you're such a pain in the ass, Hawk. You've never needed anyone."

"I don't know about that."

"So what's the deal? Now you need one?"

"I don't know. Probably not. Maybe."

"Christ, you sound like me: the Great Vacillator."

Daniel laughs.

"If you need a lawyer, you don't want me. I'm probably the worst goddamn attorney in the borough of Manhattan."

"Why do you say that? Because of the way the Isaiah Jackson thing turned out? Hell, man, you did the best you could."

"Yeah," says Matthew, "the best I could."

"I'm sure you're a hell of a lawyer, Mac."

"Let's put it this way: I wouldn't hire me if I was in a jam."

Daniel begins again to pace, back and forth across the living room. After maybe a minute he asks, "You think there's an extradition treaty between the U.S. and Argentina?"

"What?"

"You heard me."

"Yeah, okay, I guess I did."

"So?"

"So I don't know. Maybe. I could find out."

"Good."

"Why do you want to know?"

"Just curious is all."

"Bullshit."

"Maybe."

"You want to tell me?"

Daniel shakes his head. "Nope. But if you promise not to ask me again, I'll buy you some lunch and a couple cold ones."

I STRUCK BACK WITH MY OWN FUCK-A-BILLIE-FEST. Her name was Billie-Jo MacDonald. She'd been valedictorian of her high school class and the first student from her small town outside Wheeling, West Virginia, to be admitted to Cornell University. Billie-Jo was smart and pretty and perky, and for over a year she'd been trying to get me to go out with her. So finally, less than a week after I found Daniel and Rachel fornicating on Nantucket, I did.

I'm not sure how much stock I put in this astrological stuff but I learned a little about it from Billie-Jo. She had faith in the stars. The stars had told her she and I would be together, possibly even forever. Well, five months, actually four and a half, ain't exactly forever but we managed to cram a lifetime of sex and lust into that spring semester.

I won't go into all the graphic details of our sexual odyssey; Homer I'm not. But I did surprise myself daily with the kinky stuff I asked Billie-Jo to do. She proved a willing and able accomplice.

Like the time we borrowed the stepladder from my apartment building's superintendent. I climbed up to the ceiling, screwed a large eyebolt securely into an exposed wooden beam, and ran a piece of one-inch rope through the eye of the bolt. Then, using one of those fancy devices the rock climbers use, a carabiner, I think they call them, I fastened myself to the rope.

"Okay," I called to Billie-Jo, "come on up."

And she did. As naked as the day she pushed herself from her mama's womb, Billie-Jo ascended that stepladder, secured herself to the rope with a carabiner, and then confidently kicked the ladder aside. The two of us hung there in midair, giggling and tickling each other in our most erogenous zones. And I don't mind telling you that we actually managed to fornicate up there, with climaxes all around, although I've long believed that Billie-Jo faked a vast majority of her orgasms.

Anyway, this is the kind of behavior I exhibited in the last half of my junior year. Quite strange, wouldn't you say? I missed whole weeks of classes while Billie-Jo and I sought ever more creative ways to do the old in-out. We ventured into the wilds and tried our luck at the Me Tarzan, Billie-Jo Jane game. It worked pretty well until my chest pounding and yelling caught the attention of some elderly spring picnickers who immediately reported us to the park ranger. Luckily we heard him coming and slipped away before he caught us in the buff.

My grade-point average plummeted. For two and a half years it had held steady at between 3.0 and 3.2. But that spring semester proved a disaster. The long column of C's I garnered that spring undoubtedly excluded me from gaining admission to one of America's finer law schools. The system doesn't leave you much room to mess up. Rachel fucked Daniel so I fucked Billie-Jo so Columbia and Georgetown and Penn all told me to get fucked. Around and around it goes. La de da. Of course, in my case it didn't much matter. I could've earned my law degree from some correspondence school found on the inside flap of a matchbook cover and Dear Old Dad still would've brought me into the family's Wall Street firm.

I probably should've married Billie-Jo. Maybe everything would've turned out differently; it certainly would've been simpler. Only thirty-five like me, she's already like the assistant director of the American Red Cross, a real up-and-coming young star in the political arena. Maybe she'll be our first female president. Or vice-president. I should put her in touch with my little sister's soon-to-be father-in-law. Maybe they could put together a ticket for '96. Or is he a Republican and she a Democrat? Or have the fat cats decided to tell the truth and admit it's really just one big happy party and they're the only ones invited?

One thing you can count on: when Billie-Jo does run for high public office the media hounds will be out in force sniffing around for old bones she might have buried. Boy, will I be able to tell them some stories.

"Oh, yeah, I remember well that night in the raw when she chased me around the liberal arts quad and then did me dirty right up on the lap of old Ezra Cornell."

Of course, they'll probably just dismiss me as a disgruntled ex-lover looking to open old wounds, get his name in the newspapers, make an appearance on Oprah or Letterman.

Don't worry, Billie-Jo, I'll never tell. Not me. Mum's the word. I'm loyal, true blue till the bitter end. Maybe that's my problem.

Billie-Jo was convinced I was screwed up because I'd been born on the cusp. And not just any cusp but the cusp between Gemini and Cancer. And not just the cusp between Gemini and Cancer but all these other cusps as well. The stars, according to Billie-Jo's research, were all out of alignment and the planets were all in retrograde or on the far side of the moon or the sun or some such tripe at the moment I popped out of Martha's belly.

Billie-Jo blamed all of my insecurities and inferiority complexes and inconsistencies on the unfortunate moment of my birth. And who knows? Maybe she was right. It's as sensible an explanation as any other I've heard or figured out for myself.

Lying there on the floor of my Buffalo Street apartment in the middle of a Tuesday or Thursday afternoon when I should've been at my twice weekly civics lecture, Billie-Jo gave me a lecture of her own. It was late in the semester, drawing close to finals. We really should've been concentrating a little more on our studies, but as usual we were naked. And sweaty. Billie-Jo's hair looked wild. And sexy. Her scent was overpowering. Her nipples stood out like a couple of land mine detonators. I had very recently been sucking on them furiously.

"I've been reviewing your astrological chart, Matthew," she told me, "and I think I should tell you something."

Having recently ejaculated, I was calm and serene. "So tell away," I said, "I can take it."

"Well, the stars say you can expect a lifetime of dissatisfaction and aimless wandering."

"How nice for me."

"I'm serious."

"I'm sure you are."

"You'll have to work very hard not to go off the deep end."

"I'm sure I will."

"I can help."

"I'm sure you can."

We're all so fucked up, so full of bullshit and ulterior motives. We play all kinds of outrageous games with each other. We mess with each other's minds, tell endless tall tales and outright lies. Billie-Jo manipulated me. I manipulated Billie-Jo. She used me. I used her. I told her I loved her but that's only because I'd peered through that sliding glass door and seen Daniel pounding Rachel. Who knows the real reason Billie-Jo told me she loved me? Certainly I don't. But I do know she stopped telling me later that same afternoon.

We climbed up on the bed as soon as I could be resurrected. For at least the third time that day we made the springs of my old bed on Buffalo Street sing. But in the middle of the song my thoughts began to wander. Again, who knows why? They simply did. And before I could reel them in, before I could suppress my fantasy, I brought them to bear.

The tension rising, our bodies pumping, our moans and groans deep

and guttural, I let fly these few innocent words: "Faster, Rachel, faster!
Harder, Rachel, harder!"

"Rachel!" screamed Billie-Jo. "Who's Rachel?" It happened so fast,
I caught up with it only later, after she'd dressed and gone.

Nanoseconds before coming she pulled away and got off the bed. She
picked up the first thing she could find, an old broken lacrosse stick, I
believe, and while yelling the name of my one and only true love over and
over and over, she beat me across the head and shoulders with that stick;
bloodied me, she did. "Rachel, I'll give you Rachel, you son of a bitch!"

I protected myself as best I could but quite honestly I enjoyed the
blows, I wallowed in the pain. Billie-Jo couldn't see my face, and thank
God for that, because I was smiling broadly even as that broken stick
crashed down upon my naked white body.

So Billie-Jo and I went our separate ways. We tried to patch things
up, but it proved impossible. I eventually confessed that Rachel was
indeed a real person. And when tears fell from my eyes as I made that
confession, we knew things would never work out between us.

That summer Billie-Jo went back to West Virginia and I went back
to Rachel. Not that I had ever really left. I'd just slipped out the back
door and raced down the street to the candy store for a couple Tootsie
Roll pops and a bag of Sugar Babies.

"So, was she nice?"

"Who?"

"You know who."

"No I don't."

"Yes you do. Was she pretty?"

"What are you talking about?"

"You know exactly what I'm talking about. Why do you think you
have to hide it?"

"I'm not hiding anything."

It was the summer of '77. We sat on the Fredericks' front porch
drinking fresh lemonade and eating homemade peanut brittle.

"Okay," said Rachel, "you're not hiding anything. Forget I mentioned
it."

I wanted to ask her how she knew, how she could tell, but I never
did. Not that day. Or any other day. I figured she must've just seen it in
my eyes, smelled it on my fingertips.

Things slowly got back to normal between us. By normal I guess I
mean the way things had been before I looked through that sliding glass
door. Our friendship reemerged. I went to see her. She came to see me.
We talked about everything again. She talked mostly about her painting,

and I talked mostly about what would happen the following June after we graduated from college. The old future thing revisited.

We made love. We wrote letters. We talked on the telephone. Over Christmas vacation of our senior year I asked her for the first time to marry me.

It was New Year's Eve. We were staying at a guest house for skiers in Manchester, Vermont. The weather had been warm, the skiing not too good, nothing but some slush on the tops of the mountains. Most of the other skiers staying at the guest house had packed up and gone home.

So on New Year's Eve Rachel and I sat all alone in the living room before a blazing fire. We had polished off half a bottle of champagne. We were laughing and telling stories, watching the grandfather clock in the corner for the approach of midnight. And all of a sudden, out of nowhere, with no premeditation whatsoever, I turned stone-faced serious.

"Rachel?" I said, sober as the old judge.

She glanced at me curiously, then picked up her long-stemmed glass and brought it to her lips. "Yes?"

"Will you marry me?"

A very brief moment passed while she processed the question. And then she smiled. I immediately did not like the look of that smile. It had the confident glow of superiority written all over it. "Silly boy," she said, "asking me a question like that. It's just the champagne and the warmth of the fire talking."

Silly boy! Damn her. "It's not the champagne," I insisted, "it's not the fire," but it was no good, I knew it would come to naught. I pushed my cause anyway, even went so far as to list the reasons she should say yes.

But her smile had already said no. And before the fire died, before the clock chimed in the New Year, she said, "I love you dearly, Matthew. If I was ready to get married, I'd certainly marry you. But I'm not ready. Neither of us is ready. You're still a little boy. You're in a grown man's body now but you're still just a little boy."

The little boy sat there and pouted and drank more champagne. And when the bottle was empty she led him up a flight of old and rickety wooden stairs and tried to make love to him but the alcohol and his ego played tricks with his pecker, so in the end all he could do was roll over and pretend to be fast asleep.

DURING SPRING BREAK '78, final semester of my senior year, Rachel and I rendezvoused at my parents' house in Mendham. Chuckie and Martha had taken my little sister and gone off to Barbados for a week of fun in the sun. Their absence meant Rachel and I had the house all to ourselves.

Late one afternoon we decided to go for a walk. We went out the front door and started down the driveway. It was cold and cloudy. We wore coats and hats. Halfway down the drive we stopped to watch a car swing in off the road.

"Expecting someone?" Rachel asked.

I shook my head.

It was not a car but Daniel's VW camper-van. I hadn't seen him or his van in months. In fact, he'd been pretty scarce all through my college years. He'd take his tennis rackets and disappear for months at a time. I missed him, but not that much. I think subconsciously I was glad to have the guy as far away from Rachel as possible.

Now he brought his van right up alongside us and pulled open the window. "I was hoping to find you two here," he said, and smiled, "had the feeling I would."

I wondered why but before I could ask he stepped out and embraced Rachel. She didn't seem to wonder why at all.

He looked great, as usual: tan, slim, perfectly fit. He gave me a bear hug, then got right to the point. "How would you guys like to take a trip, go on a little adventure?"

"Where to?" I asked.

He had no intention of giving me an answer. "Tell you what," he said, "I'll pick you up tomorrow morning at six-thirty." He started to get back into the van.

"Wait a second," I said. "Where are we going, and for how long?"

He climbed in and closed the door. "I promise to have you back here the day after tomorrow in time for supper."

* * *

He showed up the next morning at quarter to seven. Rachel climbed into the passenger seat, I climbed into the back. We both had overnight bags with a change of clothes.

"You won't need those," he said, "I've got everything we need."

We drove to Newark Airport, left the van in long-term parking, and caught the shuttle bus over to the terminal. Any and all questions Rachel and I raised went unanswered.

We went to the Delta counter. Daniel told us to get a cup of coffee while he took care of the tickets.

"Where do you think we're going?" I asked Rachel as we leaned against the snack bar.

She shrugged her shoulders. "I don't know. But I like not knowing."

A few hours later we landed in Atlanta. Daniel went straight to the Hertz counter and signed the proper papers for a late-model Chevy, or maybe it was a Ford, I can't remember. Whatever it was, we were soon under way, driving south, Daniel behind the wheel, Rachel beside him, me in the back. We drove out of Atlanta along Interstate 75. About an hour later we passed through Macon without even slowing down.

Still no answers from our driver regarding our destination, although I'd noticed soon after leaving the airport that Rachel's questions had pretty much ceased. When I asked her if she knew yet where we were headed, she just sort of shrugged, formed a little smile with those perfect lips of hers, and said, "I don't know. Maybe."

Not too far south of Macon we turned off I-75. We headed west on Georgia State Highway 26. We passed through Henderson and Montezuma and Oglethorpe, small southern towns, nothing but crossroads and a traffic light, maybe a filling station and a place to buy some barbecued ribs.

"You know," I said, "Plains is right around here somewhere. We're not by any chance making a pilgrimage to the humble rural village of our beloved president?"

No one in the front seat said anything, but the answer turned out to be no. We weren't going to visit Jimmy or Rosalynn or Lillian or Amy or even brother Billy, who had recently hit the national limelight with his very own brand of beer. No. we weren't going as far as Plains, we were only going as far as Andersonville.

That's right, Andersonville, site of one of the most infamous Confederate prisoner-of-war camps during the War Between the States. The camp was in existence for just over a year, from early in 1864 until the end of the war in April of 1865, and estimates put the number of Union prisoners killed there at almost thirteen thousand.

We left the car in the parking lot of the Anderson National Historic Site. There weren't many cars in the parking lot that day, half a dozen at most. And a couple of those were official U.S. Park Service vehicles, no doubt belonging to the rangers working inside at the Visitor and information Center. We were visitors, Yankees, but we didn't bother to go inside for any information. I didn't know it then, but we had all the information we needed.

Daniel slung a rucksack over his shoulder, the same rucksack Victor had carried up that mountain in Austria ten years earlier. He handed another pack to me. "Having a good time so far, Mac?"

I pulled on the pack and said nothing.

Rachel had already wandered off, her step light, her eyes as wide open as I had ever seen them. She seemed to know exactly where she was going, exactly why we had come.

It was late in the afternoon of that early spring day. Only a couple hours of daylight remained. Gray clouds filled the sky. Occasionally a few drops of rain fell.

Daniel closed and locked the car. "Ready to march, soldier?"

I shrugged again.

We walked past the Visitors Center and into the Andersonville National Cemetery. Row after row after row of simple white gravestones marked the sites where all those union prisoners had been put to rest.

Rachel stayed well ahead of us, a hundred yards or more. I started to walk faster, to try to catch up with her.

"Let her go, Mac."

"What? Why?"

"Just because I think we should."

We followed her out of the cemetery along the shoulder of a smooth macadam road. An open meadow turning green with spring spread out across that rolling Georgian landscape. A stand of tall pines bordered the meadow. Somehow it all looked familiar.

"So where's the prison?" I asked.

"I think we're looking at it, maybe even standing in the middle of it."

The prison, actually a large wooden stockade made from pine logs fifteen feet high, had long since rotted or been torn down. Small blocks of stone now marked the perimeter where the stockade walls had once confined the Union prisoners of war.

There wasn't all that much left for us to see. Or so it seemed to me.

With the stockade walls no longer in existence, without the presence of forty thousand sick and starving men, the site looked remarkably tranquil, almost peaceful. There were some monuments to the dead, a few outcroppings of worn stones, and a narrow stream known as Stockade Creek, which you could easily jump across without getting your feet wet.

My head was getting wet, however. The rain started to fall more steadily. "You got any umbrellas or rain hats in these packs?" I asked Daniel.

He shook his head. "Sorry, Mac, nothing like that."

"So what's in here?"

He didn't answer. Instead he pointed across the field to where Rachel sat in the wet grass near a bend in that shallow stream.

I started in her direction but he stopped me again. "Give her a minute."

"What's this all about?"

"She never told you?"

"I don't know. Never told me what?"

"Rachel's great-great-grandfather was a prisoner here."

"A prisoner? Here?" I must've looked pretty stupid until I suddenly remembered why this place looked so familiar. It was Rachel's painting, the one she had shown me up in her studio all those years ago, the one she said she had painted from a past life. I looked around at that landscape again. The tranquillity and peacefulness vanished. I saw hordes of pale and emaciated bodies, Rachel's great-great-grandfather included.

"That's right," Daniel said, and nodded, "a prisoner of the Confederate Army."

I realized then I had never asked Rachel about her great-great-grandfather. She had given me a glimpse of that painting but I had offered nothing in return. Her connection with the past, her belief in reincarnation, had been strange and baffling to me; so I had avoided the subject, simply pretended as though this anomaly of hers did not exist. Standing out there in the open, getting wet, feeling chilled, I realized she had shown Daniel her painting as well, and that he had no doubt expressed a great deal of interest in both her beliefs and her great-great-grandfather. I was sure Daniel knew all about Rachel's ancestor. He was the reason we had traveled fifteen hundred miles.

This realization, let me tell you, caused me to lose sight of the terrible tragedy that had occurred on that piece of Georgia real estate. I stood there soaking wet and frowning, almost scowling, as I wondered what other secrets they shared.

"He died here," Daniel told me, "of scurvy and malnutrition."

I wanted to tell him I knew that, but I didn't. So we stood there for a few more minutes, thinking it over and getting wet. Then Daniel adjusted his pack and started across the field. I followed.

Rachel stood as we approached. "This is it," she said. "This is the spot. I'm sure of it. This is where he died. He collapsed right here from exhaustion as he tried to reach the stream for some water. I can see it as clearly as the day it happened. Dead and dying bodies, most of them without shoes and dressed in nothing but rags, lay everywhere, groaning and pleading for help. The bodies, even the ones still alive, were like skeletons, so thin and weak a strong wind could have blown them away."

We stood there, the rain falling faster now, and conjured up Rachel's vivid images. I'd read about Andersonville in my history class on the Civil War, but words on the page of some textbook had not brought the reality to bear. The chapter on Andersonville had reiterated the grisly facts, described the harsh conditions, graphically displayed the vast number of dead. But like tragedy we watch on television, that chapter on Andersonville passed through me so fast, I'd forgotten all about it even before I began to read about Sherman's march to the sea.

Dusk fell. We crossed the stream, found a place to hide among a stand of old pines. The plan, you see, was to pass the night there, within the perimeter of the old stockade. And to do that we had to avoid the final rounds of the park rangers, who insisted the site be cleared before they went home for their evening meal.

Images of Victor and Daniel entering the ovens at Dachau danced through my mind. I kept these images to myself. I did not want to fan the fire already burning so intensely between my two friends, engrossed as they were in the fates of their ancestors.

Not that anything I could've said would've mattered. I was a third wheel on that bike, odd man out.

As soon as darkness fell we crept out of that stand of pines and made camp with the gear in Daniel's packs. There wasn't much gear available. The idea was to re-create conditions as they had been back in January of 1865. We had a couple of worn-out blankets, no tent or tarp to protect us from the weather.

Daniel took off his clothes. He put on a pair of old Levi's so threadbare they had become almost transparent. He had a similar pair for Rachel. She undressed completely right in front of us and pulled on the jeans. They hung off her hips, several sizes too big. She covered her chest with a torn and tattered T-shirt. I was just glad to see her breasts put away behind something, anything. The mere sight of her naked body had brought on a most unexpected and unwanted erection.

"I don't have any duds for you, Mac," said Daniel. "You'll just have to make do with what you've got."

"Or strip naked," suggested Rachel. "Many of the men in the stockade had absolutely no clothes at all."

I chose to remain dressed. I had no intention of exposing my swollen member. I felt sure I'd be able to experience the suffering just fine in my damp khakis and blue button-down oxford.

We settled down under a steady drizzle for the evening meal: beef jerky and raw grits, not cooked at all, just mixed with some lukewarm water out of a canteen. Three or four mouthfuls was all I could manage to swallow. When my fellow inmates weren't looking, I threw the rest of the mess into the shadows.

More than anything I wanted to go back to the rental car. I wanted to crawl onto the back seat, fall asleep, and not wake up till we were back in Mendham, where I could get a hot meal and a warm bath. Suffering was not my cup of tea. Chandlers have never been very good sufferers.

My friends did not discuss their Dachau-Andersonville connection that night. But I could tell they had discussed it at great length in the past. When and under what circumstances, I did not know. My imagination worked overtime on the possibilities.

A strange intimacy existed between them that night. They suffered together. I couldn't get anywhere close to them. They never actually touched, never actually sought one another physically during all that wind and rain, but the power of the two of them there together, sharing that experience, was unmistakable, unavoidable. It scared me. It made me want to run. It made me want to hide.

I've seen photographs of the dead bodies strewn about the Andersonville stockade. I've seen photos of the mass burial pits, photos of prisoners so thin and gaunt they look exactly like victims of the Holocaust. They could easily have been pictures taken at Auschwitz or Treblinka or Dachau. You wouldn't want to paste one of those photographs in your family album.

When I looked at those old photographs I was overcome by the seemingly inexhaustible barbarity of our species to inflict pain and misery. But when Daniel and Rachel looked at those same photographs, they saw something very different. They saw themselves just a generation or two back. The bodies of those emaciated and lifeless men could easily have been their own bodies. They had escaped the harsh realities of history, but only in a material sense. They had no choice but to paste those terrible images in the photo albums they carried around in their minds all the time, every single day.

None of us said much that night. It was too cold and too wet, and the whole idea was to internalize the pain and discomfort. We were not supposed to bitch about how bad we had it. But I do remember one thing Daniel said. It came long after we had finished chewing on our beef jerky, long after I had resigned myself to the long and sleepless night ahead.

"This little sideshow," he whispered, "on this dirty speck of southern soil is all the evidence we need to know that horrors like Andersonville can happen anytime, anywhere.

"We're a dangerous and fucked-up species," he added a few minutes later, "that cannot be trusted."

By morning the rain had finished. We opened our eyes and watched the sun come up over the eastern hills. We ate some more beef jerky. By that time it tasted pretty good. Then we packed up our rucksacks and left the stockade. The simple irony that we were allowed to leave was not lost on me.

We walked back down the macadam road to the Andersonville National Cemetery. A historical marker informed us that more than fifteen thousand bodies were buried in the cemetery, most of them victims of the wretched conditions inside the prison camp during its fourteen months of active use.

We walked beside the long rows of graves. The white tombstones glistened in the early morning light.

Don't ask me how she knew where to go but Rachel wound her way through the rows until she stood in front of the one that bore the name of her ancestor: Corporal David Andrew Frederick. That was all it said, nothing more. The three of us stood over the stone and stared at it for several minutes.

We must've been quite a sight. Two of us dressed in rags. All of us muddy and soaking wet.

Then the time came to go. There was nothing more for us to do there. We walked slowly back through the cemetery and past the Visitors Center.

One of those official U.S. government vehicles pulled into the parking lot. Out stepped a strapping park ranger dressed in his crisp green uniform. He marched across the asphalt and right up into our faces.

He looked us up and down, a scowl chiseled on his face. "Whattay'all doin' here?" he drawled. "Y'all ain't supposed to be here in the park at this hour."

The ranger had more he wanted to say but Rachel cut him off clean with a sharp finger across her throat. "Easy, Buck. Don't tell me what I can and can't do. My granddaddy died in this filthy southern stink hole. And your granddaddy probably watched him do it." Then she stepped forward, nudged him out of the way, and strode across the parking lot.

We all three of us watched her go. Those old, muddy Levi's kept slipping down off her hips, giving us brief, erotic glimpses of her smooth and beautiful white buttocks.

RACHEL ANN FREDERICK, ALIAS MISTY GREY, *rides her bicycle along Main Street. She passes the large white house on the corner of Main and Overlook, number Thirty-six. The "For Sale" sign in the front yard has been removed. Rachel smiles and rides on.*

She pedals hard up Mosle Road, the late afternoon sun still warm on her back. At the top of Mosle she rests for a moment. She thinks about heading back to town, calling the real estate agent. She has several questions about the house.

But then she sees him sitting out by the swimming pool, sipping a beer, reading the newspaper. The questions will keep till morning.

She rides down Mosle, across the bridge spanning the north branch of the Raritan, and along Pleasant Valley Road to Hilltop. She turns left on Hilltop, then left again half a mile later onto Thomas Lane.

At the end of Thomas Lane Rachel turns into the Hawthorn Compound and leans her bicycle against the front porch. She pauses to catch her breath and wipe the perspiration from her face. Then she climbs the stairs and knocks on the massive front door. She waits, but no one comes.

She goes around the side of the house. The old VW camper-van sits in the middle bay of the detached three-car garage. Its engine compartment door hangs open. Several engine parts lay scattered on an oily rag on the garage floor.

Rachel glances into the garage, sees no one. She goes around to the back of the house, across the long green grass. She walks past the back door and out to the four-leaf-clover-shaped swimming pool.

He does not hear her approach. He swims back and forth, his crawl smooth and powerful.

On the glass table beneath the umbrella she sees an empty beer can and a copy of The New York Times. *She glances at the paper. It is open to*

*the sports section, to an article about the upcoming U.S. Open tennis
tournament out in Flushing Meadow.*

*Rachel sighs, then crosses to the edge of the pool. She pulls off her
sneakers and socks and riding shorts and dives into the water.*

*They sit now beneath the umbrella, towels wrapped around their
bodies, ice-cold cans of beer on the table. They watch the sun sink behind
the trees out to the west.*

Daniel sips his beer. "I saw Mac a few days ago."

"You did? In the city?"

"I stopped by his apartment."

Rachel runs her finger around the rim of the beer can. "How was
he?"

"Pretty well, I guess. I don't know. He's such a sad son of a bitch
sometimes."

Rachel nods, pauses, then asks, "Did he tell you I was meeting him
on Nantucket next month?"

"He did, yeah."

"On the sixteenth."

"Good thing, too," *says Daniel.* "The guy looks like he could do
with a little fresh air and sunshine. Doesn't look like he gets outside
much."

Rachel smiles, then says, "You should come, too."

"Huh?"

"You should come out to the island with us. The three of us haven't
been together since I can't remember when."

Daniel takes a long pull on the can before he answers. "Been a while
since I was out to Siasconset."

"Then come. It'll be fun."

He considers it, then shakes his head. "I better pass."

"Why? Because of Matthew?"

Daniel watches the sky to the west turn red.

"We're going to stay at least a week," *says Rachel.* "You could just
come for a few days. At the beginning. We could make the crossing
together."

"A few days?"

"However long you want."

"Maybe Mac and I could finally have that Around the Island Race
we've been threatening for the past hundred years."

"Whatever."

Daniel thinks it over while he finishes his beer.

"So you'll come?" *Rachel asks.*

"Unless something comes up with Victor."

"You mean about this other thing?"

Daniel nods.

"Is there trouble?"

"I don't know. I hope not."

"You want to talk about it?"

Daniel shakes his head, then after a moment he asks, "So, who will you be, Rachel Ann Frederick or this Misty Grey?"

"You mean out on Nantucket?"

"Right. Out on Nantucket."

She laughs softly. "Oh, probably Rachel. I think it's time for her to show her face again. Put in an appearance or two."

Daniel says nothing. They watch the sky. Darkness begins to settle.

"Speaking of Misty," says Rachel, "there's something I've been wanting to ask you."

"Yeah?"

"Remember last year, just before I left the city, I told you I was sick and tired of the act I'd been playing."

"Sure I remember. Every time you walked out of your apartment you had reporters hounding you, demanding to know if you could see or not."

"I told you I wanted to disappear, vanish."

Daniel nods.

"You told me Victor might be able to help."

"And you told me that wouldn't be necessary. You told me you were just going away for a while, to someplace where no one knew you."

"As Misty Grey."

"Right, as Misty Grey."

"Well, I'm thinking about keeping it."

"The name?"

"Yes."

"For good?"

"Maybe. Especially if Victor could create Misty on paper."

"You mean like a passport, a driver's license?"

Rachel nods and sips her beer. "Maybe a diploma or two. I sure would like to teach again. But if I apply for a position as Rachel Ann Frederick, well, the cat's out of the bag."

Daniel thinks it over, then stands. "Wait here. I'll be right back." He crosses the lawn and goes into the house.

When he returns he carries a large manila envelope. He empties the contents of the envelope onto the table. The contents are a paper trail of his fabricated life as Daniel Romankova: grammar school report cards, diploma from a Prague high school, certificate of graduation from a Czech vocational college enabling one Daniel Romankova to practice the trade of optician, tax returns, applications to travel abroad, even a copy of a speeding ticket handed out on the highway between Prague and Cheb.

They look through the stack of papers as darkness falls, as the shadows from the trees spread across the sparkling clear water of the swimming pool.

"Unbelievable," says Rachel.

"Yeah," says Daniel, "unbelievable. You want Misty Grey to have a past? I don't think there'll be a problem."

I SURVIVED ANDERSONVILLE. I caught a terrible head cold that turned into bronchitis that required antibiotics and several days in bed but nevertheless I survived.

And I survived my final semester at Cornell as well, managing, finally, to march down the aisle and accept my diploma. It was May 23, 1978, a pleasant spring day in Ithaca, New York, under a bright blue sky. A warm breeze blew off Lake Cayuga, the first warm breeze of the season. Jimmy Carter was in the White House. The Yanks were early on track for their third straight pennant. America was more or less at peace. The economy was in pretty rough shape, but I didn't give a damn about that. I had money in my pocket and a plane ticket to London.

And I had plans for the future. They might not've been the plans I would've created for myself had I been free to choose, but they were plans nevertheless. It had taken some effort but we—i.e. Chuckie, Martha, and myself—had finally found a law school willing to give me a chance. Poor grades my junior year coupled with a sub-par performance on the law boards had pretty much shut me out of the best schools, the better schools, even some of the mediocre schools.

I've decided not to use the name of the law school that accepted me. It wouldn't be fair to use the school's name after calling it middling and labeling it a second-rate institution. So I'll just tell you it was located in southeast Pennsylvania, and that its legal degree, if not exactly prestigious, was nevertheless perfectly legitimate.

I can also tell you why I chose this particular law school over the two other law schools that accepted me: because Rachel had decided to move home after graduating from Cooper Union, and this institution for the study of law was much close to Mercersburg than the others.

But I'm getting ahead of myself here. A lot happened before my first day of law school.

Wimbledon for one. That's right, Wimbledon. The Championships.

I got to sit in the friend's box and watch Daniel's first-round match. He won that match, in five sets, very exciting stuff, beat a seeded player, can't recall his name, José something or other from Spain or Mexico. The press made a very big deal about it, immediately labeled the match Hawthorn's "breakthrough victory," "an important stepping-stone," "a career booster," and so on and so forth.

Too bad it didn't work out that way. Daniel got beat in the second round in straight sets, only managed to hold serve three or four times, not too good on a fast grass court. I cheered him on, roared every time he won a point, but secretly, inside, I must admit, I had a rather good time watching him go down in defeat.

My visit to Wimbledon really began on the plane ride home from Andersonville. Daniel wanted to know what I planned to do over the summer, after I graduated. I told him I didn't know. He told me I should come to Europe, to be his warm-up partner.

"Oh, yeah, sure," I said, "I'll be your warm-up partner. A man of my tennis skills will definitely inspire your game."

He laughed and said, "Okay, maybe not my warm-up partner, maybe my coach."

"What do I know about being a tennis coach?"

He shrugged. "Okay, what about my trainer?"

"What does a trainer do?"

I carried his bags, confirmed his hotel and airline reservations, made sure his rackets got strung properly, and otherwise acted as his lackey. In return I got some, but not all, of my expenses paid, plus the privilege of hanging around the international tennis scene. Lucky me.

Still, I agreed to go. I needed to get away. I'd had my fill of family and professors and classrooms. But most of all I needed to get away from Rachel. My emotional equilibrium was way out of whack, and I blamed her. I wanted the satisfaction of leaving her behind. I wanted her to have to deal with the whole idea of Daniel and me going off together on one of our famous adventures. I wanted her to be jealous and envious. I wanted her to miss me.

I wrote to her that summer, but not often, not more than once or twice a week, and never, or let us say rarely, did I allow my emotions to shine through. Not a line of poetry flowed from my pen through those international mail-grams. I kept to the facts, usually exaggerated them slightly to heighten the tension, build the sense of adventure and intrigue. A simple pub dinner off Leicester Square when put to paper turned into an extraordinary evening dappled with strangers and night-clubs and private parties complete with members of Parliament and the house of Windsor. Very heady stuff—my imagination, I mean.

After Wimbledon Daniel had tournaments in Scotland, Sweden, and Germany. These were not big affairs; few if any of the world's top players competed. Daniel did reasonably well, reaching the semifinals in one and the quarterfinals in another. He played hard, with his old fierce determination, but he didn't practice much, some days not at all, other days for only an hour or so. He liked to swim or rent a bicycle and go for a long ride. Sometimes he invited me along, sometimes not. He used to disappear for hours, even days. And when I asked him where he'd been, he just shrugged and said nowhere.

Much of the time I was left to my own amusements. I always had free passes to the matches. But when the tennis grew boring I'd go for long walks through those old European cities or for train rides through the countryside. I'd just pick a train, any train, go in this direction or that direction, then get off after an hour or two and catch the next train back. It was pleasant and relaxing. I enjoyed having nothing to do, no one to answer to, nowhere I had to be. I didn't care where the train went or how slowly it moved or how often it stopped.

I thought a lot about Rachel on those train rides and during the hours I spent alone. As the summer slipped away, and the time and the distance between us grew, I became more and more confident that I could live without her. I convinced myself that my obsession with her had been an adolescent fling, a schoolboy infatuation.

Don't get me wrong, I wasn't about to break it off, tell her I no longer had an interest in our relationship; hell no. But from then on I intended to play it cool, not let her or anyone else mess with my emotions or make me crazy. I became a seasoned traveler that summer, or so I believed, capable of taking care of himself, of going the hard, lonely road all alone.

A rugged, rough-and-tumble American individualist with a heart of stone and huge brass walnuts was I.

By early August we'd reached Interlaken, Switzerland, a small city situated between two large, deep-water lakes, Lake of Thun and Lake of Brienz. The Alps hugged the city, especially to the south, where the famous Jungfrau reached high into the sky, its peak snow-covered even that late in the summer.

Interlaken was Daniel's last tournament before we headed home. He had to get back to the States to prepare for the U.S. Open. But in his first-round match at Interlaken he went to hit an overhead and pulled a muscle in his lower back. He tried to continue playing but after a few more games he had to default.

For two days he did nothing but lie on the floor of our hotel room. The back problem was a recurring one. Nothing seemed to help other than complete horizontal rest. But Daniel found that a most difficult chore. By the third morning he couldn't lie still any longer.

"We've got five days before we head home, Mac," he told me as he struggled to his feet, "let's go climb the Matterhorn."

I argued but of course it did no good. We hired a car to drive us over the mountains to Zermatt, actually to the narrow-gauge railroad that carries people in and out of that famous Swiss village in the southern Alps.

I might as well tell you right off: we never made our plane back to the States. Daniel got it in his head that we had to climb the Matterhorn. He wouldn't even discuss leaving until we had accomplished our mission.

We found a room on the east end of town, near one of the cable cars that carries skiers and sight-seers up the mountain. When we checked into the room the innkeeper told us we had a magnificent view of the famous Matterhorn, but over the next three days thick gray clouds shrouded the peak. We waited impatiently for the clouds to clear.

And while we waited Daniel tried to convince me to write a letter to the law school I was supposed to enter in just a few weeks and tell them I would be deferring my enrollment for one year, until the fall of 1979. At first I absolutely refused. I told him I had no intention of making such an irresponsible and impulsive decision.

"Why not, Mac? You need to do something irresponsible and impulsive. You've never taken a piss without first considering the implications. You don't wanna go back to school next month. You know that. You've been telling me as much all summer. So don't go. Put it off. What's the difference? You really think the world needs another lawyer that bad?"

The son of a bitch could really roll once he got started.

"So we climb the Matterhorn," I asked, "then what?"

"Christ, how should I know? There's a million things to do. You wanna climb, we'll climb. After this one we'll do the Eiger. Then we'll go to France and do Blanc. We'll go to Italy and do Cervina. We'll climb every goddamn peak in Europe if that's what you want. We can just climb up, tell the world to shove it, and climb down. Big deal. So what? Nobody will give a shit but you. And who else matters?"

"What about the Open?"

"Fuck the Open. I've done the Open. I'll never win it. So what? Big deal. Five hundred guys are waiting in line pushing and shoving to grab my slot. If it ain't my name on the ladder, it'll be someone else's, someone else with a backhand and a forehand."

That night I lay awake thinking about it. He was right, of course. I didn't have to go to law school, not that fall. I could put it off; it wouldn't be the end of the world.

So in the morning I did it, I just did it.

When I awoke Daniel was already gone. He liked to get up early and walk over to the tennis club. He'd hit a few ground strokes, then take a whirlpool and get a massage.

I didn't wait to tell him my decision. I sat down and drafted a letter to the dean of admissions explaining my desire to defer my enrollment until the following September. I said something about European studies, about a special educational opportunity I could not in good conscience ignore or turn down.

As soon as I finished that letter I began one to Dear Old Dad. The words did not come easily. I finally struck a chord between begging his forgiveness and outright arrogance. I informed him of my decision, told him it was something I had to do. In the long run, I assured him, my decision to forgo law school for one year would do me good. I told him it would be a character and confidence builder. I even went so far as to say I thought it would make me a better and more compassionate lawyer.

I'll bet old Chuckie just about barfed when he read that line.

Then I wrote to Rachel. I took a perverse pleasure in writing that letter. I told her we would not be returning to the States as originally planned. I told her about our scheme to climb the famous peaks of Europe. The whole question of when we would return I left vague, unanswered. "Eventually" was the word I think I used. The plan had been for her to meet us in New York, to accompany me to the Open so we could watch Daniel's matches together. Sorry, I told her, you'll have to change your plans, find something else to do. See you when I see you. Love, Matthew.

I reread the three letters, made a few changes, corrected any errors, and then sealed them carefully in their respective envelopes. I carried the letters to the post office, where I stood in line to buy stamps. Just before I reached the window, I had a moment of uncertainty. A bolt of panic flashed through me. Was I doing the right thing? Making the right move? I could still change my mind, pull back. All I had to do was toss the letters in the trash and walk away, pretend that nothing had ever happened.

But I didn't. No, instead, when I reached the front of the line, I paid extra to have my mail sent special delivery. The clerk told me the letters would be delivered within two business days. My panic passed. A wave of freedom rolled over me as I watched the clerk stamp and file my correspondence in the overseas slot.

WE NEVER CLIMBED THE MATTERHORN.

After I mailed my letters I went looking for Daniel. I finally found him sitting in the back corner of a dark cafe near the train station. At first I thought he was alone but as I approached his booth I saw another man sitting across from him. They both had their elbows on the table and were leaning forward, whispering. Their faces couldn't've been more than six or eight inches apart. I stood almost over them before Daniel spotted me.

He leaned back, worked up a smile. "Hey, Mac. What's up?"

I glanced at the man. He was older, in his fifties. He had a long, thick beard. And he looked familiar, very familiar. I glanced away, back at Daniel. "Uhh, nothing," I answered. "Just wanted to tell you I did it."

"Did what?"

"I wrote that letter. Told them I wouldn't be coming home in time for law school."

His smile turned broader. He stood up, slapped me on the back. "Atta boy, Mac. I knew you could do it. I knew you could tell those SOBs where to put it." Then he turned to his companion and said something in what sounded to me like German.

The man looked at me, nodded, smiled slightly, and mumbled something.

And then I remembered. How could I not remember? He was the man who had first appeared in the light of our campfire that night on the mountain in Austria. He had reappeared a week or so later in Vienna when he drove us across the border into Czechoslovakia. He was Victor's friend from the Old Country, the man who had dropped us off along the banks of the Danube.

Daniel saw me remember. "He remembers you, too, Mac. Says you look the same, only taller."

I laughed, held out my hand. The bearded man stood, shook my hand, then said something to Daniel.

"What did he say?" I asked.

"Nothing," said Daniel. "He has a train to catch."

The two of them embraced. Then the bearded man turned and walked quickly away.

We watched him go.

"Wanna beer, Mac?"

"Sure."

We sat down and ordered beers and hot sausage sandwiches. I decided to wait and see what my old buddy would tell me about the bearded man.

"Something's come up," he said, finally, "I gotta pull out."

"What do you mean, pull out? When?"

"As soon as possible."

"What're you talking about? Where're you going?" I felt a little panicky again, as I had back at the post office.

"I got some business to take care of."

I nodded toward the door. "With him?"

Daniel didn't look directly at me. 'See, Mac, they've been looking for this guy, and, well, they think maybe they've found him."

"Found who? I don't get it. What're you talking about?" I was confused and beginning to wonder if I might intercept those letters before they left the country.

"It doesn't matter who," he said.

I guessed not. "What about the Matterhorn?"

He shrugged. "It's not going anywhere."

"But when are we gonna climb it?"

"Tell you the truth, Mac, I've already climbed it."

"Say what? When?"

"Couple years ago. Quite a thrill. If I were you, I'd stick around and do it."

I tried to press, to push, to probe, but as always when I dealt with him, my efforts were in vain. We sat there for another hour or so, drinking beer and babbling away, but as far as the moment was concerned, Daniel had already packed up and moved on, left that quaint little Swiss mountain village and me behind.

Before I could take a deep breath I found myself alone. All of a sudden I felt the weight of being a solitary visitor in a foreign country. An hour after I watched his train pull out of the station, I realized just how much I had relied on him to take care of details, see me through the tough parts. He was the one who could communicate in German, Italian, French. He got directions, booked the rooms, ordered the meals.

I might've been the trainer but really I was just along for the ride, an extra appendage that had suddenly been severed.

I wondered for a while after his departure if he had deserted me on purpose, if this had been his plan all along. But I subdued my paranoia and eventually convinced myself to make the most of the situation. What choice did I have? Those letters were on their way.

The sky finally cleared. I got my first good look at the famous face of the Matterhorn. It looked impossible to climb, a perfectly sheer rock wall. But it had been conquered countless times before by lesser men than I. Or so I tried to assure myself.

I would need a guide to lead me up the mountain. A few days earlier Daniel had found one for us. Now I went to see him by myself. His English was worse than my Italian. We did our best. I wanted to climb. He wanted to lead me. When? Three or four days. Why not in the morning? Something about a baby or the weather, I wasn't sure.

I decided to stick it out, to stay, to be brave, to make the climb. Again, what else could I do? Crawl home with my tail between my legs?

For the next two and a half days the weather was perfect: cool, not a single cloud in the sky. I took long hikes in the mountains to get myself in shape for the big ascent. I felt so bold on the morning of the third day that I actually wondered if I could climb to the peak on my own. I hiked upward in the shadow of the face for almost four hours with that thought in mind.

Around noon I stopped to rest, to catch my breath. I was way up on the mountain. I turned around and gazed into the valley below. Zermatt looked like a miniature village, barely real. The air was as still as a statue. Not a blade of grass so much as wavered.

But then, when I turned back to continue my ascent, everything changed. A breeze kicked up, and almost immediately clouds started to roll in from the south and west.

The temperature plummeted. The breeze turned quickly to a force gale. The clouds grew dark and black. The summit of the Matterhorn disappeared. Half a minute later the whole northeast face vanished. And then it started to rain. And then snow.

I panicked. I began to run down the mountain. A squall hit and for a minute or more I couldn't see my hand in front of my face. No way could I see the trail. I could barely tell up from down. I froze, didn't move a muscle. The snow actually began to accumulate around my feet. I felt sure I would die there, freeze to death, never see Rachel again.

The squall passed. The snow turned back to rain. I started once more to run. I ran almost all the way back to Zermatt. When I reached the outskirts of the village I slowed. My entire body trembled. My heart raced. I was drenched in sweat. I wanted to go home, home to my bedroom on the second floor of our big safe house on Cherry Street in Mendham.

Finally I reached my room. I took off my clothes, climbed into bed. Off and on for the next eighteen hours I slept. Late the following morning I managed to get out of bed, shower, and dress. Down in the lobby I found several pieces of mail waiting for me.

Summed up, the information in those letters looked something like this: Daniel, writing from Vienna, told me he was flying to South America and would see me sometime: the dean of admissions at that law school in southeast Pennsylvania accepted my deferment and assured me my position would remain open until the following fall; and Dear Old Dad, writing from his plush office on Trinity Place in Manhattan on Chandler, Wright & MacPherson letterhead, more or less called me a worthless piece of horseshit barely worthy of the family name.

Nothing at all from Rachel. Not a word. And oh, how I missed her now. Forget what I said earlier about having learned to live without her. All that was out the window. Right then and there I tried to call her on the phone. It took a while but the call finally went through. The phone rang and rang and rang. It rang so many times the overseas operator interrupted, and in this snotty voice she told me she felt pretty sure no one was home.

"Go to hell!" I shouted, and slammed down the receiver.

I raced back up to my room and wrote my one true love a letter. The letter went on and on and on, page after page after page. I pledged my eternal love and devotion, assured her she meant more to me than life itself. I told her I did not want to be away from her, not ever again, not for one single solitary moment. I wanted us to be together, connected both physically and spiritually always, forever more.

By the time I had finished my love opus and sealed it tight, the post office had closed for the day. I would have to mail it in the morning. But in the morning, at the crack of dawn, after an endless and sleepless night, I left Zermatt. I packed my bags, settled my bill, got a cab to the station, and began the long journey home.

It took several days. I caught the train to Geneva. It was late when I arrived, so I had to get a room. The following morning I went to the airport and learned there was not a single seat available to New York for almost a week.

Filled with more than a little anxiety, I scrambled around that airport trying to find an airline, any airline, that would carry me back to the States. Finally British Airways told me they could get me on a flight late the following evening, out of London.

"And how," I asked the pretty girl behind the ticket counter, "shall I get to London?"

She shrugged.

I bought the ticket anyway. Surely, I assumed, I could get to London in a day and a half, almost thirty-six hours.

And I did, with time to spare. I got a train from Geneva to Paris, another train from Paris to Calais. I threw up so many times on the Hovercraft to Dover that I very nearly threw my body overboard into the cold, dark English Channel. Ah, to end the pain and misery.

Then, in the black of night, another train through Kent, stopping at Canterbury and on into London in time for morning tea. I caught the underground out to Heathrow, checked in at the British Airways ticket counter, and suddenly found myself with almost ten hours to kill before departure. I didn't care. I'd made it. I was going home.

Well, not home exactly. At Kennedy I cleared customs and caught the subway into the city. Once in the Big Apple I walked several blocks toting my two large suitcases, my carry-on bag, a Swiss watch I'd bought for Rachel, and two bottles of French wine I'd bought for her father. It seemed to take hours but finally I reached the Port Authority Bus Terminal on Forty-second Street. After waiting for several more hours I boarded a Greyhound bound for Harrisburg.

On and on I went, the miles rolling away, oblivious by this time of movement and of the blurry thoughts rotating in my head. In Harrisburg I changed buses for Chambersburg, where I changed buses for Greencastle, where I changed buses for the last time to Mercersburg. That bus ground to a halt right there along Main Street, just a block and a half from the Fredericks' big white house on the edge of campus.

The driver pulled my bags out from under the bowels of the bus. I collected my gear and began what I thought at the time was the final leg of my long journey. I didn't know then that the journey never ends.

And then I stood in front of her white house. I walked up the brick path and paused for a moment on the bottom step of the front porch. Rachel sat on the porch on a rocking chair, a sketch pad cradled in her arm. The sight of her brought tears to my eyes.

"Matthew!"

We embraced, long and hard. The first few minutes of our reunion easily fulfilled my expectations. We said virtually nothing. Our eyes and our arms did all the talking. We held each other close and tight.

But of course, eventually, the old lips started flapping. It was inevitable. She had to ask some questions. I had to provide some answers.

She listened, and then, "I just sat down to write you a letter."

Really? Just now?"

"Just this second. I only received your letter from Zermatt yesterday. It was dated over a week ago. I don't know why it took so long to get here."

She was talking about the letter I had written with perverse pleasure, the one telling her I would not be returning to the States any time soon, the one that said Daniel and I were setting off on a splendid mountain-climbing adventure of which she would not be a part.

That was my Independence Day letter, the letter full of piss and vinegar, my bold anthem to freedom and male bonding. The other letter, the letter I'd written after Daniel had left and that mountain storm had reared up and bitten off my balls, the real letter, the honest letter, lay in the bottom of my bag while I tried to decide whether or not to hand it over.

"I've only written two or three lines so far," Rachel said as she turned and picked up her pad, "but with you home I guess there's not much use in me writing anymore. Here"—and she handed me the pad—"you can read it."

She always wrote her letters on sketch pad paper. Her beautiful, flowing penwomanship was a work of art:

Dear Matthew,
    The Matterhorn! Wow! Sounds exciting! I think you've made the right decision. Law school can wait. I'll miss you, but stay as long as you

Thank God I arrived before she finished.

I stayed with the Fredericks for eight days. I would have stayed eight years. But one night at dinner, after I'd been there a week, Coach Frederick asked me in his simple nonconfrontational style, "So, Matt, you're going to take a year off from school. Any plans?"

Yes, I wanted to tell him, I plan on moving into your home permanently, but don't worry, I'll do the shopping and the cleaning and the cooking, which'll leave you more time for painting and listening to music and doing all the things you like to do. And oh, by the way, I love your daughter, and even though she hasn't said yes yet, I hope one day to marry her, but again, don't worry about it, we're not going anywhere, we'll stay right here and live with you in this big old white house.

"Uhh," I mumbled into my glass of wine, "I, uhh," aware now that the status quo I had created in seven days could not be preserved, "I, uhh, figure I'll get a job and, uhh, hopefully, uhh, earn some money."

"Excellent idea," Tom Frederick said, breaking his tradition of silence at mealtime. "It's always good to get out there and make a few dollars."

What did I expect? To take walks in the fields with Rachel for the rest of my life? To sit on the front porch in the evenings reading novels by F. Scott Fitzgerald and Jack London? To slip into Rachel's warm bedroom after lights out and make love or just hold her tight? To sleep late and never wear a watch or a necktie?

Good Lord, what a dreamer was I! I must've gone temporarily insane, lost sight of who I was. I was a Chandler, after all. I had no time to dally, no days to while away. I had to get up early and work my ass off, make something of myself, for chrissakes.

SO I WENT HOME AND FOUND A JOB. But first I had to listen to Chuckie Boy pontificate on the ways of the world and the uselessness of his male offspring. He really laid it on thick, didn't ease off for weeks. Every night at dinner I had to listen to him ride me. And all because I had dared dream of those Alpine peaks.

I got a job working for a moving company, you know, carrying couches and tables and boxes for people in transit. This particular vocation, however, did not help to improve relations between Dear Old Dad and yours truly.

"Why did you take such a piss-ass, lowlife job like that?" the closet racist demanded. "Chandlers don't work at manual labor for wages."

"Why not?" I asked.

"Because we have immigrants to do that kind of work. You think we let all this riffraff into the country out of the kindness of our hearts?"

I didn't answer. I didn't argue. I wanted to argue, wanted to call a spade a spade, but I was too timid. I felt my position in the family was too tenuous to mount a counterattack. The old man wore the captain's bars. I was nothing but a galley slave.

It took me six or eight weeks, must've been right around Thanksgiving, before I could even find the nerve to ask him if I might spend the winter in the house on Nantucket. I'd been thinking a lot about this possibility and thought perhaps I could convince Rachel to join me out on the island. I imagined the two of us living the idyllic life: sleeping late, making paintings and poetry, frolicking naked through the house.

"No," came the answer from the man at the head of the table.

And that was that.

All through the winter I moved furniture. It was mindless physical work. I enjoyed it. The simple drudgery of lifting and carrying, lifting and carrying, possessed a certain beauty, even a certain profundity. Or maybe it just seems that way now. At the time I think I hated it, loathed getting out of bed in the morning and spending the whole day with guys who called women "twats," black people "niggers," Puerto Ricans "spics," and so on and so forth.

At least once a month I spent the weekend with Rachel. Either I went to Mercersburg or she came to Mendham or we met somewhere in between. She was happy and always hard at work on a new painting. She talked a blue streak about her painting, about where it had been and where it was going. I enjoyed listening. I marveled at her enthusiasm, her discipline, her sense of purpose.

For my part, I moped and complained a lot. My big thing that winter was the future. I preferred to talk about what would be going on later in my life, sometime down the road, when I had everything just the way I wanted it.

Sure thing, Mac. Right-o. Roger and out.

Daniel popped in from time to time. He never hung around for long, just a day or two, usually disappeared again without bothering to say good-bye. As far as I knew, he didn't see Rachel at all during those months. But, of course, I knew nothing for certain. They could've been shacking up together and I wouldn't've been any the wiser.

In the spring I quit the moving company and went to work for a local landscaper. We planted shrubs and edged beds and spread this rich dark brown mulch to keep down the weeds and hold in the moisture. I loved the smell of that stuff, loved to reach my arm down into a pile of it and feel the warmth radiating through the decaying matter.

And when the soil warmed and the grass started to grow, we brought out the mowers. Through the spring and most of the summer I pushed a gasoline-powered Toro twenty-two-inch rotary mower with a side-chute grass catcher back and forth across some of Mendham's finest real estate.

I enjoyed that job: the sweet smell of gasoline, the perfectly straight lines in the lush green lawns, the final touches with the small hand clipper along the walks and around the old maples. It was simple, straightforward work, and as you climbed back into the pickup truck on your way to the next lawn, you could look back, and see what you had accomplished.

Maybe, when I'm all through sailing the ocean blue, after I've made my journey to Old Jerusalem, I'll buy myself a Toro and get a job cutting grass. Maybe out in Mendham. Or over in Peapack. We'll see. We'll just have to wait and see.

In the middle of that summer Rachel made an announcement. "I've decided to move back to the city."

"What? Why?"

"Because it's time," she answered. "Because I've done all the work I can in the country for now. It's time for me to live in the city again, as an artist this time, not as a student. My work has reached the point where maybe it will attract some attention. That won't happen here in Mercersburg."

"But but but but but..." I knew she was right but I wanted her to stay in Mercersburg. I wanted her to stay because in just over a month I would be starting law school, and law school was less than an hour's drive from that big white house on Main Street. Also I wanted her to stay because I hated New York. Too many things could happen to her in New York, too many mysteries over which I would have no control.

So what am I saying here? That I would've locked Rachel away in her bedroom for my own personal enjoyment had I somehow been able? Who knows? It's possible. Man is such a filthy, possessive beast.

But I had no way of stopping her, so off she went. Coach Frederick dipped into his savings and purchased an empty loft in Soho on Greene Street between Spring and Prince. I helped Rachel move in on August 26, 1979. The third-floor loft was mostly one large room with high ceilings and tall, narrow windows. There was a small bathroom and an even smaller kitchen and a sleeping platform at one end just big enough for a double bed and a nightstand.

I spent several days with her. We cleaned the sinks and scrubbed the floors and washed the windows and painted the walls. Every step of the way, at least a thousand times, I told her I loved her. Sometimes she told me back. Usually she just smiled. I wondered if the rest of my life would be like this: up in the air, in and out, hello and good-bye, a perpetual state of flux and fury.

She cried the morning I left to begin my legal career. Her tears gave me hope.

I'M DAMN NEAR SIXTY YEARS OLD. *When I was your age I never thought I'd be this old. But the thing is, now that I am this old, all I want to do is get older. I want to live to be a hundred, a hundred and fifty. I don't even care if I have to stop moving. Thirty, forty years ago I would've said if you took away my legs I'd wither up and die in a week. I used to think a Gypsy who couldn't move was a worthless piece of scrap. But not anymore, son. Now you could prop me up on the front porch in that old rocker and I'd sit there till hell froze over. Be nice if you or your mother or one of your sisters brought me a pipe and a jigger of ouzo from time to time, but even without those small comforts I'd sit there smiling and watching the world roll by. Plenty of things to keep my interest just in the daily rotation of the planet: sunrise, sunset, moonrise . . ."*

Victor trails off. Daniel listens and nods in the descending dusk but says nothing. They sit up in the old tree fort out in the woods beyond the swimming pool and the tennis court. The roof of the treehouse has mostly collapsed, the sides have caved in, the floor is rotten.

They were walking in the woods in the early afternoon, talking, trying to solve the world's problems, when they came upon the towering oak tree. They looked up and saw the old tree fort in the high limbs. "I'll bet I haven't been up in that damn treehouse for twenty years," said Victor.

"Me neither," said Daniel.

"Maybe it's time we changed that," said Victor.

So Daniel walked back to the garage to fetch the aluminum extension ladder. They had to extend the ladder beyond its safety zone to make it long enough to reach the trapdoor. Victor went up first, then Daniel. As soon as Daniel climbed up through the trapdoor Victor grabbed the top of the ladder and gave it a shove. The ladder teetered at its apex, then fell back, away from the oak, finally crashing to the forest floor.

"Guess we'll be here a while."

"At least till your mother finds us."

The afternoon passed.

Now dusk settles around them.

"You want to live," asks Daniel, "But is it because you're afraid of dying?"

"Hell no," says Victor, "death's nothing. I died more than once when I was a kid. It hurts and you never really get over it, but you learn to keep going."

"I know what you mean," says Daniel. "These past few weeks I keep going, but all the time I'm looking over my shoulder, checking the rearview mirror."

"You feel hunted."

Daniel nods.

Victor drifts off for a moment. He pulls a pouch of black tobacco and a pack of rolling papers from his breast pocket. With a few practiced movements, he rolls and lights himself a cigarette. "Hell of a feeling, isn't it? Being hunted, I mean. It turns you into an animal, but at the same time it puts the whole program right out there on the edge."

Daniel waits, wonders if he should just come out and ask. All afternoon he has wanted to ask. Now, finally, he does. "So do you think I'm being hunted?"

Victor holds the smoke deep in his lungs, then exhales. "What I think doesn't matter. What do you think?"

Daniel shrugs. "I don't know. I'm not sure. At the border I felt hunted. 'Trapped' might be a better word. So I retreated. A few other times I felt like I was being followed. But I don't know. The head plays games."

The light fades. They see each other now more as shadows.

"Max," says Victor, "sent someone down to have a little chat with the Indian woman."

"Heinrich's housekeeper?"

Victor nods. "It seems the individual who wasted her boss wanted the world to know he was a Gypsy."

Daniel remembers the scene in the penthouse high above the Río de la Plata. "It just slipped out. I couldn't help myself."

"According to Max she was grateful for the way Herr Heinrich was treated. I guess our old Nazi friend has been sexually molesting her for years. Old habits die hard."

"Still," says Daniel, "it was a mistake. I should've kept my mouth *shut. I shouldn't've said a word to her." He pauses, then asks, "Have I dug myself a hole?"*

"What do you think?"

"I don't need questions, Victor. I need answers."

Victor laughs. The smoke billows. "You think there are answers?"

"I think I did what I had to do, and now I'd like to get on with it."

"With what?"

Daniel sighs.

Victor smokes, blows some rings, listens. "I hear your mother," he says. "She's looking for us."

"I don't hear anything."

"You never had to hear as well as I did."

Daniel thinks about this while his father smokes. They sit quietly for a few minutes, listening to the muted sounds of a late summer evening.

"You're my only son, Daniel. I want you to live and prosper and grow old."

"And can I do that?"

"Without looking over your shoulder?"

"Yes, without looking over my shoulder."

Victor shrugs. "It wouldn't be difficult to make the little Indian housekeeper talk."

"So what are you saying?"

"I'm saying forget about that stinking Nazi. Probably everyone else already has. But watch your back nevertheless. You'll get used to it. I did."

Daniel does not respond. They sit quietly again.

After a moment Victor touches Daniel's arm and says, "Listen, she's coming."

They hear footsteps on the broken branches and dry leaves below. And then, "Victor! Daniel! This is your last call. Supper's already ice cold."

Father and son peer down through the trapdoor of the old treehouse. In the last bit of daylight they see Carolyn Hawthorn standing on the forest floor, hands on her hips.

"Looks to me like she means business," whispers Victor.

Daniel nods.

"A hell of a woman. Never would've made it without her."

She stares up at them. "Well?"

"The ladder fell over," Victor explains. "We couldn't get down."

"The two of you," she says, "a couple of natural-born liars." Then she bends down to retrieve the ladder. With no small amount of effort she rights the ladder and settles it against the oak tree. First her husband and then her son climb down out of the treehouse.

"Now what plots are you two hatching?"

They smile and say nothing.

"Little boys in great big bodies."

Daniel begins to take down the ladder.

"Leave it," says Victor. "I rather enjoyed myself up there. I think tomorrow I might fix it up some, make it a little more homey and secure against inclement weather."

The three of them stare for a moment up at the shadow of the tree fort. Then they turn away. Arm in arm in arm they walk slowly across the forest floor, back into the light of the old family home.

AND SO WHAT OF LAW SCHOOL? What can I say? What should I tell you? That it took three years? That, like undergraduate school, it quickly grew into something I just wanted to get through, something I wanted to finish? That I did pretty well but didn't really learn all that much? About the law, I mean. That after gaining an appreciation for the various types of law I didn't really find any of them particularly interesting— most of them, especially financial law, downright dull? That I had to take the law boards three times before I finally squeaked through with the lowest-possible passing grade? That I probably would've wound up an ambulance chaser in some crummy little two-bit Pennsylvania town if my old man hadn't been a prominent player in a major Wall Street firm? All true, all true.

But there must've been more. Three years, after all. There was Professor Owen Straight, a little old man with clear eyes and a quiet voice. He was all about integrity. Old Owen truly believed, even after forty years in the trade, that lawyers were ministers of justice, purveyors of the truth. "Without the law," he liked to tell us, "democracy would be a sham. You people are the protectors of the law, the guardians of democracy. When you can no longer preserve and defend the truth, your days as a lawyer are numbered. When you become part of the lie, the time has come to move on and find a less sensitive profession. Truth is nothing more than a principle, but it is that principle more than any other that you are bound to uphold."

I was far less cynical in those days, and although many of my fellow students found Owen rather dull, I took his legal pearls to heart. If I was going to be a lawyer, well, I figured I might as well try and be an honest one. Time, however, has a way of destroying even our best intentions. In the end I let Owen down, and probably myself as well.

So what else? Let me see. There were the all-nighters before exam time, and the pretty Italian girl from Pittsburgh who loved my dry sense of humor and wanted the two of us to open our own firm (and maybe make a few bambinos along the way). Her name was Maria. She made love with great passion. Too bad all I could do in return was lie there.

There were those long and dreaded days when I actually had to argue a case before a jury of my peers. I hated those days. So I determined early on in my legal career never to try a case in court. I simply did not possess the oratory skills. I would not be a litigator. I would practice law quietly, behind the scenes, anywhere but in the courtroom.

And, in fact, I was an attorney-at-law for seven years before I ever stood before a judge. Not until I stood up in the courtroom and entered a plea of innocent on a charge of second-degree homicide for my client, the itinerant black man, Mr. Isaiah Jackson, did I ever put my oratory skills to the legal test.

I saw Rachel whenever possible during my legal training. We became more and more those long-distance lovers I had wanted to be during undergraduate school. She poured herself into her work but beyond the painting she seemed to rely on me for emotional support. The city was tough and uncompromising. People lied to her, manipulated her. No one wanted to buy or display her paintings. No one showed more than a fleeting interest.

All this was new to Rachel. As a young painter she had been showered with praise, put up on that artistic pedestal. I don't think she had ever experienced rejection before. It caused her to turn to me, Old Faithful. And, of course, I did not disappoint. I gave her exactly what she wanted: unflinching and steadfast loyalty in the face of ridicule and anonymity.

Rachel was probably as pure and unsophisticated an artist as New York had seen in a generation. Four years at Cooper Union but she had never learned or cared about the subtle nuances of the New York art world. She had studied the great artists and painted painted painted. She thought that would be enough. The rest would simply fall into place. But in the early eighties she had to be educated all over again. She had to learn a whole new set of rules before she could play the game. Ability and creativity had little to do with success. It was who you knew and how you played them that mattered.

As I watched her learn how to play this new game, I found I loved her even more. She shocked and surprised me with her innocence. Until then I had been blind to certain aspects of Rachel's personality. Yes, she was vain but also vulnerable, narcissistic but also naive.

In December of 1980, right before Christmas, I was in the city fresh from my second year midterm law exams. Rachel and I sat on the floor of her loft sharing a bottle of wine and listening to "Imagine" while mourning both the death of Lennon and the recent election of Ronnie Reagan to the White House. Our mourning was interrupted by a knock on the door.

Rachel pulled open the door, and there he stood, bigger than life. I right away hated the son of a bitch for showing up unannounced, but on the other hand, I had to love him and envy him for his carefree ways and his easy smile.

"Mac, didn't expect to find you here." He gave Rachel a brief kiss on the mouth.

"I didn't expect to find you here, either."

He gave me a strong embrace, then moved straight to his objective. As always. "Got another little adventure you might be interested in."

"Oh, yeah?" I asked, remembering our trip south. "I hope this one's inside where it's warm and dry. Andersonville just about gave me pneumonia."

He laughed. "I'll tell you, Mac, I had Rachel in mind when the idea came to me, but as long as you're here I'd sure like to see you trail along."

Trail along! Bastard! How often, I wondered, does this kind of bullshit go on behind my back? I glared at Rachel but her eyes looked the other way.

"I'm not sure I can go anywhere right now," she said. "Father's coming early next week to spend Christmas with me."

So, I thought, at least this visit from the Hawkster wasn't planned ahead of time.

"If we leave right now," Daniel pushed, "I'll have you back by the day after tomorrow."

And so we went. Of course we went. We packed a bag, locked the door, and drove north out of the city in his VW camper-van. We drove into Connecticut, up through Hartford, and across the Massachusetts line. He wouldn't tell us where we were going. After a while, after I assured myself we were not headed for Nantucket, I stopped even asking; I didn't want him to think I even cared.

We drove east on the Mass Pike, then north on I-95. By this time the short, early winter afternoon had turned dusky, almost dark. We fought our way around Boston through the rush hour traffic. Then, after more than an hour of braking and accelerating, stopping and starting, we turned off the interstate onto Massachusetts State Highway 129. Not too much later I saw a sign for Salem. So did Rachel.

"Salem!" she shouted. "I should've known."

How? I wondered, but didn't ask.

We pulled into the old whaling town, now kind of decrepit and worn out, but once one of America's most vital and active seaports and before that the site of the infamous witchcraft hysteria of the 1690s.

After a few errant turns we pulled up in front of a spiffy-looking three-story brick building complete with covered canopy and a doorman dressed to kill: the Hawthorne Hotel.

"Know the owners?" I asked our driver.

"Sure," he answered, "we're thick as thieves."

Rachel laughed. We headed for the front door. I half expected the doorman to greet Daniel by name. But he didn't; he simply smiled and pulled open the door.

We crossed a plush lobby lined with crimson carpet. At the registration desk Daniel took charge. "Good evening," he said to the tall, dark-eyed, gloomy-looking man behind the desk, "you have a room for Hawthorn?"

The tall ghoul almost managed a smile. "Oh, yes, Mr. Hawthorne, we've been expecting you." He took a long, critical look at Daniel, then, with his long, white cadaverlike fingers, he pushed the registration book across the smooth wooden surface of the desk. "Would you please sign in, sir."

Daniel picked up the pen and began to write. "Oh, yeah," he asked, "do you have another room? I thought there'd be only two of us but the party got larger as word got out."

My brain immediately went to work on this bit of information, even before I heard the ghoul answer, "Sorry, Mr. Hawthorne, the hotel is completely filled." He pronounced Daniel's surname with no little amount of sarcasm.

Daniel ignored him, pushed the registration book back across the desk. "So how many beds in the room we've got?"

"Two queen-size beds, sir," the ghoul answered. He reached under the desk and pulled out a key. As he handed the key to Daniel he asked, "I'm just curious, sir. When you stop at Ho Jo's, do you register as Howard Johnson?" His pale, thin lips curled up ever so slightly at the corners.

Daniel found the slight rather amusing but I jumped to my old buddy's defense, even if he had covertly planned to use his namesake's hotel as a lust nest to defile my love. "He's a bona fide Hawthorn, pal," I said, "a direct descendent of the guy who no doubt gave his name to this dump."

The ghoul twitched, came to life. "And you, sir? Mr. Herman Melville, I presume. And on your arm the Belle of Amherst, perhaps?"

Daniel laughed and laughed. So did Rachel. I went out to the van and fetched the bags.

I suppose if the three of us were ever going to have a ménage à trois, it would've been then, during our stay at the Hawthorne Hotel on Essex Street in Salem, Massachusetts. There was certainly no lack of opportunity. A definite amount of nudity prevailed up in our third-floor bedroom. Neither Daniel nor Rachel thought anything of stepping out of the shower wrapped in a bath towel, tossing the towel on the bed, and pulling on their undergarments while the rest of us pretended not to watch by staring at the boob tube or reading the stack of brochures depicting Salem's rightful, if somewhat dubious, place in the annals of American history.

But there was no hanky-panky during our stay at the Hawthorne Hotel. We were all just friends, chums, comrades, confidants. Right. Just out for a good time and maybe a bit of historical reconnoitering. Rachel and I slept in one bed, Daniel in the other.

But what if I hadn't made the trip? What if I was back in Mendham trimming the family Christmas tree? Or down at law school preparing for the future? What then might've happened in that hotel room? Who knows? Let me just say I doubt they would have mussed both beds.

That aside, I'm sure you're wondering why we went to Salem. Why did he drag us all the way up there? Certainly not just to see how our sexual fantasies might play if we all wound up using the same water closet. No, we had an agenda. Daniel and Rachel did, anyway. I was just along for the ride.

In the morning, a cold and dreary late December morn, we bundled up and began our tour of the town. For an hour or so I thought the idea was simply to check out the old village, partly restored, where Daniel's ancestors had once lived and worked and procreated. We toured several museums and historic sites, including the famed House of Seven Gables where Daniel's great-great-great-great-grandpappy had housed his famous fictional family of American social snobs, the Pyncheons.

We visited the Salem Witch Museum, the Essex Institute, the John Ward House, the old Customs House, the First Church of Salem, and many other landmarks. But never did we visit these establishments for long. Like a couple of bloodhounds on the trail of a sly old fox, my mates sniffed at these haunts but hurried on in search of more meaty game.

Finally we paused at the old burial ground on Charter Street, just a block or so from the harbor. Something there caught their fancy. They scurried about the ancient tombs and worn headstones in a frantic search for clues. I wandered off on my own. A plaque near the entrance told me the earliest grave was dug in 1637. It contained the remains of one Francis Higginson, a passenger on the *Mayflower*. I was duly impressed.

"Here!" I heard Daniel shout. "Here it is. I found it."

"Found what?" I asked. And let me tell you, I was the only one who had to ask.

Daniel had found the final resting place of his grandfather several generations removed—not Nathaniel but Nathaniel's forebear, Mr. John Hathorne, the gentleman who had presided as judge at the infamous witchcraft trials of 1692.

So, I wondered, is this why we've come all this way, to see this eroding tombstone, to stand over this ancient mound of earth on this cold, damp December morning?

Of course not. My companions needed to find Judge Hathorne's grave only to help them follow the scent. Before I could ask even a single question they had that scent and were back on the trail. I followed close behind, wishing all the while I had a dog whistle and one of those fancy green hunting jackets with the leather patches on the elbows.

We soon left the historic area, that zone set aside specifically for tourist consumption. In no time at all we entered a far seedier section of Salem. It took only a few blocks to go from a sterilized and romanticized view of the eighteenth century to a dismally realistic and depressing view of the twentieth century.

Daniel and Rachel seemed not to notice but suddenly we were strolling through a wasted and decaying neighborhood of run-down houses and tenementlike apartment buildings. I tried to find out what historical attractions we might be searching for out in that neck of the woods but my inquiries went unanswered. The mutts were all a-lather.

We climbed a small hill along a road in desperate need of an asphalt truck and a county road crew. Abandoned cars, some of them stripped clean, rusted along the shoulder. But Daniel and Rachel paid no mind; they had their noses to the grindstone. The fox, I figured, could not be far off.

We reached the top of the hill, a small knobby knoll. I saw nothing but an empty lot in the middle of a small subdivision of one-story clapboard houses straight out of the 1950s. We entered the empty lot, stepping carefully around the broken bottles and bags of trash.

"This is it!" Rachel shouted. "This is definitely it."

"This is what?" I wanted to know.

"You're right," said Daniel, "this is it. You can still smell the stench of murderous death wafting through the air."

So what had they found this time? Not the field where Rachel's great-grandfather had been starved to death by his own countrymen; no, they'd found something even more amazing this time, something even more perplexing: they'd found the Salem gallows. Right there on the nipple of that knoll, amid the dust and decay, according to my two trusty bloodhounds, was absolutely positively the exact spot where the good citizens of old Salem had hung the women accused and convicted of conspiring with the Devil.

"You're right," Rachel agreed, "you can smell death as clearly as you could on the day those innocent women died at the end of a rope."

I couldn't smell anything; although to be honest, I've never had a very good sniffer. But I always have had a morbid curiosity, and I couldn't help but wonder why this famous site had been omitted from the local tourist map. It seemed like something we Americans would want to see, like the Statue of Liberty or the original Bill of Rights.

My friends continued to work their noses. They practically got down on all fours to catch a whiff of that gray urban soil. I wondered if they'd gone mad or perhaps ingested some hallucinogens when I hadn't been looking.

But no, something far more sinister drove them to sniff the earth.

"Here," said Rachel, "here is where I stood. Right here is where they made me stand, where they made me watch."

"Where who made you watch what?" I asked, perplexed. But I noticed Daniel did not wait for the answer. He'd already wandered off. He already knew the answer. This whole damn thing was another one of their secrets, another one of those damn mysteries I didn't know anything about.

"The hanging," Rachel answered. "They made me watch the hanging."

I was pissed off and confused. "What hanging? When?"

"When I lived here in Salem," she told me without the slightest pause for irony, "in an earlier life, in an earlier incarnation."

"What're you talking about?"

"Surely I've told you, Matthew, that I was a little girl here during the witchcraft scares and trials of 1692."

"Surely you haven't."

"Nevertheless, it's true," she said, "I was."

I opened and closed my eyes a few times, hoping to bring everything, reality mostly, back into focus. "Could you possibly give me a few more details?"

"They accused my mother of being a witch. I don't know why. Probably because she wouldn't go to church, found it oppressive and intolerant. So they accused her of casting spells and mixing potions and visiting Satan in the middle of the night."

"À la Goody Brown," added Daniel from across the way.

"Yes, exactly," said Rachel. "But unlike Nathaniel's short story, they put my mother on trial. And after the trial she was found guilty of witchcraft and sentenced to hang."

I stood there wondering if I was meant to believe this tale.

"And who," Daniel asked me in a most demanding voice, "do you think was the judge at that trial? Who do you think handed down the guilty verdict, Mac? Who do you think passed sentence on Rachel's mother? Who do you think sentenced her to death?"

I knew the answer but it took me a few seconds to say it, to get it out. I swallowed hard, caught my breath. "Judge Hathorne?" I uttered the name very softly.

"The very same!" Daniel roared.

"And they made you watch?" I asked Rachel, now totally absorbed in the tragedy.

"Yes," she answered, "they made me watch. I can still see her dangling from that old chestnut tree, her fingers and toes twitching as the rope sucked the life out of her body."

I recalled then the day Daniel had hung himself before the football game. Rachel, I'm sure you remember, had been critical of his display, had labeled it a silly, childish prank. And I had unwittingly agreed with her. I had even encouraged her criticism of his adolescent antics. But his silly, childish prank had obviously had an underlying significance for her, a significance to which I had not been privy.

How little we know beyond our own feeble confusions.

Had the two of them discussed that significance? Had they shared an intimate moment about the hanging? Of course they had. I could see it on their faces as I stood there shivering on that cold gray knoll. They had no doubt talked about it at great length, just as they had talked about the connections and similarities between the atrocities at Dachau and at Andersonville, just as they had no doubt intimately discussed God knew what else.

My brain kept buzzing as I remembered all the times Daniel had made himself the judge during our youth, how he would sit up on the umpire's chair beside the tennis court and pass judgment on his peers, especially on me. I felt sure he and Rachel had discussed all that as well.

"I made Rachel watch," Daniel said next. "I told her that the woman with the noose around her neck was not her mother at all, but an evil witch, a devil worshiper."

"*You?*"

"Yes," he answered, "me. I am, after all, a reincarnation of my ancestor. I am the one who sentenced Rachel's mother to death."

It all came clear then. I saw there were things between them I could not touch, could not begin to understand. They were connected by some strange and invisible lifeline. It concerned the past and possibly, I feared, even the future.

And I couldn't do a damn thing about it. All I could do was wonder how it had come about and hope that one day soon it would go quietly away so Rachel and I could settle down in a small house behind a white picket fence with a couple of kids and a dog and grow old together while mankind drove itself and maybe the entire planet closer and closer to extinction.

THEY WERE FRIENDS, JUST GOOD FRIENDS. Or so they insisted whenever I broached the subject.

"She's your girl, Mac," was the oft repeated pronouncement I heard from Daniel. "All you have to do is make her happy."

Oh, was that all?

And from Rachel: "Don't be ridiculous, Matthew. Daniel is like a migrating bird, like the arctic tern, almost constantly in flight. You know I love him dearly, but I rarely think of him except when he comes to nest in my little corner of the universe."

"But the two of you have secrets."

"Secrets? Is that what you call them? What about the two of us? Don't we have secrets? You and me? And what about the two of you? Don't you have secrets? Don't you think there are things between you two that I don't know about? You had fifteen years of secrets before I knew either one of you. Really, Matthew, your jealousy is your least endearing quality."

And so, no doubt, it was. I did my best to stamp out its destructive flame, and for a time I actually thought I had the fire under control. Until, that is, Daniel called me one evening and asked me if he could use the house on Nantucket.

It must've been a little over a year after our trip to Salem, February or March of 1982. I was in my last few months of law school, growing more and more eager for my tour to end, for my real life to begin. Daniel had not asked me if he could use the beach house for several years, not since that terrible time four years earlier when I had discovered the two of them frolicking and fornicating on the living room rug.

So how did I respond to his request? "Sure," I said, "no problem. Go ahead. Knock yourself out. Have a good time." And then, immediately after hanging up, I called Rachel.

"Any plans this weekend?" I asked innocently.

"Actually," she answered, "I might go home for a few days. Daddy has the flu. I think he could use a little tender loving care. Maybe someone to make him a bowl of chicken soup."

Oh, sure, I thought, a little TLC. Bullshit. "That's sweet of you," I said.

We chatted for a few minutes long distance, my blood pressure rising with each word we spoke. I thought about throwing out an accusation right then and there. But somehow I managed to hold my tongue.

I knew what they had in mind. And no way was I going to stand for it. Screwing around behind my back was bad enough, but lying about it was more than I could take. So I decided to catch them in the act, bust in on them, and put an end to their charade once and for all.

I had to stew for three days. But very early Saturday morning, before dawn, after a sleepless night, I climbed into my car and took off like a madman for points north.

I had myself a Porsche 914 in those days. Remember those sporty little midengine coupes? Mine was used, of course, probably abused by the time I picked her up. She ran on nothing but a souped-up VW Beetle engine, but push the R.P.M.s high enough and she could fly. And man could she handle. I could carve that car through the turns without ever taking my foot off the gas pedal. It was as noisy and bumpy as a subway train but those were petty details. Behind the wheel, the hardtop stowed in the rear trunk, the wind blowing, you felt like a kid driving a go-cart, slipping in and out of traffic, zipping through the curves.

Too bad I killed that little pocket rocket on the way to Nantucket. That's right, my Porsche blew up on Route 6 about five miles west of Hyannis.

For seven hours I'd been pushing that car between four thousand and five thousand R.P.M.s. All the way up Interstate 95 through Jersey and New York and Connecticut I kept the pedal to the metal, seventy, seventy-five, eighty miles an hour. I'm amazed the state troopers didn't nail me. I never even looked for cops. My brain worked on only one cylinder. And in that cylinder was this vivid image of Daniel and Rachel pounding away before the hearth.

I should've kept my eye on my gauges. If I had, I surely would've seen the oil pressure dropping. But in those last few miles I drove even faster, even harder. I wanted in the worst way to make the noon ferry. And noon was fast approaching.

Then, suddenly, *bang!*—like a high-pressure tire bursting, but in this case not a tire but the overheated pistons exploding through their valve covers and shooting forth a small but very destructive gush of refined oil, seizing that little Porsche's engine solid, turning it into a scrap of warped and useless metal.

The cops came. They snickered behind my back at my misfortune. I had to have her towed. Left her at a service station on Route 28 in Hyannis and never looked back. Caught a cab over to the Ocean Street Terminal, where I waited an hour or so for the two-fifteen ferry.

I finally reached the island late in the afternoon after a rough and stormy crossing. The churning in my stomach, along with the unexpected demise of my Porsche, made me for a time forget all about the lusty travails going on at the Chandler house on Baxter Road. But now, as I walked away from the ferry, up Broad to Main, it all came back to me. My long journey once again had a sense of purpose.

The town was quiet, practically deserted. I had to search for a taxi to drive me out to the airport. I rented another Jeep. It looked as though it might've been the same one I had rented four years earlier. The man behind the counter looked the same also. For a moment, as I signed the rental agreement, I had the paranoid feeling he remembered me as the wacko who had rented the vehicle for a weekend but then returned it in less than an hour.

I signed quickly and made my escape. During the six-mile drive to Siasconset I did not pass another car. In town I saw a car or two parked in front of the general store but those cars looked as if they'd been there since Labor Day. I kept driving, slowly, through and out of town and then right onto Baxter. My heart beat at a pretty good clip.

I pulled into the driveway. This time there were two vehicles besides mine: another Jeep and some kind of small Ford. I figured they must've arrived separately. I didn't have the sense to wonder why they would've rented two cars. No. I was too keyed up for that, too consumed by anger and jealousy. My blood pressure was far too high for rational thought. I was damn close to brain damage as I climbed out of that Jeep and started toward the house.

I reminded myself not to hold back, to throw open that sliding glass door and barge right in regardless of what perverse sexual acts played on the living room floor.

It was cold, colder even than during my last off-season visit. The wind blew from dead north, an icy breeze that sent a shiver down my spine. I reached the southeast corner of the house and stepped out into the full force and fury of that northerly. I had, of course, forgotten to bring the right jacket, had grabbed nothing but a windbreaker in my haste that morning. It was as though I wore nothing at all.

I climbed the wooden stairs and marched across the porch. All the boards were off the windows and doors on the back of the house. I didn't even look through the glass. I didn't want to see inside; I feared if I looked first I might not be able to enter, I might once again run and hide. So I threw open that sliding glass door and stepped inside.

Three large bodies sprang to their feet in surprise. All of them were fully clothed, and not a female among them. Two of them I knew: Daniel and his father, Victor. The third man I had never seen before. At least that's what I thought at first. He was an older man, Victor's age, tall and thin, almost gaunt. He held a gun, a gigantic revolver, a Magnum .357 I learned later, in his right hand. The gun was pointed at my chest.

"Jesus H. Christ," I think I said.

"Mac!?" I think Daniel said. And then, "What the hell are you doing here?"

I didn't answer. I was so thoroughly relieved not to find him fucking Rachel on the floor that I stood there speechless, my mouth hanging wide open. I stared straight ahead at the barrel of that gun. It looked huge, like a cannon, much bigger than in the movies, big enough to bring down an elephant. Then the third man must've decided I did not pose a threat because he pulled back his jacket and stuffed the revolver into a leather holster hung across his shoulder.

That's when I recognized him. He was the man on the mountain in Austria, the man who had driven us to Prague, the man in the cafe in Zermatt. He had lost weight and no longer wore a beard, but it was definitely the same man.

A minute or two passed. No one said much. Victor asked how I was. Pretty well, I told him. And your mother and father? I shrugged, said I hadn't seen them in a while.

Another minute ticked away. The living room of that beachfront house did not lack for tension. These three had not gathered for a round of golf and drinks on the veranda. No, they had other stuff on their minds, secret stuff.

"Listen, Mac," said Daniel, "what do you say we take a walk?"

"A walk? Christ, it's freezing out there. Wind's blowing a gale."

"How 'bout a drive, then?"

"A drive? To where? I just drove eight hours to get here."

"We'll just go down to the general store. Buy a couple six-packs."

So that's what we did. It wasn't an invitation, after all, so much as an order. I was being expelled from my own house.

We went out through the sliding glass door and around the side of the house and climbed into my Jeep. I fired up the engine and backed out of the driveway. We didn't say a word.

Finally, down near the end of Baxter, I had to ask, figured I had the right to know. "So what the hell's going on?"

"What do you mean?"

"What do you mean, what do I mean, you know exactly what I mean."

The son of a bitch laughed.

"Christ," I said, "you told me you were coming out here but you didn't say a word about a fucking family reunion."

"Oh, you mean Max."

"I mean the guy with the freaking gun pointed at my chest. He's the guy from Austria, the guy from Zermatt."

"You have a good eye, Mac. Maybe you're going into the wrong line of work."

I ignored him. "So who is he?"

"Max? An old friend of Victor's, from the Old Country. A little high-strung but he's okay. The war, you know. He spent some time in the camps. Don't worry about him."

"But what the hell's he doing here? In my father's house? In the middle of winter?"

"He just stopped by to say hello."

"Jesus Christ!"

Now he ignored me. "The question is, what are you doing here?"

"I came to see you."

"You came all the way from Pennsylvania to see me?"

"That's right."

"Why did you do a dumb fool thing like that?"

I knew I couldn't tell him the truth. "I guess because I'm a dumb fool."

He laughed again. We pulled into the parking lot outside the general store.

I left the engine running. "So why does he have a gun?"

"Who? Oh. You know, protection."

"Oh, right. You can't be too careful on Nantucket. There's a regular goddamn crime wave sweeping the island."

"Murder and mayhem," he said.

"And why did you guys jump when I opened the door?"

"What do you mean, jump? We didn't jump."

"The hell you didn't. All three of you jumped out of your chairs like I'd walked in while you were sitting around plotting to kill somebody."

Daniel took his time with this one. "Oh, we'll kill him all right, just as soon as we get our chance, just as soon as we can find him."

"What? Find who?"

"Just some Nazi," he answered.

"Oh, yeah?"

"Yeah."

I looked at him. I wasn't too sure what to say next.

He helped me. "Bastard was in the SS. Tortured and killed five or six thousand Jews and Gypsies. He pulled out fingernails, chopped off fingers, chopped off hands and arms. I mean unbelievable shit. Shit that would make your stomach turn, make your skin crawl."

Mine was crawling all right. I sat there and suddenly realized I had started to shiver. It was cold in the Jeep but not that cold. I had no idea whether to believe him or not. He had told me so many tales. I felt for a moment it was a ruse, another of his stories, something to throw me off the trail.

"The son of a bitch," he continued, "got out of Europe after the war. There was a whole network in place to get the butchers out. This guy made it all the way to Argentina. He had money, probably money he'd stolen from the Jews and Gypsies he'd hacked to pieces."

I couldn't help myself. "So what happened to him in Argentina?"

"He married this beautiful woman from a wealthy family. Had himself a whole slew of kids. Later on, grandkids. Owned homes in Buenos Aires and out on the Pampas. Had a three-thousand-acre hacienda. Polo ponies. Racehorses. The whole bit."

"Sounds like quite a boy." I thought he'd laugh or at least smile, but he didn't.

"For thirty-five years he's gone along his merry way. Just a regular guy. Always gives plenty of money to the Catholic church, and to the right political parties, usually the parties who don't mind killing a few people to stay in power. But we're getting close. He'll get his due."

A whole bunch of small and seemingly unrelated details raced through my brain: Dachau, Victor's collection of firearms, the mysterious comings and goings of Max, the numerous times Daniel had disappeared that summer I had spent with him in Europe . . . "And what's his due?" I asked. "What's going to happen to him?"

Daniel pushed open the door of the Jeep and stepped out. I sat there waiting. He turned around, looked at me through the window. He raised his right index finger to his throat and made a very quick slashing movement under his chin from ear to ear. I swallowed hard as he moved toward the door of the Siasconset General Store and disappeared inside.

He bought a pint of Jack Daniel's. We drove around for a while, taking sips out of the bottle. We talked about me, about what I was going to do after I graduated from law school. I kept insisting I didn't know, but we both knew. We'd known since the beginning: I'd take a few weeks off, then I'd report for duty to the offices of Chandler, Wright & MacPherson, where I would work for the next forty years until I retired, languished, and died, probably of a massive heart attack brought on by stress, overwork, and a diet high in fat and alcohol.

How nice for me.

I tried to get more information out of him about the guy back at the house with the gun and about the Nazi down in Argentina, but he refused to say another word. "I've told you too much already, Mac. You're a hell of a lot better off not knowing."

I told him that sounded like bullshit, like something from a bad movie, but no matter how hard I probed, he easily deflected my inquiries.

Dusk had fallen by the time we got back to the house. When we pulled into the driveway the small Ford was gone. I glanced at Daniel. He looked the other way.

The wind still howling, we walked around the side of the house and through the sliding glass door. Victor sat on the sofa staring out the window at the black sea and sipping a glass of Dewar's, Dear Old Dad's Dewar's. The open bottle rested on the coffee table on top of a back issue of *Yachting* magazine.

"Your guest left?" I asked after I had closed the door.

Victor nodded. "He had a plane to catch."

"To where?" I asked. "Buenos Aires?"

Victor glanced at me, then at his son. I watched Daniel carefully for some sign, some clue, some evidence of collusion. But he only smiled and shrugged his shoulders.

"Right," Victor said after a moment, "Buenos Aires. City of good air and evil water."

September 9, 1990

RACHEL ANN FREDERICK, ALIAS MISTY GREY, *paints in the darkness. It is more than an hour after midnight. Outside, the only light comes from a crescent of waning moon. Inside the loft of the old red barn, there is an almost complete absence of light. And to further add to her own darkness, Rachel has covered her eyes with a red bandanna.*

She stands before the canvas, her movements slow and deliberate. She turns, passes her narrow brush over the wide, wooden palette, and dips the bristles gently into one of the pools of colored oil. Then, with an unexpected swiftness, Rachel brings the brush to the canvas and applies the paint. Over and over this same routine passes the night.

The first very faint traces of dawn show through the windows before Rachel backs away from the canvas and removes the bandanna. She turns on a light but does not bother to look at the painting. Instead she crosses to the kitchen and puts a kettle on the stove.

She makes a cup of tea and sits at her desk. After a few moments she begins to write.

> *Dear Papa,*
>
> *I have nearly finished another blind painting. This time I have made a self-portrait. It is wild with colors and broad strokes. My confidence soars. In the painting I am huge with child; I would say easily twice my normal size. And the face, oh, wait till you see the face. Extraordinary! I do not know myself if it is joy or pain etched into that expression. Time will tell.*
>
> *As soon as the oils permit I will ship the canvas off to New York. The gallery assures me it will sell. But then, haven't they all?*
>
> *I know you think enough is enough, I should come clean, but really, I keep asking myself, why? The paintings I do with my*

eyes wide open are always signed by Misty, and have been since I arrived in this small town a year ago.

Only those I do in the dark receive my signature: RAF. So what, I wonder, is the harm? This way I get to pursue two careers: one already established and one still struggling for that big break. The combination offers so much hope and at the same time so much security.

I am sure you will offer me an alternative viewpoint on this matter. And of course, as always, I look forward to your comments, both as my father and as my friend. Where would I be without you?

October 1 has been firmly set for the date of the closing, so surely I will see you then. And no doubt I will talk to you before that. I'll call you when I get back from Nantucket.

> *Love,*
> *Rachel*

I GOT MUGGED ON MY FIRST DAY as a full-time resident of New York City. I should've seen it coming, should've seen it as an omen, should've packed up my just unpacked bags and blown town for points east and more watery.

I wanted to kill the son of a bitch, just a kid, really, a white kid, not much past puberty, after he robbed and humiliated me and ran off with my wallet containing all my IDs, a couple hundred bucks in cash, and my brand spanking new American Express card, ultimate symbol of my economic independence. And I would've killed him, would've slammed his head repeatedly against the sidewalk, had I been able to catch him, had I even pursued him.

Oh, yeah, right, Matthew Chandler, a real tough guy, a regular killer. Okay, so maybe I wasn't the one who plunged the Bowie knife into that hobo's chest in the railroad yard out in Huntingdon, Pennsylvania. Sure, Daniel was the one, it was his fingerprints on the knife, not mine, but still, I was there, I hushed it up. I was an accomplice, an accessory to murder. If I could aid and abet, couldn't I also commit? Especially under duress?

The mugging took place on December 1, 1982. That was the day I moved into my first Manhattan digs down on Tenth Street, a real wide-open spread that one, must've had almost a hundred square feet of living space, a virtual palace for opulent urban living.

Oh, I forgot, this isn't *Metropolitan Life*. Time to backtrack.

I flew out of Nantucket a few days after I found Daniel holed up with Victor and their pal Max. I flew to Philadelphia, then caught a bus back to school. For the next few months I worked reasonably hard at being a law student. And on the last day of May, with Rachel and Mom and Pop in attendance, the dean rewarded my efforts with a diploma declaring that I had the right to call myself an attorney. Hip hip hooray! My long and arduous educational journey had finally come to an end.

Sort of. I still had to pass the bar, which, as I mentioned earlier, proved no small chore. A full year slipped away before I became a sanctioned member of the New York State Bar. But that didn't matter. A little thing like failing the bar exam a couple of times didn't keep Dear Old Dad from putting me on the payroll at Chandler, Wright & MacPherson.

I had my very own office right from the start, albeit small and windowless, but my own private space with a desk and a telephone and a shared secretary nevertheless.

But before I began my distinguished law career at Chandler, Wright & MacPherson, I took eight weeks' vacation. And what did I do with all that free time? Well, for a few weeks I did nothing. I hung around the house, slept late, watched TV. I got ready for the eighties.

Then Rachel and I spent a whole month together, four delicious weeks, seven days a week, twenty-fours hours a day. We borrowed Daniel's VW camper-van and headed north. He didn't need it; he was over in Europe banging tennis balls and tennis groupies, maybe hunting down old Nazis on the run. Who knows? I didn't know.

We drove to Maine, camped for a few days at Acadia National Park. We climbed the Precipice on Cadillac Mountain, swam in the ice-cold ocean, ate fresh lobsters on a park bench right in the middle of downtown Bar Harbor.

When the crowds started to bother us, we headed inland. We drove up through Bangor and camped along the Penobscot, then north on Route 2 through Lincoln and Millinocket, and west into Baxter State Park.

We camped for almost a week at the floor of Mount Katahdin. Never once did we get the urge to climb that mountain. We just looked at it. A few times Rachel sketched it. I lay there in a meadow as soft as a pile of goose-down feathers and stared for hours at that peak and the blue sky beyond. I hadn't felt that good, that relaxed, since my first spring with Rachel down at the academy.

At night, after we cooked our hamburgers or our chicken wings on the open fire, we made love. Making love for us—for me, anyway, and I think for Rachel as well—often just meant being close: hugging, kissing, giggling, not saying much, maybe not saying anything at all. We did it in the van, we did it out by the fire, we did it under the stars.

And as you might expect, I asked her again, for the second time, to marry me.

She laughed, lightly. In the firelight I saw her lips curl up. "You don't want to marry me, Matthew," she said. "I'd be a horrible person to marry. I'm selfish, arrogant, egotistical, self-centered. I work at all hours of the day and night. Sometimes I paint for twenty-four hours straight without stopping to go to the bathroom. And you know how I hate to be interrupted, how I hate to have my concentration snapped."

"I know," I said, "I know all those things. But none of those things make any difference to me. None of those things matter. I still love you and I still want to marry you and be with you forever, all the time."

"And I love you," she said, "and I want to be with you. But not all the time, not every single day. Not married, Matthew. Being married would ruin it."

So once again, that was that. I though about trying my powers of persuasion but feared I would ruin our idyllic retreat in the back woods of Maine. Besides, I felt like time was on my side. I had my law degree, I'd soon be working in Manhattan, not far from where she lived. Once I saved some money I'd move to the city. We'd see each other regularly then, several times a week, maybe more. Little by little, day by day, I would wear her down, win her over.

My first day on the job, a Monday in early August, was one of the hottest days on record in New York City. I'd sweated through my new lightweight poplin Brooks Brothers suit even before Chuckie and I reached the offices of Chandler, Wright & MacPherson on Trinity Place.

I started to sweat on the train from Morristown to Hoboken. And I literally began to drip as I waited in line to deposit my quarters in the turnstile so I could board the PATH train to the World Trade Center. The last time I'd waited in line to reach those turnstiles was the morning Daniel and I had run off on our cross-country railroad adventure. Standing there in my suit and tie, virtually empty briefcase in hand, perspiration flowing off my brow, I distinctly remember thinking my youth had come to an abrupt and ugly end.

I commuted to and from the job with Dear Old Dad for almost four months. I saw more of him during those four months than I had in the previous eight or nine years. The guy was right there every time I turned around. And he was constantly offering advice, telling me how to walk and talk and wear my suit and shine my shoes. By the end of that first week I hated his guts more than I ever had in my whole life. By the end of my second week I wanted to quit, tell the old man to take his job and shove it. And eventually I did exactly that; it just took me most of a decade to find the courage to do it.

Life during my early days at Chandler, Wright & MacPherson can best be described as an embarrassment. I knew I had no right being there, and everyone else knew I had no right being there, and I knew they knew I had no right being there, and they knew I knew they knew... and around and around and around it went. I just tried to be nice. I think all I've ever really wanted is for people to like me.

But I was there to practice law, financial law in particular. I was supposed to make sure the big-time money brokers who were our clients stayed within the confines of the law. I was like a life guard who had to blow his whistle when the movers and shakers ventured out beyond the breakers.

My duties went far beyond that, however. It didn't take me long to realize that Chandler, Wright & MacPherson was, in reality, a counseling firm. And we offered far more than just legal counsel. We were psychologists and priests and baby-sitters as well as lawyers.

"If they come in and start crying on your shoulder," Dear Old Dad advised, "just sit there and listen. Sometimes you don't need to say a word. Often they don't want you to say a word. Let them confess their sins."

"Say what?" I was new on the job. I didn't get it. I thought I had come on board to practice law.

Chuckie explained. "The most important thing for you to do is keep track of your time. Time is money, Matthew. We bill them for the use of your time whether you're working out the details of a major corporate merger or listening to some joker moan and groan about his wife's Bloomingdale's habit or his kid's cocaine habit. It's all billable, son, every last second of it. And remember"—and he leaned a little closer—"always round off to the next highest hour. An hour and twenty minutes is two hours. Two hours and forty minutes is three hours. And so on and so forth. Understand?"

I assured the covetous pig that I understood perfectly.

"Good." He slapped me on the back, old buddy style, and added, "Another thing to keep in mind: Never commit yourself; always leave yourself an opening."

"Right," I said, and then I retreated to my windowless cubicle to reevaluate my personal values and multiply my billable hours times the firm's rather hefty hourly rate.

Behind closed doors Dear Old Dad might've ridiculed and verbally castrated the mighty men who were his clients, but when they were actually in the same room together, look out: Chuckie would turn on the old Chandler charm. He was one two-faced son of a bitch.

Many of the firms and families who used Chandler, Wright & MacPherson for their legal work had been with us since before the Great Depression. You might call it a time-honored tradition among financial folks, especially rich, white, Anglo-Saxon, Protestant, Wall Street types, to carry business relationships from one generation to the next. I assume this has to do with trust, or at least the perception of trust: my daddy got filthy rich using your daddy as his attorney, therefore I'll use you as my attorney.

A very sweet deal for all concerned.

Anyway, the mugging. I survived my four months on the commuter trail with Chuckie Chandler. And I saved my money, more than half of every paycheck. By October I was on the mad search for a Manhattan apartment, not a pleasant experience.

After checking out more than two dozen roach-infested rat traps, Rachel found the place down on Tenth Street between Fifth Avenue and University Place, just above Washington Square Park. I balked at its minuscule size when I first entered but she seemed so enthusiastic that I took a look around. It didn't take long, about thirty seconds. It was clean, I'll give it that, spotless even. And it had new carpet. So I signed.

Besides, her loft down on Greene Street was only about a ten-minute walk away through the park. I couldn't get much closer than that without moving in with her.

So on December 1, 1982, I rented a van to haul my stuff in from Jersey. I didn't have much: a bed, a few chairs, a folding table, a lamp or two, a nine-inch black-and-white TV, my stereo, some books, my clothes. Lucky that's all I had because not a whole lot more would've fit into that cell.

Rachel helped me carry everything up the four flights of narrow stairs. It was actually a pretty nice building. It had once been a very desirable address before someone chopped up the spacious apartments into small rectangular hovels. Once I stuffed my few meager possessions into the corners I barely had room to turn around. No place at all to do sit-ups.

"Looks like an excellent place to breed poverty and discontent."

Rachel told me to quit complaining. "Come on," she said, "I'll take you out for Chinese to celebrate your arrival in the Big Apple."

We walked down to Chinatown for moo shu and sweet and sour. We drank Chinese beer. I had several. More than I needed.

After the meal I walked her home. All the way up Canal Street with car horns blasting and trucks spewing noxious fumes into the cold and polluted air, I tried to convince Rachel to come back to my apartment and spend the night. "We'll continue the celebration."

"Not tonight, Matthew. I'm in the middle of something that can't wait till morning."

I'd hear that one often enough before it was all over.

Still, I worked on her as we walked up Broadway, but my efforts proved futile. As had always been the case, and would prove to be the case in the future, her application of paint to canvas was an enticement with which I could not compete.

So on an unusually quiet night in Soho, we kissed and said good night on the threshold of her loft. Five minutes later I was lost.

Don't ask me how it happened. It's pretty much a straight shot up Greene Street to the park, then through the park to Tenth. A dog could do it. But I must've turned left on Houston because all of a sudden I was over on Carmine and this kid comes out of the shadows, and as if it were a movie or something, he has on this long trench coat with his right hand buried in the pocket like he has a gun, and he says, "That's far enough, mister. Up against the wall."

I laugh like it's a joke or something but then I feel what I figure is a gun barrel press against my ribs. I freeze, move my eyes just enough to get a look at my attacker.

"Don't look at my face, stupid," he mumbles in a low voice, "or I'll blow a hole through your stomach the size of a grapefruit."

I close my eyes and start to sweat and prepare to die. But I don't die. Well, maybe just a little.

He rips my wallet from my hip pocket, then grabs the waist of my corduroy trousers and pulls downward. The waistband tears. The zipper breaks. He lets go and the pants collapse around my ankles. He laughs, the little bastard, and runs off, back into the shadows.

Humiliating? Yes. You might say that. I had to walk all the way back to my cell holding up my pants through the pockets of my jacket. But along the way I taught myself a few simple lessons. Paramount among them was this: Never, under any circumstances, appear lost while walking around New York City. Even when lost always walk straight ahead as though you know exactly where you're going. Keep your head level and your eyes slightly down. Don't look around. Don't gawk. Don't pay any attention to anyone else, not even if they're being brutalized by a pack of thugs. Mind your own business. Stay the course.

That dirty little drug addict had no doubt picked me out as a greenhorn the second he saw me. I'd been walking along with my head bobbing all over the place, trying to get my bearings, asking directions, staring at all the street signs, stopping, starting, turning around, walking in circles. He must've seen me and thought, Look at that jerk-off. He's definitely my next fix.

Welcome to the Greatest City in the World.

I SETTLED INTO THE ROUTINE. Days and weeks and months came and just as quickly went. Time moved swiftly, much more swiftly than it had ever moved for me before. This hasty passage both thrilled and frightened me.

Sally Ride flew into outer space aboard the *Challenger*, the first American woman ever to do so. Maybe it wasn't as momentous as Neil Armstrong setting foot on the lunar surface, but Rachel and I toasted the launch anyway with a bottle of French champagne and our own private two-person ticker-tape parade.

Most of that year and part of the next passed without a visit from Daniel. He seemed to have vanished, gone the way of the Ancient Mariner. Rachel talked about him sometimes, quite regularly, in fact, certainly more than I would have preferred. I did my best not to hear her, to let her tangle of emotion and nostalgia go in one ear and out the other. Out of sight, my old buddy did not seem like much of a threat.

My long-range plan began to take effect: Rachel and I spent more and more time together. I passed the night at her loft at least two or three nights a week. I had clothes in her closet, shoes and sneakers on the braided throw rug beside her front door, a toothbrush hanging in the holder above her bathroom sink.

Occasionally she even spent the night on Tenth Street—not very often; she didn't really enjoy passing time in my cell. She'd told me at the outset not to worry about the diminutive size of my domicile but I quickly learned that my apartment with its low ceilings and poor ventilation made her feel claustrophobic. She much preferred the high ceilings and tall walls of glass and uncluttered square footage of her loft in Soho.

We worked hard; it was the eighties, after all. I got used to making money. I got used to spending money. I always went out for lunch, frequently went out for dinner. My tiny fridge rarely contained more than a quart of milk and quart of orange juice, maybe a stick of butter and a box of éclairs from the bakery over on Greenwich Avenue.

I had a house charge at Barney's Men's Shop at Seventh Avenue and

Seventeenth Street. I became known as the Beau Brummel of Chandler, Wright & MacPherson. For years I had dressed in cords or khakis and a blue or white oxford. But suddenly my desire for fashionable threads became practically insatiable. Barney's clerks and tailors knew me by name.

I didn't go for the conservative look, either. I went radical. More than once the old man had to reprimand me for the unconventional cut of my suits. I owned several that I only wore to the office once. As soon as Chuckie would spot me stepping down the walnut-paneled main corridor of Chandler, Wright & MacPherson, he'd pull me aside and tell me Wall Street lawyers of our breed did not dress in flashy double-breasted Christian Dior silk suits.

"And why not?" I'd ask.

"Because I said so," the boss would answer, and then he'd strut away in his worsted pinstripes, always adding over his shoulder, "Wear it again and you're out of here."

Of course, I should've worn it the very next day, should've worn it with a pair of white patent-leather shoes and a mink fedora, and I should've kept wearing it until the old man put his threat into action. I should've forced him to fire me. It would've been the best thing in the world for me, my ticket to ride, my own personal thirteenth amendment to the as yet unwritten and undeclared Chandler constitution. Maybe it would've made a man out of me.

But what did I do? I hung Christian Dior carefully in my closet and only wore him when Rachel and I ventured uptown for a fancy night of dining and dancing.

You see, not only did I still have walnuts the size of flea eggs, but perhaps even worse, I was getting used to the good life, the high life, a life of position and money.

By this time, and I'm talking late '83, early '84, I'd passed the law boards, straightened out a couple of muddled accounts, shown a certain flair for uncovering legal loopholes, even proved a steady and moderate voice in the midst of tumultuous negotiations. I actually began to earn the respect of my co-workers. Maybe, I heard them whisper over the *whrrr* of the copier, he has that old Chandler touch after all.

Now, I must confess, a shadow of a smile rippled across my face as I slipped into my office to rub my grubby little hands together in private.

And then, in the summer of '84, while poor Walter Mondale and his pet Ferraro were out on the stump trying to scrounge up a few votes for humanity, I discovered I had power. Yes, power, that oldest of all the vices, the great corruptor, the ultimate weapon of the insecure. As if by magic, people began to listen when I spoke. They sought my counsel, my advice. They actually did what I told them to do. Poor blind sheep.

I started to walk around town like I was hot shit. I went out for power lunches and yucked it up with the power brokers over power martinis. I used to go back to the office half-drunk and crash through those double glass doors bearing the family name, this stink-eating grin on my face. I would've been thrown out on my ear except for one thing: my power plays worked. I played the power game well; it must've been something long dormant in my genes.

What the hell, you're probably wondering, is he talking about? Clients, that's what I'm talking about, new clients, fresh sources of revenue for the already swollen coffers of Chandler, Wright & MacPherson. Yes, little old me, little Mac Chandler, brought in new clients, hot new clients, rich new clients, young lion types eating raw meat over at the Exchange. I wined and dined them, fed their egos, even let them beat me at squash, and in return they gave Chandler, Wright & MacPherson all of their abundant legal work.

For my efforts I got a bigger office, one with a window overlooking Trinity Church. I got a huge mahogany desk. I got my own private secretary who screened my calls and typed my letters. I got a raise, then another raise, then another raise. By the time Reagan took his second oath of office on January 20, 1985, I was hauling in close to two grand a week.

"Don't let it go to your head, Matthew," the old boy advised.

But I did. I found myself occasionally swaggering down Wall Street. But then, in those days, everyone on Wall Street swaggered. Even the messenger boys drove Beamers and wore Perry Ellis suits. I had a 944 in fire engine red. A brand new one this time. But I didn't keep my Porsche in the city. No way. Too dangerous. I kept it out in Mendham, out in Mom and Dad's garage. I drove it only on weekends, warm and sunny weekends. I became a yuppie.

Rachel pretended not to notice. You might say she looked the other way. At least for a while. When finally she did decide to voice her opinion she would only say things like "Don't worry about it, Matthew, it'll pass." Or "Be patient, you'll get over it." Or "Every little boy likes new toys. I'm sure it's just a phase."

"What do you mean it's just a phase?" I'd ask. "What do you mean I'll get over it? Get over what?"

She wouldn't say, would only smile at me with those beautiful dark blue eyes.

Rachel continued to live simply, as always. She had little interest in possessions. If she didn't need it to stay alive or to make her paintings, she didn't have it. In this way she was like her father. And I suppose also like Daniel. I was the only glutton in the group.

In the summer she even grew tomatoes and peppers and green beans on the roof of her building. She kept them covered with a clear plastic to keep off the dirt and grime. They were the best vegetables I ever ate, always picked perfectly ripe just prior to consumption.

Little by little, day by day, contact by contact, Rachel began to create some interest in her work. By this time she knew practically every gallery owner and painter in Soho, Tribeca, and Greenwich Village. She had learned how to play the game. And at just the right time.

Every young stockbroker and money manager in town wanted to own original works of art. They spent their weekends prowling the chic galleries between Houston and Broome searching for stuff they could hang on their walls. These baby boomers had piles of cash, and they'd buy almost anything if someone told them it reeked of undiscovered genius.

So the gallery owners began to search out the work of unknown artists. Rachel, it could be said, found herself in the right place at the right time. She had stacks of paintings ready to roll out the door. And roll they did, one after another, some of them for prices that would make your mouth water.

"You criticize and cop attitudes," I liked to kid her, "on the yuppies and the way they throw their money around, but you are a direct benefactor of this economic windfall."

She always responded to my taunts in the same way. "I enjoy the recognition," she'd say, "but I could live without it."

I felt sure she could.

But she didn't have to. The paintings continued to sell, the cash continued to flow, the praise for her work grew and grew. She had several admirers who purchased her paintings in bulk, as though they feared rationing or perhaps some kind of artistic famine.

There was one young lion in particular. He was a trader, very quick on his feet, younger than yours truly, wore nothing but silk in summer and cashmere in winter, a real mover and shaker. I know for a fact he made in excess of a million bucks a year during the mid-eighties. He bought half a dozen of Rachel's paintings for close to twenty grand. Paid cash. Asked the artist out for dinner. Wined and dined her. Told her he wanted to hang her paintings in his cottage in the Hamptons. Asked her if she wanted to come out and help him hang.

She told me all this the following afternoon. Said she'd been flattered but had declined his offer. I asked her straight away if she'd slept with him. She slapped me across the face and walked out of that posh new restaurant at the corner of Bleecker and Sullivan where the young and well-to-do gathered for Sunday brunch. She left me sitting there, alone, with a plate of eggs Benedict and two still warm golden-brown croissants. She didn't speak to me for a week.

Besides painting ten or twelve hours a day, Rachel was also teaching. She taught classes at Cooper Union in oil painting and watercolors. She enjoyed teaching, just as her father did, because, they said, it constantly gave them fresh impressions on their own work.

Every few months Coach Frederick would come to town for a visit. He always stayed at the loft in Soho, which meant I was banished to my cell on Tenth Street until he returned to Mercersburg. Still, I enjoyed his visits. He always asked the right questions.

The three of us would go out for dinner, usually to Ruggero's down in Little Italy. "So," my old prep school football coach would ask, "when are you two getting married? When are you going to start a family? This old bird's ready to become a grandfather."

Yeah, I'd ask without actually asking, when *are* we getting married?

The answer always sounded the same. "You might be ready to be a grandfather, Papa, but I'm not at all ready to be a mother."

Still, in retrospect, we were practically married. I don't think you could get a whole lot more married without actually having the proper papers. We rarely made a move the other did not know about. We saw each other almost every single day. We went to the movies together, ate most of our meals together, went on vacation together, read *The New York Times* together on Sunday morning, laughed at the same cartoons in *The New Yorker*, fought over which brands of toothpaste and toilet paper and breakfast cereal to buy.

But we also had time to ourselves. Rachel could be alone when she needed to be alone. And so could I. In the terminology of the day, we both had our own space. We weren't constantly using the same bathroom or the same hairbrush or the same bed. If Rachel wanted to listen to music, I could walk a few blocks to my cell and read a book or do some work. If I wanted to watch something on TV, the Yanks or an old war movie, she could head back to her loft and take a nap or paint up a storm. We could get out of each other's way without marching off in a huff of hostility and resentment.

I wasn't willing to admit it then, or perhaps I was just too blind to see it; maybe I'm just beginning to see it now, but really we had it pretty good in those days, the best of both worlds and all that. Too bad I couldn't just leave things well enough alone. Too bad I had to keep applying the pressure, demanding more commitment.

Too bad I had to worry all the time about losing her, about having her stolen right out from under my nose. Too bad I was so damn paranoid and insecure. Too bad I was such an asshole. Too bad I didn't just treat her like a friend, my best friend, maybe the best friend I will ever have.

Too bad.

AND SO, INEVITABLY, TRAGEDY STRUCK. It struck on Monday, September 23, 1985.

That morning I woke up alone in my Tenth Street apartment. I took a shower, just like always. I washed my hair, soaped my pits, shaved my whiskers, and brushed my teeth—all under the warm stream of water pouring out of the shower head.

Rachel was not with me that morning. She'd gone back to the loft the night before, after I had made yet another push for us to have a common apartment. I used all the same arguments I'd been using for years: more practical, less expensive, more efficient, less traveling back and forth, easier, simpler, blah blah blah blah blah.

"I'm going home now," Rachel said over coffee—or was it cappuccino?—at the cafe next to the Waverly Twin Cinema. We'd just seen William Hurt and Raul Julia in *Kiss of the Spider Woman*. "This conversation," she added, "is getting boring."

"Wait," I said, "I'll walk you."

"I'll walk myself," she said, and she was gone.

I called her as soon as I got home. No answer. I called every ten minutes for the next hour. Finally she picked up the receiver. "Okay," she said without bothering to say hello, "I'm home. Safe and sound. Snug as a bug in a rug. Go to bed." Click.

I went to bed but I didn't sleep. I lay there tossing and turning and listening to the air conditioner hum and fretting about what I'd said. Rachel didn't like to be pushed, definitely she didn't like to be cornered, but dammit, we weren't getting any younger. I'd turn thirty in less than a year. And she'd be right behind me. So from midnight pretty much until the alarm went off at 6:45, I lay there between the sheets and wondered if it would ever happen, wondered if Rachel would ever turn domestic.

I got to the office at 8:30. I wanted to call her right away but there was this jerk-off client waiting for me who had to discuss some jerk-off deal he wanted to make the second the stock exchange opened for business.

It was 9:15 before I finally dialed her number. No answer. It was a Monday; she didn't have a class until the middle of the afternoon. Usually on Monday mornings she painted until eleven or twelve o'clock. But sometimes, when things were going good, she wouldn't even hear the telephone ring. The ringing would just be a vague noise in the background.

Still, I persisted. I wanted to talk. I wanted to explain. The Great Explainer wanted to set everything right. So I called every fifteen minutes. I let it ring twenty-five, thirty times every time I called. No answer.

Finally, about 11:30, after at least ten unanswered calls, I buzzed my secretary and told her I had an unscheduled lunch appointment uptown and probably wouldn't be back before two o'clock. She accepted my little white lie without question.

I caught a cab on the corner of Wall Street and Broadway and ordered the driver to head for Soho. It was a warm and muggy morning on what might've been the last day of summer. Or maybe it was the first day of fall. It was hot, that much I remember, hot and humid.

I knocked on her door. She didn't come. I knocked louder. Still she didn't come. So I got out my key. I didn't use the key she'd given me very often because I knew she considered it a violation of her private space. This time, however, I felt justified. You see, I'd convinced myself that something had happened, that she had fallen in the tub or swallowed some paint or been robbed and beaten, and was inside, unconscious and in need of emergency care.

So I unlocked the door and pushed it open. "Rachel!" I shouted. "Are you here?"

I looked everywhere, even under the bed and in the closets. No Rachel. So I sat down and waited. I waited over an hour. I read a newspaper, the *Village Voice*, I think. I ate a salad I found in the refrigerator. I drank a glass of wine. And I waited some more.

Then I went out and walked around the neighborhood. I walked up Greene and down Wooster and up West Broadway. I stuck my head inside several of her favorite galleries. She was nowhere in sight. So I walked, marched actually, over to Cooper Union. I went upstairs and asked the art department secretary if she'd seen Ms. Frederick.

The girl was busy typing a letter and smacking a piece of pink bubble gum between her teeth. "Haven't seen her, no," she answered without looking up, "but I talked to her. She called this morning and told me to cancel her class. So I hung a note on the door."

"Cancel her class! How come?"

"I dunno. Said she had personal business."

"Personal business? What kind of personal business?"

It must've been my tone that made the young Hispanic woman glance up and give me the once-over. No doubt she saw another ugly American male. "Hey, how would I know? I take messages. I don't get paid to ask questions."

I headed back to the loft. Along the way I tried to remember if Rachel had told me about any personal business on the day's agenda. I couldn't think of a damn thing.

I unlocked the door and went inside. I sat down and read another magazine, maybe the same magazine; mostly I looked at the pictures. I telephoned my apartment, thinking, wrongly, she might be there. I waited until three o'clock. Then I headed downtown, back to the office. Sitting in the cab as we sped down Broadway, I noticed the sky had turned from brown to gray. Clouds had rolled in. A breeze had kicked up. Litter swirled above the street.

"Heard the weather?" I asked the cabbie.

"Thunderstorms," he answered. "And glad of it. Maybe it'll cool things off."

I reached the office at 3:20. I dialed her number; no answer. I decided to settle down, relax, try to do some work. There were some papers to sign, some contracts that needed tightening. I remember the old man came in to see me. He wanted to know where I'd been all afternoon.

"Lunch," I told him.

"We don't take four-hour lunches at Chandler, Wright and MacPherson," he announced.

I wanted to tell him to go play with himself but instead I told another little white lie. "I was with a very important potential client, Dad. He's talking major takeovers. I didn't think it was good politics to cut him off because you don't believe in four-hour lunches."

He considered my slight, then moved on. "So who's this hotshot?"

I made up a name.

"Never heard of him. Who's he with?"

I gave him the name of a major broker.

He sniffed the air, seemed satisfied. "Keep me posted."

I assured him I would, every step of the way. As soon as he left I called Rachel. No answer. Every few minutes for the rest of the afternoon I called again.

Finally, about five o'clock, I admitted to myself what had been bothering me for the past eight hours. I hadn't really expected to find Rachel wiped out in the bathtub; that was just a smoke screen. I had expected to find her there with him, with Daniel. My old buddy. My old pal. I could feel his presence. And I knew his presence had something to do with Rachel's absence. The son of a bitch had been gone for months, but now, I could tell, he was back.

But where, I wondered, were they this time? Nantucket? Georgia? Salem? South America? Czechoslovakia? The freaking moon, for chrissakes?

I hemmed and hawed and pulled out my hair for a few more minutes, and then do you know what I did? I called the Hawthorn Compound out in Mendham. I knew the number by heart. Still do. Probably never forget it as long as I live.

"Hello?"

"Mrs. Hawthorn?"

"Matthew?" She recognized my voice immediately. It could've been fifteen years earlier. I could've been that teenager again whose heart beat a little faster every time I heard her speak.

I almost cried. But instead I wondered if perhaps she was naked and wandering among the orchids. "How are you, Mrs. Hawthorn?"

"I think you're old enough to call me Carolyn now, Matthew," she said.

And so I did. And so we exchanged pleasantries for a few minutes, caught up on all the latest news. I continued to imagine her out there in the greenhouse, pruning and watering in the buff, and for a time I wanted to confess my adolescent love for her, spill my churning guts, ask her if she might want to meet me somewhere sometime on the sly. Fortunately I refrained.

Finally I asked, "So, I was wondering if Daniel was around."

"He is, yes. . . ."

I knew it!

"He's not here right now, but. . ."

But nothing! I'd heard all I needed to hear. That son of a bitch! That wicked witch! Damn them!

"I expect him back later this evening. He has a first-round match in a tournament over at Forest Hills in the morning."

I decided to remain civil, if only to procure a little more information. "He hasn't been playing many tournaments lately."

"No, not too many. And this one is really just an exhibition, a bunch of players from the New York metropolitan area. A fund-raiser, I believe."

"I see. So where is he now? Practicing?"

"Actually, Matthew, he told me he might go into the city this morning. I figured he was going to visit you and Rachel."

One of us, anyway! "Well, I haven't seen him. Not yet."

"I just hope he's all right. He bought a motorcycle the other day. I hate those machines."

"A motorcycle!?"

"Yes, his van broke down, and when he found out it would take several weeks to order the parts he just went out and bought this cycle. I could've killed him."

"Sounds like something Daniel would do."

"I suppose."

I had to get off the phone. I'd started to sweat. My body was jumping around inside my suit. "Well," I said, "maybe just tell him I called, and uhh, have him call me sometime."

It took a few more minutes but finally we hung up.

I paced around the office, called the loft again. Still no answer.

I looked out the window. The sky had turned black. It was only 5:30, but it looked like the middle of the night. And then, suddenly, a tremendous clap of thunder exploded over the building, a bolt of lightning lit up the steeple on Trinity Church.

I trembled and left the office. More thunder and lightning. Rain fell in great torrents. The temperature felt as though it had dropped fifteen degrees since I had last been outside.

I found a cab. We started uptown. But after sitting in bumper-to-bumper traffic for what seemed like an hour, I paid the driver and headed for the nearest subway.

Half an hour later, soaking wet and fumbling with the keys to the loft, I heard Rachel's telephone ringing. I dropped the key, picked it up, shoved it in the lock. The phone continued to ring. I pushed open the door, sprinted across the wooden floor, picked up the receiver. But the caller had given up, the ringing had stopped.

I slumped down on a chair next to the kitchen table. I felt nauseated, a little dizzy. I put my head down on the table, closed my eyes. If I fell asleep, it was only for a brief moment or two, no longer. The telephone rang again.

I jumped, snatched the receiver off the cradle. "Hello?"

"Matthew?"

"Yes?"

"It's Coach Frederick."

"Yes?" My heart raced at full throttle.

"I've been trying to reach you."

"Yes?"

"There's been an accident."

DANIEL HAWTHORN, ALIAS DANIEL ROMANKOVA, *sits at the bar of the Shortwave Bar & Grill in Marion, Massachusetts, just a few miles west of Cape Cod, just a few days shy of his rendezvous with Rachel in Hyannis.*

The Shortwave is dark and smoky and not crowded. A small group of men sit and stand at the far end of the bar. They argue in Portuguese while they throw darts at a much used board on the wall.

The bartender, a middle-age woman with dark hair and an impatient manner, informs Daniel the catch of the day is cod, the soup seafood chowder.

Daniel wants to know how much.

"Not much," *she says, her accent Portuguese.* "This not Boston or Nantucket."

"Yeah, I know, but how much?"

"How much you got?"

"I got ten bucks."

"For ten bucks you get the soup, the fish, some rice, and two beers."

"What kind of beer?"

"You a wise guy?"

Daniel laughs. "No, I just wanted to see if I could get you to smile."

"I not smile in ten years."

"Why not?"

"Because ten years ago I come to America."

"You don't like America?"

"No, my husband, the one down there making all the noise, he want to come. Want to make money, lots of money. So I'm his wife. I got to come, too. But what about my sisters and my mother? They no come. Twice in ten years I see them. All we do is work. What's the use?" *The woman sighs and throws up her arms.* "So, you want to eat?"

"Sure," says Daniel, "I'll take the soup and the fish."

"Good," says the woman, "and if you don't like, you don't pay. How's that?"

Daniel smiles. "That's fine."

She brings him a cold beer in a frosted mug. He sips it and tries to understand the conversation at the end of the bar but his Portuguese is not good.

The seafood chowder is excellent, as thick and hot and tasty as any chowder he has ever had. It comes in a large iron bowl with a small bag of puffed crackers on the side.

When he finishes, she clears the bowl and pours him another beer.

The cod comes broiled. It is spiced with a pinch of curry and sprinkled with paprika. It has a clean, hot flavor. He savors every mouthful.

The Portuguese woman watches him eat. When his plate is empty she asks, "So, you like?"

He smacks his lips. "Delicious. Perfect."

She almost smiles. "Me, I make the soup. The fish, God does that." She picks up his mug. "I give you one more beer, then, when you ready, you give me ten American dollars."

"You've already given me two beers."

"I know, but I give you one more. On the house. You want to give me tip, that's up to you. I send my tips to my sisters and my mother."

Daniel sips his third beer. He picks up the mug and carries it to the end of the bar, to where the men play their games. "Can I get in on the action?" he asks.

There is silence while the Portuguese men study his face. He waits. More than a minute passes. No one says a word.

Daniel crosses the floor to the dart board. He pulls out three of the darts. "All right," he says, "so no one wants to play with me, I can handle that. But before I go, just for the hell of it, let's have a little fun."

Most of the men, he can see, do not understand a word he says. He crosses to the woman who served him dinner. "May I borrow one of your dish towels, please?"

She hands him the towel she had been using to dry glasses.

"Thanks." Daniel steps up to the firing line several feet in front of the dart board. He ties the towel around his head, covering his eyes. "Any wagers I can hit a bull's-eye?"

The men glance at one another. They seem doubtful. "You do this blindfolded?" one of them asks.

"That's right," answers Daniel. "Three chances to get one bull's-eye."

The men snicker and reach into their pockets. All of them bet against him. A total of twenty-eight dollars falls on the bar.

Daniel throws the first dart. It flies wide, sticking into the wall two feet to the left of the board. "Trouble," he says. "But I think I can get one of these next two. Any more bets?"

The Portuguese men dig deeper into their pockets. Before Daniel throws the second dart, a total of seventy-two dollars lies in a heap on the bar. The second dart hits the board, but just barely, landing in the black area outside the numbers.

"Damn," says Daniel. "Okay, one more time. Last chance to put down a bet. Anything but a bull's-eye on this throw and I match the pot."

The pile of cash on the bar swells to a hundred and twenty dollars.

"Wait," says the woman behind the bar, "what if I want to bet with you? What if I think you can do it?"

"Finally," says Daniel, "a believer. Go ahead, bet with me. If I get a bull's-eye, we split the pot. But if I miss, you pay half."

She nods. Her husband frowns. He mutters something to her in Portuguese. She scowls at him and says, "Forget you. I bet he do it."

The bar grows quiet. Daniel shakes out his throwing arm, steadies himself, and lets fly the final dart. It seems to pass through the air in slow motion. And then, suddenly, it comes to an abrupt stop, right smack in the middle of the tiny red bull's-eye: a perfect strike.

Daniel pulls off the blindfold, takes a quick look at the board, and smiles. "Drinks are on me, boys," he says as he scoops up the money and hands half of the winnings to the woman behind the bar.

THERE'D BEEN AN ACCIDENT ALL RIGHT, but before Coach Frederick could give me the details I threw up all over Rachel's kitchen table. I heard only bits and pieces of his explanation:

"...motorcycle...Jersey shore...Garden State Parkway...thunderstorm...ambulance...head-on collision...hospital...critical..."

I asked a few questions, barely absorbed the answers. Coach Frederick was leaving Mercersburg immediately, heading for South Amboy Memorial Hospital on Bordentown Road in Sayreville, New Jersey. I managed to write that down. He said he'd meet me at the hospital in a few hours, as soon as possible, as soon as he could get there.

"They're both fighters," was the last thing my old coach said before he hung up, "I'm sure they'll be okay."

And then his voice was gone, and I was all alone.

It took me some time to make a move. I stood there frozen in the middle of Rachel's loft. I couldn't move a muscle or make up my mind. I didn't know if I was scared or nervous or worried or pissed off or what. I felt like a human volcano ready to explode.

Finally, instinctively, I started to act. I picked up the keys, felt for my wallet, grabbed a raincoat. I even remembered to lock the door on my way out.

"Relax, Chandler," I mumbled to myself as I headed down the stairs, "just take one step at a time."

I had to walk over to Sixth Avenue in the rain to find a taxi. But I realized just as I stepped into the back seat that I had very little cash. So I backed out, slammed the door, and actually ran all the way over to the corner of Houston Street and Broadway to a branch of the bank that handled my financial affairs.

I had to wait in line for almost fifteen minutes to reach the cash machine. Finally, three hundred bucks in twenties and fives stuffed into my pocket, I hailed another cab. "Holland Tunnel," I ordered even before I had the door closed, "I gotta get to Jersey."

"Newark Airport?" The cabbie wanted to know.

"No," I told him, "I have to get home. Emergency." My idea was to go to Mendham, pick up my 944, then cruise down the Parkway to Sayreville.

"Where's home?"

"Fuck home," I heard myself say, "take me to South Amboy Memorial Hospital."

"Where the hell's that?"

We were in the tunnel, and making pretty good time now that the rush hour traffic had cleared. "Head south on the turnpike," I told him, "it's not far, maybe half an hour."

It took more like an hour because twice we got lost. I got pissed. The cabbie got pissed. It was not a pleasant trip. Before I paid and left his taxi we agreed never to meet again.

Inside the hospital they gave me the runaround. The people at the front desk sent me to emergency. Emergency told me, yes, a Mr. Hawthorn and a Miss Frederick had been admitted, but no, they were not at liberty to release any additional information if I was not a member of the family. I became instantly agitated, then antagonistic, demanding to speak to someone in charge, someone with authority. After a few minutes, just to get rid of me and my mouth, they sent me upstairs to administration.

Administration had pretty much closed down for the evening except for the night supervisor, this large, broad, middle-aged woman with red hair wearing a stiff white nurse's uniform. She offered the same line about me not being part of the family.

By this time what had happened had really started to hit home. I kept thinking maybe they were both dead and no one would tell me. I began to cry. Practically right in that woman's lap I started to sob. I couldn't help myself. "But they *are* family," I babbled between sniffles, "they're my best friends in the world."

It took a little while but finally she broke down. She handed me a tissue, made a couple of phone calls. "I see," she said. "Yes . . . Yes, I understand. . . . Of course, yes. . . . Thank you."

I wiped my cheeks, listened, and waited.

She hung up. "Your friends are both in critical condition, Mr. Chandler. They've had a very serious accident."

I blurted my next question, pretty much spit it all over her. "Are they going to die?"

She was calm, strong. "We certainly hope not. Everything is being done that can be done. Your friends are in excellent hands."

"Can I see them?"

"Not tonight. Probably not tomorrow. We'll have to watch their condition."

Again I blurted, "You mean if they live or not?"

She'd heard distraught persons before. "Let's not think about that, Mr. Chandler."

She told me to go home, to call the hospital in the morning. I told her going home was impossible. She handed me another tissue and told me to have a seat in the second-floor waiting room. If their condition changed, she would let me know.

I couldn't've been in the waiting room more than a few minutes when Victor and Carolyn arrived. They looked remarkably composed. I immediately began to cry again. Carolyn held me against her breast and ran her fingers through my hair.

I calmed down and told them what I knew. They told me what they knew. None of us knew much. Carolyn went off to look for the doctor, the supervisor, anyone who might be able to tell her more about her son.

Victor put his arm around my shoulder. "Hell of a thing," was all either one of us said, undoubtedly Victor, "a hell of a thing."

Carolyn returned. She had little to report.

Coach Frederick arrived. He seemed as composed as the Hawthorns, stable and utterly optimistic. His strength amazed me. He had long ago lost his wife. Both his parents were dead. Rachel was the only family he had except for a sister in California. Yet he stood there telling me they both had too much left to do to die.

I nodded on the outside but on the inside I wavered. I have always been a pessimist, always thought the worst so that whatever happened would have to be better than what I had anticipated.

Just after midnight a doctor came into the waiting room. He was tall and somber and fluid with professionalism. "Mr. and Mrs. Hawthorn?"

Victor and Carolyn stepped forward. They conferred with the doctor for maybe three minutes. Then it was Coach Frederick's turn. While Coach conferred, Victor passed on to me the gist of what the doctor had told him. "He's still critical, Matt, busted up in a thousand places, but upstairs he looks pretty clean."

"Upstairs?" I asked.

"They don't think he sustained any serious head injuries."

Relieved, I listened to Coach Frederick tell us this: "Rachel is critical but stable. She's still unconscious but the doctor says there are plenty of positive signs."

The four of us stood there then for a few minutes without saying much. In fact, I don't think we said a word. One by one we went back to our seats and sat down. No one thought for a second about going home or getting something to eat or even opening a magazine. We just sat there and waited.

That night lasted forever. So did the next few days. The parents were allowed in to see their children, but friends, even ones as old and loyal as yours truly, were kept out, banished.

Early Thursday morning, almost exactly sixty hours after he had slammed his brand-new Honda motorcycle head on into an ambulance, Daniel regained consciousness. A couple of hours later he sent word he wanted to see me.

"I told him you'd been waiting," Carolyn told me, her face exhausted but beaming.

So they gave me permission to see him. He looked like a mummy, plaster of Paris from head to toe. Only a few of his fingers and part of his face showed. I'm not sure anymore what I expected him to say; maybe an apology, an explanation, a confession.

The son of a bitch somehow managed to smile. All I could see of his face through the rolls of bandages were his eyes, nose, and mouth— nothing but a little circle of Hawthorn. But there he was, smiling.

"Hell of a thing, hey, Mac."

I nodded. "Yeah, a hell of a thing."

He might've managed that smile but I could see the pain in his eyes. He had to gather himself before he could speak again. "They haven't let you see her yet, huh?"

I shook my head. "Nope, not yet."

I hated him right then, hated his guts, wanted in the worst way to plant my fist right smack in the middle of that tight little facial circle. But a second later I loved him, wanted to embrace him, wanted to tell him how unbelievably happy I was that he wasn't going to die, that it would take a hell of a long time, months, maybe a year or more, but eventually he would heal up as good as new.

Then the hate came back. Then the love. Then the hate again. My emotions ebbed and flowed like that for several minutes, right up until the nurse came in and told me to back off, to get lost. And the thing is: my emotional tide concerning Daniel has been rising and falling ever since. I guess actually it's been rising and falling since the moment of my birth, since that day thirty-five years ago when he beat me to the punch, slipped out of the womb into the world while I hung back in the warm wet darkness hoping for a reprieve. Even now, after all that's happened, I still can't tell you if I love the son of a bitch or hate his guts.

Rachel came around the next day, early Friday afternoon. I didn't get to see her until Saturday morning. All Coach Frederick would tell me was that she was doing fine; there were some complications but she was doing just fine.

"Complications! What kind of complications?"

He wouldn't answer, told me she would tell me herself.

He led me down the hall and into her room. "I'll just come in for a minute," he said, "then I'll leave you two alone."

So in we went, Coach leading the way. I could see her there lying on the bed. She was wearing her share of plaster of Paris as well. Maybe not quite as much as Daniel, but pretty close. But from her neck up she looked undamaged, not a thread of gauze above her shoulders. I breathed a sigh of relief: her face, her beautiful face and her long dark hair, had been spared.

We stepped a little closer. The lights in the room were dim, the shades drawn. She lay very still, her eyes closed. "Daddy," she asked, "is that you?"

"Yes, sweetie, it's me. And I've brought Matthew."

I saw her mouth smile but her eyes never opened.

She reached out her left arm. It was bandaged to the wrist. I took her fingers in my hand and squeezed softly.

"I'm sorry, Matthew," she whispered, and I could see tears roll out of the corners of her still closed eyes. "I'm so sorry. I didn't mean for this to happen."

I reassured her, told her she had absolutely no reason to apologize, it was all nothing but a terrible accident. But I was an emotional basket case, totally exhausted after almost no sleep for four days. I began to cry as well. Soon we were both bawling like a couple of babies.

Coach Frederick slipped out of the room, left us alone. I squeezed her fingers tighter. Just that made us cry even harder.

That's when she opened her eyes. She hadn't meant to; she had wanted in the worst way to keep them closed, to keep them hidden away.

And I knew the moment I looked into those eyes that something horrible had happened. For fifteen years those eyes had mesmerized and controlled me. But one brief look and I could see they had lost their power; I could see something was wrong, very wrong.

I reached out to touch her. Slowly I moved my hand closer and closer to her face. The tears ran in a torrent down her cheeks. I drew my fingers to within an inch of her nose. Her eyes offered not a hint of recognition. Very gently, as gently as I possibly could, I touched the tip of my index finger against her cheek.

She flinched, gasped, and recoiled.

And then, for as long as I can remember, all either of us could do was wash away the fear with tears.

THEY RECOVERED. Slowly but surely their cuts and bruises healed, their broken bones mended, their scars began to fade. They both spent several weeks recuperating at South Amboy Memorial. I drove down to see them at least twice, sometimes three times a week.

In late October Daniel was transferred up to the hospital in Morristown so he could be closer to home and receive the proper physical therapy.

A few weeks after that, Rachel was transferred to St. Vincent's over on Eleventh Street and Seventh Avenue in Manhattan. They moved her into the city so she could receive more specialized treatment for her eyes. Also, Coach Frederick had taken a leave of absence and was living in the loft in Soho. It was much easier for him to have his daughter at St. Vincent's rather than all the way down in Sayreville.

I went back to work. At least physically I returned to the office. Mentally I was a million miles away. Clients and colleagues would sit across from me, talk about everything from tax exemptions on investment portfolios to the New York Giant's chances of reaching the Super Bowl. I wouldn't hear a word they said; barely a sound registered.

And just as I wavered in my feelings for Daniel, so also did my thoughts concerning Rachel. Her blindness, of course, depressed me. I felt sorry both for her and for me. In one fell swoop everything had been snatched away. Nothing, I felt, would ever be the same.

I thought quite a lot, and believe me, this is incredibly difficult for me to admit, about abandoning her. Maybe not all at once, but little by little, day by day, I would beat my retreat, slip out of the scene into the greater oblivion. Her blindness frightened me. It gave me the willies. I did not know how to behave around her, how much or how little to say.

Suddenly she was severely handicapped. I had no experience, and therefore no sound understanding, no tolerance, for her condition. It no doubt sounds cruel, but her blindness disgusted me. I had a difficult time even looking at her face. I preferred to turn off the lights whenever I went to visit.

Rachel didn't help. After her body began to heal, after she began to feel better physically, she grew more and more distressed, more and more despondent, about her eyes. The doctors at first said her vision might return at any time; she appeared to have suffered no physical damage to the optic nerve. But as the days and weeks passed, hope faded. In due course we all became resigned to this new sightless reality.

"Except for your eyes," I heard more than one specialist tell her, "you'll be as good as new in no time."

This provided little comfort to a young artist whose entire life revolved around her visual perception of the world. She struggled daily with anger and frustration and melancholy.

I'm sure everyone who came in contact with her during those early months after the accident experienced her confusion and her wrath, but she seemed particularly keen on attacking me. I was the dog she kicked, her scapegoat. I could do nothing right. Everything I said was ridiculous and petty, pure sentimental crap.

So when Coach Frederick decided to take her out to California, I silently rejoiced. It was January of 1986, four months since the accident. He decided to go to southern California for the warmth and sunshine, and because of the Doheny Eye Institute in Los Angeles, a clinic that specialized in psychosomatic blindness. He hoped they'd be able to help.

They stayed with Coach Frederick's sister and her family in Anaheim. I talked to her on the telephone at least twice a week. I wrote her several letters but never mailed them because I knew someone else would have to read them to her. And what I had to say I did not want read by anyone else's eyes.

Yes, I admit it, not a week after she went west I began to miss her. I wanted her back, blind or not blind. It didn't matter.

And what about Daniel? By the time Rachel went to California he was out of the hospital, back home in Mendham, more or less restricted to his old childhood bed. He had suffered a couple of compound fractures to the legs. His recovery would be slow and tedious. More than a year would pass before he finished with the physical therapy and the crutches. Except for a few short trips with Victor, he pretty much stayed put at the compound.

I sort of enjoyed thinking of him stuck out there, exiled, banished. He deserved it, I felt, after what he had done, both to her and to me.

Once in a while I'd drive out for a visit. We'd sit in the living room or, if it was warm enough, out on the front porch.

"So," I asked him one day in the early spring, "what are you going to do when you finally get back on your feet?"

"I don't know. Maybe kick your butt in tennis."

"I'll be the only one left you can beat."

"You think so?"

"I know so."

"The hell with you. I'm going to recover and win the national singles."

And I thought he might just be able to do it. He had the will, and I knew damn well he had the walnuts. But still, I suddenly resented him for even thinking about his own future when Rachel's future had been ruined, or so I thought at the time, by his recklessness on that damn motorcycle.

I tried to hold my resentment in check, but it wouldn't hold, not this time; it came flooding out, a verbal deluge I had no doubt been holding inside for years. "The national singles, huh? Well, bully for you, Hawk. But what about Rachel? What's she supposed to do? Come out and sit along the side of the court and listen to the smack of the tennis ball? I swear to God"—and I was just about screeching by this time—"you are one selfish son of a bitch!"

I didn't wait for him to respond. I knew if I did, he would use his oral gifts to nullify my pronouncements. I didn't want to be nullified. Not this time. Not again. For thirty years he'd been nullifying me, putting me in my place. This time I just wanted to hate him without being interrupted. So I stood up and stomped off the front porch and across the grass. I climbed into my fire engine red 944, fired up the engine, and accelerated out of the Hawthorns' driveway.

It's true: that little sports coupe can go from zero to sixty in about as much time as it takes to cock your wrist and look at your watch. I proved it that afternoon. I took flight down Thomas Lane. I had the pedal to the metal, the R.P.M.s right around the red line in third gear, when I hit that patch of sand and gravel on the bend right before Hilltop Road.

That slight curve had always been my nemesis as a kid. More than once I had spun out on that curve when riding too fast on my bicycle. More than once I'd wiped out, scraped up my body from head to toe.

But this time I had a lot more than pedal power under my seat. I had the horsepower of that Porsche 944. And when those radial tires hit that patch of sand and gravel, look out! The rear end began to swing. I could do nothing to stop it. I glanced at the speedometer: damn close to seventy M.P.H. "Jesus H. Christ!"

The Porsche spun off the road into the brush, then through the brush and into the woods. I held fast to the steering wheel and waited. The car seemed to spin forever but really only a few seconds passed. I felt like I was down in Seaside riding the bumper cars. At any moment I expected the attendant to shut off the electricity and bring my flight to a halt.

That's when the car slammed into the tree. That's when my head slammed into the window. That's when I blacked out.

I was all right. No big deal. Only spent one night in the hospital. Had a mild concussion and a body that felt like it had been run over by a steamroller. But my Porsche. Jesus! You should've seen my Porsche. Twisted and bent into the shape of a horseshoe. A total loss. Just threw it on the junk heap, they did, and squashed it down into an automotive pancake.

Of course, it was Daniel's fault. I blamed him. The son of a bitch. It was all his fault, the whole kit and caboodle. Like my other Porsche, the cheap one, the 914, the one I'd blown up on Route 6 driving to Hyannis. That was his fault, too. If I hadn't been trying to get out to Nantucket to catch him in the act of copulating with my woman, that engine never would've seized. And so what if she hadn't even been out there with him that time? What difference did that make? It was still his fault. Every goddamn bad thing that had ever happened to me was his fault. Not mine, not hers, his.

IN APRIL OF '86 RACHEL RETURNED from the West Coast. But she didn't come back to her loft in the city. She and Coach Frederick went straight to the big white house on Main Street in Mercersburg. I was there to meet them when they arrived. I had swept the floors and dusted the furniture and filled the fridge with food. Coach Frederick thanked me. Rachel didn't even notice. She seemed only half-glad to see me, as though the effort of reunion were barely worth the effort.

That evening I found out what she had in mind. We sat out on the porch. Coach Frederick had gone upstairs to see how his studio had fared during his long absence. It was a warm night for late April, very still. The stars showed through the trees.

I decided not to mention them. "So," I asked, "California was okay?"

"I guess."

"You glad to be back?"

"Yeah, I guess."

Her voice, as well as her eyes, were blank. But it had been that way since the accident. I was used to it. "I've been going by the loft a couple times a week to water the plants."

"Just let the plants die, Matthew."

"You don't mean that."

"Yes, I do. Just let them die."

"The next time I come out I'll bring them. You can take care of them here."

She sighed. "Don't bother."

I wasn't sure if she meant for me not to bring the plants or not to bother coming for another visit. I feared the latter, so I quickly changed the subject. "My lease expires at the end of June. I have to move."

It took her a moment to respond. "So that's good. You've always hated that place."

"Still, you know me, I get dug in." My building on Tenth Street was going co-op, and I had no desire to become an owner. So I'd decided to find another apartment. I think I'd been secretly hoping to maybe move into the loft on Greene Street.

Rachel put the quietus on that. "We'll probably sell the loft," she said. "I've been telling Daddy there's no reason to keep it. I'll never go there again."

"What? Why not?" I could barely hide my shock. "Of course you will."

"What do you mean, why not? How could I possibly live there, Matthew? Really."

"But—"

"But nothing. I couldn't live in the city in this . . . in this condition. Besides, there's no reason for me to live there now. I'm not a painter anymore. I'm just blind . . . and helpless."

I began to speak, to tell her how wrong she was to feel that way. But my words sounded hollow and uncertain. I grew silent.

We sat there in silence for most of an hour. I could hear music coming from one of the dorms. It brought on a wave of nostalgia. I let out an enormous sigh, emptied my lungs of air.

And that's when she said, "I've been thinking, Matthew."

Trouble. "Yes?"

"I don't think we should see each other anymore."

"What!?"

"I don't think we should see each other anymore. Not for a while. Not until—"

"No, Rachel, you don't mean that. You're just—"

"I do mean it." She had started to cry. "I do."

I moved to touch her. She pulled away. She stood, stumbled, fell back against the porch railing. I reached down to help her up. She pushed my hand away. "Don't!" she shouted, and I could see the pain and frustration on her face. "Don't touch me!"

I backed off, gave her room.

She struggled to her feet, felt along the wall for the screen door, pulled it open, and stepped inside. "Go home, Matthew. Just go home!"

Then, because she had grown up in that house and knew it as well as anything in the world, she raised her head and marched down the hallway and up the stairs. A few moments later I heard her bedroom door slam closed.

The following morning I returned to New York with my tail between my legs. I went back to work. What else could I do? She didn't want my help. She wouldn't even unlock her door.

The next few months were very weird. For a week or so I stewed in my own emotional juices, but May, June, July, and part of August passed in a blur of confusion and alcohol.

I was estranged from my two best friends. One I had insulted and the other had told me to get lost. So what did I do? I sought the company of strangers.

By this time you no doubt think of me as a guy who, if he wanted to have a drink or two after work, would probably go to a nice, clean, respectable bar. Or maybe to one of the clubs around NYU, say, the Blue Note or the Bottom Line or the Bitter End. But let me tell you something about old Mac Chandler you might not know: he's not entirely predictable. One visit to the Raccoon Lodge down on Warren Street and he bade all that nice, clean, respectable bullshit farewell. He was sick and tired of clean and respectable. And he damn well didn't need any high-toned entertainment. He needed cheap drinks and drunken patrons. So he became a regular at such quaint haunts as the Grass Roots Tavern over on St. Marks and the Village Idiot down on First Avenue.

At the Grass Roots Tavern I could win free drinks playing darts. About all you had to do to win was hit the board and stay on your feet. I could do a lot better than that. Years earlier down in the Hawthorns' basement I had spent countless hours learning how to throw those damn darts straight in a futile attempt to defeat Daniel at least once.

I went to the Village Idiot when I felt the need to philosophize. You could always find someone cozied up to the bar who would buy you a pint of Guinness stout and help you solve the problems plaguing the planet.

Okay, so my life had become an insipid cliché. What can I tell you. I offer no excuses.

My thirtieth birthday came and went during this three-month binge of alcohol. It came and went without a word from anyone other than my mother. Sweet mama of mine. Called to wish me many happy returns. Asked me if I'd found a new apartment yet.

Oh, my God! My lease on Tenth Street was up at the end of the month, in just over a week, and I hadn't done a damn thing about it. It had totally slipped my mind.

So as soon as I got off the phone I went on a frenzied apartment-hunting expedition. I had no idea what to do or where to look. I needed Rachel. I needed her to hold my hand, to tell me what to do, to take charge.

In the end, on virtually the last day of the month, I found this lovely flat where I still reside today. I moved here to apartment 5-C at 146 W. 17th Street on July 1, 1986. Five years, two months, and a few days ago.

I'll be here just a few days longer. Yeah, yeah, I know, you've heard that before. I've been hailing my departure since I began this tale, but really, at the end of this week I'm gone, outta here. I'm heading for open water, for the blue horizon.

My binge continued without pause during my first month in this apartment. It lasted until the end of the first week in August. That's when everything started to change again.

It was a Saturday morning, the ninth of August. It must've been ninety degrees outside, a hundred and ninety inside. I lay on the floor, hung over, a fan blowing on me from above, reading *Tao Te Ching, The Way of Life*:

> Without going out of doors,
> one may know all under heaven;
> Without peering through windows,
> one may see all there is to see.
>
> The farther one goes,
> the less one knows.
>
> The sage knows without knowing,
> does without doing,
> goes without going.

Right.

Someone knocked on the door. I thought about ignoring it but the knocker persisted. So I put down my book, rolled over, groaned, and pushed myself vertical. I wore nothing but a pair of boxer shorts. I considered pulling on a pair of khakis but the knocker pounded even louder. "All right already," I shouted. "For chrissakes, I'm coming." I unlatched and unbolted my door. "What's the big—"

And there they stood, the two of them, side by side, shoulder to shoulder.

"Didn't I tell you the son of a bitch lived here?" And then he grabbed me, pulled me close, kissed me full on the mouth. A great big Gypsy greeting.

A moment later Rachel did the same.

They were back. My mother had given them the address. He had crutches and she had a cane, but they were back. In the flesh. Close enough for me to touch.

I invited them in. The place was a mess. I still hadn't unpacked many of the cardboard boxes. I cleared a spot on the sofa, asked them if they wanted to sit.

"Maybe for a minute," answered Rachel.

I helped her find the way. I was almost glad she could not see the chaos that was my home.

"Hey, Mac," said Daniel, "nice digs," and then, as though I had just seen them the day before, "We're going down to Soho. Thought you might like to come along."

I looked more closely at her. She wore dark glasses: small, round, gold frames with rose-colored lenses, but I could tell she had a smile on her face. Maybe not a broad, toothy grin, but a smile nevertheless, the first one of those I'd seen since the accident.

So we shared a beer, then headed for Soho. I suggested a cab but they wanted to walk. Daniel said he needed the exercise.

Sometimes Rachel held my arm. Sometimes she held Daniel's arm. Sometimes she just tapped along the sidewalk with her cane.

We stopped to visit her favorite galleries. The owners lavished her with attention. They knew all about the accident. They wanted to know how she was, what she'd been doing. They told her all the latest gossip. Rachel listened and nodded and even laughed.

Daniel poked me in the ribs. I couldn't help but smile. What a sap.

Finally, late in the afternoon, we reached the loft. We threw open the windows to air the place out. No one had set foot in there for months, not since late April. The plants were all dead. I was glad Rachel couldn't see them wilted and rotting.

I had a million questions and more coming to mind every second, but I kept them to myself. Instead of asking I just watched and waited and listened. For three months I'd been secretly hoping something like this would happen.

We decided to clean up. I went out and bought window cleaner and paper towels and furniture polish. On the way back I picked up a pizza and a six-pack of beer.

We sat around the kitchen table eating and drinking and talking about stuff that had happened years ago, stuff like the time we rode the freights out to Pennsylvania, like the time Daniel hung himself on the fifty-yard line, like the time we all drove up to Salem together. We laughed and drank and pretended not to remember any of the bad stuff.

Then we started to clean. Actually I started to clean. I was the only one of us well enough to do the dirty work. Rachel did her best to polish and straighten but mostly she just tried to visualize her surroundings, tried to remember what was where, tried to figure out how many steps from the door to the table, from here to there.

Daniel pretty much retired to the sofa. I could tell he was hurting, that the long day had been a strain.

A thunderstorm rolled through in the early evening. It rained for only a few minutes, but behind the rain came a cool breeze and a slight drop in temperature. No one mentioned the storm of a year ago, the storm that had struck just before the accident.

We played some old jazz records on the stereo, Billie Holiday and Charlie Parker and Louis Armstrong's *"Just a Closer Walk with Thee."* We kept the volume low so we could hear each other if someone decided to say something. No one said much.

Around ten o'clock Daniel fell asleep on the sofa. We could hear him snoring. I turned off the music. Rachel covered him with a light blanket.

Then we stood there, the two of us, together and alone for the first time in such a long time. We were quiet and very still.

"I'm tired, too, Matthew," Rachel said finally. "Let's go to bed."

So we did. We climbed into the loft like we'd done a thousand times before. We pulled off our clothes, slipped between the sheets. I was unsure what to do. I wondered if she wanted me to keep my distance, stick to my half of the bed.

It was dark in the loft. The only light came from a street lamp down on the corner of Greene and Spring. I could barely see her face though she lay close enough for me to feel her breath against my neck.

Maybe a minute passed. She didn't move, didn't make a sound.

"Good night, Rachel," I said softly, "sweet dreams."

"Yes," she said, "sweet dreams, Matthew." Then she reached out her hand and touched my chest. My whole body tingled. I gently found her shoulder with my fingers. She did not back away. She moved closer. Soon our bodies lay pressed together.

For the next few hours we cried and giggled and apologized.

RACHEL ANN FREDERICK, ALIAS MISTY GREY, *closes her suit-case. She glances in the mirror over the bureau. A red bandanna covers her hair. A lock of her natural dark brown hair falls out across her forehead. She pushes the hair up under the bandanna.*

Outside a car horn sounds. Misty picks up her suitcase and goes out through the door and down the stairs. She sees the cab sitting at the end of the driveway.

"You call for a taxi, ma'am?"

Misty nods. Soon they are under way. The cabbie eases out onto Main Street and south out of town. "Newark Airport, right, miss?"

"Yes," says Misty.

"Right. And which airline will you be flying today?"

She hesitates. "Umm, American."

"American, fine. That would be Terminal A."

Except for a few bits about the weather, overcast with a chance of showers, and something about the buildup of troops in the Persian Gulf because of Saddam's annexation of Kuwait, the ride to the airport passes in silence.

They drive east on I-78, then south on Route 1 to the airport entrance. It is the middle of the morning. Most of the early traffic has cleared, so the cabbie has no problem pulling up in front of the American Airlines terminal.

Misty pays the fare, thanks the cabbie, and steps out. She goes into the terminal through the automatic sliding doors. Several American Airlines' agents are available to assist her but she walks past them without a glance.

She rides the escalator down to the next level and enters the ladies' room. In the privacy of a locked stall she opens her suitcase. She takes out a pair of faded blue jeans and a light cotton sweatshirt that has MUSEUM

OF MODERN ART *written across the chest. She pulls off the sundress she had put on back in Peapack after her shower. After folding and putting away the dress, she pulls on the jeans and sweatshirt.*

Now she pulls off the red bandanna. The blond coloring has been washed from her hair. For the first time in a year it is its natural deep dark brown. She brushes it gently, teases it with the tips of her fingers.

She puts on a pair of sunglasses. The frames are made of fine gold, very thin, the eyepieces perfectly round, the lenses rose-colored.

Before closing the suitcase she takes out one last item: a short stick, about a foot long, wrapped with a leather hand grip. When she twists the grip the stick telescopes out in sections until it reaches a length of almost five feet.

Rachel takes a few deep breaths, then unlocks and swings open the door of the stall. She takes a quick look around. The rest room is empty.

She glances in the mirror over the row of sinks, then away. "No," she mumbles to herself, "none of that."

Tapping the stick lightly on the floor in front of her, she makes her way out of the ladies' room and into the hustle and bustle of the terminal.

She walks slowly, her eyes open but unseen behind the dark glasses. It has been more than a year since she has acted blind in public. It feels strange, not natural at all. She closes her eyes to make it easier.

After a few minutes she stops. And waits. It takes almost half an hour, but finally someone approaches and asks if she needs assistance. She takes a quick look. The man wears a uniform, an airport cop.

"Yes," she says, and smiles, "I need to reach Continental Airlines. I have a connecting flight to catch at eleven-thirty."

"We oughta be able to help you with that," says the cop.

She has to allow herself to be passed around for a few minutes like a piece of baggage but finally she boards a bus that takes her across the airport to Terminal C.

When the bus arrives a Continental representative is waiting for her. "Hello," says a bright and cheery voice, "I'm Pam."

Pam helps Rachel off the bus and into the terminal. "And where will you be flying today, ma'am?"

"Hyannis."

"And do you already have your ticket?"

"Yes," answers Rachel, doing her best to act like a helpless child.

"All right, that'll be a Continental Express flight." Pam stops for a moment to study the departure board. "Flight 768, departing on time at eleven thirty-six. Would you like to check your bag or carry it aboard?"

"I'd rather keep it with me."

"Fine, then why don't we go straight to the gate. Would you like a courtesy car?"

"I'd rather walk."

"All right."

They make their way across the terminal, through security, and out the long arm to Gate 97. Pam never for a moment leaves Rachel's side. She chats on and on about this and that, smiling every step of the way.

Finally they reach the gate. The flight is just beginning to board. Pam steers Rachel to the front of the line. The ticket agent looks over Rachel's ticket, rips off the appropriate pages, and hands the ticket to Pam.

Rachel cannot help herself. She has to do something to salvage her dignity. "I'd like a window seat, please, if that's possible."

Pam and the ticket agent glance at one another. "Certainly," says the ticket agent, "of course."

Rachel smiles.

Just after one o'clock the plane lands at Barnstable Municipal Airport in Hyannis. Another Continental representative is there to assist Rachel, a young man this time. He carries her bag across the tarmac and through the small terminal while Rachel holds on to his arm. He hails her a cab, opens the door for her, and helps her inside.

"Thank you for traveling Continental," he says, "and have a pleasant day."

"Yes," says Rachel, "thank you." The door closes. She turns to the driver. "The Mariner Motel, please, on Ocean Street."

"Right."

Finally, half an hour later, Rachel is safely in her room at the Mariner behind a closed and locked door. She sighs, pulls off the dark glasses, rubs her eyes, and collapses on the bed.

SO WHAT HAD HAPPENED? What had changed? Time, of course. Time and a sense of reality. Rachel had finally started to come to terms with her blindness.

Coach Frederick had played a major role. His patience and understanding had overcome her sorrow and self-pity. And perhaps most important: he had convinced her to begin painting again. First a few sketches, then some watercolors, until finally one day in late June she had opened her oil paints and applied color to canvas.

This simple act was excellent therapy, exactly what the doctor had ordered. But you should have seen the results: unbelievable, stunning, magnificent. Even blind she could create beautiful paintings.

A week or two after Rachel and Daniel and I cleaned up the loft, I got to see her first blind creation. Coach Frederick drove in from Mercersburg with a carload of gear. I helped carry that gear up from the sidewalk. My second load was a large canvas wrapped in heavy brown paper. When I reached the loft I pulled off the paper. I expected to find a painting I had seen before, an old work by either Rachel or her father. The walls of the loft were filled with such paintings. But right away I could see it was something new, something unlike anything I had ever seen before.

I stood there staring at it with my mouth hanging open when Coach Frederick came through the door carrying a box of brushes and a wooden easel. "She calls that one *Sudden Storm*," he said. "Quite something, isn't it?"

All I could do was nod.

Sudden Storm was a depiction of Rachel's final visual image before the motorcycle accident. It represented the last mental photograph her eyes had taken. But before I describe the painting, let me briefly re-create events leading up to the crash. I, of course, learned of these events after the fact, primarily from the two participants.

Daniel had arrived unannounced at Rachel's loft early that morning. Another hot and humid day was predicted, so they decided to head for the Jersey shore and spend the day on the beach. Rachel was soaking up the rays and riding the waves while I tried so frantically to find her.

On their way home, driving north on the Garden State Parkway, a thunderstorm rolled in from the west. The sky turned from bright blue to black in a matter of minutes. It began to drizzle. Thunder and lightning crashed and flashed all around them. They decided to get off the parkway and find cover until the storm had passed. By this time the late afternoon had turned as dark as night. The rain fell in great, torrential sheets.

Daniel did not see the oncoming car as he eased the motorcycle down the exit ramp. He said later he saw lights and she said she heard a siren, but in the confusion of the storm they both thought it was just more thunder and lightning. But it was not more thunder and lightning; it was an ambulance driving the wrong way on the exit ramp in a desperate attempt to reach an injured motorist out on the parkway.

Just before the motorcycle crashed head on into the ambulance Rachel glanced up into the sky and saw our three faces floating there amid all those angry storm clouds.

The collision sent them flying. That was the last moment either of them remembered.

So you see the significance of the title: *Sudden Storm*. The painting appears to move as you study it, to drift across the canvas. Dark gray-and-black clouds swirl beneath a bright red-and-orange sky. You can practically hear the thunder and see the lightning and feel the rain pouring down. These effects alone would make this canvas extraordinary but the faces render it, in my humble opinion, anyway, a masterpiece.

One must look for the faces. They hide among the clouds: Daniel on the left, Rachel in the center, Matthew on the right. No bodies or limbs, just faces. Not really even any heads. Just eyes and ears and mouths. But it's us, no doubt about that. We look scared; no, not scared: horrified. And for good reason: that storm's about to tear apart our lives.

You can see Rachel Ann Frederick's *Sudden Storm*, if you want to take the time and spend the money. All you have to do is travel to the Museum of Modern Art on Fifty-third Street in Manhattan. It's on display there for all eyes to see.

But before the Museum of Modern Art displayed the painting, it hung at the Gladstone Gallery in Soho along with two dozen other paintings by Rachel Ann Frederick. *Sight and Sightless*, the gallery owners called the exhibition, for if offered works done both before and after the accident. It was Rachel's first major show, and it caused quite a sensation.

"How do you paint the wind?" That's what the art critic for the *Times* asked in his column after he viewed Rachel's work. He answered his own question by telling his readers they could find out by studying *Sudden Storm* by Soho artist Rachel Ann Frederick. His column talked about her blindness, but he insisted that even without such a handicap *Sudden Storm* would be "a modern artistic icon...a work of power, style, and supreme integrity."

The deluge began. Suddenly Rachel found herself in great demand. The *Village Voice* did a long piece on her. So did *Vanity Fair. The New Yorker* did a profile. *New York* magazine did an interview. *The New York Times* did an article in its Sunday magazine on the blind artist of Soho. Before the accident Rachel's work had been selling well but now the value of her paintings doubled and tripled, even quadrupled. She was asked to make appearances; first in New York, then as far away as Dallas and Los Angeles. A small but very exclusive museum in Paris even flew her across the Atlantic on the Concorde in return for a fifteen-minute speech on the inner mind of the contemporary artist. Ms. Rachel Ann Frederick, you might say, was becoming famous, an artist of import, a real-life celebrity in a city of celebrities.

Then, late that year, some fourteen months after the accident, some four months after her part-time return to the city, Rachel received her greatest honor. On the night of November 18, 1986, *Sudden Storm* was put on display in the contemporary gallery up on the third floor of the Museum of Modern Art. That night an original oil painting by Rachel Ann Frederick hung not far from works by Cézanne and Matisse, Van Gogh and the great Picasso.

I was on hand for the hanging. So were Daniel and Coach Frederick. I wore dark glasses just like Rachel's. Throughout the evening I kept my eyes closed and feigned blindness so I could experience the event as Rachel experienced the event.

She had to give a speech—not a long one, just a few minutes. She thanked all the right people in the art community for their assistance and their generosity. She thanked her father for his unrelenting faith. She thanked Daniel for his friendship. And then she thanked me for my strength, of all things, my strength and my courage and my character.

I cried.

I SAT IN MY OFFICE, DAYDREAMING, looking out the window at the people walking in and out of Trinity Church, when my secretary buzzed and told me Miss Frederick was on the telephone.

I snapped out of my reverie and snatched up the receiver. "Rachel?"

"Hi." She was out in Mercersburg. She still spent more than half her time in that big old white house on Main Street.

"How are you?"

"I'm good, Matthew." She sounded better than good; she sounded excited. "I have some news."

"Good news?"

"Great news." But she wouldn't tell me her news, not over the telephone. "Maybe you could come out this weekend. We could celebrate."

"Celebrate what?"

She wouldn't say. So I said, "Forget the weekend, I'll be out tonight."

As soon as we got off the phone I made arrangements to rent a car. It was late February of 1987. I remember it snowed as I drove west across New Jersey and Pennsylvania. Nearly three inches had fallen by the time I arrived at the Fredericks' house well after midnight.

Rachel was up waiting for me. She stood in the front hallway wrapped in a full-length down robe as I came quietly through the front door.

Before I could utter a word she smiled and said, "You have on your navy blue wool overcoat, gray slacks with cuff, and those fine Italian loafers polished to a high shine."

Puzzled, I just stood there and stared at her.

"And you have snowflakes in your hair and on your shoulders."

I reached up to brush away the snow when it hit me. "No!"

"Yes."

"You can see?"

"Yes," she said, "I can. Perfectly."

It was true: she could see, her vision had miraculously returned.

The best eye specialists in the country had claimed all along there was no permanent optic nerve damage; her blindness, they insisted, had been caused by a psychosomatic reaction to the accident, and therefore her sight could return at any time.

I asked her when it had happened. She avoided answering, instead responded with a question of her own. "What does it matter?"

While I wondered why it mattered, she pulled on some warm clothes and led me out into the night. We ran through the streets of Mercersburg and across the sleeping grounds of the academy. We built an enormous snowman right in front of the chapel, as tall as Rachel when she sat upon my shoulders. We dressed him up with apples for eyes and brooms for arms and finished him off with a fur hat and a cashmere scarf.

Sometime not too long before dawn we returned to the house and took off our soaking wet clothes. We hung up our coats and threw our shirts and socks into the dryer. Soon we stood perfectly naked and shivering in the middle of the kitchen. I crossed the wooden floor and held her close. Our bodies were ice cold, our hands and feet blue and practically frozen.

Before we dashed upstairs to the warmth of her bed, Rachel had something to say. "This will be our secret, Matthew," she whispered. "No one else will know but us."

"No one?"

She nodded.

Of course, her father already knew, and Daniel, she told me, would know soon. It would be cruel, she explained, to keep the truth from him.

I wondered again when her vision had returned, wondered if maybe Daniel had already heard the good news, but it seemed a bad time to press for answers. My petty anxieties seemed especially trivial in light of what had happened.

"So swear," she said, "you'll never tell anyone."

I almost asked her why she wanted to keep the news a secret; I wanted to shut it out for all the world to hear. But naked and close and staring for the first time in such a long time into each other's eyes, I said very softly, "I swear, Rachel, I'll never tell anyone."

And then up the stairs we ran, and with all the lights in her bedroom burning bright, we crawled beneath the down comforter and wrestled the rest of that morning away.

Why, you are no doubt wondering, did Rachel want to keep this miracle a secret? Why did she want to hush up the fact that her vision had returned? Well, I can only tell you what she told me. She feared important people in the New York art world would call her a liar. This business of being an artist is intensely competitive. Artists have been known to go to incredible extremes to have their work recognized. Rachel believed her enemies, who she felt sure posed as her allies, would at the very least infer that her blindness had been a hoax, a deceptive ploy to gain notoriety for herself and her paintings.

I have no idea if her paranoia was justified. But I do know that after her vision returned she made a calculated decision to remain blind in the public eye. Perhaps her ambition had gotten the best of her. Perhaps she had lost touch with reality. But who am I to say? Who am I to judge? I know only that I promised, on many more than one occasion, to go along with her charade, to keep her secret locked safely away.

A few months after the February miracle, in the late spring of 1987, I once again asked Rachel if she wanted to get married. We were up in her loft, hiding from the probing eyes of the public.

"To who?" she asked, her mouth smiling, her eyes clear and sparkling. "To you?"

"No," I said, making light of her response even though I didn't really want to, "not to me, to Daniel."

"Daniel's not the marrying kind, Matthew, you know that."

I did indeed. "Then how 'bout me?"

"You?"

"Yes, me."

"That might be interesting." She was more serious now.

I waited. "So?"

"So, what?"

"So what do you think?"

"I think I'll have to think about it."

I thought about that. "Well," I said, "I guess that's better than a simple, unequivocal no."

"I guess."

"How long do you want to think about it?"

She shrugged. "I don't know, Matthew. As long as it takes."

I let it go at that. After all the years we had been together I knew it would be a waste of time to pursue the question any further.

And so I waited. I waited through the summer and the fall and New Year's. I waited through the cold, gray months of 1988. I waited while she went right on pretending she was as blind as a bat.

I waited through the spring. I waited while she flew off to London, where some chic gallery on Piccadilly did a one-woman retrospective with more than a hundred of her paintings. I waited even after I called her one evening at her hotel on Russell Square and, you guessed it, he answered the damn telephone.

"Hello?"

"Daniel?"

"Mac?"

"What the hell are you doing there?"

"Me? I was over in Vienna meeting with Max, you remember Max? And when I heard she was coming to London, well, I thought I'd just pop by on my way home and see how things were going."

"Just popped by, huh?"

"Right."

Bastard. "So, how are things going? Where is she?"

He ignored me. "You should've come, Mac. She said you thought about it. You've missed some great weather. Sunny, not too hot. We went and saw the roses at Queen Mary's Garden. Unbelievable. Must've been thousands of them in bloom. Maybe millions. All different colors. Of course, Rachel acted like she couldn't see a damn thing. And for good reason: more than one member of the press was on our tail the whole time. I'll tell you, she's a piece of work. Really seems to thrive on this never-ending vaudeville show."

"Yeah," I said, "sure. So where is she?"

"Who? Rachel? Over at the gallery, I guess. Very big deal. They're spoiling her rotten. I've barely seen her five minutes."

"Sure," I said, "right."

And then he had to go, said he had a date to play court tennis with some lesser member of the royal family over at Hampton Court.

Son of a bitch.

I WAS STILL WAITING on the Fourth of July when that homeless black man dressed in rags walked into the offices of Chandler, Wright & MacPherson with blood on his hands and mumbled something about a dead honkie down in the lobby.

The office was closed that Monday afternoon in celebration of the nation's two hundred and twelfth birthday. I was the only one there, the only employee, anyway. I did, however, have someone with me. She and I had just made love on the leather sofa in Chuckie's office.

Perhaps a few more details are in order. We'd been downtown at a street fair doing our bit for the national birthday bash: eating ethnic foods and drinking ethnic beers and saluting Lady Liberty for welcoming all those tired, poor, huddled masses for the past hundred years.

"Lady Liberty for President in eighty-eight!" I kept shouting up and down the Battery.

"You're drunk, Matthew," Rachel informed me.

"Rachel Ann Frederick for President!"

"Now that sounds like an excellent idea."

"Let me be the first to congratulate you on the nomination." I grabbed her around the waist, drew her close, and kissed her as passionately as I had in a long, long time.

During a lull, I mumbled something like "Sure would be fun to fuck the President."

"You want to go home?" she asked.

"No," I answered, "let's do it right here. Right here on this park bench. I wanna stay for the fireworks."

"You can't have it both ways."

"The hell I can't." I picked her up and carried her off the Battery and up Broadway. I'd like to report I carried her all the way up past Trinity Church and into the offices of Chandler, Wright & MacPherson, but after less than a block she ordered me to put her down.

We walked the rest of the way up Broadway arm in arm. She hid behind her dark glasses and tapped her walking stick on the sidewalk just in case someone was watching.

The Trinity Building was dark and deserted. I had to unlock the front door. We took the stairs up to the offices of Chandler, Wright & MacPherson on the second floor. A short, carpeted hallway led to our double glass doors. The company name was inscribed across the glass in large block letters.

I unlocked the doors, threw them open, and once again lifted Rachel off her feet. I carried her across the threshold. She tossed aside her walking stick and swooned. I carried her down the long, walnut-paneled hallway, over the plush crimson carpet, past my office, past Leonard Wright's office, and straight into the office of Mr. Charles Chandler. I deposited my woman on Chuckie's leather sofa and immediately began to undo the buttons of her silk blouse.

Naked in no time, she slipped off the sofa. I didn't see her go, caught as I was with my shirt up over my head. "Catch me if you can," she said as she scampered out the door.

I tore off the rest of my clothes and let the games begin. Finally, a frivolous use for those staid and solemn law offices.

Both of us in the buff, we used those offices for a rousing game of hide-and-seek. I found her the first time under Larry MacPherson's gigantic cherry desk. She screamed when I grabbed her but I dashed off to find a hiding place of my own. I hid in the utility closet behind a pile of copier paper. But my little pleasure seeker with the long dark hair found me in no time.

"The powerful smell of your maleness," she said, "was a dead giveaway." And then off she flew, out of the closet and into the maze of legal foreplay.

When finally I found her again, she sat on my high-back leather executive's chair facing the window overlooking Trinity Church. I crept in quietly. She did not hear me. I grabbed the back of the chair and swung her around. She gasped, her eyes filled with surprise. She looked beautiful and oh so vulnerable.

But before I could ravish her I had to ask. "Would you've told me Daniel was in London if I hadn't found out myself?"

She thought about it. "Maybe. I don't know. Probably. I certainly wouldn't've kept that bit of news from you on purpose."

"No?"

"I swear, Matthew, you're so damn jealous, so damn possessive."

"Did you guys...you know...screw around?"

"What if we did?"

That caught me off guard. "I just want to know is all."

"You always want to know everything. Why?"

The answer to that seemed obvious enough to me. "Because I think I have the right to know, that's why."

"Yes, but why do you have the right to know?"

"Because . . . because I love you."

A pause. And then, with an air of sarcasm, "Oh, I see."

I wanted to slap her across the face and knock her off that chair, off her high horse. I wanted to grab her by the hair and drag her back to my cave. I wanted to beat her and tie her down and fuck her whenever the desire rolled over me.

But none of those behaviors would do. So for the third time that day I picked her up. I carried her once more to the leather sofa in Dear Old Dad's office. We made love, slowly at first, but soon with a frenzy bordering on rage. She bit my lip so hard it began to bleed.

Afterward she fell into a light sleep. I lay there and tried to sort through my emotions. Love and hate all bottled up together, an elixir for a surefire trip to the funny farm.

Once rejuvenated, Rachel tagged me on the shoulder and took off out the door. "You're it!" she shouted.

The game turned into tag. We raced up and down those hallways, in and out of those plush offices. We pushed over chairs, crashed into tables, overturned books and typewriters and telephones.

I had Rachel cornered behind the reception desk just inside those glass doors, when all of a sudden we heard someone with a very low, gravelly voice say, "I's hates to bother ya but I's thinkin' I's needs some hep. Got a honkie downstairs bleedin' like a gut-shot hog."

The honkie downstairs, lying half in and half out of the elevator, was beyond help. He was dead, stone dead. And the man who had wandered into the offices of Chandler, Wright & MacPherson, the man who had caught Rachel and me stark naked playing sex tag, the man wearing rags and whose hands were covered with blood, was Mr. Isaiah Jackson.

Isaiah had been born and bred in Harlem. I don't want to go into any great detail because I'm not real sure of my facts. I don't even know the exact year of his birth. So let's just say Isaiah had a tough life. His education was spotty, and as far as I could fathom, the best job he ever held was as a garbage man for the New York City Sanitation Department in the early seventies. Fiscal cuts in the mid-seventies, when the city teetered on bankruptcy, led to Isaiah's dismissal.

He couldn't find another job, and he hadn't saved any money, so the poor bastard soon found himself out on the street. I gather he did some screwy stuff during his first tour as a homeless person: streaked across the Great Lawn during a Shakespeare-in-the-Park performance of As You Like It, flashed some Catholic school girls, sprinted into a Burger King and just stood there next to the frying bin stuffing French fries into his mouth. These offenses landed him down at the psych unit of Bellevue Hospital.

Isaiah needed more help than he received. He had the brainpower of a nine-year-old and a slightly psychotic personality to go along with it. But the last record of Mr. Isaiah Jackson I could find before that Fourth of July when the city of New York charged him with the murder of Mr. Albert Townley was Valentine's Day, February 14, 1983. That was the day the city of New York released him from Bellevue. For the next five and a half years the guy slipped through the cracks, became more or less a nonperson, an urban ghost walking the streets of Manhattan, picking up cigarette butts and begging for loose change.

The exact sequence of events on July 4, 1988, will, of course, never be known. Isaiah admitted more than once that yes, he had stuck an ice pick into Mr. Albert Townley's chest. But he also told police he did so because he believed Albert Townley was going to shoot him. And indeed, Mr. Albert Townley did have a .38-caliber revolver on his person. Unfortunately, the police officer who first arrived on the scene testified that Mr. Townley's .38 was locked inside his briefcase.

Albert Townley had an office up on the third floor, directly above Chandler, Wright & MacPherson. He was a commodities broker, a very fat cat, drove around Wall Street in a baby blue Rolls Royce Silver Shadow with the New York license plate AL'S TOWN. I knew him to say hello but that was about all. I didn't much like him. He was a pompous ass who loved to let other people know he had money. He also loved to wear expensive jewelry. The day he bled to death in that elevator, just the value of the rings on his fingers would've been enough for Isaiah Jackson to rent a room and eat three square meals a day for a year or more.

Not that an overabundance of gaudy jewelry justifies murder. But what I'm getting at, I suppose, is this: I saw Isaiah Jackson as a victim. So I decided to represent him. I volunteered to be his lawyer, pro bono, of course, no fee required or expected.

I believe I made this hasty decision for two reasons: first, I had this feeling, right from the start, that I was supposed to help Isaiah, protect him from the evil sorcery of society. I remembered the time all those years before back at the Hawthorn Compound when Daniel had ordered my peers to erase all memory of my crimes and misdemeanors because I would need an untarnished record for the trials and tribulations ahead. It was Isaiah's trial, I was suddenly certain, that Daniel had foreseen.

And the second reason, of course, was Rachel. She encouraged me to defend Isaiah Jackson. She saw it as my duty, my calling. The plight of Isaiah Jackson, she kept telling me, was the reason I had been led down the long legal road.

The court held Isaiah on a quarter-million-dollar bond. That meant I needed twenty-five grand to spring him from the slammer. I had the cash, had it collecting dust over at the bank; I just couldn't bring myself to lay it out. I had to draw the line somewhere. I was willing to defend Isaiah, but I was not willing to be responsible for him on a daily basis. Can you imagine him living here in this tiny flat with me? The two of us, shoulder to shoulder? And yet that's exactly what I should've done. It would've been the Christian thing to do.

But Christ, I had a life to lead. I mean, I wanted to help the guy but let's face it: he was wacked out. He'd been living on the streets for fifteen years. He had no clothes, no shoes, no money. And he smelled bad, his teeth were rotten, he looked horrible.

So I left him in jail. I justified it by telling myself he was better off there than out on the street.

Sure, Mac.

The legal system moves very slowly. By the end of the summer it was clear that Isaiah wouldn't go to trial for quite some time, months even. The prosecutor wanted me to convince Isaiah to cop a plea of manslaughter, forgo a trial by jury. And I might've done it except the asshole was so smug, as though he'd learned how to be a lawyer watching "L. A. Law" or some other stupid TV tripe, that I told him to go fuck himself.

"Isaiah Jackson is innocent," I insisted. "We're going to trial."

"Christ, Chandler, he's already pleaded guilty to plunging an ice pick into the guy's chest. Manslaughter would be doing your client a favor. You go to trial and it'll be murder two."

I felt like God. "We'll chance it."

ISAIAH'S PLIGHT BECAME MY PASSION. For the first time in my life I had something I could really sink my teeth into, something that fired my emotional pistons.

I talked about his case all the time. And for months Rachel was right there with me. We had dusk-to-dawn discussions not just about Isaiah's plight, but about the black man's plight in America, and not just the black man's plight, but the plight of all minorities: women, children, old people, the whole spectrum. They were all victims of the white male supremacy.

All my life I'd been looking for a cause, and suddenly here it was. It turned me into a self-righteous pain in the ass. I told everyone exactly what I thought. People don't like to hear exactly what you think. It unsettles them, makes them hide when you come to visit.

I was not only self-righteous, I was a lousy lawyer to boot. I didn't know the first thing about trial law, even less about criminal law. Professor Owen Straight had taught me a thing or two about legal ethics but he had failed to instruct me on the nuts and bolts of putting together a defense. Or perhaps I'd just been absent from class that day.

I did some research, read some books, held some interviews, but mostly I relied on emotion. See, I believed in the absolute innocence of Isaiah Jackson, and I felt sure my sincere, deep-rooted belief would win the day.

It didn't. After all the waiting, after the pretrial hearings and the jury selection, the trial finally began. I was a nervous wreck; didn't sleep for days leading up to it. And when the judge called me to deliver my opening statement, I nearly threw up all over my voluminous pile of notes. My face literally ran with sweat.

"Isaiah Jackson is not on trial here," I eventually managed to tell the jury. "Society is on trial here. Society brought this poor, homeless black man to the brink. Society drove him into the streets, took away his dignity and his right to a livelihood. Society..."

Slowly I warmed to my subject. My voice grew bolder, more

powerful. For the next fifteen minutes I verbally castrated a world dominated by wealthy white men. I painted a vivid picture of a gloomy underworld populated by people without hope, without opportunity.

I had spent dozens of hours preparing my opening statement. Rachel had helped me every step of the way. In fact, she had convinced me that a good, aggressive offense was the best defense.

What did she know? What did I know?

Beside me sat the accused, Mr. Isaiah Jackson, in a cheap suit. He looked helpless, pitiful, barely aware of what was going on around him. As I wound down, brought my statement to a close, I studied the faces of the jurors. All of them seemed moved by what I had said. I think I fully expected them to just stand up and start shouting, "Innocent! Innocent! Innocent!"

Too bad that's not the way it works. At a trial you must ask questions, uncover facts, present evidence. Well, I'd had months to do those things but I guess I'd figured it would all be over before we ever got to the mundane, nitty-gritty part.

It wasn't long before the judge noted my ineptitude.

"Approach the bench, Mr. Chandler." He was an older man, well into his fifties, a smallish WASP all the way from the chip on his shoulder to the perfectly clipped fingernails on his tiny white hands, an old friend of Chuckie's, wouldn't you know, Columbia Law and all that crap. He leaned over close to me, did his best to hold his voice down. "Do you know what the hell you're doing?"

I muttered something unintelligent.

"The prosecutor just questioned the cop who first dealt with Mr. Townley's body," he lectured. "The evidence he gave more or less cuts your client's throat. But when I asked you to cross-examine the witness, you gave me that smug look of yours and told me you didn't have any questions. Are you a bloody idiot?"

I muttered something else even less intelligent. In fact, I think I drooled.

He ordered me to get my act together, then sent me back to my seat. The trial continued. The prosecutor continued to call his witnesses. I continued to sit there like a spectator. One witness for the prosecution after another came and went without a word from the defense.

And then I heard the judge grumble, "Counsel, approach the bench."

I shot my opponent a contemptuous look, and together we crossed the wooden floor to where the judge sat glaring down at me. Then he turned his gaze to the prosecutor. "You know what I have to do?"

The prosecutor nodded.

I waited for an explanation.

It came quickly and harshly, and not at all quietly. "I'm calling a mistrial, Mr. Chandler. Every defendant in the state of New York is required to have a fair and competent lawyer. You are an incompetent boob. I could get a damn monkey to do a better job than you're doing. I'm postponing for three months, with the possibility of continuance. Make some calls, get some help, do something besides write yourself a fancy social speech."

It went on a while longer but I think you get the drift of His Honor's remarks.

Luckily for me, Rachel wasn't in the courtroom that day. She had expected to be there, but a few days before the trial began she had headed west for the safety of that big old white house on Main Street. The city was starting to drive her crazy. For months she had been threatening to sell the loft and move out of New York permanently.

I didn't take her seriously because usually all she needed was a couple of weeks of R&R back in Mercersburg. But the pressure was building. People recognized her everywhere she went. She couldn't go down to the market on the corner and buy an apple without some artistic wanna-be soliciting her opinion on everything from *Venus de Milo* to Warhol's tomato soup cans.

Her privacy had been invaded beyond an acceptable level. She had strangers calling her on the phone and knocking on her door in the middle of the night. A very private person had become a public commodity.

Then came some bad press. I forget where it started—the *Village Voice*, I think. This reporter who occasionally wrote about art got it in his head that Ms. Rachel Ann Frederick was not really blind. He claimed he saw her sitting all by herself in a midtown cinema laughing at something that simply wouldn't've been funny unless she had been able to actually *see* the movie. He followed her around for weeks after that, unbeknownst to Ms. Frederick, of course, and on more than one occasion he witnessed small moments that indicated to him that her blindness was—how shall we say?—fictitious.

Well, as you can easily imagine, this one article led to widespread speculation. Rachel couldn't leave the loft without a dozen or more cameras capturing her every footfall. There were fresh interpretations of her paintings and a virtual war of words between the believers and nonbelievers.

"Really, Rachel," I told her, "like I've been saying for months, something like this was inevitable. Sooner or later you were bound to slip."

"Bullshit," she snapped, angry at me even though I had done

absolutely nothing. "I just have to get away for a while and let the smoke clear."

So just three days before the trial began, she slipped out of the city in the middle of the night. I encouraged her to go. I helped her pack, even helped her sneak out the back door of her building and into Daniel's VW camper-van waiting up on the corner of Greene Street and Houston. I didn't much like the idea of her going off with him but I knew she had to get out of town, and fast.

That was early April of 1989. By the middle of May she had returned, rested and ready to stand her ground. "Papa," she told me, "thinks I should come clean. But it's too late for that. They'd never believe me. They'd eat me alive."

She spent the rest of the spring and the entire summer in New York. She watched very carefully every move she made. She became the quintessential blind person. So convincing was her act that sometimes even I forgot she could see as well as I.

All of her hard work paid off because by the end of July the speculation and criticism had for the most part ceased. Apparently she had convinced the doubters that her blindness was indeed a very real part of her life. Her reputation seemed secure.

Nevertheless, the hard work was taking its toll. Emotionally she teetered on the edge. I didn't know how close she was to jumping until one night in the middle of August when I heard her tell a group of journalists at a reception at the Museum of Modern Art that she was leaving for Japan at the end of September to study and paint in a remote mountain sanctuary.

I was standing right beside her. My mouth fell open. I thought maybe I hadn't heard quite right.

But I had. The reporters wanted to know the location of the sanctuary. Rachel smiled behind her dark glasses and told them it would no longer be a sanctuary if she answered that question.

About an hour later, in the cab heading back downtown, I asked a few questions of my own. "So what's all this about a sanctuary?"

"I've had it, Matthew," she said. "I can't take it anymore. I have to get out. This is like living inside an insane asylum."

"And whose fault is that?"

"I don't give a damn whose fault it is."

"Okay. Fine." I backed off. "So are you really going to Japan?"

She actually laughed. "No, Matthew, I'm not going to Japan. Japan is just to throw them off the track. I'm not going anywhere near Japan."

"Then where are you going?"

That was a question I asked over and over for the rest of the summer. But no matter how many times I asked, she refused to provide me with an answer.

"Think of it as a sabbatical, Matthew, a one-year sabbatical. I'm going off by myself for one year to catch my breath, think a few things through, paint without pressure or interruption. It's what I need to do. It's what I want to do."

"And why can't I know where you're going?"

"Because I want to be alone. Because within a week or a month you'd be calling me, and then you'd be coming to see me, and then I wouldn't be doing what I want to do, what I need to do."

"It all sounds pretty selfish if you ask me."

She shrugged. "No doubt it is. I am an incredibly selfish person. And for that, I can only say I'm sorry."

"So how'll I get in touch with you?"

"Through my father," she answered immediately, and I knew then she had been putting this plan into motion for quite some time. "You send any letters to him and he'll forward them to me."

"What if I just want to talk?"

"In an emergency I'm sure we can work something out."

"What if it's not an emergency?"

She looked at me and sighed. "Come on, Matthew, this is something I need to do."

That part of my personality prone to violence jumped to the fore and demanded I vent my anger with some physical abuse. But the bumbling coward in me proved more culpable. "So," I asked, "what about Daniel?"

"What about him?"

I swallowed hard. "You're not going off with him, are you?"

"No," came the quick, annoyed response.

"Do you think you'll see him?"

She took a deep breath, probably wondered how she had ever gotten involved with such a pitiful pain in the ass as me, and said, "No, Matthew, I don't plan on seeing him. I don't plan on seeing anyone. Daniel has no idea where I'm going. I doubt he even cares."

And so, on the last day of summer, her loft rented to some gallery owner's assistant, Rachel left the city. I didn't know it then but she would never spend another night in Soho. That part of her life, and my life, was over.

DANIEL HAWTHORN, ALIAS DANIEL ROMANKOVA, *parallel parks the VW van and steps out into the cool, windy late summer afternoon. He stands on the high ground above Onset Beach, a few miles west of Cape Cod. To the south lies Buzzards Bay. Dozens of sailboats dot the water, some with their spinnakers billowing in the breeze.*

Across the street he sees the Bayview Motel. Daniel crosses the street, climbs the half dozen steps to the motel office, and pulls open the door. He waits by the front desk.

Half a minute later a man not much older than Daniel comes in behind the desk from a back room. "Good afternoon. Can I help you?"

"Do you have any rooms?"

Before the man can answer, a young boy, maybe seven or eight, comes running into the motel office. He jumps up onto the desk and looks directly at Daniel. "Hi, mister. Do you know how to sail?"

Daniel smiles. "Say what?"

Before the boy, who has red hair and a face full of freckles, can repeat his question, the man, the boy's father, sweeps him off the desk with his forearm. "Let the gentleman catch his breath, Rex. How many times do I have to tell you not to assault the customers?"

Rex does not seem to mind the reprimand. He smiles, showing a wide gap between his front teeth. "Sorry, Pop, I just sure would like to learn how to use that boat."

"What kind of boat you got, kid?" *Daniel asks.*

"Just this little sailboat."

The boy's father explains. "We found the boat washed up on the shore. It was kind of beat up, had a busted rudder and a torn sail, but otherwise okay. Trouble is, I've never been on a sailboat in my life. We're from Albany, just bought this place early in the summer, so it's not like I was brought up near the water. The wife's back in Albany now, ill health *in the family, you know, so I haven't been able to get away to take Rex out in the boat."*

Daniel listens to the man's tale. "That's something," he says. "So what about a room?"

"I've got one or two vacancies."

"How much?"

"Just for the night?"

"You never know. I might stay a month."

The motel owner thinks it over. "It's off season, I could give you a special rate."

"How special?"

The motel owner hesitates. "Say sixty-five."

"Sixty-five bucks a night! That's highway robbery."

"With this view of the bay I get a hundred and ten during the season."

"I'll give you fifty."

"Sixty."

"Fifty-five cash, including tax."

"Deal."

They shake hands. The motel owner gives Daniel a key. "My name's Green, Harrison Green. You can call me Harry."

"Okay, Harry, thanks." Daniel starts toward the door.

"Hey, mister?" It's Rex.

Daniel turns around. "Yeah, kid?"

"You never told me if you could sail or not."

"Crewed with Turner aboard Courageous on his America's Cup victory. How does tomorrow morning at nine o'clock sound? We'll take a sail around the bay."

Rex breaks into a broad grin, then fixes his eyes on his father.

Harry casts a wary eye at Daniel. He wears a look of concern. "All right," he says finally, "as long as you wear your life preserver at all times."

When Daniel walks into the motel office a little after nine o'clock in the morning, he finds young Rex raring to go. The boy has on his swimsuit and a yellow slicker and a pair of old Keds. Harry looks nervous about the expedition. "The wife would kill me," he says, "if she knew I was sending the boy off to sea with a complete stranger."

"I'm not a stranger anymore, Harry," Daniel tells him, "I just spent the night under your roof."

The old Sunfish is chained to a piling down on an inlet off the bay.

Rex carries the new tiller and the centerboard. Daniel carries the mast and the sail and the aluminum boom.

They unchain the small boat and push it across the mud and sand to the water's edge. "Okay, kid," says Daniel, "I'm gonna show you how to rig 'er up, so pay attention."

Rex nods, his eyes wide with enthusiasm. He looks ready to sail around the world.

"First we secure the mast." Daniel shows Rex how to do it. Then he takes down the mast so the youngster can put it up himself. They do it like this every step of the way. First Daniel raises the sail, then he lowers the sail and hands the halyard to Rex. The boy is a fast learner. He understands right away how the gooseneck works to maneuver the sail and how to tie off the sheets to the cleats along the gunwales.

Daniel pushes the sailboat out into the inlet until it floats. Rex wades into the shallow water and climbs aboard. Daniel hands the boy the tiller and the centerboard. "All set, kid?"

"All set, Captain."

Daniel climbs over the side. There isn't much breeze in the inlet, but out on the bay he can see the water kicking and rolling. He orders his mate to use the centerboard as a paddle to help push them out into open water. Rex obeys.

Daniel attaches the rudder and tiller to the bracing on the stern of the boat. He tells Rex to set the centerboard, and then he brings the boy aft to show him how to secure the rudder to the transom. A few moments later the breeze grabs the sail and drives them out into the bay. Rex screams with pleasure as the boat shoots forward.

Instead of lecturing Rex on how to read the wind and trim the sail and operate the tiller, Daniel tells the youngster to sit back and enjoy the ride. They sail first on a broad reach out to the west. Then they come about and take a close-hauled tack to the southeast. Daniel hasn't sailed in a while, several years, anyway, but Mac taught him well; he handles the boat with skill and dexterity. Sailing, he knows, is like riding a bike: you never really forget.

Rex wants to go faster. He has no fear whatsoever. He wants to crash the bow straight into the oncoming wakes. He wants to heel the boat over until the top of the sail kisses the surface of the water.

"You're gonna make a hell of a sailor," Daniel shouts into the wind.

Then it's the boy's turn. "This is the stick," Daniel tells him, pointing to the tiller, "and this is the string," he adds, handing the mainsheet over to the youngster. "Steer with the stick, get speed with the string. That's all you need to know to sail."

Rex doesn't hesitate for a second. He grabs the tiller and takes command.

The sail drags and luffs, and more than once the small boat drifts in circles, but Rex doesn't care. Neither does Daniel. He keeps his mouth shut, figures the kid'll ask questions when he's ready.

Then Rex pushes the tiller too far to starboard and the wind catches the sail just right and flips the boat over, sending both captain and crew sprawling into the bay. They both come up laughing and bobbing in their bright orange life preservers. "You okay, kid?" Rex looks a little bewildered but otherwise just fine. He nods his head up and down.

Daniel stands on the centerboard and shows the boy how to right a capsized boat. Rex, starting to shiver, assures Daniel he can do it, then quickly climbs into the cockpit. Daniel swims under the boat, grabs the centerboard, and flips the boat over.

When he surfaces he finds Rex breathing hard and looking kind of pissed off. "Why'd you do that?"

"Because I know I can do it. Now I wanna see you do it. You don't wanna go out sailing by yourself, flip over out in the middle of the bay, and then discover you can't right the boat. You gotta know what you can and can't do in life, kid."

They get back to the motel early in the afternoon. They find Harry pacing out on the sidewalk. "I was about to call the Coast Guard. Figured something awful had happened."

But young Rex is just fine except for a sunburned nose and an empty stomach.

"Where were you all this time?"

"Sailing, Dad, we were out sailing."

"Kid's gonna make a hell of a sailor," says Daniel. "It'll be tough to keep him fixed on land." Then he turns and walks back to his room for a long hot shower.

He showers until the water runs cool. He rubs himself vigorously with a towel, then dresses in baggy canvas trousers and a cotton sweater. He packs up his leather satchel and goes downstairs to the motel office.

Harry stands behind the desk. "You got that boy all worked up."

"He's got the bug."

"I'll say. I better learn myself before he gets away from me."

"Good idea."

"Maybe one day this week you could take me for a spin around the bay."

"I'd love to Harry, but I'm checking out."

"Checking out? Now? This afternoon?"

"Just as soon as I give you back your key."

"But I thought you were gonna stay a while. Maybe a month."

Rex comes in from the back room. He has jelly on his chin and a peanut-butter-and-jelly sandwich in his hand. He sees the leather satchel on the floor. *"You're leaving?"*

"That's right, kid," says Daniel. *"I'm headin' down the road."*

"But I thought we'd go sailin' again. Maybe tomorrow."

"You're on your own now, Rex. You can teach your old man the ropes."

"But, but . . . but I don't know the ropes."

"Sure you do. Just don't be afraid."

Rex wipes the jelly off his chin. He tries to make himself taller. *"I'm not afraid."*

"Atta boy."

Harry is busy writing something on a piece of paper. He finishes and pushes it across the desk to Daniel. It is the bill for the room.

Daniel checks it over. *"Fifty-five bucks. That's what we agreed, right?"*

"Right."

Daniel borrows Harry's pen, turns over the bill. *"Let's see,"* he mumbles, *"five hours at, say, thirty-five an hour. . ."* He writes it all down and pushes the piece of paper back to Harry.

"What's this?" Harry asks. *"A hundred and seventy dollars. For what?"*

"That's my fee for teaching Rex how to sail. Less the fifty-five I owe you makes it a hundred and twenty. Pretty cheap, really. Most sailing schools get fifty and up an hour."

Harry keeps staring at the piece of paper. *"This is ridiculous."*

"No, it's not," says Daniel, *"it's perfectly reasonable. Really."*

"You're serious?"

"Absolutely. I'd prefer cash if you can swing it."

Harry's not real sure what to do. He rubs his hands together, stammers a time or two, glances at his son. He pulls open the cash drawer under the desk. *"I doubt I have that much cash. The people in room two charged their stay on a credit card, and room three hasn't—"*

Daniel holds up his hand. *"Forget the money, Harry. Call it square. I had a good time sailing, anyway. Could hardly even call it work."*

Harry looks relieved. *"You sure?"*

Daniel nods. *"Maybe next time I pass through you can put me up for nothing."*

"Sure, no problem."

Daniel and Harry shake hands. Rex wipes his sticky fingers on his shirt. He shakes hands with Daniel also.

"Keep your sails full of wind, kid."

"Yes, sir, Captain."

Daniel picks up his satchel and leaves the motel. He crosses the street and climbs into his van. He fires up the engine and heads east for Cape Cod and his rendezvous with Rachel.

I WROTE TO RACHEL AT LEAST TWICE, sometimes three times, a week. Just as she had ordered, I sent the letters to Coach Frederick and he forwarded them to his daughter.

She usually wrote to me once a week, long, rambling letters about painting and creativity and the wonderful new life she had created for herself. She had even taken on a new identity, an alias, some stranger named Misty Grey.

I looked forward to her letters with great anticipation, but in the end they never failed to disappoint, to leave me feeling low and blue. I suppose I opened each of those letters hoping to find a woman broken and in desperate need of my emotional support. It never happened.

So all alone once again, I rode the Broadway local down to Wall Street and the offices of Chandler, Wright & MacPherson. What else could I do? I loathed my work with the rich and powerful more than ever, but during the final months of '89 and the early months of '90, I existed in a kind of physical vacuum. I was more robot than man. I operated like a piece of computer hardware. The alarm sounded in the morning: I opened my eyes, performed my various functions for the next sixteen or seventeen hours, then crawled back into bed and closed my eyes. A dead man could've done it.

When I could find the energy, I worked on the Isaiah Jackson case. In the first trial I had taken the social approach, presenting Isaiah as a victim of society's bigotry and neglect. We all know how far that defense got me. So at the next trial I decided to stick a little closer to the facts. Whatever they were.

A wide range of circumstances kept pushing the trial date farther and farther back on the judge's docket. I felt bad for Isaiah languishing in prison but at the same time I was glad for the reprieve. The idea of going back into court and making a jackass of myself did not exactly stir within me powerful emotions of joy and passion.

I'd been looking for another attorney to help me with the case but thus far I hadn't found much interest. "No dough, no go," was the general response I received from my well-heeled Wall Street colleagues. But finally, late in January, just a few weeks before the trial date of February 15, 1990, I found my man.

His name was Charles "Chuckie" Chandler, Dear Old Dad, the one and only.

He walked into my office late that winter afternoon and closed the door. The day had already turned to dusk. A few wet flakes fell from a steel gray sky.

"What the hell am I going to do with you?" he asked. "My gut tells me you're a pain in the ass, a goddamn malcontent." Chuckie rarely used such hard language. He must've been in turmoil over his boy's predicament. He continued, "But your mother says you're a romantic, insists you have a good heart."

Three cheers for Martha. I felt a tear form in the corner of my eye.

"She says helping this black man is the right thing to do." Pause. And then, "I don't know about that, I think it's damn possible he's as guilty as Brutus, but I do know a Chandler always comes to the aid of another Chandler."

I wanted to stand up and give my old man a bear hug but it just wasn't in me, the genes just couldn't comprehend it. So I just nodded and said, "Thanks Dad."

No time for sentiment. Attorney Chandler wanted to get right to work. "Bring out the case folder, Matt," he demanded, "we don't have much time."

We worked deep into the night. We even ordered in Chinese food. And near the end of the session he disappeared for a few minutes, and when he returned he held high a bottle of Glenlivet. "Keep it in my bottom drawer," he confessed, "for occasions just like this."

Isaiah Jackson's second trial for murder lasted three days. Charles Chandler represented the defendant. I sat behind the defense table, relegated to a secondary role. This was done partly to impress the judge but also because I would later be called as a defense witness.

In his opening statement, attorney Chandler used an approach similar to the one I had used. But he toned down his rhetoric, spoke in a much less accusatory voice. He talked about equality and justice, and more than once he referred to Isaiah as a victim.

Isaiah's months in prison, however, had not been kind. He did not look like a victim. He looked mean and ornery, and he couldn't stop sweating. It wasn't his fault. Outside it was cold and raw and damp, but inside that courtroom it felt like a furnace. The thermostats had gone haywire, driving the temperature well into the eighties.

The prosecution opened its case by parading before the court a series of witnesses who described in graphic detail how the deceased, Mr. Albert Townley, had died. It came down to this: an ice pick had been plunged into his heart, causing cardiac arrest and death.

We all knew Isaiah had done the plunging; he had admitted as much. But had he done so in self-defense? That's what we were there to find out.

The prosecution called the cop who had first dealt with Albert Townley's dead and bloody body. He insisted there had been no gun in evidence at the scene of the crime. He claimed that only later did he discover a .38-caliber revolver in Townley's briefcase. "And that briefcase," he said, "was locked. I needed a hammer and chisel to get it open."

Attorney Chandler rose to cross-examine. "I ask you, sir, if the .38-caliber revolver in question was locked inside Mr. Townley's briefcase, how then did Mr. Jackson know the gun existed?"

"Objection, Your Honor!" shouted the prosecutor. "Calls for speculation."

"Overruled."

The cop shrugged. "Hey, I dunno. A lucky guess. A desperate grab for motive."

"A lucky guess?" asked Dear Old Dad, the sarcasm in his voice filling the courtroom.

Again the cop shrugged. "Look, what can I tell you? Fourteen years on the job I've never once heard a guy admit he did it. They always got an excuse. The dead guy always had a gun or a knife or a broken bottle. In this case, when I got to the scene, there was no gun, just an ice pick sticking out of the dead guy's chest. What more do you want from me?"

Nothing, thank you very much.

Chuckie tried but he couldn't budge the officer's story. Even I began to wonder why the cop would lie. If he'd seen a gun, why wouldn't he just say so?

That night, back in the office, Chuckie said as much. "Doesn't look good, Matt. A jury always believes a cop in a case like this. And I'll tell you, I think maybe your boy did it. He probably got pissed off when Al wouldn't fork over some cash, one thing led to another, and pretty soon out came the ice pick."

Ouch. "So what are you going to do?"

"I'm going to put you on the stand. Let you tell your side of the story: how Isaiah came up to the office, how he calmly told you there had been an accident. I'll wonder out loud why a cold-blooded murderer would do such a thing. Why would he report his crime? Why wouldn't he just run for his life? Hopefully we'll create a little doubt in the minds of the jurors."

I nodded, and then he hit me with this: "I've subpoenaed Rachel."

"Rachel! Why?"

"Just to corroborate your story. She'll be testifying after you."

"I don't think that's such a good idea, Dad." I felt myself start to sweat. I had to think fast. "I mean, she didn't see anything. She couldn't see anything."

"It never hurts," he said, "to put a handicapped person on the stand. It might give your boy a little breathing room."

My boy. Great.

During the night Chuckie changed his mind. He decided to call Rachel to the stand first, not me. I didn't know how he had found her so fast—through Coach Frederick, I learned later—but there she was, bigger than life.

She entered the courtroom wearing dark glasses. A red bandanna covered her hair. She held on to the bailiff's arm. He led her down the aisle to the witness stand. Her head did not wander left or right. She took the oath: swore to tell the truth, the whole truth, and nothing but the truth. So help her God. And then she proceeded to lie lie lie.

I had not seen her for months. She looked relaxed and bright with color.

After a few preliminary questions, defense attorney Chandler asked the witness, "You are blind, is that correct, Miss Frederick?"

"Yes," came the answer, loud and clear.

"And you were also blind on July fourth, 1988, the date of the incident in question?"

"Yes," she answered, and without a moment's hesitation.

"Can you please tell the court what happened that day inside the Trinity Building."

I had this sudden twinge of paranoia that my love might recount all the sordid details of our sexual exploits that wild and woolly day. But no, she carefully avoided the juicy parts.

In fact, Rachel did not really have much to tell. "I was in the reception area of Chandler, Wright and MacPherson," she explained calmly, "with Mr. Matthew Chandler when Mr. Isaiah Jackson came through the door and told us there had been an accident. Almost immediately Mr. Chandler and Mr. Jackson left the office and went down the stairs to the lobby. Since I am blind and only would have been in the way, I stayed behind."

"What did you do after Mr. Chandler and Mr. Jackson left the office?"

"I dialed 911 and asked for an ambulance."

"And then?"

"And then I waited for Matthew. . . for Mr. Chandler to return."

That much was true. Rachel had called 911. She had waited upstairs while I went down to the lobby. The truth and nothing but the truth, except for the bit about her blindness.

The prosecutor had no questions for Miss Frederick. Harassing a handicap would only cause him trouble.

The judge called a fifteen-minute recess. I caught up with Rachel out in the corridor. There was already a small throng of reporters taking her picture and hurling questions, mostly concerning her whereabouts during the past several months.

I found an empty room, where we had a moment's respite. "I'm sorry," I said, "I had no idea you would be called to testify."

She was angry. "This is humiliating," she said, "and totally unnecessary. I don't see why—"

Dear Old Dad stuck his head through the door. "Matthew, we need to talk. And the two of you really shouldn't be discussing—"

"Okay, Dad, I'll just be a second. Be right with you."

He growled at me and closed the door.

"Can I see you," I asked, "afterward?"

"No," she said, "I'm leaving."

I fumbled around for the right thing to say. "Are you all right?"

"I'm fine."

"But is everything okay? Do you need anything?"

She wasn't buying it. "You should go, Matthew. And so should I."

I started to panic, feared if she got away, I might never see her again. "But when can I see you? I just want to talk, spend a little time together."

She thought about it, softened. "I'd like that, too." Then, after a moment, "If you can promise you won't tell a soul, I'll meet you in Mercersberg on . . . on say, the first day of spring. That's only a few weeks from now. We'll take a long walk in the fields together."

I promised to tell no one, then assured her I would be there. She kissed me lightly on the lips. Before I could return the kiss she slipped away, left me standing there yet again with my confusion and my expectations.

And then it was my turn to lie, to commit perjury.

I didn't tell any grand lies, nothing that would have changed the outcome of Isaiah Jackson's trial. But lies nevertheless.

"Please tell the court," said Charles Chandler, "what happened in the Trinity Building on the afternoon of July fourth, 1988."

"Miss Frederick and I had stopped by the office," I lied, "so I could pick up some papers for a case I had pending."

"And while you were there what happened?"

I told pretty much the same story Rachel had told earlier.

"So," continued the defense attorney, "you followed the defendant downstairs. What happened when you reached the lobby?"

"Mr. Jackson and I came out of the stairwell, and right away I saw the body of Albert Townley lying near the elevator. I started toward him but before I got very far two policemen came rushing through the front door. One of them crossed to the body and the other one herded us out onto the sidewalk. We stood there, just the two of us, Mr. Jackson and myself, for three or four minutes. Before long the police had the whole area roped off."

"And during this time did Mr. Jackson make any attempt to escape?"

"None whatsoever."

"What happened next?"

"I gave a brief statement to the police, then I was given permission to go upstairs and get Miss Frederick."

"Thank you, Mr. Chandler," said my father. "No further questions."

I took a deep breath and started off the stand, happy the ordeal was over. But then Dear Old Dad sat down, and the prosecutor, the guy I had told several months earlier to go fuck himself when he tried to get me to settle out of court, stood up and strode toward me.

"Isn't it true, Mr. Chandler," he asked, nice as can be, "that you and Miss Frederick were stark naked when the defendant showed up at the offices of Chandler, Wright and MacPherson on the afternoon of July fourth, 1988?"

Wham! Anyone in that courtroom who had dozed off was suddenly brought wide awake by the accusation.

"What!?" I asked. How the hell, I wondered, did he know about that? I shot a glance at the old boy. His lower jaw had fallen down around his navel.

Fortunately his legal instincts brought him back into the action. "Objection!" shouted Dear Old Dad. "Irrelevant."

"Overruled."

"Were you and Miss Frederick naked?"

I swallowed hard and whispered, "Yes."

The bastard made me say it louder, loud and clear.

"Yes," I said, "we were."

The jury gasped. Just like that I had become a useless witness for my buddy Isaiah.

Mr. Prosecutor had shot me dead, but his vendetta continued. "Tell us, Mr. Chandler, did you see a thirty-eight-caliber revolver in the lobby of the Trinity Building on July fourth, 1988?"

I waited for the objection but Chuckie had melted into his seat. He was both seething with anger and bright red with embarrassment. I was on my own.

"No," I answered, "I didn't. But I never really got close—"

"You were in the lobby, not more than ten feet from the body."

"Yes, but—"

"And did you see a gun, any gun at all?"

I shook my head. "No, I never saw a gun."

He could have stopped right there, victory was his, but he was intoxicated with the sound of his own voice. "So you didn't see a gun. And we know Miss Frederick didn't see a gun. After all, she was blind, isn't that right, Mr. Chandler?"

Chuckie definitely should have objected at this point. Not only was the question totally irrelevant but the son of a bitch was badgering me. Too bad Dear Old Dad had drifted off. His eyes had gone blank.

I saw my old law professor, Owen Straight, turn over in his grave. Owen wanted me to tell the truth. And I wanted to tell the truth, for several reasons. I wanted to tell that prosecutor he was dead wrong, Miss Frederick had been able to see just fine that day. I wanted to tell the truth to spite Rachel for putting me in such a compromising position. And I wanted to tell the truth so I would be able to live with myself once the trial had come to a close.

Before I answered I had enough time to realize that Owen had been right: truth is nothing more than a principle. If I could lie about this, then surely I had it in me to lie about most anything. It seemed quite possible to me at the time that my whole life might be nothing but a lie, a long and futile path of deception.

"Yes," I nevertheless told the prosecutor, "that's right. Miss Frederick was blind. No way she could have seen a gun."

That bastard didn't even know he was forcing me to lie; he thought I was telling the truth, the whole truth, and nothing but the truth. So help me God. He was just using his dominance over me to drive home his point about the gun. "Then it's fair to say," he said, talking now directly to the jury, "that neither of you saw a thirty-eight-caliber revolver. You saw only the dead body of Albert Townley, lying on the floor of the lobby with an ice pick in his chest?"

My torment belonged only to me. All I could do was nod.

✳   ✳   ✳

After the judge sent the jury to the jury room, Dear Old Dad herded me into that same room where earlier I had rendezvoused with Rachel. He was not a happy trooper.

"Goddamn you, Matthew! Running around naked in the office of Chandler, Wright and MacPherson! What the hell were you thinking about? And why the hell didn't you tell me? For chrissakes, if I'd known about that, I never would have put you on the stand."

I just stood there and hung my head, stared at the dusty floor.

"They're going to find your boy guilty. And as soon as they do we're going to pack up our briefcases and get the hell out of here." He slammed his fist down on the wooden table in the middle of the room. "Look at me!" he ordered. "Look at me, you stupid bastard!"

But I couldn't. My head weighed a thousand pounds. Try though I did, I couldn't lift it.

The jury convicted Isaiah in less than two hours.

When the verdict was read Isaiah barely changed his expression. I don't know, maybe he was glad, maybe he liked it in prison. A bed with clean sheets, three square meals a day, a roof over his head.

He turned and shook my hand. "I wants to thank ya, Mistuh Chandler. Ya done all ya could. It's God will."

I didn't believe any of that for a second.

They handcuffed him and led him away.

Chuckie and I watched him go. The old boy, calmer now, looked relieved to have the affair finally brought to a close. And who could blame him? It certainly hadn't been his finest hour. Nor had it been mine.

MY MOTIVES HAD BEEN ALL WRONG. I thought my defense of Isaiah Jackson had been inspired by a desire to help the downtrodden, to see justice served, to give something back to the system that had given me so much. What a load of crap. My motives were selfish, pure and simple. I wanted to make Matthew Chandler look good. I wanted to make Matthew Chandler feel good. Altruism be damned; I doubt very much such a scheme even exists.

After the trial I grew gloomy and depressed. I felt sorry for myself. I felt like a loser. I was moving into my mid-thirties, and everywhere I looked I saw dead ends and darkness.

My mood picked up some near the end of March, on the first day of spring, when I traveled out to Mercersburg for my reunion with Rachel. It's hard for me to believe but that was a year and a half ago already. It seems like only a few brief weeks ago.

We spent three days together. We talked a little about the trial, not much. We avoided any and all mention of perjury.

I told her I hated New York: the homeless people living in the subway stations and the crack addicts freezing to death on the benches in Washington Square Park and the noise and the greed and the filth and the meanness. I told her I hated my job and I hated myself for being such a dishonest and mediocre lawyer. And then in the very next breath I told her I missed her and loved her. I asked her when was she coming back and when was she going to answer the question I had asked all those months, all those years ago.

"What question is that, Matthew?" She looked puzzled. Her eyes sparkled. She looked as lovely and as healthy as I had ever seen her. She had changed her hair. It was short, like a boy's, and blond; no doubt part of her new identity. I hated to admit it, just as I hated to admit that her months away from the city, away from me, had obviously been a success, but her new appearance made her even more beautiful than before.

"Never mind," I answered.

"You mean about getting married?"

I nodded.

She held me close. I felt like a little boy.

"I'll make you a deal," she said after the embrace.

"A deal?"

"Yes. Last fall I told you I wanted a year, one year, all to myself."

"So?"

"So it's been six months. Let's wait another six months and see where we are."

I made some quick calculations. "Six months?"

"Yes," she said, "September."

An idea came to me. "Maybe we could meet at the house in Siasconset?"

She thought about it. "That's perfect. We'll have a vacation."

"Right," I said, "a vacation." I was already getting excited. "We'll sit on the beach, go for walks, listen to the breakers roll up onto the sand."

"It sounds wonderful."

"So it's a date?"

She nodded. "Absolutely."

I felt better. I started to relax. I had something to look forward to, something to keep my sights on.

My depression, however, lingered. It manifested itself in my inability to maintain an erection. Rachel and I spent hours together during those three days in Mercersburg, much of the time naked and close, but not once did we have intercourse. I kept apologizing but the more I apologized the smaller it got. I wanted to cut the damn thing off.

Rachel didn't say much, just giggled a little and told me not to worry about it. She said it didn't matter, that it made no difference.

Right.

Impotency aside, I returned to the city feeling reasonably good. Six months didn't seem like such a long time. And after that, well, I felt sure everything would come up roses.

I even went back to work with a renewed vigor. Perhaps vigor is too strong a word, so let us just say I gave the firm a decent day's work for the first time in a long time. Occasionally, a day or two even went by when I didn't think about Rachel. Or Daniel.

I couldn't even remember the last time I had seen him. But then, in late August, just a few weeks before Rachel and I were to meet on Nantucket, he knocked on my door. I was sitting here in my hovel trying to deal with yet another hot and humid New York summer.

"Hold on to your hat," I called, "I'm coming."

When I opened the door and saw him, I wasn't sure if I was glad to see him or not.

Still, I invited him in. "How did you get into the lobby?" I asked. "The front door is supposed to be locked."

He shrugged. "Some guy carrying a guitar let me in." He gave me a bear hug, just like old times. "So how you doin', old buddy?"

I sort of rolled my eyes. "Pretty good, I guess. And you?"

"Can't complain."

Neither of us was very comfortable.

I watched him closely. He looked edgy. Maybe it was just my imagination.

"I heard about the trial," he said. "Sorry."

"Fuck it," I said. And then, "Who told you?"

He thought about it. "Must've been Carolyn. I guess she got it from your mother."

"Sure." I didn't believe him, not for a second.

He took a long, slow look around the apartment. His eyes fixed for most of a minute on Rachel's two oil paintings hanging on the wall.

I told him I was going out to Nantucket with her.

He nodded.

I asked him if he'd seen her. He said no. I didn't believe that, either.

I had the feeling he was maybe waiting for an invitation to join us. No way was he about to get one from me.

But then he shifted gears. "I might need a lawyer, Mac."

"A lawyer? Why?"

"Something's come up."

"You wanna tell me about it?"

He didn't. He just wanted to know if there was an extradition treaty between the United States and Argentina.

I asked why he wanted to know but he wouldn't answer. I knew it had something to do with that old Nazi he and Victor had been tracking down in Argentina for the past hundred years, but beyond that I could only speculate.

Then those old motives came into play again. I stood there and told him, my oldest pal in the whole world, that I would find out what I could about any extradition treaties between the United States and Argentina, but in the back of my head I was hoping the son of a bitch was in deep shit with the authorities all the way from Buenos Aires to Washington, D.C.

That's swell, Mac. Really nice work.

He hung around most of the afternoon. We went out and drank a few beers.

"So where you headed now?" I asked him as we stood next to his old VW camper-van parked along Seventeenth Street outside my apartment.

"Mendham," he told me. "Have a few things I need to discuss with Victor."

"Well," I said, "I'll see you around."

"Right," he said, "see you around."

Finally, a few weeks later, the time came to roll. I packed my bag and flew from New York to Nantucket. I rented a Jeep, ready as always to take that drive out to the lonely wastelands of Great Point. I imagined the two of us out there, spreading a blanket on some desolate beach, sharing a bottle of wine, then making love with the sun setting and the sand still warm with the day's heat.

I reached the house in Siasconset on Friday September 14, two days before Rachel was scheduled to arrive. I cleaned and dusted that old beach house from top to bottom. I filled the refrigerator and the cupboard with Rachel's favorite foods. I stocked up on wine. I made sure the old stereo still worked. I put fresh sheets on the bed.

The next day I rested, sort of. I took a long walk on the beach. I drove around the island in the Jeep. And late in the afternoon I went over to the yacht club on South Beach Street, where Chuckie kept his sloop and I kept my catamaran.

I hadn't sailed my catamaran in a couple of years but I hoped to have the opportunity during our stay on the island. And just in case that opportunity arose, I decided to check the rigging, make sure the boat was safe and seaworthy.

The old cat had some problems, neglect mostly. The right rudder was just about shot, practically broken off. The mainsheet traveler was rusted solid, so the mainsail had only limited maneuverability. The trampoline had a few holes in it and was growing threadbare along the starboard hull.

The main and rear beams, which held the two hulls together, posed the worst problem. They, more than anything else on the boat, needed to be replaced. In heavy seas with strong winds, the beams could possibly fail.

The sailboat had some other minor deficiencies as well, but nothing I considered vital or dangerous. No sailboat, not even a brand-new one, is a hundred percent perfect. I wouldn't've sailed that cat up to Nova Scotia or down to the Keys, but it definitely seemed safe enough for a cruise around the Sound.

The morning dawned. A low fog hung over the sea. I sat out on the deck with a mug of coffee and watched the sun rise out of the fog. I decided right then and there to ask Rachel if she wanted to spend the winter with me in Siasconset. I'd quit my job, lock up my apartment, and pass those months writing poetry and wandering along the beach. Rachel could paint as many hours each day as she desired. I would promise to leave her alone.

I shaved and showered, brushed my teeth twice. Long before I had to leave I climbed into the Jeep and headed across the island. I drove slowly, tried to relax. I drove into town on Washington Street, turned right on Commercial, left on New Whale, and found a parking spot outside the A&P. I still had an hour to kill before the ferry arrived.

I walked up Main Street on the old cobblestones once used for ballast on the great wooden whaling ships. I bought the *Boston Globe* and sat on the steps of the Pacific National Bank Building. I glanced at the headlines. The news seemed far away, like some remnant of fiction written long ago, something to read for a moment's diversion.

Eventually the hour passed. I headed down to the wharf. A few other islanders had gathered to meet the ferry. We could see it not too far offshore as it rounded Brant Point and entered the harbor. The pilot sounded the horn, announcing its presence to all those who might lie in its path or be interested in its arrival.

Slowly the ferry approached, swung around, and backed into its berth on Straight Wharf. The crew secured the lines, fixed the gangway. My eyes raced from passenger to passenger as I tried to find her familiar face.

And then, as you already know, as I have already told you, I found not only her face, but his. Try as I have over the past twelve months to replay that moment in a more positive light, I simply have not been able to change the reality of the situation. He is always there, right at her side, his hand upon her shoulder. No matter how hard I try to erase him from the picture, the Gypsy reappears. . . .

He sees me in the crowd. He waves and smiles. The son of a bitch. If I had a gun, say, strapped to my hip, a six-shooter, I'd pull it out and blow him away, blow him right off the canvas.

In another age, in some distant time, I would've been permitted, expected even, to defend my honor by putting a couple of bullets through his heart. Not so in this age of false civility. In this day and age I am supposed to smile and take it on the chin.

And so I did. And so I do.

RACHEL WAKES TO THE SOUND OF A FOGHORN *blasting off Hyannis Point. She rolls over, glances at her watch—7:20—and wonders why Daniel has not arrived.*

She showers and dresses and prepares for another day of blindness. At the front desk she leaves a message for Daniel, then goes into the restaurant for breakfast. Fog rolls through Hyannis harbor but already the sun has started to burn off the mist.

When she returns to her room Daniel has still not arrived. She waits another half an hour, then, just after nine o'clock, she repacks her bag and leaves the motel.

She walks down Ocean Street using her stick. A man offers his assistance. He helps her across the street and up to the ticket window, where she purchases a one-way ticket on the 9:30 ferry to Nantucket.

At 9:15 she boards the ferry. Still no sign of Daniel. She hopes nothing has happened, that everything is all right. She watches through her dark glasses as the other passengers board the ferry and settle into their seats.

A young man sits beside her. She pretends not to notice him.

"Excuse me," he asks, "are you Rachel Ann Frederick, the painter?"

She cannot believe she has been recognized. It seems almost impossible. She has the uneasy feeling the young man has been following her for the past year, has documented every move she's made, has captured her whole other life as Misty Grey on videotape.

"Yes," she answers, "I am."

He smiles. "I thought so."

She waits.

"I'm an artist," the young man says, "and, well, I just wanted to tell you how much I admire your work. Especially the paintings you've done since you, well, since you—"

"Since I went blind?"

The young man lowers his eyes. "Yes, since you went blind."

She sees through her dark glasses now that he is shy and harmless. His red face and sweaty palms give him away. "Thank you," she says, "I appreciate your kindness."

"Well," he says finally, "sorry I bothered you. I'll leave you alone now."

She starts to invite him to stay and talk, but she hears familiar footsteps hurrying up the gangplank. "It's no bother," she says. "Thank you for stopping."

The young man stands, moves off.

Daniel drops onto the empty seat. "Damn," he says, slightly out of breath, "almost didn't make it."

The gangplank is hauled in, the captain blows the whistle, and the Nantucket-bound ferry pulls slowly away from the dock, away from the mainland.

GREETINGS, GREETINGS, HUGS AND KISSES ALL AROUND.

"Oh, Daniel's come," I didn't say but definitely wanted to, "how nice, how wonderful, how special. Just what I'd been hoping."

More hugs and kisses, and how was the ferry? Oh, just fine. The Sound was as calm as a bathtub. How nice, how wonderful, how special.

The bullshit flowed for a good five minutes right there on the wharf. The three of us knew the scene was fucked up, not at all what it was supposed to be. But our little threesome delicately avoided touching it—even Daniel, king of come-as-you-are.

The crew off-loaded the luggage. Daniel waded into the crowd to claim the bags.

As soon as he was out of earshot: "What the hell is he doing here?"

Rachel, playing the role of the helpless little blind girl by clutching pitifully on to my arm, avoided answering with another hug and then a long, hard kiss.

That kiss continued until I heard him say, "Easy, kids. You'll excite the masses, work them into a frenzy."

I looked at him standing there smiling with Rachel's suitcase in one hand and that old leather rucksack in the other. I couldn't help myself. "So," I asked him, "where you staying, Hawk? I'll drop you off."

This kind of sarcasm does not offend Gypsies. Daniel let loose a hearty laugh, gave me another hug, and said, "Mac, I told Rachel you'd be glad to see me."

I took Rachel's hand. We eased our way through the crowd. Daniel followed with the bags. We crossed the A&P parking lot to the Jeep. For a change I drove, Rachel sat beside me, and Daniel sat in the back. I could see him in the rearview mirror. He looked curious, alert, as though all this were just another adventure. And I suppose, in a way, it was.

I swung the Jeep out into the line of traffic and headed back to Siasconset.

The conversation moved as though under the weight of an unwieldy burden. Mostly we talked about the weather, the island, the crossing, crap like that. Then silence.

He broke it. "I was thinking on the ferry on the way over here."

My good manners forced me to ask, "Oh, yeah, about what?"

"About that Around the Island Race we've been threatening for the past twenty years."

I immediately remembered the time he and Buckley and I had become stranded in a dead calm out on the Sound. He'd challenged me to a sailboat race that day, and from time to time ever since he had renewed that challenge, usually just to rile me up, piss me off.

"Yeah?" I asked. "So?"

"So I think the time's finally come to have that race."

"Touché," was all I said, "I accept the challenge." And then, for the remainder of the ride out to Baxter Road, I sat there conjuring up images of his sailboat foundering out on the Sound and me heaving-ho nearby, tossing him a lifeline, but snatching it away a moment before he could grab it, a little game of nautical cat and mouse.

As we climbed out of the Jeep and walked toward the house, I wondered about our sleeping arrangements. I decided to take charge of the situation.

So as we stepped through that infamous sliding glass door and into the living room, I announced, "Rachel and I will sleep on the third floor. Daniel, you can either sleep in the second-floor guest room or on the Hide-A-Bed in the den."

No response. Seconds ticked away. The planet circled the sun. Around and around.

"Your choice," I added.

Another brief silence, then Rachel made her announcement. "I'd prefer to have a room of my own, if that's possible."

Oh, of course. Fine. . . . I didn't say a word, not a single solitary goddamn word.

Daniel took the Hide-A-Bed, Rachel took the guest room, and yours truly took his old room on the third floor. Daniel and I were like slices of bread with Rachel the meat in between.

Was there trouble in the air?

I was ready to hurt somebody, I can tell you that.

"I'd like to maybe go up and lie down for a while," Rachel said.

So I carried her suitcase up the stairs. We went into the guest bedroom. She sat down on the side of the bed and took off her dark glasses for the first time.

I thought she looked pale, tired around the eyes. "You all right?"

"Just a little dizzy," she said. "Probably the crossing. A short nap and I'll be fine."

I stood there in the doorway with the million or so things I wanted to say. But before I could say a word, Rachel leaned back, put her head on the pillow, and closed her eyes.

Quietly I closed the door. Back downstairs I found no sign of Daniel. Had he done us all a favor and flown off to Budapest or Buenos Aires? No such luck. I saw him standing out on the deck, leaning against the railing, sipping a beer, staring out at the sea.

I stepped through the doorway, out into the sun. "I'm still working on that information you wanted about the extradition treaty between the U.S. and Argentina."

He drained the beer and crushed the can. "Forget the treaty, Mac."

"What do you mean, forget the treaty? I figured you must've whacked that old Nazi and now the authorities are hot on your trail."

He laughed. "Excellent imagination, Mac, but I'm afraid you figured wrong. Forget that old Nazi. Forget the treaty. It's all over, finished."

That was not what I wanted to hear. I wanted to hear him grovel. I wanted to hear him beg for my legal expertise. I wanted to hear a full and complete confession. I wanted to be the judge for a change. And maybe the jury as well. Dream on, Mac.

We listened to the waves breaking on the beach far below. I hated him right then, wanted in the worst way to stick an ice pick in his chest. But I couldn't do that, so instead I asked, "That hobo, the one out in the railroad yard in Pennsylvania?"

"Yeah?"

"Did you really kill him? Plunge that Bowie knife into his heart?"

Daniel looked at me. Our eyes held for most of a minute.

"What do you think?" he asked.

I didn't know. I couldn't tell. Were those the eyes of a cold-blooded killer? I shook my head, then changed my mind and nodded, very quickly, just once.

"Don't sweat it, Mac," he said. "Ain't a damn thing in this world we can be absolutely sure about."

"No?"

"No."

"There's one thing," I said.

"Oh, yeah? What's that?"

"That you're a selfish and insensitive bastard."

*   *   *

The rest of that day lolled. I felt as if I were anchored in the middle of the ocean on a small boat. The water was calm. The boat bobbed gently, rising and falling, rising and falling. The late summer sun beat down on my unprotected head. I felt only semiconscious, slightly delirious, occasionally nauseated. My brain responded to the emotional overload by simply shutting down and demanding alcoholic beverages.

I had been prepared to attack Daniel with all the verbal savagery I could muster, but he had merely smiled at my reproach, slapped me on the back, and gone in for another beer. What do you do with a guy like that? What do you say?

Rachel awoke from her nap feeling much better. We ate lunch and went for a swim. We had a few cocktails and ate dinner and drank a few more cocktails and went to bed. Each of us wandered off to our own floor, our own private chamber.

I was drunk enough that it was not pleasant to lie down and close my eyes. The whole world spun a little too fast. So I stood over by the window and watched the moonlight flicker across the surface of the sea.

Then I thought I heard someone downstairs, so I went over and very quietly pulled open my door. Was she going to him? Was he going to her? Did they have plans to rendezvous and ball each other's brains out?

I crept out into the hallway and down the stairs and along the wall. I could see the door of the guest bedroom standing open. I quietly made my way along the hall. And then, when I reached the doorway, I literally jumped into the room and flipped the switch operating the bright overhead light. But the light exposed nothing. Rachel's bed was mussed but quite empty, not a soul in sight.

So, she had gone to him. I would catch them in the act and cut off their private parts!

I headed for the stairs. Along the way I passed the bathroom. The door was closed, light filtered out through the cracks. I heard a noise coming from inside. I pressed my ear to the door. I heard clearly that horrible sound the human body makes when it dispels the contents of the stomach back up through the esophagus and out the mouth.

Rachel, I concluded, must've had too much to drink. Too bad. I suppressed a smirk and retreated to my bed.

In the morning, however, I learned that an overindulgence in alcohol had not been the reason for Rachel's midnight retching. No, something else far more intoxicating was at the root of her nausea.

When I ventured downstairs not too long after dawn, Daniel was already up and dressed. He was just finishing his breakfast of coffee and toast. "Morning, Mac. Sleep well?"

"I slept like shit. How 'bout you?"

"Never better." He got up from the table and deposited his dishes in the sink. "I made a pot of coffee. Help yourself, it's piping hot."

I mumbled something.

"Listen," he said, "I'm heading into town. Got some people I have to see."

I didn't want to hear about it. "Good. See ya later." I turned my attention to the coffee.

"Probably be gone most of the day. You think I could use the Jeep?"

The fucker had nerve, no one can deny him that. "No," I said, and poured myself a cup.

"No problem," he said, "I'll hitch a ride."

"Or take a bike," I suggested. "There's a couple out in the garage." I imagined some sleepy-eyed island fisherman in a '68 Ford pickup honeycombed with rust wandering onto the shoulder of Milestone Road and knocking my old buddy off his bike and into one of the island's few remaining cranberry bogs, where he would be lost to us forever and ever.

"Good idea." He grabbed his jacket and headed for the door.

"Hey, Hawk?"

"Yeah, Mac?"

"Don't forget our Around the Island Race."

"Hey, don't worry, old buddy, I'm counting on it. How does tomorrow sound?"

I nodded. "If the weather's good, we'll do it in the morning."

"You have two boats?"

"I've got one. We'll rent another."

He gave me a thumbs-up and opened the door. "Gotta go, Mac. Later."

It was almost noon before Rachel finally got out of bed. I was sitting on the sofa staring at a magazine when she came slowly down the stairs. "Good morning, Matthew. Is it still morning? It feels so late, like I slept for a year."

I'd been planning to ignore her but heard myself say, "It's about eleven-thirty."

"Sorry I slept so long."

"I figured you would. You must've tied on a pretty good buzz last night. I heard you getting rid of it."

She sat down on the sofa, not far from me. "Oh, you mean the throwing up?"

"Sounded like you were having a hell of a good time."

She smiled. "Yes, but it wasn't the alcohol. I think I only had one drink. Maybe two. I shouldn't've had any."

I must've had eight or ten and probably should've had more. "So what was it then, something you ate? I think we all ate the same thing: shrimp and rice and salad."

She shook her head. "No, it wasn't the food, either."

"What, then? Some kind of a bug? You want me to take you to see the doctor?"

"Relax, Matthew. I don't need to see a doctor. But I could use a cup of tea."

I tossed aside the magazine and crossed to the kitchen. I put the water on to boil. "Do you want something to eat? I bought some fresh croissants."

She ate two croissants, a bowl of cereal, a banana, some grapes, and a scrambled egg.

"Jesus," I said as I watched her polish off the egg, "I don't think I've ever seen you eat like that, not in twenty years. You want anything else?"

She shook her head. "No thanks. Maybe just another cup of tea."

"You've developed quite an appetite this past year."

"Really just in the last six weeks or so."

"But you're still so thin. You must be getting plenty of exercise."

"I bought a bicycle. I ride almost every day."

"Maybe that's why you've developed the appetite of a lumberjack."

"I don't think so, Matthew."

"No? How come, then?" I had my back to her. I stood innocently at the stove, preparing her a second cup of tea.

"I think because I'm eating for two."

"What?" I swung around, but believe me, it didn't sink in, not right away.

"I'm eating for two."

"What do you mean, you're eating for two?"

"I'm pregnant, Matthew. I'm going to have a baby."

"Pregnant! No, you're not pregnant! That's impossible."

She smiled. "Oh, it's very possible. In fact, it's definite."

"But but but . . ."

"I knew right away. I could feel it happening practically from the moment of conception, but I had to wait several weeks before I could get a reliable test. The doctor finally gave me his medical blessing just a few days ago."

"A few days! But but but we haven't been together"—my brain was doing some very fast arithmetic—"since March . . . almost six months ago . . . and even then we didn't . . . I mean I couldn't . . . Christ!"

Things had looked pretty bad the day before when I watched Daniel walk down that gangplank. And things had gotten a little worse when Rachel announced her desire to have a room of her own. But this, this was a nightmare, a goddamn dream gone wild.

"It's been about two months," I heard her say, "the middle of July." She lifted her T-shirt. "If you look closely, you'll see I'm just beginning to show. I have a very slight—"

"No!" I shouted. "No! This isn't happening. You're not even here yet. You're coming later. Tomorrow. Alone. Without him. . . . Is it him? . . . It is, isn't it? It's him!"

She didn't say a word or make a move.

"No!" I screamed. "I don't believe it! I refuse to believe it. How? When? Why? Why, Rachel, why?"

"I wanted it to happen, Matthew. I wanted to get pregnant. I'll be thirty-four years old in a few months. My time has come."

I went blank for a few seconds, maybe a few minutes. I may have asked her to explain, or she may have simply decided to explain on her own.

"This past year," she said, "you've wanted to know where I was, where I lived, where I went after I left the city. Now I can tell you. I've been living in a beautiful old barn, Matthew, an old and renovated barn in a small town."

I listened, numb.

"Believe it or not, I've been living in Peapack."

"Peapack! Peapack, New Jersey?"

"That's right, just over the hill from Mendham."

"With Daniel?"

She actually laughed. I wanted to strangle her, rip her insides out. "No," she said, "not with Daniel. He had no idea where I was. But in July he found me. Stumbled upon me, would probably be more accurate."

"Stumbled upon you?"

She nodded. "Late one afternoon I was sitting alone in that small park in Peapack. Do you know the park I mean?"

"The one with the pond?"

"Yes. I was just sitting there when suddenly I heard his van. He stopped to take a walk around the pond. He had no idea he would find me there."

"What!? Do you really expect me to believe that? That he just happened upon you by chance, by sheer luck?"

"You can believe me or not, Matthew. That's entirely up to you."

"I don't believe a fucking word you say."

"I didn't do this to hurt you, Matthew. I did this for me."

"Well bully for you, Rachel. Or whatever the hell you call yourself now."

"Don't be a child about this, Matthew."

"Oh, right, excuse me. Let me have a minute to put my life back together and then I'll take it like a man."

"That's not what I mean."

"I know what you mean, you bitch!"

"You've always tried to simplify our relationship, Matthew, make it something black and white, something it wasn't. You've wanted from the very beginning to put the two of us in our own little pond, our own private little fish bowl. And yet you've known for almost as long that I refuse to swim in circles. I need to keep swimming upstream, Matthew. I need to—"

"Enough with the swimming bullshit!" I screamed. I was losing it, fast. "I know what you need. You need to fuck him whenever you feel like it. Fuck him and screw me. I know all about what you need. I've seen what you need. I've seen it with my own eyes."

"What are you talking about?"

I should've cut my losses, maybe turned and marched out of the house, returned to fight another day. But that would've constituted a retreat, and I was in no mood to retreat. There would be no more retreats. I was on a kamikaze mission. Nothing could stop me now.

"What are you talking about?" she repeated.

"I was here. I saw. . . with my own eyes. Right through the sliding glass door I saw."

"Saw what?"

"Saw you! Saw him! Saw both of you! Fucking naked!"

"What! When?"

"You know when! You know exactly when!"

"I know you're acting like a madman, Matthew. I know you're acting exactly like the kind of man I have always despised: jealous and possessive and violent. Why don't you hit me? You know you want to! So just do it. Get it over with!"

"I've never hit you."

"Well bully for you too."

That slowed me down.

"For almost fifteen years you've been trying to get me to marry you. Well now, right now, at this very second, take a good long look at yourself and you'll know why I've never said yes."

But I couldn't look, not right then, not at that moment. "It's because you've always secretly wanted him."

"Oh bullshit, Matthew. Bullshit bullshit bullshit. Do you have any idea how many times I've even seen Daniel since we graduated from Mercersburg? Maybe fifty times. In all these years maybe fifty times. That's all. And most of those times you were there. We were all together. The three of us."

"I wasn't there when you were here!" I shouted. "And I damn well wasn't there when you two slammed into that ambulance!"

"No, and thank God you weren't."

"Thank God my ass. I don't believe a word you say."

"Well then, I feel very sorry for you, Matthew."

"Don't bother."

She let that pass, gave the room a few moments to breathe.

My whole body trembled. I wanted to run out the door, sprint across the lawn, jump off the cliff. I had so many accusations to make, but absolutely no energy to make them.

"He doesn't know yet," I heard her say.

"He doesn't know what yet?"

"That I'm pregnant."

I looked at her, really looked at her for the first time since she'd made the announcement. "You haven't told him?"

"No."

"Why?"

"I'm not exactly sure. Maybe because I'm afraid he won't care."

"He probably won't."

"I don't know. Not that it really matters. I don't want anything from him. He didn't ask for this."

"No, not Daniel." I started to spit again, but now I had my anger pointed in a slightly different direction. "He never asks for anything. He just takes. He just wants to get his rocks off. He doesn't give a shit about anyone but Daniel."

"You haven't got that exactly right, Matthew, and you know it."

"I know he's a self-centered bastard and an egomaniac."

"He's the best friend you've ever had."

"Bullshit."

"He'd do anything for you."

"Including steal my woman."

"I'm not your woman, Matthew. That's what you've never understood, what you've never been willing to accept. I'm your friend, not your possession."

"He's still a shit."

"You don't mean that."

"The hell I don't."

"Be serious, Matthew. You've always put Daniel up on a pedestal, granted him almost mystical status. But you refuse to see his dark side, his difficulty in finding a place where he belongs. Daniel is a Gypsy, emotionally and genetically, in a settled and stagnant society. You pretend it's otherwise, but your old friend is as troubled and confused as the rest of us. Maybe more so."

"You act like you know him better than I do."

She paused, then whispered, "In some ways I do."

And I knew she was right, she did.

SOMEHOW WE MADE IT THROUGH THAT DAY.

By the middle of the afternoon we were sick and tired of the whole affair, sick and tired of one another, of the charges and countercharges. We both had headaches and stomachaches and heartaches. My voice was shot from ranting and raving. Rachel said she was exhausted and started back upstairs to take a nap.

"Bitch," I mumbled as she reached the second-floor landing. She paused, sighed, then continued down the hallway to her room. She closed the door very softly.

I stood there for a moment, seething, my temples pounding. Then I went out the sliding glass door and across the lawn to the edge of the cliff. It had been years since I had descended the cliff to the beach below. I had always been afraid of falling, of splattering myself on the hard, wet sand. But Daniel had always insisted. He would goad me until I got up the nerve and went over the side.

That day, however, I went over the side and made the descent without hesitating. My fears had vanished. And when I hit the beach I started north at a brisk pace, almost a jog.

My whole life swirled in front of me. I grabbed hold of everything that had happened up until that moment, my entire past. I stomped on it, buried it in the sand, then dug it up and threw it out over the breakers into the wild sea beyond.

I focused on my hatred for Daniel and Rachel. Everything she had said about me back at the house was bullshit. Total bullshit. I was a decent guy, honest, trustworthy. I'd never hit her, never been violent, never done anything to hurt her. I had backed her every damn step of the way. I had supported her and praised her. I had lied for her and goddammit even committed perjury for her. Perjury, for chrissakes! All I had ever wanted to do was love her, make her happy, make her safe. My intentions had always been perfectly honorable.

And him, the bastard. He was no friend of mine.

They were the enemy, both of them. I had the desire to find a gun and shoot them both dead, but I decided they didn't deserve my wrath; they weren't worth the aggravation. No, I'd just go back to the house, and nice and easy in a cool, calm, and collected voice I would order them to get the fuck out and never come back. Never.

I kept moving north along the water's edge. I ran faster and faster, my eyes now focused on the sea. To the sea, I knew, was where I was headed. For all my thirty-four years I had been reaching for the sea, mentally and physically preparing myself to sail into the horizon.

I began to formulate a plan. I worked on it for hours. In the end the details proved pure and simple: I would blow them off, once and for all; then I would buy myself a seaworthy sailing vessel, go back to the city, settle my affairs, tell Chuckie the time had come for me to go; then I would head for the sea. I would sail along the coast of South America, around the treacherous Cape Horn, then west across the great green Pacific, through the Coral Sea and along the Australian coast, then east across the Indian Ocean, around the Cape of Good Hope, and finally back into the beautiful blue Atlantic, north and then west through the Sargasso Sea, landing, eventually, back where I had started, perhaps back here on this very beach.

That was my plan. And I was determined to see it through.

By the time I got back to the house dusk had fallen. Stars had started to fill the evening sky. Coming across the lawn, I could see a light burning in the living room. As I climbed the steps to the deck, I slowed. I lost some of my momentum, some of my confidence, some of my vim and vigor. I felt very small and weak and alone.

The sliding glass door was open to let in the evening breeze. Just as I was about to step inside I heard her laugh. I stopped. She laughed again. It was just a quiet laugh, like a laugh you might have after a good cry. I listened, strained to hear.

Daniel's voice reached me but not clearly. He was telling her a story but I couldn't get the gist of it. All I knew was that his story was making her laugh.

In I went. It was my house, after all. I'd tell them to get the hell out.

But I didn't get my mouth open before Daniel went on the offensive in his usual upbeat, enthusiastic voice. "Hey, Mac, where you been? What're you scowling about? House being attacked by bats?"

They sat on opposite sides of the sofa, an empty space of maybe three feet separating them. I remember thinking I wanted to fill that space. What a sicko.

My brief hesitation provided Daniel with another opening.

He stood, came at me, looked me straight in the eye. I wanted to punch him in the face, land a solid right jab in the middle of his smiling Gypsy mouth. It all of a sudden hit me, right then, at that moment, that this whole stinking mess was all his fault.

"Really, Mac, where you been? There's something we need to talk about."

What? I wondered. Had he gotten the word? Did he know the Bitch was pregnant? Did he want me to pay for the baby doctor, maybe put the kid through college, law school?

But very soon it was clear she still hadn't told him, hadn't uttered a word to him about the goings-on in the house earlier in the day. For a guy guilty of high crimes, he had managed somehow to remain incredibly innocent.

"What?" I asked, my scowl now etched deep into my face. "What do you want to talk about?"

"The race," he said, "I wanna talk about the big race."

"Yeah? What about the goddamn race?"

He stood right in front of me. I could smell his breath. It smelled of grapes, of wine, my wine. "It's gotta be tomorrow, Mac, tomorrow morning."

I started to ask why but suddenly didn't give a damn. My thoughts began to swirl all over again. It all came clear. I knew what I had to do. For the very first time in my life, I glimpsed the future. "Tomorrow morning," I said, "no problem."

"You won't pussy out on me, will you, old buddy?"

"Fuck you, Hawthorn," I said, "tomorrow we race around the island."

He laughed and gave me a great big Gypsy bear hug. "Now you're talkin', Mac."

The morning dawned cloudy and cool. I was up and at it even before Daniel. I went into the kitchen and turned on the radio, listened to the local weather report. It didn't sound like the greatest day to sail: skies would be changeable with the possibility of showers, gusty winds, and choppy seas; not too bad for an accomplished sailor but hell for rookies. There was a small craft advisory in effect but I decided to keep that bit of the forecast to myself.

I ate some breakfast, then rousted Daniel from his roost. I didn't say a word about the weather. To hell with it. Today was the day. Tomorrow be damned. I wanted to get this show on the road. And so, I reminded myself, did he.

We started out of the house before Rachel ever showed her face.

At the sliding glass door Daniel hesitated. "Maybe we should wait till she gets up."

"Why?" I demanded to know. "She won't want to come."

"No, but..."

"But what?"

He shrugged. "Hell, I don't know. Just thought it would be nice to say good-bye."

"Christ," I said, "you want to sail or you want to hang around the goddamn house all day with the girls?"

He sighed, slapped me on the shoulder, then followed me out the door. We drove all the way into town without saying a word.

We had a tough time finding a boat worth renting that late in the season. Most of the rental shops had closed until spring. We had to settle for a catamaran even older and in worse repair than my own. The boat was seaworthy but lacked several key pieces of equipment, including trapeze lines and wind indicators. No way would that boat sail at maximum speed or efficiency. So after considerable discussion, it was decided I would race the rental boat and Daniel would race my boat.

And who made that decision? I did.

Daniel had only this to say: "Both these boats seem pretty fucked up to me."

"What's the matter, Hawk," I asked him, "looking for an excuse to back out?"

The son of a bitch just laughed. "No way, Mac. Not a chance."

So finally, late in the morning, we tacked out of the harbor to begin the race.

The course was simple: we would sail north and east through Nantucket Sound along the beaches of Coatue and Coskata. We would then sail out of the Sound around Great Point and into the Atlantic. Then, hugging the shore, we would head south along Galls Beach and Squam Head and Sankaty Light straight into Siasconset.

We had given up the idea of completely circumnavigating the island. It would take too long, and we were already getting a late start. So the race would end at Siasconset Public Beach, where we would drag the cats ashore and have them trailered back to the marina. Daniel called me a castrated chickenshit for cutting the length of the race virtually in half, but in the end he agreed that half a race was better than none.

"You'd better agree," I told him. "I'm doing it for you. I know how to sail. You're nothing but a damn land jockey, barely know a jib from a jibe. We're gonna get two miles up Coatue Beach and you're gonna beg me to head for shore."

His laughter boomed across the harbor, echoed over the surface of the water. "So you think you got bigger walnuts than me, hey, Mac?"

"Damn right," I shouted back.

He raised his sail and took hold of his tiller. "Then may the man with the biggest set of walnuts win!"

We passed slowly through the channel and out into the Sound. As soon as we reached open water and moved off the shelter of the land, a southwest breeze pushed us steadily toward Great Point. Both boats pretty much ran with the wind. We headed farther out into the Sound to shorten the overall distance around the Point, which reached out and back to the northwest like a giant fishhook.

Regardless of my old buddy's verbal bluster, he was not an accomplished sailor. I had to heave-to frequently so as not to get too far ahead. He kept losing the wind. I thought about sailing off, leaving him in my wake, but that meant abandoning my plan, and I did not want to abandon my plan. Besides, I enjoyed watching him struggle with the fluky winds and the tricky crosscurrents. So instead of sailing off, I sailed around him in circles as he fought to find and hold the breeze.

Each time I circled past his starboard bow I heckled him. "Hey, Hawk! You landlubbing son of a bitch! You ready to call it quits? You ready once and for all to admit who's the better sailor?"

He just kept up that goddamn laugh of his, kept insisting that in the end victory would belong to the Gypsies.

I flipped him the bird, tightened up my main, and sailed ahead. For the next half an hour I kept my distance, sailed alone. I could see the sail of the other boat off my port beam but I paid little attention. My mind worked once again on the past, on all the times the two of them, especially Daniel, had used me and deceived me and manipulated me. She was a bitch but he was a knave, a scoundrel, a goddamned evil demon in Gypsy clothing. He had corrupted her. I felt sure that if not for him, she and I would be happily married and settled down in a nice suburban home with a small army of little kids playing in the backyard. I hated her but I hated him even worse. I foamed at the mouth and plotted my revenge.

I scanned the horizon, found no boats at all besides his. It was just the two of us out on that dark and rolling sea. "Okay, Chandler," I told myself right out loud, "time to make your move."

I came about, set my sail just off the wind. The wind had shifted out of the south and now blew directly across the Sound from due west. I found it and tightened my mainsheet. I sailed directly at him.

I had in mind to cut his boat in two, split his trampoline right down the center, separate his hulls, and thereby render his vessel useless. I wanted to send the son of a bitch flying and screaming into the sea. I wanted to watch him flail amid the whitecaps. I wanted to hear him call for help, beg for mercy.

And what would I do then? I wasn't sure. I didn't know.

He piloted my old catamaran from the starboard hull. He waved to me as I bore down on him. And then he smiled.

That smile smacked me right between the eyes. All our years together, our entire youth, slammed head on into my brain. I had no choice; at the very last moment I pushed away the tiller, loosened my grip on the mainsheet, and veered off course. I slipped by his outward hull with only the slightest hint of contact.

"Jesus Christ, Mac," I heard him shout, "what the hell are you doing?"

I tried to laugh it off but the sound caught in my throat. Nothing came out.

"What the fuck's the matter with you?"

I once more came about. I found and caught the wind.

Okay, you castrated chickenshit, I told myself, if you don't have the walnuts to dump the son of a bitch in the sea, at least kick the crap out of him with the news she used to kick the crap out of you. It was a cheap and petty alternative to my original plan but the situation demanded I do something.

I ran up alongside my adversary's boat.

"You okay, Mac?" he asked. "I thought you'd lost it there for a second."

I ignored him. "Hey, Hawk," I asked my old childhood chum, "the Bitch tell you yet what she's gone and done?"

"Who? Rachel?"

"Yeah, the Bitch!"

We had to shout, what with the wind suddenly beginning to blow a gale.

"Why do you call her a bitch?"

"Because that's what she is!"

"What's the matter, Mac?" His voice sounded just a little bit scared. "You gone loony on me or what?"

The sea began to swell and toss around our little boats.

"Fuck you!" I shouted.

"Christ, Mac, what's this all about?"

Poor Daniel. His face had lost its color. For the very first time in my life I actually saw fear in the Gypsy's eyes. Too bad. This time they had gone too far.

"You're gonna be a daddy, Daniel!"

"What?"

"That's right, old buddy, you lucky dog! Baby's on the way! Ball the Bitch once too often and that's what happens!"

And then I pulled in my tiller, tightened up my main, and sailed off. I left him in my wake, my laughter, the laughter of a lunatic, echoing between the raging water and the black storm clouds spreading out across the Sound.

I SAILED FOR THE TIP OF GREAT POINT, determined still to finish and win the race. The other catamaran followed but fell farther and farther behind. I could see her sail as she crested the swells.

For the past hour the winds had been shifting, swinging from the southwest to the west to the northwest and now almost directly out of the north.

The sky had turned ugly. Where earlier the clouds had been gray but very high and thin with occasional patches of blue, now fresh clouds blew over the Sound as the wind pressed in off the ocean. These new clouds were black and thick and extremely low. It felt more and more like rain.

I decided I had to warn him. I came about and ran downwind. I sailed as close to the other cat as I dared. "A storm's coming!" I shouted. "Feels like a nor'easter! Maybe we should beach and find shelter! Wait it out!"

Daniel shouted his reply but the wind snatched and scattered his words.

I cupped my hands around my mouth and yelled as loud as I could. "Maybe we should head for shore!"

He had plenty to say in response, but his words did not reach my ears. All I heard for sure was something about the minuscule size of my walnuts.

And then the son of a bitch began to laugh, a high and hearty laugh, so I pulled in my sail and headed back against the wind. It was slow going, one short tack after another just to make minimum headway. I figured if I could get around the Point, I'd be okay. At least then I'd be able to turn south and make a run from the storm.

I lost him off the Point. I saw the top of his sail as he tacked past the lighthouse, but then I dipped into a deep swell and when I came up the other cat was gone.

The water ran rough, almost wild where the Atlantic crashed into the Sound. It took all my skills and experience as a sailor to bring that catamaran safely through the chop. I sailed away from shore, out into the ocean. Finally I found calmer water.

After a brief rest and some time to consider my options, I turned back to the west, back into the chop. I knew I couldn't just sail away to safety.

I sailed as close to the wind as possible, my eyes constantly searching the horizon. In the distance I spotted the lighthouse but not a trace of the other catamaran. I thought about the main and rear beams holding the two hulls of that cat together; they had not been in good shape. I wondered if those beams would be able to withstand the fury of this running sea.

The wind, blowing carelessly now from every direction, and more viciously than it had all day, made it virtually impossible to sail back around the Point. I tried several times but each time I swamped and almost capsized. I knew I'd be in big trouble if I went over in that swirl of water, so I backed off, let the wind and the current push me back out to the east, back out into the Atlantic.

Where was he, goddammit! Why hadn't he made the turn?

I rested and caught my breath, then made a long slow tack to the north, hoping to find that catamaran drifting across the Sound, perhaps in the direction of Cape Cod. But before I got very far it started to rain: first just a drizzle, then a cold and steady stream, and finally a torrential downpour. Visibility quickly fell to just a few hundred feet. I had to sail for land. I had to get ashore, and fast.

I headed south. The wind had kicked all the way around to the north-northeast by this time, so sailing almost due south was relatively easy even with the seas high and running. I thought about putting ashore along the Galls but decided that would be futile. There was nothing along that deserted beach, no homes or hotels. I would probably have to walk several miles before I found a soul, before I could locate a telephone. So I kept sailing.

The rain increased. The wind blew harder. As I had expected, a nor'easter was rising up out of the Atlantic. Within an hour the sea would be absolutely inhospitable to all small crafts, especially sailboats.

I sailed past Squam Head, saw not a soul upon that wide white beach. Everyone had retreated from the storm, gone inland on a search for shelter. I wondered again where he was, wondered if that shaky cat could hold together, if he could somehow coax that old boat up onto the shore.

Had he capsized? Was he flailing about in the chop? Was he lost at sea? I asked myself these questions over and over as I steadied the tiller and held the mainsheet against the rip of twenty- and thirty-mile-an-hour gusts. I asked, but I couldn't answer. I kept thinking he must have made it to shore. He must have run that catamaran up onto the beach in the shadow of the Great Point Lighthouse. He was no doubt cold and wet and miserable, and maybe injured and a long way from a warm meal and a hot shower, but nevertheless he was okay. I felt certain I would see him again before nightfall.

But did I want to see him? Did I want him to survive the storm? All night long I had been awake plotting his death, thinking up ever more creative ways to bring about his demise. I had come up with the plan to cut his sailing vessel in half, to spill him into the cold dark sea as soon as we drew far enough away from land. Lying there, staring at the ceiling, listening to my heart pounding and the waves crashing onto the shore, I had convinced myself that my old buddy deserved to die.

But now, out there in the middle of it all, the end as close as the rising waterline, my conviction began to waver.

I sailed past the Sankaty Head Lighthouse with my sail practically ripped clean off the mast. The tiller was all but broken in half, hanging together by a bare thread. Another mile and I doubt I would've made it to shore.

Several hundred yards south of the lighthouse I rolled through the surf and pulled that broken boat up onto the sand. For just a moment I paused and stared out at that dark and violent sea. For some reason I felt sure I would see him out there, coming in right behind me. Daniel would never allow a small thing like an ocean to stand in his way. But the Atlantic had turned mean and ornery, a black and ferocious swirl of rain and wind and wave.

I sprinted south along the beach. My eyes searched the oceanfront dwellings along the top of the cliff for signs of the Chandler family home on Baxter Road. The rain and mist made it difficult to see. I must've run half a mile before I finally saw the back of the house. I trudged through the soft, damp sand to the base of the cliff. It had been years, twenty years or more, since I had actually ascended that vertical wall. Climbing up had always been even scarier for me than climbing down. But believe me when I tell you, I did not take the time to contemplate my fears on that stormy late summer afternoon almost exactly one year ago.

I crested the cliff and pulled myself up onto the grass. I sprang to my feet and ran as fast as I could across the backyard. I climbed over the deck railing and reached for that sliding glass door. For just a moment I paused, and remembered. But an instant later I pushed open the door and stepped into the house.

"Matthew!" She jumped off the sofa, came at me, her eyes wide open and wild with fear. "Where have you been? Where's Daniel? What's happened? The radio says to prepare for a full-force gale, fifty-and sixty-mile-an-hour winds!"

I ignored her, swept her out of the way. This, I knew for sure, with absolute certainty, beyond a shadow of a doubt, was her fault, all her fault.

I raced into the kitchen and grabbed the phone off the wall. I called the cops. I called the Coast Guard. "Help!" I shouted to those who answered. "SOS! A boat! A sailboat! A catamaran! Lost! Off Great Point!"

Those who answered calmed me down, asked me the right questions, received the right answers.

The rescue effort was under way.

There was nothing more I could do.

FOR THREE DAYS THEY SEARCHED. On the morning of the third day they found one of the hulls of my catamaran washed up on Coskata Beach, about two miles to the southwest of the Great Point Lighthouse.

As I had feared, my catamaran had broken apart during the storm. And now, or so it seemed, he was dead, lost at sea.

Was I responsible? Am I responsible? Is his death my fault? Did I kill him? I knew that sailboat wasn't safe, knew it wasn't seaworthy. Nevertheless I encouraged him to race that boat around Great Point, probably the roughest, toughest eddy of water in Nantucket Sound. I encouraged him, challenged him, made it a matter of ego and honor and all that broad-shouldered, hairy-chested bullshit.

But no one blamed me. Of course not. It was all a terrible accident. He was my oldest and dearest friend, my best friend in this whole wide wicked world. No one would have thought to blame me for his untimely death. No, everyone grieved with me, grieved for me, supported me in my time of sorrow.

Including Rachel.

In public we presented a brave and united front. We sat side by side and answered any and all questions. She of course wore dark glasses to cover her eyes and a hat to cover the short blond locks of her conspirator, Misty Grey. We even went so far as to hold hands when the local pastor dropped by to offer his condolences and say a short prayer for our dear departed friend.

But in private, behind closed doors, we fought like a couple of alley cats. Actually I did most of the fighting, all of the yelling and screaming. Rachel barely uttered a sound during my fits of rage. She remained uncharacteristically quiet, almost docile. Her silence only infuriated me more. I bombarded her with innuendo and accusation. I called her a whore and a witch and a vamp. She just sat there and took it, didn't say a word.

Five days after Daniel had been lost at sea they still had not found his body. Rachel told me she could not take it anymore. She wanted to get off the island, slip away and return to her secret life. "There's nothing more I can do here."

I gladly drove her to the airport. We did not leave the house until almost midnight. She had a ticket on the last flight of the day off the island. I didn't know where the flight was bound. And I didn't much give a damn, either.

We sat in the Jeep outside the terminal. I left the engine running.

"Matthew," she said, "we don't want to leave it like this."

"Get out," I said.

"You're pushing me away but inside you know that's not what you want."

"Shut up!" I snapped. "Just shut up! You don't know what I want."

"But I think I do."

I thought for a second I might hit her. I took a deep breath. "Just do me a favor," I said, "just get out. Now!"

Finally she did. The second she stepped away from the Jeep I slammed the transmission into gear and zoomed away. All night long I drove back and forth across the island. I drove like a maniac for a few miles, but then I slowed and just wandered, aimlessly, without reason or destination.

Just before dawn, out near Madaket, I ran out of gas.

I remained on the island for another week. I answered all inquiries, tried to clear up all necessary details. The search for his body continued but any hopes of finding him alive had faded.

I wrote some poems, walked on the beach, began my research for my sail through the seven seas. I read and reread Captain Joshua Slocum's classic *Sailing Alone Around the World.*

And on my way back to New York, driving Daniel's VW camper-van, as Victor had asked me to do, and feeling more and more like a full-fledged Gypsy wanderer, I stopped at a small boat yard. It was in the town of South Dartmouth, Massachusetts, on Buzzards Bay just south of New Bedford.

At the home of Marshall Catboats I talked at great length with the manager, Mr. John Garfield. He gave me all the pros and cons of trying to sail a catboat across the ocean. There were definitely more cons than pros, but nevertheless, at the end of our talk I signed a contract to have his yard build me a Marshall Mariner, a twenty-two-foot, sloop-rigged sailboat with a ten-foot beam and four hundred and thirty-eight square feet of sail, by far the largest catboat Marshall made.

The contract specified several custom-designed features to make my sailboat more comfortable and more seaworthy, including all the latest electronic equipment, four twenty-five-gallon water tanks, boat hook, bilge pump, fog horn, anchor, and side shrouds to keep out the water in the event of heavy seas. We also decided to rig the sails in such a way that would make them easier for a man sailing alone to handle.

I left that boat yard almost giddy with excitement and expectation. A tragedy had swept through my life but I headed south for New York a happy man.

Happiness. Right.

If it was happiness I had felt that day, let me tell you, it did not last long.

The reality and finality of Daniel's death began to take hold, began to gnaw at my gut and eat away at my brain. Just as had been the case in life, so now it was in death: I could not escape him. Day and night he remained at my side. He followed me everywhere I went, even into my dreams. I couldn't look in the mirror without seeing those eyes of his grinning back at me. All day every day he had a firm grip on my walnuts. If I took a step or made a move he didn't like, the son of a bitch would squeeze until he brought me back in line.

I felt like that old Gypsy must've felt; you know the one I mean—the one who forged the nails used to hang Jesus from the cross.

April 15, 1991

RACHEL ANN FREDERICK, ALIAS MISTY GREY *leans over the crib.
She picks up the infant boy. He is not more than three days old. Just today,
this morning, she brought him home from the hospital.*

*She rocks him gently in her arms. He falls asleep. She crosses the
room, looks out the second-story window. Outside, in the backyard of
the big old white house on Main Street in Peapack, New Jersey, she sees the
first daffodils of a new spring.*

*She settles the baby back in his crib. While he sleeps she paints. His
bedroom is her studio.*

*Late in the afternoon Coach Frederick returns with the groceries.
He fixes dinner. The three generations dine together.*

*In the evening, after the wine and the soft jazz, the mother and her
son return to the bedroom. They lie naked on a blanket on the floor.*

*The house is quiet except for the spring breeze blowing through
the open windows.*

*Grandfather Frederick sketches in the guest room at the end of the
hall.*

The baby falls asleep.

*Rachel stands, crosses to a large table where she keeps her paints and
brushes. Beneath a pile of old sketches she finds a pad. She stares for a
time out at the darkness, thinking, waiting. . . . Finally she begins to
write.*

> *Dear Matthew,*
>
> *I wonder: do you read my letters? Do you even open the
> envelopes? Or do you simply discard my correspondence into the
> trash unopened, unread, unnoticed? Do you hate me that
> much?*
>
> *I want you to know about the baby. Maybe you don't want*

to know, maybe you couldn't care less, but still I want you to know. He was born on April 13, 1991, at three o'clock in the afternoon. He weighed almost seven pounds, strong and healthy. No doubt he is the most beautiful baby ever born. His name is rather long: Thomas (for Father) Matthew (for you) Daniel (for him). A fine name, don't you think?

I hope one day you will come to see him, come to see me, come to see us. I want you to see my house. I know you would like it. It is so much like the house in Mercersburg, and I know how much you always loved that house.

The curtains snap in the cool breeze. Rachel stands, startled. For just a moment, as though in a dream, she expects to see Daniel fly through the open window.

But the breeze dies. The curtains hang still. Rachel crosses to the baby. His eyes open wide. She sees right away they are his eyes, Daniel's eyes, clear and bright and curious, a Gypsy's eyes. She smiles.

The eyes fall closed. The baby sleeps. Rachel crosses to the window, stares out at the darkness. Nothing. No one. She sighs and returns to the letter.

Papa is here to help with the baby. He is well and sends his best, and hopes, as I do, to see you soon. He is still whitewashing over his paintings; I am not. Always further to go.

I know you live your life now, Matthew, as if I were dead, as if I had been on that boat with Daniel. But I was not on that boat, Matthew. I hate the sea. You know that. I am not dead, Matthew. I am alive and well.

I suppose I could go on and on, tell you how much I miss you, how much I think about you, but I fear my words mean nothing to you; I fear my words do not even reach you. So I will close this letter, Matthew, by saying I am sorry. I hope you are well. Please, let me know.

Love,
Rachel

Misty sighs as she signs her other name. The baby stirs. She picks him up, holds him close to her breast. He suckles, as the night, another night, passes.

COURAGE, ULTIMATELY, IS A CONFRONTATION WITH FEAR. I discovered I had courage that night on the Danube when I became separated from Victor and Daniel. But my discovery came only after fear had raced down my spine and embedded itself in my naked, shivering soul.

As I prepare to raise my sails and head for that distant horizon, I find myself once again gripped by fear. It is the same old story, the one about the minuscule size of my reproductive organs. I know that just as I once threw myself out into space to become a full-fledged member of Daniel's tree fort club, so now I must throw myself out upon that deep blue sea.

I write these last few lines here at the Chandler family home in Siasconset. I arrived only yesterday. Hopefully I will be leaving as soon as tomorrow. Chuckie and Martha are here to see me off. We have silently made an uneasy peace.

I settled my business in the city, gave away my few remaining possessions. I gave away everything except for a few clothes, my nautical charts, and a stack of paintings by Miss Rachel Ann Frederick. Those paintings have all been carefully wrapped and sealed and put away in a safe and secure place. I thought for a time I might one day sell them if I needed the money, but I know now I never will. I would starve to death, waste away to nothing, before I would part with those paintings.

As for Daniel, well, I have nothing in a material sense; I have only his stories, the tales he told me, the adventures we shared. My memories of Daniel, I hate to admit but must, are the greatest and most exciting memories of my life.

The ghosts of my two old friends continue to haunt me. As well they should. I should have believed in our trinity. I should have seen us as something new and enlightened. I should never have seen us as two males vying for the love of a female, not with all the sexual and emotional bullshit piled on top of that ancient arrangement.

I let the trinity slip through my fingers.

And now I am all alone.

Yesterday morning, at the crack of dawn, I sailed my brand-new Marshall catboat out of Buzzards Bay and across Nantucket Sound. She sails like a dream: strong and steady, yet light as a feather dancing over the surface of the water. And boldly written in black letters across her transom: FREEDOM III.

I am ready to go. My galley has been filled, my nautical charts endlessly perused. All that remains for me to do is wave good-bye, raise the jib, clear the harbor, and steer east for that mythical horizon. I no longer seek a journey around the world. I have gone long enough in circles.

I will steer for the Azores, pass through the Strait of Gibraltar, cross the Mediterranean Sea. I will anchor at Tel Aviv, then travel overland to Jerusalem and make the Walk of Sorrows to the crucifixion site at Golgotha. It will be a voyage of repentance.

Of course, who knows? Perhaps the moment I am out of sight of land my courage will fail. Perhaps I will panic and head for port. It would not be the first time. But I have resolved this much: I will not retreat. I may hug the shore but I will not retreat.